The Raven Stone
(A Novel)

By Michael Rea

ISBN: 978-0615879536

Other Works by this Author

Justice, A novel, (science fiction)
The Colonel, A novel, (historical fiction)
Connected: Remaining Human in a Networked World (non-fiction)

www.workshopforwriters.com

Table of Contents

Chapter One

Where am I? I'm standing in a meadow, but where? I don't remember this place. It is familiar, but not lucid. Not far away, just beyond the reach of the light, is the edge of a forest, foreboding and dark. Twilight is descending and a mist is rising from the ground... Every object, every shadow is swallowed up by the gray. Nothing is clearly seen, everything fades into the depths of the wood beyond. Is it real, or not?

What is that, just at the edge of the glen? It's a woman, all dressed in white. Who is she? Do I know her? She is veiled, a bride. She is beautiful, ethereal and alluring. What is she doing here? What does she want?

Her hand rises from her side, graceful and delicate. Gently she waves to me. She wants me to come to her. But as I approach, she turns and walks into the wood. I follow, but she remains at a distance. I fail to draw close. Why does she bewitch me so? She pauses a moment, and turns to face me. Again she waves for me to follow. I can almost distinguish her features beneath the veil. I can see her eyes, dark and penetrating. Then they are gone, she turns and walks away. Deeper into the forest we go. Where is she taking me? I want to know, I need to know?

There is nothing like walking across campus when the temperature is thirty below. He was just not a morning person. Staying up late at night was no problem, but in the morning he was barely conscious. He was on his way to see his advisor. Combine ridiculously cold weather, with a morning of rebuke from Professor Winslow and he felt he was near hell, a cold hell. It seemed interminable, stretching forward with no warmth of spring in sight.

The English building, his intended destination, sat right on the main quad, opposite Davenport Hall. It was only about three fourths of a mile from his house on Nevada St., but in weather like this, it seemed much further. As he passed the Kranert Center, he was provided with a little respite from the blustery and biting wind coming down from the north.

Not only was he cold, frozen to the bone, he was also tired. He had another one of those dreams last night. It was so weird and it gave him the creeps. He could never remember having dreams that repeated themselves. In fact he could rarely remember most of his dreams at all. What made this one so unique was how vivid and real it seemed, and how he remembered every detail when he woke up. It was not a nightmare exactly, but he always woke up feeling weary, as if he had been walking, or even running, in his sleep.

As he passed Noyes Lab he stopped and looked east across the quad. The trees reached to the sky with a million fingers, ice and snow their only adornment. It was on mornings like this John wished he had learned to be a coffee drinker. Right now he was in desperate need of some caffeine, not to mention something hot. He used his entire six foot frame and lengthened his stride. He decided to take a direct route across the snow covered lawn, rather than follow the diagonal sidewalks; anything to bring a quick end to his journey. The crusted snow on the ground crunched beneath his weight. Despite the exertion, he tried not to breathe too hard. The air was so cold it felt as if it was actually freezing the inner lining of his respiratory passage. He was looking forward to the warmth of the English building.

It is the winter of 1983 and John Ridley was in his fourth year of graduate school at the University of Illinois. He was not exactly sure what brought him to this place and time, why he was in graduate school, but here he was. Pursuing a Ph.D. in English Literature seemed a bit of a curious endeavor to him, when he stopped to think about it. He had a hard time seeing himself as an academician. While at Wheaton, he had a rather difficult time deciding on a major. He had a wide variety of interests, and could have chosen other majors, but he had a hard time settling on anything, until, almost by default, he fell into the English major. It was not until graduation was looming that he realized he had no idea what to do with a degree in English. Teaching school did not seem appealing, but what else was he going do? Become a writer? That seemed too risky, so here he was stumbling across the frozen tundra of the Illinois winter, wishing he were at home in his nice warm bed.

There was a blast of warm air as he passed through the main entrance. As if by habit, he loosened his scarf and undid the buttons on his overcoat. As he entered the office, his Professor Winslow was intently pouring over a manuscript, his reading glasses perched on the end of his nose, as they usually were. He wore a tweed jacket with elbow patches, over a blue oxford shirt, blue jeans, and penny loafers. It seemed as if this was the same outfit he wore every day. It was possible that he had several blue oxford shirts, but he was a bachelor and John's skepticism led him to believe that the former were true.

The first time John met the Professor, he knew it would be a good fit. Choosing a thesis advisor and thesis project was never an easy task, but John knew right away that he had made the right choice. The Professor was an expert in John's area of interest, Medieval British Literature, and he had a sort of old sage wisdom about him that was appealing.

John had always been interested in the origins of legend and myth. This probably all started the first time he learned about the legend of Robin Hood and then discovered Sir Walter Scott's adaptation of this legend in *Ivanhoe*. The Professor suggested that he pursue this interest and consider researching the origins of ancient ballads and legends and the use of oral traditions in the development of the British novel. It would be important to find out if the legends had any basis in fact, as well as the way in which they may have affected the work of the authors who made use of them.

It was a difficult task to determine whether ancient legends have any basis in real events or real persons. The classic example was the legend of King Arthur. Most authoritative sources seemed to imply that Arthur was not an actual person, but instead the mythical personification of several, or perhaps many different rulers, during the early history of England. There did not seem to be any physical evidence or historical record that a king named Arthur had ever existed. Perhaps the best written history of England, composed by the Venerable Bede, made no reference to Arthur at all. However, the lack of written record was not enough to rule out the existence of this traditional king, since written histories of any kind were very rare during the Middle Ages. Oral histories were much more common, and they usually came in the form of poems and ballads.

By the 12th century, written histories were becoming a little more prominent, possibly because of the influence of Bede. It might also have been due to the establishment, by William the Conqueror, of the usage of surnames among the nobles. This practice resulted in the construction of family pedigrees and histories. These records, in part, would be useful in providing collaboration of the story line of an oral history conveyed in poems and ballads. This could be illustrated by the legend of Robin Hood. Although this story was also viewed to be a legend, there had been found at least some written pedigrees and histories that supported its authenticity. For example, the pedigree of the kings, showing

8

that there really was a King Richard and Prince John, was enough to give some credibility to the legend.

Most researches into the Robin Hood legend began with the premise that the name was significant, and even if there was no Robin Hood, there might have been someone with a similar name in the historical records. The most popular reference was made of a Robert Horde, who was an outlaw in England. Unfortunately, Robert Horde lived more than a hundred years after the time that Robin Hood was supposed to have lived, and therefore it called to question any connection between the two.

Through his research, John had come up with another theory. He believed that Robin Hood was not a name at all, but a description. It was a derivative of the words "robbing hood", making reference to a thief who wore a hood to cover his face when engaged in his profession. Contained within the royal pedigrees and histories of the royal family of England, there was mention of a man by the name of Fulk Fitzwarin, who had grown up with Prince John. At some point during their teenage years, the two boys had a falling out that resulted in a perpetual feud. When Prince John came into power, he decided to confiscate all the property owned by Fitzwarin, which was his prerogative as the ruling authority, and to banish him, causing him to flee into the forest and become an outlaw. Just prior to being outlawed, Fitzwarin was betrothed to Maud Le Vavassour, a young widow. Maud had been part of a marriage of convenience to the Chief Butler of Ireland, but upon her husband's death, her father purchased her marriage rights and then in an attempt to reattach her to the royal family, promised her in marriage to Fulk Fitzwarin. When Fitzwarin fled into the forest, tradition tells that Maud chose to follow him and live the life of an outlaw with him. It seems that even though the marriage was arranged, she had, in fact, fallen in love with Fitzwarin. To John, this seemed a likely source for the legend. Fulk Fitzwarin may actually have been Robin Hood and Maud his Lady Marian.

The Professor kept reading to himself, as if John was not even in the room. John tried to stand patiently, while he waited for the professor to acknowledge his presence. Finally, he decided he could not wait any longer.

"Hello, Professor", John said, somewhat hesitantly, not really sure that the professor had seen him.

"Oh, hello John!" replied the professor, a little startled. "I did not hear you come in. Is it that time again already? I was just catching up on some editing for the ELH (Journal of English Literary History). Come on in and have a seat."

"Thanks Professor, what are you reading?" John tried to sound interested as he slumped down in the chair facing the professor's desk.

"Oh, never mind that, nothing of importance, just some musings really. I have some great news, John. Now where did I put that letter?" The professor began shuffling through the mound of paper on his desk. "It was just here. What did I do with it...? Oh, here it is..."

"What is it?" John asked, somewhat curious.

"It's your acceptance letter, you've been granted the summer fellowship for the study abroad program at Oxford."

"Oxford! As in Oxford, England? What fellowship?" John asked in bewilderment. "I didn't apply for any fellowship, what are you talking about?"

"The fellowship for the summer study abroad program at Oxford," replied the Professor. "I am sure I told you about it. I thought I would put in a good word for you. After all it is a great opportunity. Don't you remember? It is for this summer"

Besides his wisdom, the professor was also known to be a bit absent minded. He would become so distracted in his work, at times, he would forget things, or in this case, remember things that had never happened. "Sorry, Professor, I guess I had forgotten about it. Maybe you could remind me of the details."

"Well, like I was saying, this is an incredible opportunity, a full fellowship, covering all your expenses to attend the

Summer Institute in Medieval Literature, at Oxford. It begins the second week of June and runs to the first week of August. It will allow you to follow up on your research into the origins of ancient English oral traditions. You must go."

"But Professor, don't you remember! Annie and I were planning to get married in August. I can't leave for the summer, right when were supposed to be planning a wedding."

"Ridiculous, John. She'll understand. This is an incredible opportunity. Besides she doesn't need you around. Women want to do the wedding their own way, you would only be in the way."

"I'm not sure Annie would look at it that way. I mean, it is not as if I wouldn't want to go...but really, how could I? Our wedding is in early August, I would be getting home just a few days before. It just sounds like really bad timing. "

"Look," the Professor became a little more adamant. "There is no way that you are going to be able to complete your thesis work sitting here in your office, or hanging out in the library. As good as our library is, and even with interlibrary loans, you are never going to be able to find answers to your questions without going to the source. After all, you are researching legends and myths that have not necessarily been published. You must go to England, it is the only way. You go and talk to Annie about it, I am sure she would agree with me. You'll see; it will all work out."

John knew that there would be little benefit in continuing the argument. The professor was obstinate and a fierce debater. It wasn't as if he could make John go, so arguing would just be pointless. "Okay... I'll talk to her, we'll see..." John relinquished.

"Fine, fine... so tell me, how is your research going? Have you uncovered any more puzzles?"

"Well, it's still pretty slow going. It seems as if every legend is veiled in mystery or rooted in myth in some way," John decided to put aside the discussion of the fellowship. He

11

would need time to construct a better argument against going if he were to make any headway with the Professor.

"Why do you think that is?" The Professor started to get into his teacher mode.

"Well, at least a part of it can be attributed to language", John replied.

"I see," the Professor stroked his chin thoughtfully. "What do you mean by language?"

"Well, it is not just the language. I think it has to do with the fact that these ballads were passed along orally. This, by circumstance, created inaccuracies, or embellishments."

"How so?"

"In any culture the language is woven together with metaphor, idioms and slang. To compound the problem, during the Middle Ages in England there was a blending of many languages, the Celtic, Norman, Saxon, and Pict. As oral traditions were passed on from generation to generation, among a people that had blended vocabulary, it was quite possible that words and phrases were mispronounced, often enough that by the time the ballad was written down, the writer had to interpret what sometimes may have sounded like gibberish."

The professor sat quietly. John knew that the dead air meant that he was supposed to keep going. "Of course, the mystery was a part of the advantage to the novelist like Scott."

"What do you mean?"

"Well, in any good novel there has to be some tension, some kind of conflict. This is better achieved if not all the answers are provided up front. Without mystery, there are no unanswered questions; which means there is no plot, which means there is no story."

"Exactly," affirmed the Professor. "Now you see; the novelist is both researcher and story teller. The one can't exist without the other. But eventually, the novelist wants to know the answers to the questions. The story has to be brought to a conclusion. You can't leave it open ended.

Whether tragedy or comedy, it must be brought to a conclusion. But even if a ballad has mystery, unanswered questions, that is, there must be truth. What really did happen? Is it possible to find out the truth? What evidence is available to us to either affirm or dispel the myth? Take for example, this ballad concerning this… Who was it?… A Sir Albany, I think."

"A right… I think you mean Sir Albany de Featherstonhaugh", John confirmed.

"Right, Sir Albany of Featherstonhaugh," the Professor continued. "Even if we can confirm that he was a real person, there are still questions left unanswered. Why was he killed? What was his relationship with the party that killed him? Can this be found out nearly 500 years later? Is there a reason why the oral tradition leaves out the details? Is it because the details were not considered critical to the story? These are all important questions."

It was the professor who first put John onto Scott's lesser known work *Marmion*, which contained a ballad about the Ridley clan, and the border wars. This intrigued John, especially since he had the same surname as the characters in the ballad. He had never really been all that interested in his family history, but when he thought that he might have a connection to these characters, he could not help feeling curious, wanting to dig deeper into the details.

"How are you going to make sense of it all? How will you know if it really happened?" The professor asked after a momentary pause.

"I know what you're getting at. You're saying I have to go to the source, and in this case the source is somewhere in England." John knew that the discussion would somehow get back to this. No matter how many times it happened, John always forgot that the professor's questions were not merely questions, but they always led somewhere. He was 'Socrates in sheep's clothing'.

"I think we're done here," said the Professor. That was the signal for the session to end. "I've got work to do…I have to get back to this manuscript, and I think you have some soul searching to do. Don't take too long with this. There really is only one decision to be made, so get on with it. Have a nice day John. I will see you next week."

John took this as his cue to leave. "Goodbye Professor, I will talk to Annie and let you know what I decide." He got up from his chair and walked to the door. The professor muttered something under his breath that sounded something like "what's there to decide."

*****

It was late in the afternoon and John did not really feel like going to the library in this weather. Besides, he was meeting Annie for dinner at the Pizza Haven, on this end of campus, in just a couple of hours. Walking all the way across campus in below zero temperatures, and then having to return, as it was getting dark, seemed a poor idea. He decided he would go back to the T.A. office and get a little work done. That way he would not have to leave the building and brave the cold, until it was absolutely necessary. He had some papers to grade anyway.

After about an hour of red marking student essays, John pulled out the copy of Sir Walter Scott's *Marmion* he had checked out of the library. He quickly thumbed through it to the ballad that he and the professor had been discussing earlier.

THE DEATH OF FEATHERSTONHAUGH

Hoot awa', lads, hoot awa'
Ha' ye heard how the Ridleys, and Thirlwalls, and a',
Ha' set upon Albany Featherstonhaugh,
And taken his life at the Deadmanshaugh?
There was Williamoteswick,
And Hardriding Dick,
And Hughie of Hawdon, and Will of the Wa',
I canno tell a', I canno tell a',

And mony a mair that the deil may knaw.

The auld man went down, but Nicol, his son,
Ran away afore the fight was begun;
And he run, and he run,
And afore they were done,
There was many a Featherston gat sic a stun,
As never was seen since the world was begun.

I canno tell a', I canno tell a';
Some gat a skelp, and some gat a claw;
But they garr'd the Featherstons haud their jaw,
Nichol, and Alick, and a'.
Some gat a hurt, and some gat nane;
Some had harness, and some gat sta'en.

Ane gat a twist o' the craig;
And gat a bunch o' the wame;
Symy Haw gat lamed of a leg,
And syne ran wallowing haine.

Hoot! hoot! the auld man's slain outright!
Lay him now wi' his face down; - he's a sorrowful sight.
Janet, thou donot.
I'll lay my best bonnet,
Thou gets a new gude-man afore it be night.

Hoo away, lads, hoo away,
We's a' be hangid if we stay.
Tak' up the dead man, and lay him anent the bigging.
Here's the Bailey o' Haltwhistle,
Wi' his great bull's pizzle,
That supp'e up the broo', and syne ----- in the piggin.

In his notes, Scott had described that there had been a
feud that existed between the two families, Featherstonhaugh
(haugh is from the middle English meaning hollow or corner

15

of land) and Ridleys. And that the characters Willimoteswick, Hardriding Dick, Hughie of Hawdon and Will of the Wa' were all members of the Ridley clan. The reference to Thirwall was another prominent family of Northumberland that must have been allied with the Ridleys at the time. The clue to the location of this supposed murder is found in the last stanza when Haltwhistle is mentioned, a village on the south Tyne river in Northumberland.

Scott further explained that he first came across this ballad, when an old woman of 80 years sang it for him. She had first heard it as a young child and said it had often been sung by the men of the borders (referring to the border between Scotland and Northumberland) around the fire at night.

Did it describe a real event or was it just a legend? Was it a myth that had some basis in fact? Did these individuals actually exist, and if so when did they live? Most importantly, what was the feud about? Perhaps the professor was right. The only way that John would ever find answers to these questions would be to go to England. But, why did it have to be this summer? Couldn't it wait?

One thing was for sure, the places mentioned in the ballad were real. While browsing in the library, John had come across a geography book that contained images of maps of England from the early 1800s. The map of Northumberland showed the location of Featherstonhaugh Castle, Thirwall Castle and Willimoteswick Castle. All of them were a short distance from Haltwhistle on the Tyne River. Researching a little more he discovered that the entire area was called Tynedale and included two other rather large towns, Hexham and Newcastle. Down deep, John did feel a longing to go England. He was intrigued by the history of the place. Like any young boy, he had always been attracted to the swashbuckling tales of knights, damsels in distress, castles and dragons. What were these places really like? After such a long time had past, would he be able to discover anything new that would unravel the mystery concerning Sir

Albany? Something stirred in his heart, a longing for adventure, a need to find answers. The more he thought about it, the more appealing it became. He had nearly convinced himself, and yet he was troubled. What was he going to tell Annie?

John was looking forward to seeing Annie, although he wasn't exactly sure how he was going to tell her the news. The news presented by the Professor was really poor timing. Annie had been gone the entire fall for a semester abroad in Ecuador and now John had to tell her that he would be gone all summer. It was not going to go over very well. As it was, Annie had not quite seemed herself ever since she had returned. At first John just attributed it to jet lag or the readjustment to school. He wasn't sure what it was, but something seemed a bit off. Clearly this news was not going to make it any better. The more he thought about it the more anxious he became. He tried to work out the words in his head, but no matter how long he thought about it, he could not come up with a way of easing into it.

*****

Inevitably six o'clock rolled around and he crossed over the street to Pizza Haven. It was Wednesday, and even though the restaurant sat right on the edge of campus town, it wasn't very busy. He was able to get a table right away. He was able to get a booth that overlooked Lincoln St and as the waitress seated him, he went ahead and ordered their usual. He was pleased to get the booth, it offered a little extra privacy and he had a feeling he was going to need it. Annie had a seminar from four thirty until six, and it would take her at least 15 minutes to walk across campus. If everything worked out, the pizza would arrive just about the time she sat down.

He was reading when Annie slid into the seat across from him. She smiled awkwardly and mumbled something like, "Sorry, my lips are a little cold, it is pretty bad outside today."

"How was your day?" It seemed a bit of a trite question, but John was a bit nervous and grasping for words.

"Oh... it was pretty good, although the weather is a bit extreme," She replied as she stripped off her coat, gloves and scarf and laid them on the bench seat beside her.

"Yeah, I know what you mean," John agreed. "I couldn't feel my nose when I got to class this morning. I thought it was going to fall off."

"That's a pretty thought." Just then the waitress arrived with the pizza. "Oh, good, I'm starved!" She exclaimed.

John took Annie's hands in his and said a little prayer over the pizza. He then grabbed the spatula and served a piece for Annie and then for himself. They began eating without further comment about the weather. They were both so preoccupied with their meal, it grew uncomfortably quiet. John did not really know where to begin and for her part, Annie seemed preoccupied. As was his usual habit, when faced with a difficult problem, he was procrastinating. He did not really want to start this conversation. He looked out the window trying to gather his thoughts, but it was not working, the sun had long since set and there was nothing outside to see, but cold and dark. He looked back at Annie, she looked away, down at her plate. He let the silence linger a little more. He just sat there watching her eat, and said nothing.

Annie was strikingly beautiful, with long dark hair and deep blue eyes that completely captivated him whenever she looked at him. She was wearing a navy turtleneck sweater, suitable to guard against the cold, but also just snug enough to compliment her feminine figure. It was not noticeable to John whether she ever wore any make-up. She had a natural beauty that required little in the way of enhancements. If she wore jewelry, it was always subtle and non-distracting. She was very pleasant to look at and had an endearing personality to match.

Slow, but sure, the pizza began to disappear, and they began to make small talk, about things like how was your day? What are you doing tomorrow? Did you see so and so?

18

How was this class or that one? All of this kept delaying the inevitable. He knew that he was going to have to say something, but how was he going to tell her about England? He just couldn't? But he had to. How should he begin? He kept waiting for the opening? And then, just as he was beginning to think he could avoid it altogether, the opening came.

"How did your meeting go with Professor Winslow?" She asked.

It was now or never. "How should he start?" he thought to himself.

There was only one way to begin, he would just have to spit it out. "It went pretty well," he began, "although, he did kind of drop a bomb on me."

"What you mean?" she asked.

"Well unbeknownst to me, the Professor had recommended me for a summer fellowship, get this, at Oxford, no less. I mean really, there are times when I never really know what to expect with him. He claims that he had already told me all about it, but I don't ever remember discussing it. I mean, I think I would remember us discussing a trip to England. He expects me to go to England THIS SUMMER, for ten weeks; just when we are supposed to be planning our wedding."

"It sounds like a really good opportunity. Why are you so upset?" she appeared a bit more supportive than he could have imagined.

"It is a good opportunity," he continued. "It's a great opportunity, it is just horrible timing. I mean really, how could I consider going? I would be getting back just a couple of weeks before the wedding. I could not do that to you, it would not be fair. The whole time I was gone I would be thinking of you and how I left you to do all the preparations for our wedding on your own. I could never forgive myself."

"That's really sweet John, but I think you should go," she said rather quietly, looking down at the table, refusing to meet his eyes.

"You think I should go?" he asked surprised. "Really! I don't know what to say. I thought you would be disappointed. I guess the professor was right. He said you would be okay with it. I didn't believe him. He sat there and said you would not mind, and that I would only be in the way. I thought he was crazy." He was beginning to ramble now, which he always tended to do when his emotions got the best of him. "So you really don't mind, you think I should go?" he asked one more time.

"Yes, I think you should go," she replied despondently. "It is too good an opportunity, and you shouldn't...you can't pass it up. In fact...," she paused before continuing, "there's something I need to tell you as well."

John could tell by the tenor of her voice that something was bothering her, but he did not think it had anything to do with his news. She seemed genuinely anxious about something, even to the point of being detached.

"I should have talked to you about this earlier," she began. "I don't know why I haven't. I suppose I've been frightened, or worried. I don't know why I have waited this long. It really isn't fair to you or me. I kept trying to tell myself that I didn't want to hurt you, but truth is, I have just lacked the courage."

"Well what is it?" He was starting to get a little nervous. He did not like the way she sounded, and he could sense that this conversation was going to end very badly.

"Don't interrupt me please," she started again. "This is hard enough as it is." She paused for a moment. The silence allowed her to gather her thoughts. She looked up at him and stared sorrowfully into his eyes. "John, I don't think we should get married... I'm sorry, I know this is going to come as a shock. I don't' exactly know how to begin. The last thing I wanted to do was hurt you. I do love you, but I can't marry you." A tear started to trickle down her cheek. Her voice had become quivery.

For a moment he sat in stunned silence. "I don't understand," he was in a bit of shock. "What happened? Did I do something? I mean if you love me, why can't you marry me?" He could see more tears welling up in her eyes. He hesitated..."is there someone else?" He could not believe he was even asking this.

Slowly, she nodded her head up and down. She started to say something, but she was stumbling over the words. "I mean... it just sort of ... happened. I don't know how to explain it..."

"It just sort of happened! How? Who is it? What do you mean... it just sort of happened!" He was trying not to yell, but his emotions were all jumbled up. For one moment he had been nervous to share his own news, the next moment he was listening to something inconceivable. He could not believe his ears. The room was spinning, and he could feel his emotions getting the best of him.

"Shhh....," Annie cautioned, looking around at the other people in the restaurant. She took a deep breath, attempting to compose herself. "I met him in Ecuador. We were both part of the same program. We spent nearly every day together. We were just friends. He new that I was engaged, I mean, he is not that kind of guy. We tried to keep our distance, but the more time we spent together the more our friendship grew. I would not let myself think of him romantically. I kept telling myself, I'm in love with John, and we are going to get married."

"When I came home in December, I found myself thinking about Tom; that's his name, Thomas Moore, like the priest. I began to realize that I was falling in love with him. I couldn't believe it myself. I kept asking, God, what are you doing? How could this be happening? It is not right? Then he came to visit me at Christmas. He poured out his heart to me. He had fallen in love with me. He knew that I was engaged, but he just had to know if there was any chance that I had feelings for him. He proposed to me, and in my shock I said yes. It was as if in that moment we knew, it was meant to be."

"But, then there was you, how was I going to tell you? I can't tell you how many times since we have been back that I have tried to tell you…every time I tried, the words would not come to me. I really never intended to hurt you. It was the last the thing I ever wanted to happen…," she let the words trail off.

John just sat dumbfounded for minute. He could not get his mind around it. He did not even know how to react. He could feel his ire rising, but he tried to keep his emotions in check. Annie was already in tears. Making her feel worse was not going to make him feel better. He was hurt, but somewhere down deep he realized that it was not permanent, that he would eventually get over it. It was like there was a little voice in his head saying, 'it's going to be okay, it was never really meant to be.'

"I guess I had known all along there was something wrong," he tried to sound calm and reassuring. "Ever since we came back at Christmas, you have not been yourself. I guess I thought it was a little hangover from the trip, and that you just needed some time to readjust to campus life again. It never occurred to me that it was anything more. I don't know what to say," he went on. "I can tell there is no going back, you seem too sure of yourself. I just don't know how to react, I'm sad. I'm angry. I'm confused. I don't know…what am I supposed to do?"

"Nothing, John, don't you see? You didn't do anything wrong, neither did I. It is better that we find out now, rather than later. It was just not meant to be. God has other plans. We don't always understand them, but in the end they are right."

John knew she was right. Men tend to think they are in control of their lives, and in some ways they have some control, over small moments, but in the really big things, God always brings them back to his plan. It was mysterious, but it was also comforting. He knew that this was why, down deep, he already knew this was right. It wasn't that it was any less painful, but sometimes the pain we experience, is due to our own failure to listen to God, and go down paths that move us a little away from God's plan. It was right, but it was hard. He wanted to cry out, to lash out, but it was pointless.

"I really believe," Annie continued, "God intends for you to go to England. It wasn't your plan, but He new, even before we had this conversation that you needed to go. I'm not trying to make excuses, and I am not trying to convince you to go, just to ease my own guilt. I feel horrible, but at the same time, I am convinced that this is right. Going back to Ecuador with Tom is God's plan for me, going to England is God's plan for you. Only God knows where it will take you, but that's just the point, who do you want in control, Him or you?"

"You don't have to feel guilty, Annie", John was beginning to come to grips with the reality of the situation. "I know you would never intentionally hurt me. I will survive. You will just have to give me some time...So you're going back to Ecuador?"

"Yeah, I am going to finish out this semester, and then we are going back to Ecuador. We have been offered an opportunity to work in an orphanage. We plan on leaving some time in August, as soon as we are married."

"Wow! Just like that. And working in an orphanage, I never knew you had it in you." John did not know what else to say.

"I'm sorry," Annie returned. "It all happened so fast. I know it seems a bit brash, but it is what I need to do. Please be happy for me."

The waitress came with the check. It was just in time. John felt a bit drained emotionally. He needed some alone time to think through what had just happened. Annie picked up the check, "I think maybe I should get this, given the circumstances and all."

John didn't feel it necessary to argue. He stood up and put his coat on. Annie did the same and then reached out to give him a hug. He held on for just a moment. She whispered in his ear, "I'm really sorry." As she said this, she placed something in his hand. She then turned and walked to the cashier. John turned and walked to the door and stepped out into the frigid cold. He looked down in his hand. It was a piece of folded up tissue. He felt beneath the paper, but he didn't need to look at it. It was Annie's engagement ring. He slipped it into his pants pocket without even looking inside. He didn't turn to look at Annie as he sensed her exit the door behind him. He didn't want her to see that he had tears in his eyes.

*****

For the next several days John was in a daze. He couldn't seem to focus on anything. He went through the motion of teaching his classes, but could hardly remember any of the discussion points later. He felt lost. He liked having a plan and knowing where he was going, but right now, all his plans and aspirations seemed meaningless and disjointed without the prospects of Annie sharing in them.

He kept replaying their conversation over and over in his mind. He'd tried to remain calm and amiable when she had begun to talk about how this was God's plan all the time. Even though he initially agreed with her in his heart, as he had time to reflect, he began to wrestle with the whole 'God is sovereign' thing. The reality is, that when things are going well the sovereignty of God makes perfect sense, but the minute that disappointment or even tragedy strikes, believing God is sovereign is not always that comforting, and sometimes it is even confusing and frustrating.

If God is sovereign, and if in this case, he really didn't want Annie and John to get married, then why have them go through the whole dating thing and eventual engagement, if it was never meant to be? It was not as if John or Annie had been deliberately trying to choose to disobey God, and disrupt His plans when they first became attracted to each other and started to date. And John did not remember any little voice in his head telling him 'no, don't do that' when he decided to ask Annie to marry him. Neither John nor Annie could be described as carefree and haphazard in their decision making. They were relatively rational individuals. The thing was, if in fact God had other plans, why did He allow them get so serious, knowing they would have to suffer through the present pain. It didn't make sense.

John had become so comfortable with thinking about his future with Annie, and now that he was confronted with a future without her, he didn't know how to move forward. Every day he thought through all the arguments to their end and he came to the conclusion that maybe she had never really loved him in the first place. This haunted him. The thought that it was all a lie, made him angry. Why would she do that?

As each day passed, John became more despondent as he sank into a continuous cycle of feeling depressed, then pitiful, then confused, and then angry. He knew he should let it go, and he tried. But just as he thought he was starting to let go, he would bump into Annie on campus or at church. Each time, it was immensely awkward. They would greet each other, and then make some small talk about the weather or school. Every time he looked at her, he would see in her eyes this sort of woeful 'I'm really sorry' look. He began avoiding church, just so he would not see her. Not just her. There were also those looks from everyone around him. Those horrible 'Isn't it sad about John and Annie looks' as if they knew every detail. He just wanted to get away.

The prospect of leaving for the summer and going to another country was beginning to look better and better every day. He had already told Professor Winslow that he was going. Of course, the Professor had believed that John was going all along, so the news did not elicit any sort of celebratory congratulations. He chose not to tell him about his breakup with Annie. The last thing he needed was consoling from a sixty-something. He decided to let the professor find out his own way.

John had never been to Europe. It had always seemed to be beyond his grasp. His parents were typically middle class, and would never have done anything so extravagant as splurging on a trip to Europe.

He had grown up in Beaver Falls, Pennsylvania, a day's drive from Urbana. His dad had a good job, working for the water department. It was secure, and came with government benefits. He had a younger brother, and together the four of them had lived simply in a three bedroom Georgian home, with detached garage, in a fairly normal residential neighborhood on the edge of town. They had all pretty much stayed close to home, and there was never any room for extravagances.

He would never forget his mom's reaction to his going to grad school. "Are you sure you know what you're doing?" she had whispered to him as he left for U of I. His father was the first to ever have gone to college in his family and no one had ever achieved an advanced degree of any kind, let alone a Ph.D.

Even though he had never been to Europe, John had dreamed about it. He loved to travel and explore new places. His parents had taken him and his brother to Washington D.C. one summer. It was one of his favorite memories. He had always wished they had traveled more.

Now John had three reasons to go to England: one to fulfill his travel fantasy; another to have an opportunity to complete his thesis research; and finally, most importantly, to get as far away from U of I and Annie as he possibly could.

John did have one daily comfort. It came in the form of his friend Stephen Hansen, one of his fellow graduate students in the English department, and one of his roommates at the "Nevada House" (that's what everyone called the house he shared with two other grad students on Nevada Street). Every time they got together and Annie's name came into the conversation, Stephen would promptly chime in, "would you forget about her. Why do you keep beating yourself up about it? You are better off without her. I mean, can you really see yourself traipsing off to Ecuador and spending the rest of your life working with under privileged kids in some out of the way hell hole." Although Stephen was a bit crude, he always seem to make John feel a whole lot better about the situation.

February gradually eased into March, and with March came spring break. The weather finally began to warm up and the trees began to show their new growth. John loved the spring, and his spirits were lifted at the thought. Graduate students did not always take advantage of the school breaks and go home-even though they were not teaching any classes-it was a great time to focus on research with very little distraction. In this case, however, John felt the need to get away and go home. He was looking forward to it, although he did not look forward to those first few moments of his mom showering him with pity in her not so subtle way. He had not told his parents about Annie right away, but he knew that it was better to tell them before he actually went home, so he had called them the Sunday before he left and gently broke both pieces of news; that he was no longer getting married and that he was going to England for the summer. It was not surprising that his mom was beside herself and was having great difficulty coming to grips with both.

John's last class on Friday ended at eleven. He immediately went back to the house, threw all his laundry into a large basket, and then into the trunk of his Toyota Corolla. He grabbed a few books, a small suitcase, with what few clean clothes he owned, and his guitar. On his way out the door he shouted goodbye to Stephen, who was sprawled on the living room couch, vegging out and listening to some Fleetwood Mac.

As he made his way down the walk, he could here Stephen shout, "Don't forget to bring me back some of your mom's apple pie. You forget and I will never speak to you again."

It was about a 10 hour drive to Beaver Falls.

Chapter Two

He could see her through the trees. She was standing on top of a rise, facing away from him, but he new it was her, all dressed in white, a veil covering her head. He began to run towards her. As he approached, she turned to look at him. As he drew near he slowed and then stopped, unsure if he should go any further, not wanting to frighten her. He wished he could see her face. Who was she? As she stood facing him, looking at him, it was as if there was an impenetrable wall that would not let him proceed any further. He longed to know her, to be close enough to touch her. He did not know her, and yet she was not entirely unfamiliar; something he could not explain. He took another step, but she remained distant. He wanted so much for her to remove her veil. He yearned to know her. Was she real? Did she know who he was? Why was she here, all alone?

*Just then her head tilted as she looked to the sky. He followed her eyes to the trees above. There, twenty feet above her, sitting on branches directly above her, were three crows. No wait, they weren't crows, they were too big. They were **ravens**. As he looked at them they turned and looked back toward him and then suddenly, without warning, they sang out, a loud screeching, unearthly sound...*

John awoke suddenly to a car horn blaring outside on the street. It was Saturday morning and he was in his own bed at home. The covers were all twisted, as if he had been wrestling with them all night, and he was a little damp from perspiration.

He looked around the room and saw his posters and memorabilia, still displayed on the walls and bookshelves. His mom had not touched a thing since he had first left for Wheaton, almost seven years ago. He sat up and let his feet drop to the floor. He ran his hands through his hair and scratched his head, rubbed his eyes, and tried to get rid of the last remnants of sleep from his mind.

He had had another one of those dreams last night. It had been three or four weeks since the last one and he had been hoping it had been the last of them. They left him weary and confused. What did it mean? Was he totally losing it? He did not dare tell anybody about it, they would think he was crazy. Each time the dream seamed more vivid, and yet at the same time, more mysterious. It all seemed so real, which made it all the more disturbing.

The smell of bacon frying reached his nostrils. That could mean only one thing, his mom was making his typical welcome home breakfast, bacon lightly crisp, eggs over easy, with a nice stack of fluffy pancakes on the side, smothered with old fashioned maple syrup. His mom was not in the habit of cooking breakfast all that often. They had always been your typical, down a bowl of cereal as you ran out the door to school, kind of family. Never the less, his mom always made a point to make him a huge breakfast the morning he arrived home for a visit. He assumed it was to get him to come home more often.

He had got in pretty late last night, so he hadn't had much time to talk to his parents. This meant that he was going to have to face the music, this morning, at breakfast. This left a bit of a knot in the pit in his stomach that no pancake breakfast was going to fill. He slowly stood up from the bed and stumbled down the hallway to the bathroom. The wooden floor was cold to his feet, but at the same time all too familiar, he was home. He splashed some water on his face to clear the cobwebs and then looked at himself in the mirror to be sure he was somewhat presentable. Determining that his appearance was adequate for family presentation, he made his way downstairs and into the kitchen.

As John entered the kitchen his mom had her back to him and his dad was sitting at the table reading the newspaper, as was his morning habit. As he started to pull a chair out from the table he whispered a quiet and muttered, "good morning".

"Good morning John, welcome home," his dad said now peering over the top edge of the newspaper. "Did you sleep okay?"

Immediately his mom turned from whatever she was doing at the stove and briskly walked to the table, where she promptly bent down and gave John a big hug and kiss on the cheek. "Yes, welcome home Johnny (that was what most everyone in the family called him, and even though he preferred John, he never said anything to discourage it), it is so good to have you home," she added. "It has been too long," even though it had only been since Christmas.

John did not feel the need to make a point of this. "It's good to be home, Mom. What's for breakfast?"

"Your favorites," she replied (she didn't need to go into detail).

"What's new in school?" his father asked, with a kind of smirk on his face.

"Oh Bill, stop making small talk," his mom interrupted. "Johnny, we wanted to hear about you and Annie. Is the wedding really off? I mean, maybe it's just sort of a lover's spat. You know these things happen. Whatever it is, tell her you're sorry, and then give her a little time to get over it. Every relationship has its difficult moments."

"No, it's really off, Mom." He really did not want to get into this. "She met someone else...she is marrying someone else. Can we just drop it?"

"I don't understand," his mom was not going to give in. "How did she meet someone else? She was engaged to you. How does someone meet someone else, when they are engaged to someone already? That just shouldn't happen."

"You're right Mom. It shouldn't happen, but it did. They met in Ecuador. It wasn't really like Annie meant for it to happen... I mean, she did not really mean to fall in love with someone else, to create all this hurt and confusion, it just happened," John sounded as if he was trying to convince himself, as much as his parents.

"But you were so right for each other," his mom continued the barrage. "We loved Annie. She is exactly who we would have picked for you. She was a perfect fit. We were so happy for both of you." Now it sounded as if his mom was more disappointed for herself than for John.

"I know, Mom, it seemed right. But I guess it was never meant to be, or at least that was what Annie thought," it was his only defense. "Now can we drop it? I really don't want to talk about it anymore. Let's talk about something else. Dad how is everything at work?"

"But, Johnny," his mom did not want to let go. "We just want to help. It just seems so strange that it's over, just like that. It is just so hard to believe that the two of you don't love each other anymore. I mean, how do you feel about this? We just want to know." This made John blush with anger. The last thing he wanted to do was talk to his mother about how he was feeling.

"Now Carol," his dad interceded. "He says he doesn't want to talk about it anymore, let's change the subject. Hey Johnny, what is this we hear about you going to England?"

His Dad actually seemed interested, or maybe it was just an easy way to change the subject. His mom started serving the pancakes. John had already sampled the bacon, and he was starting to feel hungry. He started smothering the pancakes in butter and syrup as he talked.

"Yeah Dad, it looks like I am going to England," he retorted. "Pretty crazy huh? I can hardly believe it myself."

"Do you want some orange juice, Johnny," his mom interrupted. He could tell she was still thinking about Annie.

"Thanks Mom, I'd love some," John replied, hopeful that the conversation had taken a turn.

"What exactly are you going to be doing in England, again?" his dad asked.

"Well, the opportunity to go came because I was chosen for a fellowship to attend a summer long symposium at Oxford University," he continued. "It is really a very cool opportunity.

There will be scholars from all over the world attending, many of them grad students like myself, and many of them coming from the U.S., I imagine. We will have opportunities to attend seminars, participate in discussion groups, and generally take advantage of the resources of the University Libraries. It could prove to be very helpful for my research."

"Sounds like you're pretty excited about it," his mom said trying to sound pleased.

"I wasn't at first," he went on. "It seemed like a long ways to go to do research. But then the more I thought about it, the more I realized it was a great opportunity, and the travel, going to new places, could actually turn out to be a lot of fun. So I guess you would say that I have gotten used to the idea, and yes I am getting excited about it."

"How are you going to pay for this?" This was the practical side of his Dad coming out.

"That's the great part about it Dad, nearly all of my expenses are covered. Even more importantly while I am there I will have a little free time to go and explore and follow some leads on my research. I should have time to actually leave Oxford and travel to other parts of England. It's quite adventurous when you think about it." John did not go into the details of his research with his parents, so he was trying to keep the discussion somewhat superficial. He was not sure they would exactly understand or at least they would not see it as meaningful. There was no need to get into it with them.

"Completely paid for, sound great!" his dad was now on board.

"Seems like a long way to go just to do *research*," his mom put a little accent on the word research as if she still did not understand why it was so important. "Are you sure you are going to be safe. Traveling by yourself in a foreign country can be dangerous you know."

"Of course it will be safe, Mom," John tried to be reassuring. "It's not like a third world country or anything. Besides they speak English, I won't have any difficulty getting around. It'll be fun, an adventure. After all, you did not seem so worried about Annie going to Ecuador." Oh no, just as he said it John knew it was mistake.

"Well I would have been worried had I known she was going to meet someone else and break off your engagement. Of all things, what kind of person would fall in love with someone else when they are already engaged," she fired back.

"Now let's not go there again. It's best to leave it alone Carol," his dad came to the rescue.

At that point, John thought it better to stop talking altogether. Keeping the conversation going only meant risking the possibility of it circling back to Annie. He sat quietly, pretending to be occupied with his breakfast, stuffing his mouth full of pancakes. After a moment of dead air, his mom picked up the conversation, again, with trivial news about his home town. This was interlaced with stories of the new mall being built, and an acquaintance from church that had passed away. And then there were the announcements of John's classmates from high school who had recently become engaged, or married, or even some who had had babies. He was not sure if his mom was doing this to make a point or if she was simply spouting random news. He tended to think it was the former, not the latter. In any case, he was not going to take the bait. He just remained quiet occasionally offering an "um" or "is that so".

After a while, the conversation turned from news about Beaver Falls, and turned to news about his family. Both his mother and father had come from large families and, as a result, John had a whole slew of cousins. He thought the number had grown to almost thirty and that did not include his cousins once removed. Not only that, but John still had three grandparents living and his father's paternal grandmother, Great-Grandma Ridley was still alive. All this being said, every family reunion was ridiculously huge, between the aunts and uncles, cousins, and second cousins, etc., John found it difficult to remember anybody's name.

"...and did I tell you, we heard that your dad's cousin James Ridley is planning on selling the family farm in Ontario," his mom was now rambling. "You know, the old homestead that has been in the family for years. Speaking of which, your father called your Great-Grandma Ridley last week to wish her a happy birthday. It's her 90th you know. And anyway, we mentioned that you were planning a trip to England. She seemed very interested. You know, she rarely shows any emotion, but she seemed genuinely excited for you. She was born in England you know."

"Yeah, I think I remember something about that," John used to visit his great grandmother quite often, when he was younger. However, he had probably only seen her twice in the last five or six years. He had always liked her. She was relatively kind, not too talkative, except when she had a story to tell, and then it was always something substantial and engaging.

"Well, anyway," his mom continued, "she was hoping you could visit her before you go to England. It would mean so much to her. She may not be with us much longer. I can't say when you will have another chance."

John's great-grandmother had moved with her husband from the family homestead, to the town of Brussels, in Ontario, about 30 years earlier. Her husband, John's great-grandfather, died 12 years later, leaving her widowed. She had a son who lived nearby in Brussels. He

kept an eye on her, but he must have been approaching seventy, himself. She lived in a small Victorian home, in a quiet neighborhood, and she seemed to be doing pretty well for someone advanced in years. Her health seemed good, she was still very alert, and so, the family did not see any reason to put her into a home. The trip from Beaver Falls to Brussels was about eight hours. This did not seem very appealing at first, but then again he might never get to see her again. It would be the perfect opportunity to get away, and it would mean he could avoid talking all week about Annie.

"Yeah, maybe I could go see her," John agreed. "You're right. I may never get another chance. I could leave on Monday, spend Tuesday with her and return on Wednesday."

It had not occurred to his mom, that by making such a suggestion, it meant John would be homeless, but she was trapped now. "...uh, yeah, good, that will be great. We will have to call her tonight, to let her know you are coming."

*****

After breakfast, John put on his running shoes and went for a jog. He was not a disciplined athlete, but while in college it seemed like all of his friends had taken up running to keep in shape. Although running had never been appealing to him, in fact he thought it kind of boring, he had begrudgingly joined in. Now he just did it as a force of habit. He would only run three times a week or so, and only for one and a half to two miles, but it was enough to keep him in reasonably good shape for his other athletic pursuits. He would much rather play a little tennis or better yet a pick-up game of basketball, but it was unlikely that he would be able to do either while he was home in Beaver Falls.

After his jog, he showered and changed and then went down stairs to the family room. His dad was already perched on the couch in front of the T.V. watching college basketball. It was the second week of the NCAA tournament. John had lost interest in the tournament since Illinois had been upset in the second round. However, right now basketball seemed a great diversion, especially if it meant keeping his mom from bringing up Annie again.

He and his dad used to watch basketball together a lot when he was in high school. It was one thing they had in common and could enjoy together. Now sitting there, listening to his dad rebuff the coaches on the screen for their bad decision making, made him feel right at home. There were games on all afternoon, and John's mom knew better than to interrupt. As the afternoon waned, John decided to go upstairs to his room and get caught up on some reading until it was time for dinner.

Dinner went rather smoothly. There was little talk of Annie or England or anything else for that matter. His dad began the dinner conversation by complaining about the referee call at the end of the last tournament game of the day.

Since John and his mom had not been watching at the time, they could not comment. His dad was left to rant and rave for several minutes, without any support or rebuke, after which he just sat quietly and stewed. Needless to say, his dad tended to get a little too caught up in the action. All and all, the dinner was relatively quiet by his family's standards. After dinner, John returned to his studies.

The next morning John attended church with his parents. The family had been attending First Baptist Church for as long as he could remember. It was a large red brick church that sat just a block away from the campus of Geneva College. The current pastor had been there for John's entire life, and it seemed as if John had heard every one of his sermons at least twice. This morning was no different than most. It was a rather typical service, a couple of hymns with a couple contemporary praise choruses mixed in, a special number by the choir, announcements, an offering, followed by the pastor's sermon. Just like clockwork it ended right at noon.

As John exited out the main door of the sanctuary, he made his way through the foyer to the outside and then stood on the walk at the front of the church. As per their usual habits, long time members of the church and friends of the family came by to say "hi" and welcome him home. This time it was a little different. Every conversation began with, "I am so sorry to hear about you and your fiancée, what was her name, Annie?" John could not believe his ears. How had they heard so quickly? He had only told his mom and dad last week. He gave a furtive look at his mom after about the fourth person made the same comment to him. He could tell by the look in her eyes that she was trying to assure him that it was not her fault, "that she had only told one or two people, at most." When the ordeal finally ended, John slouched down in the back seat of their Dodge Monaco, avoiding eye contact with any onlookers, and choosing not to say anything.

His mom slid into the front seat and turned to look over her shoulder, "I probably should have mentioned that I invited the Nelsons over for lunch today, Johnny."

'Perfect!' he thought to himself. It was not unusual for his parents to have friends over on Sunday afternoon. In fact he had pretty much come to expect it, but did they really have to this Sunday, and did it have to be the Nelsons. Had she done this on purpose? The Nelsons had a 25 year old daughter, Linda, still living at home, who he just happened to date when they were in high school. It was one of those things where they had been classmates in school, attending the same church, they just sort of fell into a dating relationship their junior and senior years of high school. Now, she was still single and working as a receptionist at a dental office, or something.

It wasn't so much that John didn't like Linda. It was just that they hadn't dated in over eight years and yet every time he saw her, he could swear that he saw that look of "hope" still in her eyes. Maybe he was reading too much into it, but it seemed to him that she had never gotten over him. No doubt, she, like everyone else at church, had heard of his break-up with Annie, and that would only serve to encourage her "hopefulness".

When the Nelsons arrived, John got up from his comfortable chair in the living room to greet them. Mr. Nelson shook his hand vigorously while giving him an enthusiastic, "good to see you John." Mrs. Nelson smiled and leaned over and gave him a little kiss on the cheek, as was her habit. Linda trailed behind sheepishly, not meeting his eyes directly. She seemed a bit embarrassed and stepped right up to John, gave him a hug and said, "it's always good to see you John," just soft enough so that only he could hear.

His mom immediately directed the entire crowd to the dining room to sit down. A pot roast had been simmering in the oven all morning, and dinner was ready. John's family had always had a heavy lunch or dinner on Sunday afternoon. It was an old tradition that was slowly fading away with most families, but that did not deter his mom. She always had a good portion of the Sunday dinner prepared and ready before they ever left for church on Sunday mornings. It was typically pot roast, ham or some other meat that would take a long time to cook. When summer rolled around, his dad would often barbecue something on the back patio. There was always plenty of food in anticipation of the guests, and it usually meant a lot of 'Sunday leftovers' the rest of the week.

Dinner went surprisingly well. It was as if the Nelsons understood the etiquette of not bringing up painful news a little better than his own parents. And with guests present, his mom and dad were on their best behavior. There was not one mention of Annie during the entire meal. At one point, Linda asked John about his future trip to England. He didn't really mind this. Once his parents had gotten over the initial shock, they had been quite civil about the whole thing, and he was actually beginning to enjoy talking about it, anything was better than 'Annie'.

Since Linda had asked the question, John decided to go into just a little more detail about his research. He explained to the whole group that he was not only going to be at Oxford, but one of the main reasons he was going was so that he could explore Northumberland and Scotland.

At this, Mrs. Nelson asked, "Are you going to visit any castles?"

"Well, yes, I guess I am," he replied. "Northumberland is supposed to be thick with castles and I hope to visit Willimoteswick, a castle once owned by a family by the name of Ridley. Perhaps we may even be related to them. I'm not sure, but it would be kind of cool to find out that we were."

"That sounds exciting," Mrs. Nelson continued. "Castles are so romantic, so much history. So, you really think you might be related to the family that once owned this castle?"

"It's possible. I suppose I will be able to find out, once I get there," John replied. "I know that our ancestors originally came from England, but that's about all I know. Isn't that right Dad?"

"That's as much as I know as well," his father joined into the conversation. "My paternal great grandfather, John Ridley, was born in England, I think. But I don't know any of the details. He was dead before I was of an age to really know him, and my grandfather, rarely talked about our English heritage."

"I must say, I am a little jealous John, I have always wanted to go to England," Mrs. Nelson then turned to her husband and gave a playful slap on the shoulder. "When are *you* going to take me to England?"

Mr. Nelson was obviously thinking of something else and he kind of jumped with a start, "Now see what you've done John, I won't hear the end of this for weeks. The last thing I need is to be badgered about some trip to England. It's a ridiculous waste of money if you ask me." Mr. Nelson tended to be very frugal.

"Sorry Mr. Nelson, I will try to be more careful about what I talk about in the future," John said with a wry smile. "Did you see any of the basketball yesterday?"

"Now don't try changing the subject you two, and John, you never mind Mr. Nelson. You go on talking about England and any other places you want to. Maybe this one will get the message," as she pointed at her husband.

The dinner conversation started to wind down and John's mom entered with some plates of apple pie a la mode. He was always amazed at how she would slip out quietly in the middle of conversations without anyone noticing and then she would be back in a flash with dessert. She was kind of spoiling John at this point, she new that apple was his favorite. In his mind, no one came close to making apple pie like his mom.

"Maybe you young people would like to take your dessert to the den," his mom stated, as if suggesting something. "It's time you leave us old people alone."

This was her way of providing a way out for John and Linda. He was not sure if she had ulterior motives or not, but he really didn't mind. Linda and been fairly respectful and at a distance all during dinner. He didn't think there was any risk in spending some time alone with her.

"Shall we," he offered, grabbing both plates of dessert at the same time and allowing her to lead.

As they sat down on the couch, he set the pie in front of them on the coffee table, and she began the conversation, "Your research sounds really interesting, John. I think, like my mom, I am also just a little envious. England sounds as if it will be wonderful."

"I must admit," John, began, trying to appear humble, "at first I wasn't sure that I wanted to go. It was really my advisor's doing. But then, after I began to get used to the idea, I really began to get excited. I mean...I have always enjoyed traveling, and Europe has always been on my list of places I wanted to go. I just never thought I would get there... It seemed too far out of reach, too expensive. But enough about me, what is new in your life, are you still working for Dr. Anderson?"

"Yes, I am still his receptionist," she said smiling. "The truth is, I rather enjoy it. I like to interact with the patients, you know put them at ease, especially since most of them hate to go to the dentist. Unfortunately, I may not be able to stay there much longer."

"Why not? He's not retiring or anything," John thought that Dr. Anderson couldn't be more than fifty five, but he might be wrong.

"No, it's not him, it's me, I am engaged to be married," she said it rather nervously as she held up her ring finger.

John could not possibly hide his surprise, "That's ... great Linda! Really great!" John couldn't believe he hadn't noticed her ring at the dinner table. He must have been too preoccupied. "I am really happy for you," he collected himself. "Who's the lucky guy?"

"It's okay John," she was consoling him, "I was a bit surprised myself. It all happened rather quickly. His name is Mark Simpkins."

"How'd you guys meet?" John kept the conversation going as he tried to act nonchalant.

"We met last summer," she continued. "His parents had just moved here to Beaver Falls, and he was going to graduate school at Penn State, getting his Master's in education, so he can teach high school history. He came to stay with his parents for the summer and we met at the church Fourth of July picnic. He started asking me out and we dated some during the summer. When he returned to school, we started writing back and forth. We saw each other one or two weekends and then Thanksgiving, and when he came home at Christmas he proposed and the rest is history. We plan to get married in August."

"Wow! That's unbelievable," John slowly released the air from his lungs. "Why didn't you say something earlier?"

"I'm sorry, John," she said blushing slightly. "I wanted to, but I didn't really know how to start. In fact, I made my parents promise they wouldn't say anything. I didn't know what you would think."

"I am very happy for you," John did mean it. "I would never want anything but the best for you. You should know that."

"Thanks...I heard about you and your fiancé, John," she finally let the cat out of the bag. "Just so you know, I think it stinks. She doesn't know what she gave up."

"It's okay, I'm almost over it now. Distance makes the heart grow colder... or, er, maybe I have that wrong."

She smiled, "You just wait and see, John Ridley, there is some very fortunate girl out there who will be the one lucky enough to land you and then all the other girls will be jealous."

"You always seem to know the right thing to say," and she always did. For as long as John had known her, Linda had been the kindest and most diplomatic person he had ever been around. It was her greatest quality.

They sat and chatted some more, mostly about old times, and catching up on the latest news of the "old gang" they had both grown up with. Before he knew it, it was time for the Nelsons to leave. As they were leaving, Linda gave him a personal invitation. "I would love for you to come to our wedding John," she pleaded. "It is August 14. Make sure you are back from England by then."

"I will do my best, Linda," John promised, as she turned and walked down the front sidewalk to the Nelson's car. Just as she was about to get into the back seat, she turned toward John one more time and gave a slight smile. There was that look again, a hopeful look, only this time it wasn't for her... it was for him.

*****

John chose not to go to the evening church service with his parents that night. His mom was not happy about it, but he knew she would get over it pretty quickly. It was going to be nice to have a little quiet time. Besides, he was going to be leaving fairly early the next morning for Canada. His mom surely understood that.

He spent the evening catching up on some more of his reading and then he decided to jot down a few notes for himself. If he was going to visit his great grand mother it would be good to think over some of the questions he wanted to ask. Things like 'Where did the Ridleys come from? And did she know the name of any of his ancestors?' It was kind of funny, he had never really had that much interest in family history before, but now that he had started investigating it seemed to have grown in importance. He began to feel connected to the research. As if it told him a little about himself that he didn't already know.

His parents came home around nine. They had probably gone out with some friends after church. He could hear them in the hall outside his door. They chose not to check in on him, even though he knew his mother was probably itching to do so. He did not bother to say good night to them. He would see them in the morning before he left. He read for another hour and then decided it was best to try and get a good night's sleep.

He was able to get off by seven-thirty the next morning. He only packed a light bag, knowing that he was only going to be gone for a couple of days. He grabbed a quick bowl of cereal for breakfast and then gathered his things to leave. His dad was just finishing his coffee and was about to leave for work himself. He said a quick goodbye and was about to slide out the door when his mom stopped him in his tracks.

"Wait, before you go," she said rather quickly, realizing his desire to get on the road. "Take this with you. It will make a nice midmorning snack on the road," as she handed him a paper sack.

He could tell by the weight of it that it was one of her home baked cinnamon rolls. "Thanks Mom, see you in a couple days. Bye Dad, see you later."

"Say hi to Grandma for us," his father returned.

Once he was on the freeway, John clicked on his favorite radio station and settled in for the long drive. He would stop for lunch in Niagra Falls at a place that had always been a favorite pit stop for his family.

'Oh-oh-oh wishin' you were, wishin' you were here...'

"Chicago, V, I think," John said out loud when he recognized the song. He always liked to guess the artist before the DJ came on and announced it. It helped to pass the time.

John's mind wandered as he drove and listened. He really didn't know that much about his family heritage now that he thought about it. His dad never really said too much, nor did his grandparents, for that matter. They always had plenty of stories to tell, but they were always about their own life experiences, not about their parents or grandparents. He knew that at some point the Ridleys had immigrated to Canada and purchased two farms, one of which was still owned by a distance cousin, James Ridley. He thought they came from England, sometime around the mid 1800s, but he wasn't even sure of that.

'The stars are shining, the sky is bright, and I would really like to see you tonight...'

'England Dan and John Ford Coley' he thought to himself as the hits kept coming. He was trying to remember his great grand mother's maiden name, 'Barker or something like that. I wonder how they first met. Let's see, if she is ninety years old now, that meant she must have been born in 1893. Wow! What was that like? Canada had to still be pretty primitive then. What was it like growing up on a farm in the middle of nowhere? They must not have had running water. Outhouses, did they have outhouses?' It was hard for him to comprehend how difficult it must have been.

'Longer than there have been stars up in the heaven...'

"Seriously, Dan Fogelberg!" he said aloud. "Is that all they ever play on this station anymore, romantic drivel?" he complained, as he started pushing the buttons on his radio to find another station. Romantic, heart wrenching clichés was hardly what he was in the mood for.

'Knights in white satin...'

"Moody Blues," he announced. "Now that's what I am talking about. This is real music."

That is pretty much how the entire trip went. A stop for lunch in Niagra, intermingled with John's attempts to locate radio stations that would play music suited to his present mental state. The hours slipped by and slowly, but surely, he came to the town of Brussels, in the northern part of western Ontario. Anybody who knows anything about Ontario knows that the southwestern part of the province is all there really is. The major portion of the province to the north was just wilderness and a very sparse population. This was true of all of Canada, with 90 percent of the population living within fifty miles of the U.S. border.

As he got to Brussels, he pulled out the directions his dad had written out for him. Even though he had been to his great-grandmother's house several times, he had never driven there himself. He thought he would recognize it once he saw it, but he was thankful for the directions. As he turned down Fourth Street, he recognized the huge maples lining either side of the street. Even though they did not have their new spring growth on yet, they were still impressive as they stood out as sentinels for this quiet neighborhood.

Great-Grandma Ridley's house was a small Victorian house, cream in color, with ginger bread laced siding around the windows and beneath the sharply angled roof line. It had a covered porch with a couple of rockers sitting to one side of the front door, and a small serving table perched between. John trudged up the stairs carrying his overnight bag. He knocked at the door. He could hear a faint, "I'm coming," from somewhere inside.

The door opened slowly and there stood his Great-Grandma Ridley. Her hair was up and tied back in some sort of bun. It was the only way John had ever seen her hair. She could not have been more than five feet tall. She was a little hunched over, but still had a sparkle in her eye.

"Hello John," she greeted. "It's so good of you to take the time to come see an old woman. Come in, come in."

"Hush Grandma (he had never gotten used to calling her Great-Grandma), you're not that old. In fact, you don't seem to age at all," John knew that it was always the polite thing to do, compliment the elderly.

She gave a little chuckle as she led him into the house. 'That smell,' John thought to himself. It was always there. He could not quite describe it. It was not bad or good. It was sort of a mixture of sweet, something like perfume, something baking and something old all at the same time. He was not sure what it was, but it was always there whenever he entered this house. It never changed. It was familiar; it helped him to know where he was.

Grandma Ridley turned, "Take your bag up to the first room upstairs, that's where you'll be staying. I don't get up the stairs much anymore, so you will have to fend for yourself up there. The bathroom is on your right, you remember. Everything you need is there."

"Thanks Grandma, I will be fine. Don't worry about me, I know my way around. Don't go to any trouble. I can take care of myself."

"Fine, fine," she replied. "I am sure you'll do fine. You go on up stairs. Take your time. I know you have had a long trip. We have plenty of time to catch up. You go and freshen up. We'll talk later."

Although it was a bit of an abrupt greeting, John new better than to argue with her, it was just her way, straight to the point. He grabbed his bag and started upstairs. He was kind of glad. He would actually like to clear a little of the fog in his head left by the trip. He scoped out his room, made a little visit to the bathroom and got himself fully settled before descending the staircase. As he neared the bottom of the stairs, he was surprised to discover another visitor, or in fact, two. Sitting on the couch in the living room was a young woman in her mid twenties and she seemed to be nursing a baby. He could not be sure, because the baby's head was covered with a small blanket.

"Oh, hello, you must be John," she greeted, as he reached the bottom of the stairs. "I'm your cousin Jenny and this is Emily," nodding at the baby. "I would get up, but I'm afraid it is impossible. It seems every time we take a little trip, the minute we get out of the car, Emmy here wants to eat. There is just no getting around it."

"Hi...," was about all John could get out before his grandmother entered the room.

"Oh good, I see you two have met," she said as John was still standing, a little dumbfounded. "Jenny is the grand daughter of my oldest son William, God rest his soul. William was your grandfather's brother, which makes Jenny your...a... well, I guess it makes her your cousin, twice removed or something, I never know how that works."

"We have actually met before Grandma, several years ago at the reunion at Rocky Park. We were just kids," she had stood up now. She had removed the baby blanket and John could now see the baby's head. Jenny held her against her shoulder and gently rubbed her back.

"Yeah, I sort of remember that," John agreed. "I didn't recognize you without your pigtails."

"And this," Grandma stepped toward Jenny and the baby and attempted to look the baby in the eyes, "this is my first great-great grandchild, Emily. Isn't she adorable?" As she spoke Jenny turned so her back was facing them and they could both see the baby's face.

46

"Uh huh," John tried to sound genuinely impressed. "She *is* beautiful." As far as he could tell all babies were beautiful, or at least, he knew better than to suggest otherwise.

"Well anyway, I invited Jenny to come and stay with us a couple days, her husband being away and all. I thought she could use the company and I need the help in the kitchen," Grandma continued. "It has been a long time since I have had to cook for anybody but myself."

"Oh Grandma, you do fine," Jenny encouraged. "I don't know many other ninety year old women who get around as well as you do."

"Pish, posh, stop trying to butter up an old woman," Grandma said sheepishly. "We need to stop jabbering and get dinner going. This poor young man is probably starved."

"Right behind you, Grandma. Here John why don't you hold Emily while I go help in the kitchen," without any warning, Jenny handed the baby into John's arms. He must have looked a little surprised because Jenny assured him, "Don't worry, she is a dream. She'll probably just go to sleep anyway. If she gives you any trouble, just holler."

Jenny and Grandma Ridley went to the kitchen to prepare dinner. John adjusted the baby in his arms slightly to be sure he was supporting her head, and then he sat down in a rocking chair near the front window. She was now smiling up at him and seemed to be content for the moment.

He was fairly comfortable with babies. It probably came from being around them so much, whether at family reunions or church events. He rocked gently. Emily was beginning to drift off to sleep, so he didn't feel in the least alarmed about his situation. He could feel her breathing steady and then her eyes started to droop, once, twice, three times, there, she was asleep. She *was* a beautiful baby, especially while she was sleeping so peacefully. After a few moments, Jenny returned to check on him and Emily. John was glad, because he realized that he was beginning to doze off a little himself.

"Caught you two napping, huh," she said quietly as she leaned close to him. "Here, let me take her." She reached down and gently lifted Emily into her arms. She then lightly stepped to the other side of the room and laid the baby down into a basinet.

"There, she should be fine for now," she whispered. "Why don't you join us in the kitchen? Dinner should be just about ready."

John got up from the chair, stretched his arms and legs a little and then followed her into the kitchen. He sat at the kitchen table, while his grandmother and Jenny completed the final preparations for the meal.

"I hope you didn't go to any trouble on my account, Grandma," he said politely.

"Oh, it's nothing, just a casserole I put together that has been heating in the oven. Jenny did the rest. She brought some homemade cherry pie I think you'll like." John could see Jenny smile over her shoulder, as he looked in her direction.

"That sounds great," John assured. "Jenny, Grandma mentioned that your husband…ah I guess I don't remember his name… is away somewhere."

"Stewart Pogue, Stew I call him," she explained. "He is in the RCAF and had to go to England for six months for some sort of special training operation. He just left and won't be home again until the end of August. It seems a bit silly to me that they had to send him half way around the world just for training, but that's the military, you know."

"Wow, six months! That seems like a long time," John tried to sound empathetic. "Especially, after you have had your first baby. That's kind of rough. Where in England is he stationed?"

"It is kind of rough, but that's what you get when you marry into the military," she said courageously. "He's some place called 'Spa-dee-dam' or something. Somewhere in the north, I think. I don't really know."

"Dinner is served," Grandma Ridley chimed.

The ladies took their seats and Grandma Ridley said a short prayer before they began eating. The initial conversation began with stories about John's relatives living in Canada. His Great Grandmother Ridley had four sons and three daughters. Two of her sons, one of which was his grandfather had immigrated to Pennsylvania. Her remaining children all remained in Ontario, the oldest having inherited the farm.

"Why did my grandfather go to Pennsylvania?" John asked.

"Your grandfather and his brother George decided to go to work for the railroad. They heard that the Buffalo to Pittsburgh Rail was hiring in Buffalo, so they left home. They initially worked as conductors on the line before they landed jobs as ticket agents or something, George in Punxatawney, and James, your grandfather, in Eidenau," She explained. "They met their wives and settled down to have families. Meanwhile, their father and older brother continued to work the farm back home."

"What about Great-Grandpa Ridley, how did he end up on the farm?" John asked.

At this Jenny's ears perked up, "I would like to know about this as well Grandma. I don't think Granddad ever said much about where our family came from."

"My husband, William, did not like to talk very much, and truth be known he did not know that much about his family history," she began. "His father, your great-great-grandfather James Ridley, would not talk much about his parents. There was some bad history that he felt was better to leave in the past."

"What do mean, what sort of history?" John inquired.

"William's grandparents, as well as my paternal grandparents, were all born in England, and immigrated to Canada in the 1850s; came over on the boat together. My grandparents were both born in Bristol. My grandfather, Henry Barker, purchased a farm in Grey Township, not far from the Ridley farm. It was passed on to my father and it is where I grew up.

I'm not sure of the exact place in England where William's grandparents were born, but I know that there was tragedy that followed there trip to Canada. James Ridley's father, Joseph Ridley-let's see, that would be your three-times-great-grandfather- had married in England and they had one son, John, your namesake, before setting out for England. Sadly, his wife died on the journey. When he and his young son arrived in Canada, he decided to remarry by wedding his wife's younger sister, who had traveled from England with her parents, on the same boat. This was your three-times-great-grandmother. She had three children, the oldest of whom was James, your great-great-grandfather, William's father. Once again, tragedy struck. At some point she became religiously insane and she drowned her two younger children in the river before taking her own life. This left her husband to raise his two older sons, who were half-brothers, alone.

James Ridley was old enough to remember the deaths of his younger siblings. He never talked about it. He would simply refer to the moment as 'that dark day'. I often wondered if he didn't feel some sort of guilt over their death. I'm not sure."

"How tragic," Jenny gasped. "I had no idea. I don't think I have ever heard this story before. What could have brought a mother to drown her own children?" At that moment they could hear the baby stirring in the living room and Jenny got up from the table to tend to her.

"Whatever happened to Grandpa's Uncle John?" John asked.

"When he was older, he purchased part of the farm, here in Grey Township, from his father," she explained. "However, neither of his sons were interested in farming, and so they left. I believe they went north to work on the railroad in New Liskeard, but I'm not really sure. The last I heard, their sister, she was about my age, had married and had gone to Saskatchewan to start a farm there. We never heard from any of them again. John Ridley died before the birth of your grandfather and the farm he owned reverted to his brother James and then eventually to your great-grandfather William, his nephew. Today, the farm is owned by Jenny's uncle James, but he is thinking about selling it. If he does, it will pass out of the Ridley family for the first time in over 130 years."

Jenny came back into the kitchen with the baby, who was awake. Little Emily provided a little diversion from all the talk about family history. Grandma Ridley served up the cherry pie with a little ice cream on the side; and then they began asking John about his parents and his brother. At one point, they mentioned that they had heard that he was engaged, but he side-stepped the inquiry by stating that "it just didn't work out". He got the impression that they understood not to pry any further.

After he had caught them up on the latest news from Pennsylvania, they began asking about his pending trip to England. He explained that he would be gone all summer and that it was all a part of the research he was doing on British literature. He didn't have to extrapolate any further.

Jenny asked, "Maybe you could stop and say hello to Stew for me while you are there?"

"I don't know Jenny," he didn't want to make any promises he couldn't keep. "I'm not sure exactly where he is. You would have to get me more details. Even then, I will be pretty busy." He noticed the disappointment in her eyes. "But, I suppose I could try," he added abruptly.

She smiled a little. It was clear that it was important to her.

The conversation was waning and it was starting to get late, but John had one more question, "Grandma, do you have any idea where Joseph and John Ridley were born? That is, where in England?"

"I don't really know, John, but I do have some papers and things that William left behind in an old trunk," she answered. "It's in the attic. You can help me get it down tomorrow and we can take a look together."

"That sounds fun," Jenny said. It seemed as if she was becoming more interested in the family history than even John was.

"Well, I'm afraid I 'm not as young as I used to be," Grandma Ridley said. "It's past my bedtime. I must say good night. You know where your room is, Jenny. John, are you settled? There should be towels in the closet in the bathroom. Do you need anything else?"

"No I'm fine, good night Grandma, we can talk more tomorrow. Thanks for dinner and the family history as well."

He turned to Jenny as he was getting up from the table. "Thanks for the pie, Jenny, it was excellent. Sleep tight everyone."

"You're welcome, John," Jenny returned. "I hope Emily doesn't keep you awake tonight. She is still not sleeping through the night."

"Don't worry about me. I'll probably sleep right through it. Good night." With that, John excused himself and went up to his room. He could hear the rattle of the last few dishes placed in the sink. He spent some time reading and he heard Jenny talking to Emily as they walked by his door a few moments later. Evidently mother and daughter were going to be sleeping just down the hallway.

*****

June 24, 1853, H.M.S. Chimborazo

    To my brother James,
    We have now been at sea for five weeks, and still we do not see the end in sight. It has been a difficult crossing, all the way battling a tempest that has more than once threatened to disassemble our small vessel. I write you now, anticipating the worst of all circumstances. It has become realized that not all will survive this fateful voyage.
    This morning the captain officiated the funeral of one of the young sailors, it was the second time the body of a young man has been quietly slid into the sea this week. The ship's doctor has informed us that it is typhoid. Four others lie in their sickbed, or perhaps deathbed, below decks. And now, just as we are hopeful of approaching the end of our voyage, I am confronted with my greatest fears. My dear Mary is now showing similar symptoms of those previously afflicted.
    I look to the horizon, gazing into the distance, hoping for even the slightest glimpse of the shoreline of New York. It seems that the only hope for my beloved is to reach our destination and to secure medical expertise not available on this God forsaken ship.
    My poor darling Mary, so young, so frail, so consumed with fever, she can not recognize her loved ones. In this desperate hour, when she might find comfort from the playful laugh of our young son, she finds none, for he must remain separated from his mother, perhaps forever. How thankful I am that my wife's sister is here to provide loving care to young John. She remains a steady bastion of hope in an otherwise hopeless circumstance.
    I fear that I have made a dreadful error in bringing poor Mary on this voyage to the promise land. She was not meant for such hardship, and even now I am weighed down with the guilt and remorse of knowing that I may have been the cause of her end. In my own arrogance I felt myself invincible, able to overcome any obstacle, not realizing that I had condemned my wife-and perhaps my son as well-to death on the high seas. If only God in his gracious mercy would grant this pour soul a reprieve from having to watch his dearest loved one suffer so. If

only our Heavenly Father would intervene in this most desperate hour and preserve the life of our Mary, so that my son would grow up knowing the love and care of his mother unto manhood.

Even now, I feel as if my prayers have fell on deaf ears, no not deaf ears, for our Father hears all, but perhaps on the ears of One who has purposed these events. I fear that we approach a time which our Heavenly Father has predetermined the passing of my Mary from this world to the next. For each there is but one appointed time, this I know. I do not comprehend the coldness of this fate, but I am resigned to accept it just the same.

Still, in the recesses of my heart, I continue to hold onto that flicker of hope that Mary may yet be saved. Yes, I continue to hold on, for I can not imagine going forward through life without her at my side. She has always been my star shining brightly, a beacon casting illumination into the darkest recesses of my soul. Even now, do you remember when I confessed to you from the onset of our engagement that she was my whole world and I could never love another.

Alas, it is quite possible that should the Lord deign to take her home, that I myself may not be long for this world. This plague passes through the ship like the angel of death in Egypt, and without any sign of land on the horizon, we may all be doomed. I do not fear death, and should the Lord take me, I might find it a blessing to go home with my beloved. And yet, I must make every effort to remain here for now, for the sake of our young son. May God be gracious to me and grant me this courage.

If I am not long for this world, this will be the last time I will write to you. Greet our brother for me and kiss my sisters, and convey to them how much I love them, especially to young Bella. I am sorry that I did not get to see her grow into a woman. Tell her that I love her and I miss her greatly.

Pray for us brother, for even if we survive this voyage, I am quite sure there are many hardships still ahead. Mary's parents and her sister Dorothy all send their greetings.

God Bless,
Your Brother, Joseph Ridley

Chapter Three

It is twilight, the forest is dark. There are voices all around, but none are discernable. He must keep running. The edge of the forest must be nearby. He can sense it, but he can't see it. Is it just ahead or perhaps to his left or his right? He can't stay here, he must keep moving. Something is wrong, he is not sure what it is, but it is not safe. There is a mist that is rising from the forest floor and he can hardly see where he is going? Is that a clearing up ahead? He runs toward it. When he arrives at the edge he can hear someone crying. It is her. She is there sitting in the grass, barely visible through mist. Three ravens sit surrounding her. As she turns to look at him, through the veil he can see her eyes, dark and penetrating. The ravens flap there wings and begin to rise. And then they erupt with a horrifying scream...

John awoke. It was still dark in the room. From down the hallway he could hear a baby crying. It took him just a moment to remember where he was...

He was at his great-grandmother's house and the baby crying was Emily. It must be time for her to be fed. He turned and reached for his watch. It was a little after two in the morning. He could not believe he had another one of *those* dreams. He couldn't be sure, but it seemed as if they were becoming a little more frequent. None of it made any sense. At first it was just the woman dressed in white. Now the dreams were being frequented by these annoying ravens. What could it all mean, if anything? He decided to go down stairs to get a glass of milk. He always felt that a little milk settled his stomach.

A few moments later, John returned to his bedroom. He could hear Jenny softly singing a lullaby to Emily. As he listened to the gentle melody, he began to wonder what it must be like to be a young mother with her husband thousands of miles away. She was courageous and at the same time, so content. He could tell that she was very comfortable in her role as wife and mother. She had no ambition other than to love her husband and to lovingly raise a family with him. It seemed simple, uncomplicated. He sort of envied her. He was not really that ambitious. He realized there was a certain kind of prestige that came with having a doctorate, but he had never been really that comfortable with it. At times, he wondered what the real point of going to graduate school was. In the big scheme of things, what did having a Ph.D. in English have to do with anything? It wasn't as if it was evil, but was it good, was it meaningful. It all seemed a little vane, a chasing after the wind. Perhaps that is what King Solomon meant when he said there was "nothing new under the sun". In any time period, men choose to pursue their own ambitions.

As he lay in bed, his thoughts began to drift a bit and he started thinking more about his family history. There was something very intriguing about all of it. No, intriguing was not exactly the right word. It was mystical, supernatural. When he began to think about the stories of the lives of his parents, grandparents, great-grandparents and so on, he was struck by the statistical problems posed by the conditions that were necessary for each couple, husband and wife, to get together. He had never thought of his existence as being merely a chance phenomenon. He believed he existed for a purpose, that his life did in fact have meaning. However, looking at it from the perspective of looking back to his ancestors gave a whole new meaning to purposeful existence. He had a total of 16 great-great-grandparents and in order for him to have been born, eight different couples had to have the right chain of events happen in their lives in order for them to meet marry and have children. How many times had they been confronted with death and survived. And why had they survived, when so many of their family members had died prematurely? Given the complication of his own recent past, he realized that it was no longer possible for him to look at human events as merely chance phenomenon. There was too much at stake. Where was God in all of this? Does He intervene in human affairs? Does He really care?

As he continued to ponder these things, he grew drowsy, and before long he drifted off to sleep. This time he would experience a restful sleep, without any more dreams or babies crying.

*****

The next morning John decided to go out jogging before breakfast. The air was cool and the sky was overcast, as it often was in Ontario, but it did not rain during his run. He felt invigorated by the time he returned to the house. He could smell bacon on the stove when he entered the front door, so he quickly dashed upstairs and took a quick shower. Fortunately, the bathroom was not occupied; he thought Jenny and Emily might still be sleeping. He imagined that Emily had been up at least once more during the night, but he could not be sure; he had been dead to the world and had slept right through to morning. He put on his clothes and was headed down the stairs when he heard the bathroom door close behind him. He hoped he hadn't woken Jenny.

He greeted his grandmother as he entered the kitchen and then assured her that she shouldn't go to so much trouble. She did not need to be making breakfast for him. He was a grown man and he could fend for himself. She ignored his pleas and promptly told him to sit down and eat. Just as he was finishing, Jenny entered the kitchen carrying Emily. Jenny promptly placed her daughter in John's lap and made her way to the counter where there was a pot of coffee brewing. He thought it kind of funny that she was so comfortable allowing him to hold her baby. She was definitely not one of those paranoid mothers, who treated their babies like china dolls.

"I'll be glad when Emily learns to sleep through the night," she said, between yawns, as she added a little cream and sugar to her cup. "Would you like some coffee John?"

"No thanks, Jenny, I'm fine. I don't drink the stuff."

"I hope Emily didn't keep you awake all night. I wouldn't want you to get the wrong impression about her, she really is an angel," as she leaned over and kissed the baby on the forehead.

"No I was fine. She woke me up once, but I fell right back to sleep. Really, don't worry about it. I'm sure it's tougher on you. You're the one that has to keep getting up all night."

That opened the door to allow Jenny to go on a long serenade about the joys of being a new mother. John sat and listened patiently, pretending to be interested, but his mind was elsewhere. The truth was, he was more than anxious to take a look into the trunk that Grandma Ridley had promised they could explore.

After breakfast, Grandma Ridley led John up to the attic where she pointed out an old chest buried beneath some old magazines and things. John cleared it off and then lifted it from its resting place. It was not too heavy, but its size made it a bit awkward to carry. Gradually, after resting a few different times, he was able to get it down the attic stairs and then down the stairs to the ground floor, setting it down in the living room next to the coffee table.

Jenny was sitting on the couch. She was all a glow with anticipation. Grandma Ridley sat down beside Jenny as John went into the kitchen and grabbed a chair from the dining set. When he returned to the living room, he sat down across the coffee table from the ladies, in close enough proximity to the chest so that he would be able to open it and empty the contents onto the table. He then pried open the latch and carefully opened the lid.

The chest contained a variety of items, some which appeared to be very old. There were stacks of old letters tied together with string. They appeared to be from different sources; some from friends, others from family, and others from people in the farming industry. John and Jenny leafed through the letters, looking for anything that might be interesting, but Grandma insisted there was nothing of importance in the stack.

The chest also contained some very old pictures. There were some pictures of Grandma Ridley when she was very young, perhaps even in her teens. There was a photograph of two older men standing together in front of what looked like an old Model T.

"Grandma, do you know who this is?" John asked, pointing at the photograph.

"That's a picture of John and James Ridley, your great-great-grandfather and his older brother." She answered. "That was taken just a couple years before John passed away. It was probably the last picture taken of him."

There were a few other pictures as well, some of which were John's great-grandfather when he was younger. There were also several personal items: like a mother of pearl handled straight razor that looked very old; a bone handled hunting knife; and some wire rimmed spectacles; old magazines, some of them with various advertisements that were dog eared or marked with a paper clip; an old bolo tie; as well as a couple copies of the farm almanac. There were some books as well, two of which immediately caught John's eyes. Both of them appeared very old, as the covers showed some heavy wear and age.

"These look interesting," commented John, as he lifted them out of the chest. "This one seems to be a Bible," referring to the one on top.

"That was the family Bible, passed down to William from his grandfather," Grandma Ridley confirmed. "I had almost forgotten about it. William kept it in this chest to keep it protected. It is very old."

The cover was very worn and frayed on the edges. John opened up the cover. The title page indicated that it was an English Standard Bible and had been printed in 1832. He turned to the next page. It was a dedication page that had been inscribed with the following:

Presented to
  Joseph Ridley and Mary Topping
  In celebration of their marriage, this day,
  23rd of April, 1850 at St. John Lee Parish, England

"This is great, it's a clue to where the Ridley's came from in England!" John exclaimed.

"I'm not sure I'd ever noticed the inscription before," said Grandma Ridley. "This is your three times great-grandfather and his first wife, the one who died on the trip from England to Canada. It was her sister Dorothy, that later went insane."

"But where exactly is St. John Lee Parish?" asked Jenny.

"I'm not sure," John replied, "however, I may be able to find out." He then handed the Bible to Jenny, and his eyes focused on the title of the book beneath. "What is this?"

The title of the book was *The Ancient Ryedales by G.T. Ridlon.* John opened the book up to the title page. The copywrite date indicated it had been published by the author in 1884. Beneath the initial title was a subtitle:

...and their descendents in Normandy,
Ireland, Great Britain and America, Comprising
the Genealogy for about 1000 years of the families
of Riddell, Riddle, Ridlon, Ridley, etc.

On the next page was a lithograph portrait of the author. Beneath the picture was hand written the following note:

To John Ridley, in gratitude for your
indispensible assistance in providing the history of
the Ridleys of Hexham. G.T. Ridlon, 1888.

John immediately turned to the table of contents and began scanning the chapter titles. They were laid out by name and location. Riddells of Scotland, Riddells of Ireland,..., Riddles of Pennsylvania,..., (and then he saw it) Ridleys of England, (and a few lines down the page), Ridleys of Willimoteswick. His heart began to pound and he felt a bit of a lump in his throat. He could hardly believe his eyes.

"This is what I've been looking for," he said with a gratifying sigh.

"What is it?" asked Jenny. "What did you find?"

"I can't be sure, but it looks like I have found part of the answers I have been looking for, answers to questions having to do with the research I have been doing. I think it also holds a clue to the origins of our family in England," he explained. "This book appears to be an entire history of the Ridley family. It's almost too good to be true. It was published in 1884 and seems to trace the histories all the way back to the Norman Conquest of Great Britain, that is sometime around the eleventh century."

"I don't understand. How is it connected to your research," Jenny asked. "What do the Ridley ancestors have to do with...a...your studies in English literature?"

"It's this mention of the Ridleys of Willimoteswick," he pointed to the table of contents in the book so that they could both see. "Sir Walter Scott mentions this place in his notes to one of the ballads I am researching. It, at least in part, confirms that the ballad may be about real people or at least real places. I can't be sure until I actually study this more. I'm really sorry," John said remorsefully, "I hope you don't mind if I excuse myself for a little while so that I can do some reading. I am really intrigued by this book and the answers it might provide."

"Go ahead John, we totally understand," Grandma Ridley assured him, while Jenny nodded her head in agreement. "You take your time, we aren't going anywhere."

"Just be sure you save some time to share what you find with us," Jenny added. "You're not about to keep this all to yourself."

John closed the book and took it with him as he left the living room. As he climbed the stairs to his bedroom, he could hear Jenny say, "I wonder what else is in this old chest." He knew it was a little rude to just get up and leave them there like that, but he could not help himself; he felt a little comfort knowing that they would at least have the rest of the things in the chest to occupy them.

*****

When he got to his room, John sat back on the bed and immediately opened the book to the chapter on the Ridley's of England.

> *This family pedigree reaches back to the time of William the Conqueror, Ridley Hall, the earliest known residence of the family, was in Cheshire, a place previously owned by the Knights Hospitalers...The ancient property continued in the main line of the Ridley family till it ended in an heir female, who became the wife of Robert Danyel, who quartered his arms with those of Ridley...*

> *Ridley, or Ridleigh, as the name was originally spelt, being a local name. William the Conqueror required all residents to assume surnames at his accession, in order to properly keep the records; and the family at Ridley Hall, if then resident there, probably adopted the name at that time...it is possible that their ancestor came with William from Normandy.*

'So the Ridleys may have been from Normandy, and they initially settled in Chestershire,' he thought to himself, 'interesting.'

> *A junior branch of the ancient family of Ridley of Chestershire emigrated to Northumberland, and became settled upon extensive lands in the valley of the Tyne, long before the elder line became extinct at Ridley Hall. Just how their lands in Tynedale came to them has*

not been learned; neither what place they made their first residence in that County. They were certainly possessed of the castle and estate of Willimoteswick as early as 1280, and probably much before that date. Evidently daughters of Hudard de Willimoteswick were married to the Ridleys...Willimoteswick means the mote or keep of William...Willimoteswick Castle is situated on a wooded knowl, at the meeting of the South Tyne and Blackleugh Burn...The estates of Willimoteswick were held by the Ridley family through a long succession of strong knights until 1652, when in consequence of their steady adherence to the cause of King Charles, all their land and seats in Tynedale were confiscated and wrested from their hands...

'Now were getting somewhere,' thought John as he continued reading. On the next page was a picture of the ancient castle. And then, when he turned the page again, he could not believe his eyes...

The Ridleys and Featherstones of Featherstonhaugh Castle, were at deadly feud, and for many years seem to have watched for every opportunity to shed each others blood, as will appear from the following account of an engagement at Greenscheles Cleugh where on the 24th of October, 1530, the Ridleys killed Albany Featherstonhaugh, an event which was made the source of a strange ballad...

And then there was the ballad; word for word the same one that Sir Walter Scott had published in Marmion. He recalled that Scott had died in 1832, so the author of this book was clearly familiar with and had access to Scott's work. The question was whether Ridlon would have referenced the poem if he had thought that it was only a legend. It was clear that the author believed the event to be real. This suggested that the Ridleys did in fact murder Sir Albany Featherstone. But why, or more to the point, what started the feud?

John read on, but there did not seem to be any explanation for the feud. The author went on to explain that his source for the ballad was Sir Walter Scott and therefore, John was not actually in possession of an independent source, but a secondary source from the same place. It was not necessarily confirmation of the factual event, but it did supply some support. He read on. The author provided additional support from notes he had discovered in the works of Sir Walter Scott, unfortunately the notes were in Latin, and John's Latin was a little weak. He was going to need some help with this part.

John continued reading the remainder of the chapter, but it was mostly about a second Ridley Hall established in Northumberland as well as other places of residence of the Ridley family including Unthank Hall, and Hardriding. The section about Hardriding was of particular interest since it was mentioned in the ballad, but John's head was already beginning to swim. He decided to go back over the section on the Ridleys of Willimoteswick several times, jotting down some details and making sure he had not missed anything. He took copious notes in his notebook as he read.

The next section of the book was on the genealogy of the Ridley family in England, and even though John was anxious to get to it, he realized he needed to take a break. It was almost noon; Jenny and Grandma would be wondering about him. He stuck a sheet of paper in the book where he had left off, closed it and headed downstairs.

When John arrived at the bottom of the stairs, he could see his great-grandmother playing with the baby on the couch. Emily was propped up with a couple of pillows and Grandma Ridley was shaking a tiny stuffed bear in front of her, while leaning over and pretending to play peak-a-boo. It was kind of a strange sight, this old woman playing games with a baby, it caused John chuckle to himself. It occurred to him, sitting here on the couch were two individuals removed from each other by five generations. The history that would expand the entire lives of these two individuals was a very significant thing. The elder had seen the first automobile, the first airplane, the invention of the television and a man walk on the moon. There was no way of telling what the younger one would experience in her lifetime, but if it was anything comparable, it was going to be astounding.

"Grandma, you look like you are having more fun than she is," John said as he approached them.

"I suppose it keeps me young at heart," she answered. "She is a dream," as she turned back to give her attention to the baby. "Jenny is in the kitchen making lunch. We figured your stomach would get the best of you."

"I must admit, I am a little hungry, but mostly I just needed a little break, my head can only absorb so much information in one sitting."

"Well you can tell us all about it over lunch," Grandma insisted. "But right now you're going to have to pick this baby up and bring her to the kitchen. As much as I love her, I don't dare try to lift her. She's getting too big for these frail old bones."

"Don't worry Grandma, I have her," as John walked around the coffee table and swept Emily up in his arms. "See there, light as a feather."

Together John, Emily and Grandmother Ridley walked into the kitchen and sat down at the table. John held Emily on his lap so she could see her mother, as Jenny finished putting the food on the table.

"What would you like to drink, John," Jenny asked.

"Do you have any pop," John asked.

"Of course, Grandma had me pick up some Pepsi, special for you." Jenny set a bottle of Pepsi in front of John and then lifted Emily from his lap and placed her in her high chair. "Okay it is time to fill us in, what did you find out?" she asked.

He didn't mind sharing with them what he had learned. Talking about it out loud kind of helped him to sort it all out in his mind. Even as he repeated what he had learned he found himself feeling a little amazed that he actually had been able to find evidence that traced the Ridleys all the way back to the eleventh century. While he continued to share, his grandmother got up from the table and disappeared into the living room for a moment. When she returned she was carrying a large, old, dust covered atlas.

"I have had this old atlas since I was a school girl. I thought it might be helpful for us to look at a map of England." She proceeded to open the atlas to a full page map of England and Northern Europe and laid it down in front of John. While she looked over John's shoulder, Jenny scooted her chair closer and looked on.

"This part of northern France is Normandy," John explained pointing to the map. "According to the history, it is believed that the Ridleys came to England with William the Conqueror, who was also the Duke of Normandy. Chestershire is here on the western edge of Great Britain, right next to Wales. Northumberland is here in the north, bordering Scotland. Evidently, the Ridleys first settled in Chestershire," again pointing to the map, "and then a branch of the family ended up at Willimoteswick Castle, here near the Tyne River, in Northumberland.

"How do we know where our family is from?" Jenny asked.

"We have some clues from the inscription in the Bible. At the same time, the book contains genealogies of the Ridley family in England. Hopefully, I will be able to connect the two. I have not had a chance to read through the entire thing."

As lunch was ending, John was running out of things to share. "I think I am going to take a little walk, get some fresh air. I need to clear my mind a little bit."

Grandma asked, "Since you're going for a walk would you mind going down to the market and getting me a few things. I've made list."

"Sure Grandma, after all you two have been doing for me, it's the least I can do. What do you need?"

The sun was peaking through the clouds as John left the house carrying the list his grandmother had given him. The market was just a few blocks away and so John took a leisurely pace. He wanted some time alone to think. It was nice to get outside and clear his mind a bit. As he walked, he started to daydream about England. It was getting easier for him to come to grips with the fact that he was actually going. He kept trying to imagine what Oxford must be like. It would be a little like walking back in time. It was a very old university, rich in history and tradition. And there was the trip to Northumberland, the land of castles. The more he thought about it, the more excited he was about the prospects of exploring its rich history and the history of his family. It was no longer just about his research, he was beginning to open the door to a story that he was a part of and he wanted to see it to its conclusion. He felt that with each step, he was discovering something new about where he came from and who he was. It gave him a bit a rush. It was a bit like investigating a mystery. Each door he opened provided the answer to one question while prompting him to ask several more.

When he returned to the house, he found Jenny napping on the couch with Emily asleep in her basinet, nearby. He quietly stepped into the kitchen. He set the bag of items from the market on the counter and looked out the back window where he could see his grandmother bending over pulling weeds from her garden. 'Ninety years old and still gardening' he mused, feeling a deep profound respect. He would be fortunate to live as full a life, enjoying each moment as it came. After watching his grandmother for a couple of minutes, he turned away, very quietly, and climbed the stairs to his room. He sat at the writing desk in his room, opened the book to the section he had marked earlier and began reading again.

There were several generations of the Ridleys of Chestershire listed. He haphazardly scanned through the list for something that would be significant to him. After skimming it over he skipped ahead to the section titled the *Ridleys of Willimoteswick, Northumberland.* The first named mentioned was a Thomas Ridley who was the son of Sir Thomas Ridley of Cheshire. This Ridley had possessions of lands in Tynedale before the family came into possession of Willimoteswick Castle. The first mention of Willimoteswick came in the fourth generation when Odard Ridley, the grandson of Odard de Willimoteswick became heir to the castle through his mother.

This same Odard of Willimoteswick was shown to have witnessed a charter signed at Hexham Abbey in the time of Henry II (1206-72). The Ridleys came to possession of Willimoteswick as a result of the marriage of his daughter to Anthony Ridley, Odard Ridleys father.

At this point he was beginning to realize that he was having difficulty keeping the names all straight in his head. There was too much repetition. He decided to create a chart that chronicled the Ridley pedigree, indicating only the major heirs.

Generation One- Sir Thomas Ridley of Cheshire
Generation Two-Thomas Ridley of Tynedale
Generation Three-Anthony Ridley of Willimoteswick
Generation Four-Odard Ridley of Willimoteswick

John read on until he came to the eleventh generation and then he paused.

> *Sir Nicholas Ridley was successor to Willimoteswick... He was styled the "broad knight", probably in consequence of his gigantic physical proportions. He was the high sheriff of Northumberland in the first, second, third and twenty-third years of the reign of Henry VI...He was chief of the clan when they murdered Sir Albany Featherstonhaugh, as appears on a view of the body by the coroner of Northumberland that year-1530...This was the Sir Nicholas addressed by the Bishop Martyr when imprisoned at Oxford as the "bell-wether" of the Ridley family, and is faithfully admonished by his pious nephew and namesake respecting his religious faithfulness.*

'So, this is the Ridley of Willimoteswick, in the ballad,' he thought to himself. 'Now I have the date and the person, but not the reason. And who is this Bishop Martyr?'

John jotted down some notes including: 'find the definition of bell-wether' and 'look for additional information on the "Broad Knight" and the role of the sheriff of Northumberland. How did one get to be the sheriff and who was he accountable to?'

He read on for a couple of pages at which point he discovered identity of the Bishop Martyr. There was picture of a Rev. Nicholas Ridley and on the following page, listed in the twelfth generation, was the description of Rev. Nicholas Ridley, son of Christopher of Unthank Hall, brother of the aforementioned Sir Nicholas. 'So Bishop Ridley was the nephew of Sir Nicholas Ridley'.

John read on. The biography of the Bishop indicated that he had been appointed Bishop of London by Henry VIII. He was supportive of the reformation and the forming of the Church of England. He also worked with Thomas Cranmer to help write the first "Common Book of Prayer". When Henry VIII was succeeded by Edward VI, Bishop Ridley served the young King as one of his advisers. When the King died, Ridley supported Lady Jane Grey for succession. As a result, when Mary, who was Catholic, ascended to the throne of England, Bishop Ridley, along with Thomas Cranmer and Hugh Latimer, were imprisoned in the tower of London; all three were later burned at the stake for their support of Protestantism.

On the pages that followed, John found a picture of the 'Martyrs Memorial' at Oxford. It indicated that it commemorated the death of Bishop Ridley and the others. 'At Oxford, I can hardly believe it,' he thought to himself. 'I wonder if it still there?' He went back and reread the biography of Bishop Ridley once again, taking notes as he went. He was particularly curious about 'Unthank Hall'. It seemed like a very strange name. He made a note to try and find it on a map, as well as its meaning or origin.

In the thirteenth generation was mentioned a Thomas Ridley, who married Elizabeth Ridley, daughter and sole heir of John Ridley of Walltown. This John Ridley was no doubt a descendent of "Wil' o' the Wa'" mentioned in the ballad. In the 14th generation he found a Thomas Ridley, son of Nicholas, who was styled of Hardriding. This was the first mention of Hardriding and this Thomas was most likely the descendent of "Hardriding Dick". Hardriding was also mentioned in the fifteenth, sixteenth and seventeeth generations, as well.

As John continued to read down through the generations, he began to realize that he was working backwards. There was no way he could make a connection to his family by starting with the earliest generations and moving forward. He realized that he must start with himself and move backwards. He knew that his three times great grandfather was born in England. He needed to start there. He turned back to the inscription in the front of the book. 'Thanks for your help with the Ridleys of Hexham' is what was written. He turned back to the table of contents. There it was, *Ridleys of Hexham, England*. He turned to the page.

[The Ridleys of Hexham, Northumberland, are descended from the old Willimoteswick family,-descendents from a younger son of the main line representation, consequently they have not preserved any authenticated pedigree. All efforts to procure full statistics of the branch have proved fruitless.]

James Ridley was descended from some branch of the Northumberland family (most likely Hardriding)

    Joseph, brother of James,
    George, brother of James,
    Ann, sister of James.
      Next Generation-
      Elizabeth, daughter of James,
      Isabella, daughter of James,
      Mary, daughter of James,
      Margaret, daughter of James,
      Ann, daughter of James,
      George, son of James,
      William, son of James,

Joseph, son of James, born in Hexham, 1831,
married to Mary Topping, emigrated to America.
He secondly married Dorothy Topping, sister of
first wife. Mr. Ridley is a farmer and resides in
Grey, Ontario, Canada.

There it was, the entry for John's three times great-grandfather. As he scanned down the list of names he noticed the naming pattern. With each generation, all the way down to his own, the Christian names of both men and women had been repeated several times. Here the author suggested that the Ridleys of Canada, through Hexham, were most likely descendents of Hardriding. 'Was it possible, that John could, in fact, be a direct descendent of the Ridleys who were responsible for the murder of Sir Albany Featherstone?' In one afternoon, he had discovered that his ancestors included both a hero, in the name of Bishop Nicholas Ridley and a villain by the name of Sir Nicholas Ridley.

He took a moment to go over his notes. So far he had been able to determine that the characters of the ballad in Marmion were real people and could be referenced in the Ridley pedigree. At the same time, all evidence seemed to suggest that the murder of Albany Featherstone was a historical event, as indicated by the coroners report (he found it interesting that there were actually coroners in the sixteenth century). He had also surprisingly discovered that he not only had the same surname as the individuals in the ballad, but he could be directly related to them. Despite all this new information he was still left with many unanswered questions, some of them new. What was the cause of the feud between the Ridleys and Featherstones? Why did the Ridleys murder Sir Albany? Would he be able to fine the coroners report mentioned in the genealogy? Could he find the charter witnessed by Odard of Willimoteswick, at Hexham Abbey? Where was St. John Lee Parish? Could he find any records that would connect the Ridleys of Hexam with those of Hardriding?

*****

71

That night at dinner, John did the best he could to outline the family history for Jenny and Grandma Ridley. The two of them listened intently as he shared the entire history. It was a little difficult to keep it all straight given the constant repetition of Christian names and that it covered fourteen generations or more. There was no way, that when he had begun this journey, he would ever have expected to learn as much as he had. When he arrived at the part about Bishop Nicholas Ridley, he gave as much detail as he could remember. The story left the same impression on them as it had on him. They had all been raised in Protestant churches, of one form or another. They felt a certain obligation to the reformers and what it had meant to their own religious heritage. It was hard for any of them to imagine that, as a result of the conflict that existed between Catholics and Protestants, in sixteenth century England, there were some who were actually burned at the stake for their faith.

They ended up talking about this at such length, that John decided to read a few of the more significant parts of the story of Bishop Ridley's life and death. None of them knew very much about the Bishops of the Church of England, nor could they recall ever hearing of Bishop Latimer or Bishop Cranmer, but they still understood the level of authority they would have commanded in the church at that time. As John read the passage concerning the death of Latimer and Ridley, he came to an account of the actual conversation between the two just prior to their deaths. Latimer was quoted as saying, *"Take heart Master. Ridley, play the good man, for today we light a candle in England, which, by God's grace, shall never be extinguished."*

"How sad," Jenny whispered, as she listened intently to John as he read. "They were so brave, and had such powerful conviction that they were standing for what was right. I can't imagine what it was like for those in the crowd who were watching. Surely, they must have known the character of these two men and their innocence."

"Some would have surely," Grandma Ridley agreed. "However, bigotry and prejudice are powerful things, and they often blind the eyes of men to the truth that is right in front of them. They were not burned at the stake for having committed a crime, they died because they represented something, an idea; an idea which those in authority, like the queen and her minions, were afraid of."

"You're right Grandma," John added. "The burning at the stake of these individuals was not merely an execution, it was a symbol of cleansing, a purification by fire. Those who were Catholic believed that the reformation was of the devil and it needed to be purged. Despite the horror of it, they thought they were doing the right thing, protecting the Christian faith from heretical teachings. It would have been more horrifying for them to allow these bishops to lead the people astray. It is difficult for us to comprehend, because we are Protestant. We can still see the level of passion in this dispute demonstrated in the violence still evident in Ireland."

"Regardless, of their doctrinal teachings, to be burned to death seems extremely cruel and unjust," Jenny could not get past the horror.

"Perhaps, but the Queen also meant for these horrific deaths to send a message. Remember they were not only Protestant, but they had also supported another to succeed to the throne. She had to be at least a little put off over this act of treason. In any case, I think this has been plenty for one evening. I think talking about it any further will only serve to have us all suffer from nightmares tonight," this was John's way of suggesting it was time for bed.

"You're absolutely right, young man," Grandma Ridley said in agreement. "I think we passed my bedtime some time ago. I must call it a night. Make sure you turn off the lights, you two." She got up from the table and left the two of them alone.

"Well, what do think, Jenny? Are you off to bed as well?"

"Yes, I am, but I don't think I will be able to avoid the nightmares; too much water under the bridge, if you know what I mean."

"I'm sorry Jenny, I didn't mean for the story to get so morbid, just before we go to bed and all."

"Don't be silly. I'll be fine. I was just being a little facetious. The truth is, I've enjoyed it immensely. Thank you so much for coming. I am sure I would never have learned any of this had you not been here. These stories are important and I am glad we will both be able to pass them on to our children."

"Well good night then," John said, as he got up from the table.

"Good night, John." Jenny lingered at the table a little longer. He could tell that she was thinking more about what they had learned together.

*****

That night John slept soundly. He thought he heard Emily wake in the middle of the night, but he could not be sure he was not dreaming. In any case he never came fully awake until morning. The next morning he had a light breakfast and then it was time to say goodbye. He was actually feeling a little melancholy about it. He kind of wished he could spend a little more time with Grandma Ridley. He had come to understand that she had a great deal of wisdom, and he was afraid he might not see her again. At the same time, he had really enjoyed seeing his cousin Jenny again. He was of the impression that if they were able to spend more time together, they would become great friends, not merely distant relatives. He gave his grandmother a hug, and then bent down and gave Emily a little kiss on the forehead, as she sat munching on some cheerios, in her high chair. Jenny got up from the table and gave him a hug as well.

"It was good to see you again John," she said in parting. "I hope it won't be as long 'til we see each other again."

"Goodbye, Jenny, it was good seeing you again, too. I will try to see if I can stop in on Stewart while I am in England," he thought it was the least he could say. "Goodbye, Grandma," he said, as he started to leave the kitchen. "Thanks for everything and I will try to come and see you when I get back from England."

"Goodbye, John," he could hear over his shoulder as he went out the front door.

Before getting into his car he stopped and turned and looked back at Grandma Ridley and Jenny, as they stood waving on the porch. He wondered when he would next see them. He started up the Corolla, and clicked on his radio, settled back in his seat and then began the long drive home. All and all it had been a very productive trip and he was glad he had come.

Chapter Four

The forest was dark now. Even though the moon was full, its globe was broken up by the tree branches overhead. On the path ahead there were small patches of moonlight that lit his way. He kept walking forward, he didn't know why. Something was pushing him on. It was more than just an urge, it was a need; he had to keep walking, going deeper into the forest.

As he came to a slight rise he could see a small clearing ahead. There was a bridge that traversed the river he could now hear in the distance. There she stood, at the foot of the bridge, her back was to him. There was something wrong, he wasn't sure why. He approached, she did not move away as she had before. He drew close, she turned. Wait, it was not the bride; it was not the same girl he had seen so many times before. It was an old woman. He had mistaken her long silver hair for the veil. Her face was weathered and wrinkled. Her eyes looked crazy and as she smiled she showed teeth that were yellow and decayed. She frightened him.

As he stood motionless, she spoke to him with a voice that was not much more than a hiss. 'Remember, Remember,' she repeated several times. 'You must follow the ravens, the ravens, you must follow the ravens.'

John slowly crawled out of bed. His radio alarm was blaring out the morning news; at least it seemed like it was blaring. It was another one of *those* nights. He had had another dream, only this time it was different. There was no beautiful bride, but instead an old hag that still sent a chill down his spine as he thought about it. What did it all mean? Could he be having premonitions? Was that even possible? How did dreams work? Why do we dream the things that we do? What is the connection between the subconscious and conscious?

It was Monday morning and John had just returned from his home in Pennsylvania the night before. He was teaching a Comp class at eight, so he would have to hurry; as always he was running a little behind. He grabbed a glass of milk and a left over chocolate donut from a box on the table. It was a little dry, but it was all he had time for this morning. He rushed out the door and heard a 'welcome home' from one of his housemates as he skipped down the front steps.

It was overcast and there was a drizzle falling from the sky. It made for a dreary walk to campus. There were very few students out and about this early on the first day back from break. John used the time to reflect on his trip to Canada.

He sort of wished he had been able to spend a little more time. He wasn't sure he would ever see his great grandmother again. Although she still seemed active and in good health, he knew that death was creeping up to her doorstep. He had always been impressed with her. She was of such strong character and courage; she had seen and endured much in her lifetime. He knew, down deep, that there was still much to be gained from her wisdom and experience. He hoped that he would have more opportunities.

His first class was a little dull. Only half of his students had actually made it back from spring break. His first impulse was to just dismiss class, but he realized that was not particularly fair for those who had made an effort to be there. He decided to use the opportunity to do a little Socratic exercise, getting the students to think through the process of writing a persuasive essay. Despite the early hour, the students were relatively engaged and when it was all said and done, it was a productive moment. His second class went about the same.

In the afternoon, he decided to go over to the Foreign Language department to see if he could find someone that new some Latin. The Foreign Language building was just across the quad from the English building so he didn't have far to go. As he entered the building, he noticed Annie sitting on a bench in the corner of the foyer. He immediately cringed. He knew there was a chance of running into her here, but the last thing he wanted was for her to think he was hanging on and looking for opportunities to bump into her. He tried to pretend he didn't see her and turned down the hallway to the right hoping she hadn't noticed him, but it was too late.

"Hi John," she greeted, as she looked up from whatever she was reading. "What are you doing here?"

"Oh, hi Annie," he greeted, hoping to hide the fact that he was blushing. "I was doing some research and I needed some help with a Latin translation. I wasn't expecting to see you here." He immediately wished he hadn't said it.

"You do remember that this is my department and my office is in this building, don't you?" she mocked. "Hand it over."

"Yea, I remember," he was definitely turning red by now. "Hand what over?"

"The Latin you need translated. I am sure I can handle it."

John pulled the book from his back pack and opened to the place where he had marked the note of Sir Walter Scott. Annie took it from him and then pulled a pen from her bag and began jotting down a translation.

> "24 Oct. 22 do Henrici 8 vi. Inquisito capt apud Hautwhistle sup visum corpus Alexandri Featherston. Gen, apud Grensilhaugh felonici interfecti, 22 Oct, per Nicolaum Ridley de Unthauk Gen. Hugon Ridley, Nicolaum Ridley et alios ejusdem nominus. 36 to Herici 8 vi, Utligatio Nicalia Featherson, ac Thome Nixon, etc., etc. pro homicitto Will Ridley de moral."

Annie offered the following translation:

> The 24th of October in the 22nd year of Henry the VI, according to the chief inquisitor in view of the corpse of Alexander Featherstone a felony

murder in another place by name Grensilhaugh,
by Nicholas Ridley of Unthank, Hugh Ridley,
Nicholas Ridley.

In the 36th year of Henry the VI (12 years
later), Nicholas Featherston and Thomas Nixson
and others without hesitation commit homicide on
Will Ridley.

"Does this help?" she asked handing him the translation.

"Yes, thanks, it does," he said, as he read it to himself. "It's about what I thought, but I wanted to be sure. Thanks again. It was good to see you Annie." He got up to leave.

"John, have you decided if you are going to England?" she asked.

"Yes, I'm going. Actually, I'm starting to get pretty excited about it. I'll be leaving mid-June, returning the first of August."

"Good, I am glad. Send me a post card, if you think about it. I would really like to hear how you are doing."

"Sure, I'll do that," he said, while leaving; as if he was really going to send her a post card. He realized he was being a little rude, but he really didn't want to prolong this conversation.

"Bye John," he heard as he left the building.

*****

Later that evening, John visited the U of I main library to look up the nineteenth century Atlas of Great Britain he had found earlier. He loved to go to the library and find a quiet place to work, with no diversions. It was large enough to lose yourself in, and deathly quiet. He had no difficulty focusing here.

He found the atlas where he had left it and carried it to a nearby table, where he promptly sat down and turned to the map of Northumberland, the northern most county in England. He began scanning the map, looking along the Tyne River, at the southern edge of the county. He found Haltwhistle on the west and used he finger to trace out the line of the river running eastward toward Newcastle. Just below Haltwhistle, he found a notation for Featherstone Castle. Just to the north, he found Thirwall Castle, he thought he remembered reading something about a connection between the Thirwalls and Ridleys, but he couldn't remember where. He would have to check his notes later. As his finger moved eastward, along the Tyne, he found Unthank Hall just to the south. A little further eastward, he found Willimoteswick Castle, and then Ridley Hall. Then just to the north, he found Hardriding, right next to the village of Bardon Mill. A little further on, the river passed through Hadydon Bridge and then Hexham. There it was, just on the north side of Hexham, St. John Lee. His heart began to palpitate as he felt an adrenaline rush. It was exactly what he had hoped to find.

He took out a piece of tracing paper from a folder he had in his back pack, and placed it over the map. He traced out the outline of Northumberland and then the line of the Tyne River flowing from the west to the east. He marked each of the major towns, Haltwhistle, Haydon Bridge, Hexham and Newcastle. Then he went back and marked the locations of each of the residences of the Ridley family. Then he marked Featherstone and Thirwall Castles, as well. He lifted the map and looked at the original again. He placed the tracing paper back over the map and traced the outline of the Roman Wall that sat just to the north of the Tyne. And then, as an afterthought, he also marked the position of Wall Town. When he was satisfied that he had made notations for all the key places, he gently folded the piece of tracing paper and placed it in the inside cover of his copy of the *History of the Ancient Ryedales.*

He sat back and thought about each of these names and places and then he began to make a mental picture of his itinerary for his visit to Northumberland. He could not wait to share his most recent discoveries with the Professor at their weekly meeting on Wednesday. He felt that he had accomplished more in the past week than he had in several months. It confirmed what he had come to understand about research; it was a continuous series of lulls followed by brief moments of exhilarating results. It was these few brief moments of inquiry and unexpected discoveries, which created just enough inspiration to carry one forward through the next valley of obscurity. The more questions that could be elucidated, the more energy and incentive there was to continue the work. It was always those inevitable lulls, those dead end trails which led nowhere, that could make research seem mundane and endless. This was not one of those moments. Right now he felt hopeful of what the next overturned rock would reveal.

The Professor was pleased to see that John had made progress in his research, but as usual, he demonstrated little enthusiasm. It was a wrong expectation to think he would offer any praise, and John had grown accustomed to his ways. The Professor rarely showed any real excitement about anything, and if he did, it was always for the most trivial things. Generally, he was stoic, sitting there behind his desk, rubbing the stubble on his chin and asking those infernal questions, never satisfied with the response, but always asking more and more questions. It was very irritating. John always knew what the Professor was doing, trying to lead him to the answers without actually telling him, and of course he would always take the bait. He would get sucked in by some seemingly obvious question that he would answer without thinking, and before he knew it, he was on the Socratic road.

"So John, you have connected the dots," the Professor began, "you were able to confirm the historicity of the death of the Albany Featherstone, described in the ballad in Marmion."

"It seems so," John affirmed. "I have at least two sources. However, it could be that the one source was only repeated by the author of the second source, kind of a chicken and the egg problem."

"But you don't know what the feud was about?"

"No, not exactly."

"Where did you say the Ridleys came from?" the Professor asked.

"Normandy." John knew this was going somewhere. "It appears they came over with William the Conqueror."

"Yes...from France. I see, and what about the Featherstones?" the Professor asked.

"I think I read somewhere that they were Saxons, but I'm not sure," John answered. "I know what your thinking, but I don't think that was it. It seems unlikely to me that this was just a Norman-Saxon feud."

"Why not? Don't you remember the story of Robin Hood?" the professor asked.

"Of course I do, it just doesn't seem to make sense. I mean, this took place in 1530. The Normans invaded England in the middle of the 11th century. It would require that this feud between a Norman and Saxon family would have lasted for four centuries."

"So what you're saying is, you think that the feud was continued because of some other event. That prejudices could not possibly continue on for hundreds of years. Is that it?" another question by the Professor.

"I think what I am saying is, I don't think the feud was just about family origins and history, but had to be about something else, something more contemporary to the participants. Perhaps it was revenge, perhaps something else, or maybe it was just what appears to be obvious, cold blooded murder."

"Perhaps, I suppose it is unlikely that bigotry could remain for hundreds of years, a bigotry that stirred the emotions enough to cause murder, or perhaps revenge. That kind of bigotry would have to have a very significant origin, more than the place of ethnic origin, something like religion perhaps." the professor whispered, letting his voice trail off.

"Okay, I give up." John kind of rolled his eyes. "I know what you're getting at. Protestants and Catholics have been at each other for centuries, and there are still people dying over it in Ireland. Christians and Muslim have been at it even longer and there is no telling how many others have died because of religious bigotry. It's just hard for me to believe that the Ridleys still thought of themselves as Norman and the Featherstones thought of themselves as Saxon after four hundred years. By the sixteenth century they were all English."

"And the Irish were Irish and the Scotts were Scottish," the professor muttered under his breath just loud enough for John to hear. With that little parting shot the Professor ceased the questioning. He changed the topic all together and asked John if he had started his preparations for his trip to England. John explained that he had already filled out all the paper work for the Institute and he had called a travel agent and left them instructions to find a plane reservation departing around June 15th. That would get him to England a few days earlier than necessary, allowing him to get settled before any of his classes began. The fellowship covered all of his travel and living expenses and he would be staying in one of the dorm rooms set aside for the fellows.

The Professor seemed satisfied. After a few suggestions for John regarding his itinerary, he dismissed John and went back to whatever he had been reading when John had entered. John got up and left the office, without turning around, but he sensed there was a slight smile of satisfaction on the Professor's lips.

As he left the building he could see some thunder clouds looming in the sky above Noyes Lab. He knew it was just a matter of time before the storm hit. He began walking briskly across the quad in hopes he would be able to reach home in time. By the time he reached Krannert Hall, the sky had turned dark gray, then without warning a lightning bolt streaked across the sky. Within moments, thunder sounded with an ear pounding Boom! John actually flinched, looking upward for the source. Right on cue the sky let loose and the rain began to fall in torrents. It was too late, he was caught. He ducked beneath a large oak tree to avoid getting drenched. He looked up the street to see if he could locate a possible refuge from the rain. Across the street was a bar. It was not a place he frequented, however he had been there once or twice with colleagues from his department. He decided to risk it. He ran across the street and ducked into the front door, shaking off as much rain as he could as he entered. Thunderstorms like this rarely lasted for very long, so he knew that he would only need to stay for a short time. He sat at a table in the corner and ordered a coke.

He reached into his back pack and pulled out the brochure for the Institute for Studies in Medieval and Renaissance Literature. If he traveled on the 15th of June, he would arrive five days before the Institute began on June 20th. That should be enough time to see some sights in London and get himself settled at Oxford. Students were allowed to check in on Saturday, June 18th.

The Institute was two two-week sessions, with a week break in the middle. The brochure indicated that the break was intended for independent studies and touring by the participants. It was perfect. It would allow him to travel to Northumberland during the middle week, which would give him more than a week to explore. He had asked the travel agent to see about train tickets leaving Oxford on the second of July, and returning on the 10th. (He later learned that there was no need for reserved tickets since the trains and buses in England ran with great frequency) He would take the train to Hexham, and then travel by bus to the other towns he planned on visiting. It seemed like a good plan. He had set aside plenty of money in savings to pay for the train and for his overnight lodging and meals in Northumberland.

The Institute would end on July 22nd. John had decided that his return flight should be on or about August 1st. This would give him a little extra time in England at the end, just in case he needed it. The additional expense would be worth it. He wasn't sure when he would get a chance to go to England again and so he would make the most of it.

Summer rainstorms rarely lasted very long and this one was no exception. John peeked through the front window and could see that the sky was becoming lighter and that the rain had stopped. It was safe for him to continue on back to the house. He jotted down a few notes to himself, stuck his notepad into his backpack and decided to brave the elements one more time. As he left the bar, he could smell something pungent in the air, and he began to feel sticky all over. Instead of cooling the air, the rain had only served to make the warm day steamy.

John walked as quickly as he could toward home, believing if he hurried, he could avoid anymore showers. As he walked, he thought through his schedule for the next few weeks. It was now March 23rd. There were seven more weeks in the semester and then he would have a brief break to go home before getting on the airplane bound for England. It could not come quick enough. He needed to get away.

*****

The weeks dragged on at a snail's pace. There were times when John felt he was just going through the motions in his teaching. It was hard to focus. Every essay he read seemed like the one before. At the same time, there was very little he could do on his research where he was. He was distracted, unfocused and he felt as if he had exhausted all the available resources. He was in a lull, wandering aimlessly, without any real motivation. Going to England would not only create the space he needed to get away from Annie and everything that reminded him of her, but it also offered the promise of reinvigorating his research.

When school finally ended in May, John packed up all of the things in his room, stuffing it into boxes. Everything, that is, except what he would need for the trip. He had decided to sublet his room in the house for the summer to an incoming graduate student. It would provide a little extra income, but it meant storing his stuff in the basement. After cleaning out his room, and saying goodbye to his housemates, he packed up the Corolla, one more time, and headed for home.

He spent just a little more than two weeks at home and that was more than enough. It was not long before both of his parents were driving him nuts. It was not as if he did not love and appreciate his parents. However, he was now an adult, accustomed to his independence, and his parents had difficulty understanding boundaries. They would plan things without asking him and then he would have to politely go along with it. They could not adjust to the blurred line between him being their son and him just being an adult guest in their home.

The departure date for England was June 14th. When it finally arrived, he was both relieved and anxious to get on the plane. His parents delivered him to the Pittsburgh airport a couple of hours before his scheduled departure, at 2:40 PM. His mom was trying to be brave as she gave him a hug and told him to "be careful", as he got in line to board. His dad patted him on the back with a "have a great time son, send us a post card." And that was it.

He was now on the plane, leaning back in his seat, relieved to be getting out of Beaver Falls, and genuinely excited about his upcoming adventure. His first flight was fairly brief, followed by a short stop over at JFK, before the long flight to London's Heathrow Airport. Once the plane left the ground at JFK, the stewardesses served dinner, and then shortly thereafter, pillows and blankets were distributed and the lights of the cabin were turned low. John sat quietly, staring out the window into the blackness of the night. The sound of the jet engines all but drowned out any sound in the cabin. He felt strange, out of his element. There was something dreamlike about plane travel. It probably had something to do with the distance traveled; combined with moving the clock forward, as one time zone after another passed by unobserved. As he continued to peer through the window, he noticed the stars above; they seemed vast. A wave of uncertainty swept over him; he felt alone.

He looked back into the cabin. It was dark and quiet, with the occasional glow of personal reading lights scattered about. The plane was going to get into London at 7:30 AM, the next day, and so he decided it would be best if he tried to get as much sleep as possible. It was not easy. As he was drifting off, he could here soft voices in background. And then there was the occasional rocking of the plane, as it passed through variations in the air that caused it to dip or waver in its path. He found himself drifting in and out of sleep, unsure of whether he was getting any sustained rest.

Between these moments of disturbed sleep, he spent his time reading a *Guide to London* that he had purchased at a bookstore at the mall, in Champaign. The travel agent had made reservations at a hotel near Hyde Park, where he would spend the first two nights. This would give him an opportunity to explore London, and so he spent the time creating a sketchy itinerary for his first two days. Fortunately, his hotel was in close proximity to Victoria Station, where he would take the train to Oxford on Friday. The flight was relatively uneventful, and despite everything, he convinced himself that he had gotten enough sleep. Before he knew it, the plane was touching down on the runway at Heathrow.

By the time John had located his luggage, and passed through customs, it was a little after nine, local time. He decided to find a place in the airport where he could get some breakfast. He was pretty sure he would not be able to check into the hotel before mid-afternoon, and so there was really no reason to hurry. While looking for a café, he found a place to exchange his currency; taking advantage of the accessibility. After a leisurely breakfast, with his luggage in tow he found the boarding area for the Underground. The trip from Heathrow to his hotel took about fifty minutes. When he arrived at the hotel in South Kensington, he found it was still a little early for check in, so he left his luggage at the desk and took a walk through Hyde Park. The weather was surprisingly pleasant, a little cool, but not raining. In fact, the sun was trying to peak through in places. Given the time difference and the jet lag, the exhilaration of the walk was a necessary stimulus. After the brisk walk, he found a bench near the fountains where he could sit and read, and watch the people passing by. He began to feel drowsy and the need to get up and move. He explored the local area, visiting a few shops and scoping out a few different places that seemed suitable eateries.

When he finally returned to the hotel and checked in, he was beginning to drag, but he knew it was important to stay awake as long as he could, to get acclimated to London time. He took a hot shower, and then he forced himself to eat some dinner at a pub around the corner from the Hotel. The entire meal was a blur. He felt like he was in a waking dream. He couldn't focus on anything. As much as he tried to fight it, his body was telling him that it wanted to sleep. When he returned from dinner, he could no longer stay awake so he gave up and went to bed.

He slept hard and woke up very early the next morning. The sun was barely peaking above the horizon. After a simple breakfast of tea and rolls, he decided to get an early start exploring London. He caught a double-decker bus tour of the city. The weather remained pleasant, so he was able to sit on the upper deck enjoying the view of the city. It seemed like a very 'touristy' thing to do, but he really didn't have that much time and he figured it would at least allow him to see the highlights. The tour passed by Piccadilly, Trafalgar and most of the prominent museums. He had the freedom to depart the bus at any time and rejoin the tour later. As the bus passed through Covent Garden, the guide explained that they would soon be entering London. John had not realized that the city of London only made up a small portion of the entire metropolitan area.

When they stopped in front of St. Paul's cathedral, he decided to get out. As he stood on the front steps, he couldn't help but smile. He had a sudden memory flash into his mind, remembering the scene of the beggar women selling feed for the pigeons for a tuppence in *Mary Poppins*. It was just as he remembered it.

Once inside, he found a stairway that climbed up into the dome. There was balcony that stretched around the entire circle of the dome. He took a moment to sit and take in the entire cathedral from this vantage point. He began to hear voices, an almost whisper. A man and woman were speaking to their son, cautioning him not to get too close to the railing. John could hear them plainly as if they were right next to him. He looked around. Sitting opposite him, on the other side of the dome, were a young couple and a boy of about six. Somehow the sound was being reflected around the curvature of the dome.

As John was leaving the cathedral, he noticed an inscription on one of the pillars in the hall, *Bishops of London*, followed by a list of names. There it was, about a third of the way down, Nicholas Ridley, 1550-1553.

He rejoined the bus tour. In minutes they were passing over a bridge leading to Big Ben and Parliament. On the other side, the bus came to a stop again, this time in front of Westminster.

It would be impossible to describe John's first impressions when walking the grounds of Westminster and then entering the front entrance? Awestruck just didn't seem a big enough word. His first impulse was to just stand and gaze, to soak it all in. Every little part, from the tile on the floor to the railing of the pews, to the support columns ascending to unbelievable heights; every part, every detail, was intricately designed. Besides the incredible beauty, there was also the magnificence of the engineering required in both the design and construction of such an impressive edifice. He remained standing in the nave for several minutes, gazing upward at the arches that supported the ceiling; arch after arch, interlaced in perfect unity and symmetry, providing a stark contrast to the diagonal checkerboard tiles of the floor beneath his feet.

He walked along the northern aisle, pausing to admire the artwork that decorated the walls and supports. Westminster Abbey was not legally considered a cathedral, but instead, a Royal Peculiar; the place of worship of the ruling monarchy. Through the centuries, Westminster served as both a coronation sight for the monarchs of England and the burial site of both royals and aristocrats, including famous scientists and artists of the British realm. Turning into one of the alcoves, he came upon a memorial dedicated to a number of famous British authors, including the likes of Chaucer, Shakespeare, Dickens, Tennyson, Kipling and others. He later learned that it was called the Poet's Corner, and the memorial was for those who were actually buried at Westminster, Chaucer having been the first. Also in the nave were memorials to famous scientists, only two of which he had ever heard of, Charles Darwin and Isaac Newton. As he continued exploring, he eventually came upon the coronation throne, very old and somewhat strange in appearance, bare wood, with a gilded lion at each of the four corners of the base. It served as the seat of coronation of every British monarch for more than 700 years. Beneath the seat was a cavity, where the coronation stone was placed. This stone, which resides in Scotland until a new monarch is crowned, was once believed, according to some ancient tradition, to be the pillow of Jacob, the patriarch of Israel.

The entire visit to Westminster was more than inspiring and he was glad that he had taken the extra time to explore it. Once he left the church, he opted not to rejoin the bus tour, but instead decided to walk a bit, by way of Buckingham Palace. He had a good map of London in his guidebook and given that he was still feeling the effects of jet lag, he figured the walk would do him good. He passed a small park that stood between Trafalgar and the palace. In the middle of the park was a small lake, and in the lakes there were swans swimming, enjoying the summer the day.

He arrived at Buckingham just before noon, as the guard was in the middle of its daily change. He watched the procession and then proceeded down the mall that led to Trafalgar where he found a quiet café where he could get some lunch. After lunch, he picked up the tour bus again at Picadilly and decided to take in a few museums. By the time he returned to his hotel that evening, he had completed a very full day, sleep came easy.

*****

The next day, John took the Tube to Victoria Station and boarded a train, just before noon. The trip took about an hour and half. When he arrived at the Oxford station, he grabbed a cab to take him to Keble College, where the fellows in the Institute were supposed to check in. The distance from the station was not that far, but given that he had his luggage, he didn't feel like walking. As the cab passed through town and then the university campus, he found himself glued to the window, taking in all that he could see. Everything seemed so old and so big, it was surreal. If there hadn't been cars on the road, he would have thought he had stepped back in time. Most of the university buildings seemed to him ancient. Many could boast of a history that had lasted centuries. He could hardly wait to start exploring the campus.

The cab dropped him at Keble College, in front of what was called the Porter's Lodge. The college was completely surrounded by a wall. There was a small opening, a door, in what appeared to be a much larger wooden gate. As he stepped through the opening he noticed the sign for the porter to the left.

He was a stout man of about fifty, with closely cropped hair and tiny round spectacles. He stood behind a counter and was dressed in a black suit that showed a little wear in the elbows of the jacket. He looked the part.

"Hello, my name is John Ridley," he introduced himself, "and I am a visiting fellow for the Summer Institute."

"Did you receive a letter of confirmation in the post, Mr. Ridley?" The porter asked, with a rather thick accent.

John handed him the letter. The porter turned and began browsing through a box of packets on the credenza behind his desk. John looked around the porter's office, taking in the details. Just then, a young man about his age entered behind him, also carrying luggage.

"Hi, my name is Ian McGowan," the stranger greeted.

"John Ridley," he responded. "Are you here for the Summer Institute?"

"Yes I am?" the stranger responded.

"Where are you from?"

"Duke University," he replied, "Durham, North Carolina, how about you?"

"University of Illinois, Champaign," John said trying to sound as if he was proud of it. "When did you get here?"

"Arrived in London this morning and came straight up by train," Ian continued, as John glanced back at the porter behind the desk to check his progress. "What about you? When did you get in?"

"I came in on Wednesday. I spent a couple days in London. I imagine you are a bit jet lagged, huh?"

"Nah, not too bad," Ian smiled. "I tried to get a little shut eye on the plane. I imagine I'll feel it tonight though."

"Here you are, you have an ensuite room in De Breyne, DB4, and here is your key," the porter explained. "Here is a map of the campus. Please feel free to explore the college grounds and let me know if you are in need of anything. You are right here," pointing to the map, "If you go out the door and through the passage to your left, it will open onto Liddon Quad. Make a left through the breezeway, into Pusey Quad. Then go through this walkway in front of the library, which will take you to Hayward Quad. The building here on the left is De Breyn. Your room is on the second floor. Meals are provided in the Dining hall located here (pointing at the map.) You should find whatever linens you need in the closet in your room. In this brief is additional information about your schedule including meal times. An opening reception is held at 7:00 PM on Sunday evening in the garden quadrangle here. Do you have any other questions?"

"No I can't think of anything. Thank you. It was nice to meet you Ian," John said turning to his new acquaintance. "I suppose we will see each other later."

"Yea, nice to meet you, too."

John placed the information packet beneath his arm, picked up his back pack and suitcases and made his way to the rear exit that opened onto Liddon Quad. He stopped as he exited the building to take a second look at the map. Since he was standing still, he took a moment to take in his surroundings. The buildings surrounding the quad were huge brick buildings that completely wrapped around the quad. The brick was a little reminiscent of U of I, but the quad was entirely enclosed by buildings and quite unique. The neatly manicured lawn sat recessed six feet beneath the level of the walkway that surrounded the quad. Staircases descended down to the lawn on all four sides, connecting a crossing walkway. The architectural style was much older than anything back home. Across the quad there was a chapel with high arching stained glass windows and several spires reaching skyward. It was a very impressive structure, and John made a mental note to investigate its interior when he had the chance.

He felt a little strange in this place. He had been on several different university campuses, but there was something different about this one. It was not only the physical appearance of the buildings, but it was also the ambience. There was an ancient history and tradition here that went beyond just external appearances. Even though he would only be here for a short time, he felt somehow connected to it, connected to the past.

After this momentary reflection, he picked up his bags and started walking towards Pusey Quad. Just as he started he heard steps behind him. "Hey, wait up," it was Ian. "Turns out we are practically neighbors...what are the odds," he said as he caught up with John.

"Yea, that is a coincidence, I suppose," John agreed. Although, he really didn't think it was much of coincidence at all, since all of the fellows were probably going to be staying at the same location.

As they walked, Ian, without any invitation, began to share a good portion of his life story. John listened respectfully. He figured he would either hear it now or later, and now would be as good a time as any. Ian stood about five ten, a little shorter than John. He had short, curly, strawberry blond hair that was cut reasonably short. He wore round, wire-rimmed glasses that he had to keep pushing back up on his nose. Every time he did so, he would raise his eyebrows and stretch his nose as if it made the adjustment easier. It appeared to be a nervous habit more than anything practical.

Fortunately, their walk was not that long, so Ian's autobiography was cut short when they arrived at the residence halls. De Breyn Hall, and Hayward Hall, next to it, were much more modern than the rest of the campus buildings. John was struck at how strange it looked. Hayward was four stories high and the front of the building was entirely made of glass. Some of the windows had there blinds open, revealing rooms whose front walls were entirely window. The front of DeBreyn was a sort of concrete block. In contrast to the surrounding red brick buildings, these dormitories looked strangely out of place.

Ian and John passed through a passage way that led into a courtyard in the center of the dorm, only to reveal the interior walls facing the courtyard, were just like that of Hayward, entirely of glass. The new friends found the stairwell labeled DB4. There was a card on the wall with their names and two others, indicating the present occupants of the section. As they about to enter another young man emerged through the door, nearly knocking Ian of his feet.

"Hello there," Ian greeted. Shyness did not seem to be one of his attributes.

"Hello," the stranger greeted, looking up, appearing surprised.

"My name is Ian McGowan, and this is John...Ridley wasn't it?" Ian proceeded with the introductions, without hesitation.

"That's right," John added, "nice to meet you.

"I am Sean Hoskins," the stranger responded.

"Where are you from?"

"University of Washington," Sean answered. "Go Huskies," he added in what appeared to be a little of a mocking tone.

"I'm from Duke and John's from Illinois," Ian said. John was more than happy to let Ian carry the conversation. He just wanted to get to his room and get settled. The jet lag was starting to catch up again. He had a hard time understanding why Ian was not feeling any of the effects, or at least he was not showing it.

"Nice to meet you," Sean returned. "I imagine your rooms are upstairs." He half-heartedly pointed up, and then continued his journey to wherever he was going.

"A bit of a reserved chap, I suspect," Ian said, in a sort of mocking British accent as they started up the stairs.

John just smiled.

The two of them struggled, a little, getting their luggage up the stairs, but they eventually made it. It turned out that their rooms were on different floors, Ian's directly above. John left Ian to his own interests and stepped through the doorway into his own room. He set his bags down and kind of fell back onto the bed. He just lay there for a moment, staring up at the ceiling. Then gradually, he gathered himself and pulled himself to his feet. He unpacked his bags and hung some of his clothes in the armoire that stood against one wall and then he placed his sundries in the drawers beneath. There was a desk with a lamp and a small mirror hanging on one wall to complete the furnishings. The bed was a bit springy, but he did not think it would make a bit of difference. He found the linens in the closet and was just about finished making the bed when Ian appeared at the door.

"Y'all settled?" he asked, with a bit of a southern accent. From his earlier autobiography, John remembered that Ian was not really from the south, so the "y'all" was a bit over the top. "This place is great isn't it?"

"Not bad, I suppose," John answered. It seemed Ian's natural disposition was cheery and optimistic, even when jet lagged.

"Hey, would you like to take a walk and check out the campus?"

"No thanks, Ian, I think I might just hang out here for a little while, sort of get my bearings and all," John needed a little down time.

"Suit yourself, maybe a little later we can go to dinner together."

"Sure, sounds good," John figured it would do no harm having dinner together on the first night.

After Ian left, John stood peering out the window at the quad below and the buildings opposite. He could hardly believe he was here. He felt the urge to pinch himself. As he stood there he caught a glimpse of Ian going down the walk, back towards the Porter's lodge. He took out the copy of *Kennilworth,* by Scott, he had brought along and sat back on the bed and began reading. Before long, he felt himself drifting off. Rather than resist, he simply lay back in the bed and let the drowsiness take hold.

Chapter Five

The path opened before him into a glen. He was climbing a slight rise. As he arrived at the top, the sun was just setting off to his left. Looking ahead down the lane, in the distant twilight, he could see what appeared to be a castle, a dark silhouette against the grayness. He could just make out the battlements lining the top of the exterior walls. At the front entrance, there was a tower gate and in the top of the tower, a window and in the window, a light, silhouetting the shape of a young woman.

There was a gentle knock at the door. John opened his eyes slowly, to see Ian's head peer around the edge of the slightly opened door. "Anybody home?" Ian whispered. "Hey John, are you asleep?"

"Not really," John said sleepily, "just kind of dozed off. What time is it?"

"A quarter of six. I thought I'd better wake you. I think they start serving dinner at around six. I didn't think you would want to miss it," his voice started to climb from a whisper to a normal level.

"Quarter to six, really? I guess I must still be a little jet lagged. Let me freshen up a bit and I will be right with you."

As John and Ian were leaving, they passed Sean in the hallway and invited him to join them. He just shrugged his shoulders and without saying a word, followed them. The three of them walked across Hayward Quad to the dining hall. Rising from the solid wood floor were long tables that were formally set with china and linen napkins. The walls rose to a ceiling that must have been twenty feet high. It was constructed with huge panels between wide semicircular arches. Providing light to the room were huge arching windows along each of the walls. Between each of these windows was a collection of portraits. The walls were paneled with dark wood. Once again, he felt as if he had just stepped back in time.

The tables were very long, with bench seats on either side, enough to seat thirty to forty at each table. The three of them found some empty seats at one of the tables and as they sat down, they introduced themselves to the other fellows sitting nearest to them on either side. The dinner conversation consisted of sharing personal backgrounds and career aspirations. As these personal biographies began to wane, the conversation transitioned to talk about literature, which naturally led to favorite authors. Sean seemed to be a fan of Beowulf, while Ian could not stop talking about C.S. Lewis. Visiting Oxford was a dream-come-true for him, since Lewis had taught here; a professor of Medieval Literature.

After dinner, Ian talked John into doing a little exploring. Sean made some excuse and returned to De Breyne. From the dining room they were able to pass through the Library and then out through Porter's Lodge, to Parks Road. Opposite the college, on Parks Road, was the Museum of Natural History. Walking south, they passed by St. John's College, one of the oldest colleges of the University. John had read that there were over thirty different colleges that were a part of Oxford University, each having their own history and traditions. St. John's had an extensive garden park that bordered Parks Road. They decided to cut through the park and explore a little of the historic college campus. They passed through Canterbury Quadrangle and then through to the front quad and main entrance of St. John's. As they emerged onto St. Giles St., John noticed to their left a tall obelisk in the center of the road. He decided to check it out. As he approached it, he realized it was a memorial of some kind. Located on the front panel was an inscription.

Martyrs Memorial

*To the Glory of God, and in grateful
commemoration of His servants, Thomas Cranmer,
Nicholas Ridley, Hugh Latimer, Prelates of the
Church of England, who near this spot yielded
their bodies to be burned, bearing witness to the
sacred truths which they had affirmed and
maintained against the errors of the Church of
Rome, and rejoicing that to them it was given not
only to believe in Christ, but also to suffer for His
sake; this monument was erected by public
subscription in the year of our Lord God,
MDCCCXLI. (1860)*

"Nicholas Ridley...are you related to him?" Ian asked,
looking over his shoulder at the inscription.

"I'm not exactly sure, it's possible," John was amazed that
he was actually standing here in front of the memorial, just
weeks after discovering the story of Bishop Ridley.

"Do you know the story behind this memorial?" Ian asked.

"Most of it," John paused to reach back in his memory to
recall the story he had read in the history of the Ridleys.
"Nicholas Ridley was the Bishop of London, during the reign of
Henry VIII. Along with Cranmer and Latimer, mentioned here,
he helped to establish the Church of England. He and Cranmer
were credited with writing the First Common Book of Prayer,
during the reign of Henry's son Edward. If you remember your
English history, Edward, like his father was Protestant, but he
died at a very young age. Bishops Ridley and Latimer then
supported Lady Jane Grey to succession. This was because they
did not want Mary, who was the older half sister of Edward, to
become queen. Mary was the daughter of Catherine of Aragon,
and therefore Catholic. She gained in power, obtained control
of the government and then she threw Lady Jane Grey in the
tower of London; eventually having her beheaded for treason.
Ridley and Latimer were also arrested and asked to recant the
protestant faith. When they refused, they were sentenced to be

burned at the stake. Hundreds of Protestants in England were executed by one form or another, thus the nickname given to the queen was 'Bloody Mary'."

"Interesting story," Ian mused. "Imagine being burned at the stake, what a gruesome death. It's hard to believe that a civilized people considered this an appropriate form of execution."

"I think it was reserved for executions having to do with heresy. They thought that the flames would either cleanse the soul or begin the eternal torment of hell." John explained. "If I remember right, Bishop Ridley's brother-in-law actually tied gun powder around the neck of the Bishop so the end would come quickly. As they were lighting the fire, Latimer turned to Ridley and said something like 'take heart Master Ridley for today in England we shall light a candle which shall never be extinguished.' And so it was. Mary was the last of the Roman monarchs in England."

"Incredible," Ian said.

John took one more moment to look upon the face of the statue of Bishop Ridley. He wondered if it was a true likeness and whether there was any actual direct connection between his ancestors and the Bishop. Christian martyrdom was so far removed from his own life experience that it made it difficult to comprehend. It was even more difficult, given that the conflict was between two Christian churches. Was the threat of heresy so disconcerting that it created an atmosphere of fear, even to the point of paranoia, or was this really more a case of political intrigue and was not about religion at all. The more he studied history, the more he realized that these lines were often gray and difficult to decipher. In this case it was even possible that the victims believed themselves to be dying for a just cause that was thoroughly religious, while the persecutors also believed themselves to be in the right, but that their cause was political and about loyalty to the throne.

The sun was starting to approach the horizon so John and Ian continued their walk up St. Giles St. Fortunately, Ian had remembered to bring a map, otherwise they may never have found their way back. Just beyond the walls of St. John's was a walkway called the Lamb and Flag Passage. This walkway passed through to Museum Street, on which De Breyne Hall was located. It was turning dark just as they returned to the dorm.

"Goodnight, Ian, thanks for the company," John said.

"Yeah, thanks John, I enjoyed it as well, goodnight. Thanks for the history lesson."

John retired to his room and closed the door behind. He sat down at the desk and pulled out his journal. He had committed to journalize his experience in England on a daily basis. He knew that this was a once in a lifetime experience and in the end he would be glad for making the effort. He had been too tired in his hotel in London to do any writing, so he decided to start by recapping the past three days. This, of course, required a bit more effort than usual. When he got to the part about the memorial he paused for a moment's reflection.

> *...I am not sure why I feel this connection to Nicholas Ridley. I don't know if we are related, I'm not sure that really matters. There is something heroic about his story. It's not so much that I need to know if we are connected as much as I simply need to be connected. I feel this urgency of wanting to be a part of something significant, something real. Dying for a cause, seems to be meaningful, however having the strength of conviction to die for something is even more meaningful and real...*

He put aside his journal, and got ready for bed. He read a little more before drifting off to sleep.

*****

The next morning, he rose very early and went for a jog. He decided to go north on Parks Road, just to explore a different part of the campus. He circled back down St. Giles and then took the Lamb and Flag Passage back to the residence hall.

100

He showered and changed and then walked back to the dining hall where he had a relatively quiet breakfast. After breakfast, he spent the rest of the day exploring downtown Oxford. When walking back on Parks Road he passed Bodleian Library. He had heard about this library from the Professor. It was supposed to be one of the oldest and largest libraries in Europe. The collection of printed material dated back to the 16th century, and there were also manuscripts in the collection that dated back to the 11th century. It literally contained millions of volumes. Like most of the colleges, the library was a large building that was built around a central courtyard. From the courtyard, John noticed there were several entrances, each marked with a sign over the door indicating a specific discipline. One was labeled Schola Morale Philosophie, another Schola Geomtriae et Arithematicae, another Schola Metaphysicae, and so on. Outside of the Old Library sat the most ornamental building in Oxford, the Radcliffe Carmera. He looked forward to being able to explore the library further.

After dinner that night, Ian came and sat down beside him.

"You going back to the room?" he asked, kind of catching John by surprise. Ian had been conspicuously absent all day, so he wasn't sure if he was more surprised to see him now, or that he hadn't seen him earlier.

"Oh, hi Ian," John greeted, showing his bewilderment. "Yea, I thought I would do some reading or something."

"I've got a better idea, why don't you come with me?" he invited.

"What did you have in mind?" John asked.

"You'll see, come on." Ian got up from the table and started for the door.

John shrugged his shoulders and followed. He figured it couldn't hurt to go along. As they left the dining hall, Ian led him down Black Hall Road and then down Museum Road and then through the Lamb and Flag Passage. Instead of turning down St. Giles, they crossed the street where they found themselves standing in front of a pub called the Eagle and Child.

"Do you know what this is?" Ian asked.

"Should I?"

"Come on let's go inside," Ian insisted.

John was not sure why Ian was so excited about a pub, but they were in England after all, so he followed him through the front door. They were seated at a small table towards the back next to a small fire place. He took a moment to look around and take in the setting. It was about what he expected to see in an English pub, nothing particularly unique, poorly lit, dark wood all around. He couldn't see why Ian insisted on coming here. On one wall, above the fire place, there were some pictures. There were two black and white portraits, which looked somewhat familiar, but he couldn't say for sure whether he recognized them. In between was a framed, handwritten document of some sort.

"Do you know who they are?" Ian asked pointing at the portraits.

John shook his head no. "I can't quite place them," he said.

"C.S. Lewis and J.R.R. Tolkein," Ian said with a smile, he was almost giddy. "They were both professors here at Oxford, and this is the very pub in which they and others used to gather. Have your read Lewis or Tolkien?"

'What, Lewis, again?' John thought to himself. He decided to be diplomatic and not let on to his indifference. "I think I read *The Lion the Witch and the Wardrobe* in middle school, and then *The Hobbit* in high school. I loved *The Hobbit*."

"I read the entire *Chronicles of Narnia* before I was in 6th grade," Ian said. "After that, I became a huge fan of C.S. Lewis. He might be why I became an English major. I think I have read everything he has ever written, at least twice. Have you ever read *Screwtape Letters*?" John shook his head no. "It's an absolute must. Of course I think my favorite is *That Hideous Strength*, the third in his science fiction series. Have you heard of it?" He didn't wait for John to respond. "I first read *The Hobbit* in high school as well. It wasn't long before I had devoured the entire *Lord of the Rings* series. I was captivated, I couldn't put it down. Imagine both of these literary greats sitting here in this very pub, talking over a pint. I wonder if their students ever understood the significance of their friendship."

John was surprised by Ian's level of enthusiasm. It was certainly cool that Lewis and Tolkien used to visit this pub together, but it wasn't that astounding. They were professors after all. It was not as if they were members of the *Beatles* or something. He sat quietly as Ian continued to ramble on about how these two authors had been the most influential in causing him to study English Literature. He clearly was in awe of the entire moment. John thought it was best not to interrupt and allow him to revel for a while longer.

Ian ordered a pint of ale and John decided to have tea. They sat and talked for a while, Ian dominating most of the conversation. At some point he began jabbering on about a work by Lewis entitled *The Great Divorce*. "The image of heaven he creates is quite insightful. Clearly, he was illustrating the importance of knowing that heaven is more substantial, more real, than even earth. It changed the way I looked at life and the journey toward heaven..." he paused reflecting. "Of course it wasn't just Lewis and Tolkien. There were others as well, Charles Williams, T.S. Eliot and then there was Lewis' brother and Tolkien's brother as well. They called themselves the Inklings. It was reported that they would often chide each other about their work. Lewis received the most reproach for having written children's books, even though he himself had never had any children..."

Ian went on and on, but eventually he started to wind down. They had been at the pub for an hour when John suggested that they head on home. Ian seemed disappointed that it had to end, but the frown on his face didn't last long. He must have realized that he would be in Oxford all summer and there would be plenty of more opportunities to visit the *Eagle and Child*.

They left the pub and crossed over St. Giles to the entrance of the Lamb and Flag Passageway (John later learned that the Lamb and Flag Pub was also frequented by Lewis and the rest of the Inklings). In five minutes they were back at De

Breyne. John said his good nights and went straight to bed. He read a little, as he always did, but soon drifted off to sleep.

*****

The next day was Sunday. John decided to walk to Christ's Church Cathedral for Sunday services. He figured it would be a little different than anything he had experienced in his home church or at TCBC in Urbana. He was not disappointed. The cathedral was impressive. It was beautifully ornate, intricate in the details, another masterpiece of architecture and engineering. It was reminiscent of Westminster, but smaller and with its own character and artistry. The service was much more liturgical than John was accustomed to. It made him feel that his modern American evangelical experience had been lacking in reverence and formality. He found himself listening intently to every part. It was fresh and new and meaningful. At one point, he found himself looking up at the ceiling while he listened. Everything seemed to draw his attention upward, as if he were being drawn to heaven.

The first few days of the Institute kept him pretty busy. That evening everyone attended the reception and orientation at Sloane Robinson Hall. Monday began with lectures in the morning by Professors of Keble College, followed by seminars in the afternoon on various writers. As the week moved forward, John found himself falling into a bit a routine, attending classes, participating in seminars and discussion groups, and in his spare time, exploring the University. In the evening there were social gatherings to encourage the fellows to mix with the faculty. It was not until Friday afternoon that he found some time to go back to the Bodleian Library to do some research.

John went to the main desk to ask for some help. Before entering the actual collections area he had to sign a declaration in which he promised not to remove any materials from the library and that he would not deface any document in the collection. He thought this a bit strange at first, but when he realized that the collection contained books and manuscripts that were hundreds of years old, he realized the need for such a protocol.

Having just recently visited the Martyrs Memorial, John decided to do some research into the life and work of Bishop Ridley. Although it was off track from his actual research, he thought he would take advantage of the opportunity. The Library was surely to have material covering the life of the Bishop, and as it turned out, he wasn't disappointed.

The librarian initially brought him biographical materials concerning Nicholas Ridley. There were a couple of biographies published in the late nineteenth and early twentieth century. There were also a couple of collections of biographies, John Foxe's Book of Martyrs, and the Encyclopedia of Eminent Christians, both of which also contained information concerning Hugh Latimer and Thomas Cranmer.

The first biography confirmed that Nicholas Ridley had been born at Willimoteswick and had lived at least part of his life at Unthank Hall. John took copious notes on any material that provided something new. While he was working, the librarian returned and said that he had found older material which actually contained published works of Bishop Ridley. However, he would have to go to the basement between Bod and the Radcliffe Camera. He could peruse the documents in the reading room of the "Radder".

The librarian directed him to a special collections room where an assistant helped him to locate several documents. One was a first printing of the original Book of Common Prayer compiled by Ridley and Cranmer. There was also a collection of papers written by Bishop Ridley concerning church policies, including criticisms of the Roman church. John browsed through the titles, but nothing really caught his eye. He would have loved to read some of them, but he didn't really have the time to do that now.

Moments later, the assistant brought him a collection of correspondences of Bishop Ridley that had been published by his nephew in the late sixteenth century. He was intrigued. He carefully opened the cover and turned to the contents list. There were a few letters that had been written to his colleagues

Latimer and Cranmer, as well as a couple other bishops. However, the majority of the letters were ones that had been written to family members. Contained in the collection were several that were addressed to his brother Hugh Ridley. John looked at the dates. They began in 1525 and continued to about 1554. John remembered that the Bishop had been burned at the stake in 1555. He started reading through the letters beginning with the first one. When he got to the fourth one he browsed the page and immediately noticed the mention of Sir Nicholas Ridley about half way down the page.

May 15, 1530

My Brother Hugh,

It was good to receive your recent correspondence. Thank you for your continued diligence in keeping me informed of recent events within the family. Please convey my love to your lovely wife, and to your children. I continue to remember them with the greatest of affection, and I long to see them all. If you would be so kind as to remember me to our sisters as well, assure them that I have not forgotten them, and I fully hope to have the opportunity to address personal letters to each of them individually in the near future.

I continue to be very busy in my office as Bishop. Each day I pray to God that he might keep me humble, and never allow my elevated position to create within me a proud heart that would only serve to dishonor my person, while failing to bring honor due Him; while at the same time it would only serve to discourage the laity for whose benefit I have been given this charge. I continue to remain in good stead with His Majesty, which is no easy accomplishment, considering he is a man whose temperament can swing like the pendulum.

I was deeply saddened to hear of the news brought to me concerning our uncle and the Lord of Featherstonhaugh Castle. It is difficult for me, as a man devoted to the cause of God, to know that there continues so great a feud that exists between the families of Ridley and Featherstone. The Lord has instructed us to live a life of peacemakers, not warmongers. Where in this conflict is there any consideration for the message of our Lord to "love thy neighbor". Surely the Featherstones and Ridleys are neighbors in even the most simplest of terms, and are not exempt from this exhortation of our Lord and Savior.

To consider that for nearly 400 years two such prominent families could continue in such a struggle of prejudice and bigotry. What once was a conflict of property rights and privileges has now become a struggle over petty differences, even over the privilege of the position of High Sheriff. How I grieve over the innocent blood that has been shed in so many temporal events.

And now, you bring me news of another tragedy, of a magnitude that is difficult to imagine. It was highly irrational for so great a man such as Sir Albany to have believed that the unfortunate accidental death of his son was somehow the fault of our young cousin Thomas. It is unfathomable that Sir Albany would find it necessary to be the vigilante, acting as the judge, and take it upon himself to play the part of the executioner upon the life of a youth who has yet to reach manhood. Sir Nicholas and his brethren were left little choice, but to come to the aid of the poor lad.

It was highly unfortunate that the Broad Knight was not able to bring a resolution to the horrible event without additional blood shed. Sir Nicholas was completely justified in his actions to save the young boy, and must be completely

*exonerated in his actions, even though these
actions resulted in the grievous death of so
honorable a man as Sir Albany. Please assure our
uncle that I bear no ill will toward him as a result
of these unfortunate events and now as always I
continue to revere him as the bell-wether of the
family. Please have complete freedom to convey
these sentiments to him on my behalf.*

*I will continue to pray for Sir Albany's oldest
son who is now left alone in his grief, and my
prayers will also petition the Most High to grant
peace to the land and families of these most
prominent families.*

*May God's Peace and Love Shine on You
Daily,
Your Loving Brother,*

Nicholas Ridley

John could hardly contain his excitement. He could feel his
heart pounding in his chest. How could he have ever imagined
that he would begin unraveling the mystery surrounding the
murder of Sir Albany Featherstonhaugh through the
correspondence of Bishop Ridley? It was almost too good to be
true. Was this in fact the truthful account of the cause of the
death of Sir Albany? Or was this merely the perspective of the
Ridley clan. It seemed unlikely that the Bishop would have
embellished the events, given his position. Perhaps he hadn't
been given an accurate rendition of the event. It was hard to
know for sure. John knew that there were always two sides to
any story. He was still going to need to continue his research
until he had exhausted all sources and all possibilities. The next
step had to be to look further into the source of the ballad
discovered by Sir Walter Scott. His time in the 'Bod' (The
Bodleian Library was endearingly referred to as the 'Bod'.) was
up for now, so he would have to return at a later date. He

quickly copied the last couple of paragraphs of the letter by the Bishop, and then packed up his stuff and left the library.

*****

The following Sunday, John decided to visit Christ's Church for Evensong, a service of worship held in the early evening. The service was entirely led by the organist and choir. John could not remember having ever heard a true pipe organ before. Given the perfect acoustics of the chapel, the organ music reverberated throughout, creating a stereophonic atmosphere. Although the music was a bit antiquated, and not to John's particular tastes, the pageantry-including the white frocked robes of the choir-and the beautiful setting, made for an inspiring experience.

The choir sat on either side of the chapel, in two rows of wooden pews, separated by a waist high, solid bannister. The sopranos and altos sat in front on either side, with the tenors and bases in the second row behind. It was an all-male choir, the soprano and alto parts carried by young boys who were about seven to ten years of age. John was sitting in the third row back, just to the right of the altos and tenors. He had a clear view of the sopranos and bases who sitting on the other side. He was immediately struck by the youthfulness of the boys in the front row, and then amazed by their confidence and precision as they began to sing. He had enough musical knowledge to appreciate the difficulty of the pieces they were singing and their ability to stay on pitch. If anything, it was the older men who were struggling to stay in tune with their young counterparts. The music was amazing. He couldn't help but be impressed by how the young the boys were and how they never took their eye off their director and as the pitch of the music rose and they came to the end of each line, their mouths would be formed in perfect ellipses. Even the highest notes seemed effortless and always perfect in pitch. He closed his eyes and listened to the harmonies filling the air, ascending heavenward. The voices died slowly, the organ as well, and then without warning, they rose again in crescendo, louder and louder, higher in higher filling every place within the cavernous cathedral.

There were moments when the congregation was asked to participate in responsive readings, led by an officiating vicar. The music would begin again, and in the end the congregation was asked to join the choir in two hymns, one of which was a Wesley hymn that John recognized. There was a short sermon at the end- something about allowing your actions to be a product of what you really believe-and then it was over.

As John started his walk back to the dormitory, it started to drizzle. It was a light rain, as was common to England, and so he didn't really mind. The sky was a very dark grey, and the twilight was soon to become night. One by one, lights were turning on all over the University. He turned and looked at the light filtering through the stained glass windows of the cathedral. Against the darkened sky, the images in the panes were brilliant. As he walked up Commarket Street, the street lights were reflecting off the wet pavement, creating a glassy sheen.

There was a café on the left and so he decided to duck in out of the rain, and take a little refreshment. As he sat looking out the front window, he noticed a small church across the street. The sign in front was lit, and even through the light rain he could make out the words, St. Michaels. He could see lights on inside and so he decided to investigate. He finished his tea, and then stepped outside, skipping across the street, trying to spend as little time as possible exposed to the elements.

The front door of the church was open, and so he went on inside. At the back of the church there was a young priest who was busy gathering some papers that had been left on the back pews, perhaps remnants of a worship program from earlier in the evening.

"Excuse me father, I don't mean to intrude, but could you tell me what church this is?" John asked, trying to speak softly.

"Oh hello," The priest looked startled as he turned to face John. "I didn't know that anyone was here. This is St. Michaels of Northgate. The tower is the oldest structure in Oxford.

110

You're welcome to look around if you like and the tower is still open," he pointed to the open stairwell.

"Thank you, I think I will." John browsed through the chapel and then climbed the stairs of the tower. In the tower, there was an old door that had a brass plaque nailed to the top of it. The inscription read, "The door of the prison cell of Bishop Thomas Cranmer, when imprisoned in Bocardo Prison with Bishop's Latimer and Ridley, prior to their martyrdom in 1555".

John could hardly believe his eyes. He had no idea that any such thing even existed. He copied down the inscription before descending the stairs again, making special note of the name of the prison. Thanking the priest before he left, he stepped through the front door, out into the night.

Everywhere he looked the University was all aglow, as night began to stretch across every street and alley. The buildings had an abundance of nooks and crannies that were completely enveloped in darkness. He imagined that at any moment some sinister character could emerge from the shadows, and he found himself feeling a little anxious. He knew that he was only imagining things, but unconsciously he increased his pace. Along with his slight trepidation, there was also a heightened adrenaline rush. It was exciting and mysterious, frightening and beautiful, all at the same time. This was the England he had imagined.

When he finally reached his room, he felt slightly invigorated, partly from the rain and partly due to the adrenaline. He decided to spend some time writing in his journal. He had been so busy that he had not consistently made his daily entries. He spent some time catching up on the previous few days, including a brief description of the letter by Bishop Ridley.

...I was surprised and excited to find the letters of N. Ridley. They were so personal and endearing that it created for me an image of the Bishop as a man who loved his family. I was very impressed with the way in which he reached out in

empathy to his uncle. It suggested to me that Sir
Nicholas was not as horrible and unfeeling a
murderer as Scott had suggested.

Knowing the kind of man the Bishop was, I
am even more moved by the story of his
martyrdom. The fortitude he displayed in the face
of the ordeal of his trial, imprisonment and
eventual execution, leaves me with a sense of pride
that I share the same surname of such an eminent
and faithful servant of God...

...as I listened to the Evensong in the
beautiful surroundings of Christ's Church
Cathedral, I was brought closer to understanding
worship. Worship is not merely a ritualistic
tradition, but is an offering, a sacrifice. In this case
the offering was a presentation of all that the
musicians could offer of truth, goodness and
beauty. Worship therefore becomes what we can
offer back to God of our talents and treasures,
which is a reflection of the image of God in us. I
think it must have been the same for Nicholas
Ridley. Was the sacrifice of his life blood in the
consuming fire an act of worship? Would it have
mattered at all to God whether the truth was on
the side of Protestantism or Catholicism when the
Bishops Latimer and Ridley gave all they had;
believing in their heart that they were making the
sacrifice on behalf of the truth of the Gospel of
Christ? I wonder what God thinks of these things...

On Wednesday, John was able to return to the Bodleian
Library. He had done some research in the Keble College
Library on Sir Walter Scott, but hadn't found anything
particularly enlightening. He had decided that the Bod was
probably still is best source. He asked the librarian for any
poetical or lesser known works of Scott, preferably containing
notes by the author. The librarian was able to find several early

collections of Scott's poetical works with notes, containing *Marmion* and *Lady of the Lake* among other things. They had been published in the mid 1800s, but they did not offer anything new.

While John was rereading a portion of Marmion, the librarian returned with a rather old book with a surprising title, *Letters on Demonology and Witchcraft*. He was unfamiliar with this work. This edition had been published in 1829 and seemed to be a first printing. He opened to the first letter...

> *Origin of the general Opinions respecting Demonology among Mankind— The Belief in the immortality of the Soul is the main inducement to credit its occasional re-appearance—The Philosophical Objections to the Apparition of and Abstract Spirit little understood by the Vulgar and Ignorant—The situations of excited Passion incident to Humanity, which teach Men to wish or apprehend Supernatural Apparitions—They are often presented by the Sleeping Sense—Stoy of Somnambulism—The Influence of Credulity contagious, so that Inviduals will trust the Evidence of others..*

'Supernatural Apparitions-They are often presented by the Sleeping Sense' caught John's attention immediately. His mind immediately jumped to the images he had recently experienced in his dreams. It was as if Scott was speaking directly to him. Were his dreams premonitions? Did they have meaning? Were they connected to reality? He read on. Scott was offering a rational explanation into the strange and mystical associated with the occult and fantasy. It was sort of warning against the dangers of the occult, while at the same time an expose on false myths such as fairy, elves and apparitions. It was not as if Scott was arguing that these things did not exist entirely, but that from his research, most were a product of myth and superstition.

John did not read the entire text, but scanned through the topics of each of the letters and reading only the bits and pieces that tweaked his curiosity. When he came to Part X-A Condemnation of the Unjust Treatment of Falsely Accused Witches-he noticed a short testimonial of Scott concerning an incident that he had first hand knowledge of. It occurred in 1800 when an old woman was accused of witchcraft for having issued a curse at a local farmer only to have the farmer experience a personal calamity immediately after. The old woman was then accused of witchcraft, for which Scott claimed the calamity to be a mere coincidence. What caught John's eyes was not the actual story, but what was written in the margin; a note inscribed, presumably by a one time owner of the book. To his surprise, he read the following phrase:

I wonder if this is a reference to Beardie Grey of Featherstonhaugh?

Once again, John could hardly believe his own eyes. There it was written clearly, Featherstonhaugh. Who was this Beardie Grey? Was she a witch? What was her connection to Featherstonhaugh? It seemed, with each new revelation, he was confronted with more questions, new mysteries. He made a note about Beardie Grey in his journal with the hope of finding out more about her.

He spent the rest of the afternoon browsing through a few other books. As he was wrapping up, the librarian who had been helping him, checked on his progress.

"How is everything going, Mr. Ridley?" he asked.

"You have been very helpful, thank you. I am almost through." John replied. "Can you recommend any other sources, perhaps one of the other libraries here at the University?"

"I have checked with the other libraries. I am not sure there is much of anything else here. Is there any chance that you might be making a visit to Edinburgh?"

"I had not planned on it," He said, "why do you ask?"

"The library at the University of Edinburgh is known to have an extensive collection of Sir Walter Scott's work and personal effects. The collection includes some early manuscripts, his notes, and correspondence. I am sure you would find it very interesting."

"Well, maybe I will have to make a special effort to go there then," John said as he contemplated how much time he would have to travel to the North. "Thanks, I will think about it. And thanks again for all of your help."

"My pleasure, Mr. Ridley, let me know if there is anything else I can help you with. Have a pleasant evening."

"Thank you, you also," John gathered his belongings and headed back to the dormitory.

That night he began to think through his itinerary for his travel into Northumberland. He figured if he used his time efficiently, he might be able to make a day trip to Edinburgh. On Friday he walked to the train station to confirm his time of departure for the next day. While he was there he decided to check on the train schedule from Haltwhistle to Edinburgh.

The Last Days

The bishop sat alone in his room, deep in thought, contemplating the events unfolding. Tomorrow morning he, and his friend and colleague, would once again be paraded before the Queen's own form of an inquisition to present one last defense. Of course it was not really a defense, the course of these proceedings had long since been determined, before they had even began. It was not this tribunal of churchmen that he now faced who were his judges, but instead the Roman Queen, who, like her father, believed herself to be God's chosen judge.

It seemed a strange thing, in one moment be entrusted with the spiritual oversight of an entire nation and in the next moment to be stripped of the priestly robes and condemned to prison; the only change in circumstance having been the passing of the throne from a dead brother to his sister. The religious diversity of a doomed marriage, which first created resentment between a brother and sister, had now divided an entire nation.

A knock came at the door and the bishop rose to his feet. "Excuse me Doctor Ridley, Mr. Shipshide is here to see you." The apologetic intruder was Mr. Irish, Lord Mayor of Oxford and his host, or should it be said jailer.

The bishop had been imprisoned for several months now, first in the tower, then in Bocardo Prison, and now in the comfortable lodgings of this Lord Mayor. It was not clear why he had been afforded this special circumstance over his companions in trial, Hugh Latimer and Thomas Cranmer, but here he was just the same.

Mr. Irish was not much of a jailer. Truth be known, he supported the bishop's cause, and if it had been in his power, would have released the prisoner long ago. Just the same, it was fortunate that he had been able to convince the Bishop's council to release Dr. Ridley into his care, given the promise of the bishop that he would make no attempts to escape. Despite being on trial for heresy and betrayal, there was not a person in England who would ever believe the bishop capable of going against his word.

"Thank you sir, tell him that I will be with him shortly," the bishop returned. It was an odd time of night for a visitor, when most would be preparing to retire. However, these were unusual and trying times, which demanded unpredictable behavior.

Nicholas knelt beside his bed briefly before leaving to meet his brother-in-law. He had no doubt that he would soon be meeting his maker, but that did not hinder him from his usual routine of spending a moment in prayer each time he left, or each time he entered his bedroom. He had continued this habit from the moment he had left Pembroke College as a young man. Even though he was nearing the end of his journey, he saw no reason to stop now.

"Our Heavenly Gracious Father, grant me grace and peace as I anticipate the moment that I shall be united with my Lord and Savior in glory, imminent as it may be. I am not long for this world, and yet I have no fear, no sorrow; for I know in Whom my faith rests, and am convinced that thou art faithful to deliver thy servant from death unto glory.

I humbly confess my trepidation for the flock with which thou hast entrusted me. Give me the wisdom and fortitude to provide them with words that will comfort and strengthen them in their grief. Thank you for the love and companionship now shown by my sister's husband. He has not left my side and has been a source of refuge and light. Grant him peace as he plays witness to these grievous events and may he be a comfort to my family in their sorrow.

To Thee, be all glory and honor, in the name of our Lord and Savior, Jesus Christ, Amen"

The bishop rose, paused but a moment to regain the feelings in his knees and then gingerly stepped out into the hall. Slowly he descended the stairs to the ground floor, it seemed the years had caught up with him and his movements were now made with the caution of a toddler. As he reached the bottom step his brother-in-law stood up from his chair near the fire place in the front sitting room.

"George, how good of you to come, even at so late an hour," the bishop said as he took his brother-in-law's hand.

"I am your servant, Nicholas, as you well know, any moment of any hour." George Shipside was the husband of the bishop's next oldest sister Alice. She was nearly ten years his junior, and although he would not have considered it proper to have a favorite amongst his siblings, Alice was the closest thing to it. From first hearing of the bishop's imprisonment, the beloved Alice had commissioned her husband to go to her brother's aid and attend to his needs. She would have gone herself had she not had the greater responsibility of remaining at Unthank and caring for her children.

"Tomorrow will no doubt be the last attempt by the council to extract from my lips a false confession; one that I have no intention of delivering, much to their disappointment. What happens next, I can only imagine. I find it very likely that my friends and I will be sentenced to burning and it is unlikely that there will be any stay of execution. How quickly they will move to this pseudo-justice, I can not say. Fearful that I may not have another opportunity, I have taken this moment to write some parting words to your wife, my sister, as well as the rest of my family. Will you be my messenger one last time?"

"Of course…but is there no hope, no chance of clemency?" George asked.

"I am afraid not brother. There was never really any hope of it. The court I now face is but a puppet court, erected for appearances only. They have made every effort to secure my confession, all the time believing it would never come. The only consternation is that it has gone on for this long. No, tomorrow Bishop Latimer and myself will be judged heretics and condemned to death, and soon after our friend, Bishop Cranmer."

"But will no one come to your defense? Will not the people cry with a loud voice of your innocence? How can these Romans proceed without fear of reprisal?"

"Alas, I am afraid there will be none. It is true that there are many who would come to our defense, but their conviction can not overcome their fear. I judge them not their weakness, for not all are called to make such a sacrifice."

"But I know one who would gladly risk all on your behalf. Let me send for your uncle 'The Broad Knight'. He will raise an army and come in your defense. With such a bastion to lead them, many would fall in line and join our cause."

"No brother, I can not allow this. You are right that my uncle would not hesitate to stand in my defense, and perhaps others would follow him. But I can not allow my trial to be the trial of others. I would not wish for others to die in my stead. I must bear this cross alone, well, nearly alone. I am sure that my two dear friends would be of one mind on this. If death may come, let it come, we are prepared."

There was a moment of silence. It was as if George Shipside was searching his own soul for some kind of resolution other than the one that seemed to be fated. The strain was great, and he began to weep. In the corner of the room sat Mr. Irish, head lowered, slowly turning from side to side, and though unobserved, it might be known that tears were welling in his eyes as well.

"Now, now, George," the bishop broke the silence. "There is no need to grieve. It is appointed to each man a time to die. It is no different for me than any other. Today I am blessed to be here with you, but tomorrow I shall be with my Lord."

There was another moment of silence.

"The Lord's gain; is this world's loss, brother," George whispered.

Early the next morning, the Bishop was led by guard once more to St. Mary's Church, to appear before the Bishop's council. Those who had been assembled as his judge had at one time been his partners in the mission of the church. Dr. Whyte, bishop of Lincoln led the proceedings. He began by outlining major points of doctrine espoused by Bishop Ridley and which now had to be refuted by the defendant. These doctrines were entirely of a reformed nature, having to do with the authority of the papal see of Rome, the transubstantiation of the elements of the Eucharist, the use of indulgences in the propitiation of the quick and dead.

The bishop had prepared his defense on paper, or might it be said, his justification for having held such doctrines. When given the opportunity to speak he began reading his final dissertation. He began, "My lords, you know my mind fully herein; as for my doctrine, my conscience assureth me that it is sound, and is according to God's word; and which doctrine, my Lord being my helper, I will maintain so long as my tongue shall move, and breath is within my body; and in confirmation, thereof, I am willing to seal the same with my blood."

Dr. Whyte made one last appeal, "Will thee not, given this one last opportunity, confess that the Pope is the head of the one true church?"

Ridley replied, "I marvel that ye will trouble me with any such foolish questions, you know my mind concerning that usurped authority of that Anti-Christ."

"You refuse to recant of thy heresies then," the Bishop of Lincoln stated one last time.

Nicholas, looked down upon his dissertation and began once again where he had left off a moment before. "No doctrine, nor tradition of the church shall stand against the authority of God's Holy Word..."

"Enough of this," Dr. Whyte interrupted. "We need not hear any more of these ramblings. Be silent."

Bishop Ridley stopped and stood tall before the council, without the least hint of reverence.

After examining Bishop Latimer with similar results, the two were called together to face the council one last time. Dr. Whyte read the judgment, "Nicholas Ridley and Hugh Latimer, (their titles having been stripped) you have been found to be guilty of heresy against the one true Catholic church, and therefore have been sentenced to death by burning; to be carried out at the appointed place outside the wall of Baliol College one week hence. May God have mercy on your souls."

And with that the trial was over.

The bishop was pleased that the council had seen fit to leave the guilty a week to contemplate their sins and seek repentance. Although he had no plans of repenting of anything, since there was no sin committed, he was thankful for the time to be able to communicate one last time with his friends and colleagues who would remain behind. He had completed his correspondence with his family, but there were many others he hoped to leave some parting words. Most of these letters were to fellow Christian

120

brothers in bonds. The time was well spent writing, and each day he continued to receive visitors.

On the eve of the black day, he prepared himself for dinner by bathing and then doing a thorough job of washing his hair and long flowing beard. At dinner were Mr. and Mrs. Irish, Mr. Shipside, Catherine Willoughby, Duchess of Suffolk, and her husband, Richard Bertie. Lady Willoughby had long been a supporter of Ridley and Latimer both in spirit, and materially. Her and her husband had flown to France to escape the clutches of Queen Mary, but had secretly returned at this moment to stand by the side of the condemned in their last moments.

"I wish there was more we could do Master Ridley," Lady Willoughby spoke.

"You have done more than most, milady; without your support, Bishop Cranmer and I could not have continued to do our work. And even now, you and Mr. Bertie risk prison yourself by being here."

"It is a very slight risk, I think, the Queen's attention are drawn elsewhere for the moment. She has little to gain by pursuing an insignificant person as myself."

"It is true. The duchess has very little to fear here. She is safe for the moment," interjected the Mayor.

"Well, if that be the case, then we must put away fears and enjoy this wonderful evening," the bishop stated rather cheerfully.

"You seem in good spirits Master Ridley, how can this be?" Lady Willoughby asked.

"And why should I not be in 'good spirits', for tomorrow I must be married, and you my friends, you are all invited. And my sister, will she be there? Has she recovered from her journey?" he asked turning to his brother. Alice, upon hearing of the verdict, could bear it no more, and leaving her children behind she had made the trip from Northumberland, arriving just that day.

"She is resting now. Yes, I dare say she will be there, with all heart," Mr. Shipside replied.

Despite the bishops attempts to bring levity to the moment, thus demonstrating his fortitude and strength, the rest of the dinner party were beside themselves with anxiety and grief. As the evening continued, some began to weep. Each tried to hide their sorrow, but it was impossible for it to go unnoticed by the bishop.

"Quiet yourselves," the bishop said reassuringly, "though my breakfast shall be somewhat sharp and painful; yet I am sure my supper will be more pleasant and sweet." He paused for just a moment and then, "I think it is best that we retire, we all need our rest."

"Would you like for me to stay with you the night?" his brother asked.

"No, no, that you shall not; for I intend, God willing, to go to bed and sleep as quietly tonight as I ever did." And with that they all said their good nights and departed each other's company.

An armed force was assembled the next morning to assist with the execution of Ridley and Latimer. It was believed that a tumult might arise that would stall the proceedings. And so it was, on the 15th of October, 1555, the Bishop was led forth by the Mayor and the bailiffs. Dr. Ridley had on a black gown, much like the one he wore as bishop. Upon his head was a velvet cap and on his feet, slippers.

As he approached the place of execution, he was met by his friend, Hugh Latimer. When he saw the stake, he held up his hands and said to Latimer, "God will either assuage the fury of the flames as he did for the three in Babylon, or else strengthen us to abide as he did for the venerable Polycarp." Given the opportunity he knelt down and prayed most fervently.

A sermon was preached, after which Nicholas wanted the liberty to reply to the discourse, but he was denied. He would only be allowed to speak if he would now deny himself, revoke his opinions and confess himself a heretic.

"Well," he began, "so long as breath is in my body I will never deny my Lord Christ and his known truth; God's will be done for me." He then arose. "I commit our cause to Almighty God, who will indifferently judge all."

He then removed his robe and turned and handed it to Mr. Shipside. His brother-in-law then turned and handed it to the Mayor. Mr. Shipside then turned back to the Bishop and tied a small bag of gun powder around his neck. He then gave the

Bishop a kiss on both cheeks, "for me and for Alice," he whispered, all the time tears streaming down his cheeks.

"Take heart, brother, and give a kiss to my sister for me," the Bishop returned.

Nicholas then stood upright. He commanded a striking pose of confidence and strength, unexpected in a man his age. Those gathered stood in awe as he spoke one last time. "O heavenly Father, I give unto Thee most hearty thanks, that Thou hast called me to be a professor of Thee, even unto death; I beseech Thee, Lord God, have mercy on this realm of England, and deliver her from all her enemies."

Latimer and Ridley embraced, and spoke some quiet words, that no other could hear. The smith then took and bound Nicholas around the waste to the stake with a chain, and then did the same with Latimer. Nicholas took the chain in his hand and said, "Good fellow, knock it in hard, for the flesh will have its course." The faggots were then lit and the fire began to grow.

It was at this moment that Bishop Latimer could be heard above the groan of the crowd, "Be of good cheer, Ridley, and play the man; we shall this day, by God's grace, light up such a candle in England, as, I trust, will never be put out."

"Unto thy hands, O Lord, I commend my spirit," Nicholas cried out, and then Latimer followed with the same. Unfortunately, the fire had been ill-constructed and some of the wood was yet green. The fire indeed grew, but only below. The heat was intense, but not consuming. The result was a horrifying spectacle as only the bishop's limbs were singed. Suffering greatly he cried out, "I can not be consumed. Oh for God's sake, let the fire come unto me."

It was a dreadful scene, most could not watch as they turned away in horror. The Bishop suffered greatly and it seemed little could be done. He cried out to God again, and then again, to relieve his suffering. Then suddenly a man standing nearby with a hook leaped toward the fire and snagged some of the faggots near the base and pulled them away. The fire then shot upward, the bishop literally leaning toward it with all his remaining strength. There was a small burst, his head fell forward and he was heard no more.

By this time the entire throng of onlookers was in tears. In the midst of them, standing alone in white was a woman, mature in years, but youthful in appearance. She was not crying, her continence, one of peace and tranquility. "Goodbye, brother," she said softly, "today you shall be in paradise, and tomorrow we shall meet again in that wonderful place."

She turned and walked away. As she did so, she held up the letter in her hand and read it once more.

"Farewell my dear brother, George Shipside, whom I have ever found faithful. Farewell my sister, Alice; I am glad to hear thou dost take Christ's cross in good part. By grace, our Lord and Savior suffered, even unto death; that those faithful, shall be spared from judgment. Do not grieve me my state, nor weep for my sufferings. Shall I be condemned to the fire that burns for a short time, be reminded that it is but a moment in comparison to the eternal joy of my reward. If I cry out in my pain and tribulation, it is because I have come near to knowing the full measure to which our Lord and Savior suffered on our behalf. Do not cry, but remember me to your children and to their children also. Confirm my love for them.

Say farewell to my beloved brother John Ridley, of Walltown and his wife my gentle and loving sister, Elizabeth. And to their daughter Elizabeth, my niece, I bid farewell, whom I love for the gentleness God hath given her, which is a precious gift indeed.

Farewell to my sister Elizabeth, wife of my brother, Hugh of Unthank Hall, with all your children, my nephews and nieces. Since the departure of my brother, my mind was to have been a father unto them. God bless you all, I now go to join your beloved father.

Farewell, my beloved uncle Sir Nicholas Ridley of Willimoteswick, and my aunt. I thank you for your kindness, shewed both to me and my siblings; so I pray you, good uncle, as my hope and trust is in you, continue and increase in the maintenance of truth, honesty, righteousness, and all true godliness, and to the utmost power to withstand falsehood, untruth, unrighteousness, and all ungodliness, which are condemned by the word and laws of God.

Farewell, all my kindred and countrymen-farewell in Christ altogether.

Nicholas R.

"Farewell, my brother, I did not cry, even when I heard you cry out in agony for our God to deliver thee. Even now, I shall not cry for thy departure, for I know thou art in glory. However, allow me this, tomorrow I shall cry for myself, for my children and for all of England, because we have lost what is most precious; a righteous man."

The Martyrs Memorial, Oxford, England.

Chapter Six

There was someone following him, but he couldn't see who it was. The mist was too thick. He could hear the pounding of hooves. It was someone on horseback. He started to run. He was afraid, but he didn't know why. Who was following him? What was he afraid of? The fear gripped him as the sound of the horse's steps grew closer. Then all at once without warning he tripped and fell; he hit his head on a large moss covered rock. It stunned him for a moment and he had difficulty regaining his senses.

As the fog began to clear from his mind, he sensed the rider and horse were now too close, escape was not possible. The mist was lifting slightly and he could see moonlight filtering down through the trees. He slowly rose and peered over the top of the rock. He could see him now. It was a rider on a coal black stallion. The rider had something in his hand; as he turned, the moonlight glimmered off the blade of a sword. He crouched back down behind the rock. His heart was pounding. What was he going to do? He had no weapon; no way to defend himself. What did the rider want of him? As he sat motionless, listening to the beat of his own heart, he noticed something on the rock. There was a thread of moonlight reflecting off its surface. He reached out his hand to touch the slight indentations of an engraving. It was some sort of writing...

John's travel alarm went off, it was set for six. He figured this would leave him plenty of time to get to the station. His train left at a little after eight. He was taking an early train back to Paddington station in London and then catching an express train all the way to Newcastle, in Northumberland. From there he would have to change trains again to go Hexham, where he would be spending the night. If he made all his connections, he would arrive in Hexham around three in the afternoon. That should give him plenty of time to find a place to stay and to pay a visit to the St. John Lee Church.

The train ride from Oxford station to Paddington was uneventful. John actually took a little cat nap. Every time he had one of *those* dreams, it left him drained the next day. It was if he had actually been running all night. He getting worried. They were becoming more frequent. He was actually beginning to think he was going a little crazy. Was he having some sort of premonition? He thought again of Scott's words. He had looked up the word somnambulism. It meant sleepwalking. John was not sleepwalking exactly, but his dreams seemed so real. It was as if he was awake inside his dream; he was 'dream waking'.

When he arrived at Paddington, he only had a few minutes to make his connection to Newcastle. He jumped off the train and half jogged to the next platform. As he arrived at the train he saw the conductor at the entrance to the car.

"Is this the train for Newcastle?" John asked.

"Sorry sir," the conductor replied. "This is platform five. You need to go to platform six, the next one over."

"Thanks," John said over his shoulder as he turned and hurried back up the platform and around the train to the next platform. He was not sure how he had made the mistake of going to the wrong platform. Now he was cutting it a little close. The train had not left yet, he just needed to get on board.

He gave a sigh of relief when his feet touched onto the steps of the last train car. He heard an intercom announcement indicating that the train was just about to depart. As he reached the top of the stairs there was a conductor who examined his ticket briefly and then pointed for him to enter the coach. As he entered, he noticed that it was nearly full. As he made his way down the aisle he found one empty seat next to a young woman sitting in the seat by the window.

"Excuse me, is this seat taken?" he asked politely.

"No, it is free," she replied, and then returned to the book she was reading.

John placed his bag in the overhead luggage space, pulled a book of his own from the side pouch and then sat in the seat. He was a little disappointed about having an aisle seat. He was hoping to catch some of the scenery as they traveled north. Fortunately, the windows on the train were quite large and he had a relatively unobstructed view.

As they pulled out of the station, John occupied himself with a little reading. As they left London and the outskirts of the city, he looked up from his book and watched as the scenery passed by in the window. It was a little overcast, but not raining, so the visibility was fairly clear. As he looked out of the window, occasionally his eyes would drift to the young woman sitting next to him. She must have been in her early twenties. She had shoulder length auburn hair that she had tied back into a pony tail and she was wearing a pink oxford blouse with a navy pleated skirt that went to the knees. She was quite attractive and he found himself staring. He noticed that the book she was reading was quite old and had an embossed binding. Even more intriguing it was in French, not English. The few words he had heard from her did not betray a French accent. Just then she looked up at him, he was caught.

"Uh...I'm sorry, I didn't mean to be looking over your shoulder," John could feel the blood rush to his cheeks as he fought for the words. "It's just, this is my first time in England and I wanted to enjoy the scenery." Just as he said it, he wished he had not. He didn't want her to think it was some sort of come on.

She smiled at him, "I don't mind. You're an American aren't you?"

John was relieved. Maybe she hadn't actually caught him looking at her. "Yes, I am, I guess I don't hide it very well."

She smiled again. It was very natural and becoming. "That's alright. You don't need to hide it. Would you like to sit next to the window? We could switch."

128

"That would be great," John answered. In reality he would have preferred not to switch at this point. He could see the scenery outside without any difficulty, and now he would no longer have an excuse to look in her direction.

As they switched seats and got resettled, she introduced herself, "I'm Abby Brown, by the way."

"John Ridley," he returned. She kind of made a funny face. "Something wrong?" he asked.

"No," she said, "it's just that Ridley is a very common name where I come from.

"Really, are you from Northumberland?" It seemed a reasonable assumption, since they were headed to Newcastle.

"Yes...yes I am. I am returning home to Haltwhistle. I have been visiting an aunt in London. Where are you headed?" she asked.

"Well, tonight I will be staying in Hexham," John replied. "In fact, I hope to learn a little about my ancestry. Eventually I will make my way to Haltwhistle, as well."

"I suppose you will be stopping by Ridley Hall, then?" she asked.

"Yes, I will, do you know it?"

"Yes, I have been there a few times." Again she smiled. "Is that why you are here in England, to do research into your family history?"

"No, not exactly. I have been at Oxford for a summer program in Medieval Literature."

"So, you're a student then?"

"Yes, actually a graduate student, I am working on a doctorate in English literature. I thought I would take advantage of this opportunity and do a little research while I'm here. The family history is just sort of a side trip. I didn't know that my ancestors came from Northumberland until just a few months ago. But while I'm here, I can't pass up the opportunity."

"So, you're going to be a professor?"

He blushed, a little. He had never had it put that way before. Even though he was getting a Ph.D. he never really thought of himself as a professor. "Yes, I guess I am." He tried changing the subject, "I noticed you were reading something in French, you don't sound French."

"No, I'm not," she smiled. "I took French in school and I like to keep up on it by reading it on occasion."

"What are you reading?"

It was her turn to blush a little. "Promise you won't laugh."

John smiled and shook his head, "Why would I laugh?"

"Okay, but only if you promise...it's a copy of *Robin Hood, The Outlaw,* by Alexander Dumas. I found it in a used book store in London."

"Why would I laugh at that, I love Robin Hood," John let out a slight chuckle anyway.

"Oh, you know, it's not the kind of tale that should be appealing to 'proper' young ladies."

"Too much sword play I suppose," John played along.

"Exactly," she affirmed.

"So, you're a fan of swashbuckling tales of adventure?" John tried to push her buttons a little.

"Not exactly," her countenance changed slightly from embarrassed to slightly serious. "When I was a young girl I fell in love with the book *Count of Monte Cristo* by Dumas. As a teenager, once I had become proficient in French I read it again in the original language. I then began to explore other works by Dumas, including the *Three Musketeers*, and a number of his lesser known works, as well, including *The Black Tulip* and the *Knight of Mason Rouge*. Whenever I can find them, I will read them in the original French."

"Why Dumas?" John was growing captivated. "Why not Hugo, you know *Les Miserables*?" It had been his experience that girls tended to like Hugo more than Dumas.

"Have you read Dumas much?" she asked.

"Just a little, *Monte Cristo* and the *Three Musketeers*, and that's about it," he had to admit.

"I think I enjoy him because of the characters. They are real, but at the same time they are almost super real. In one moment, they make me laugh an in the next they make me cry. There is also the connection which Dumas accomplishes in making the bridge between fiction and history. The historical accuracy of his novels always leaves me wondering whether they are really fiction. I find myself thinking this could have actually happened."

At this point John was mesmerized. Not only was she attractive, but she was intelligent, as well. He smiled slightly, "interesting, I guess I will have to read a little more Dumas."

"Have you ever heard of the sequel to the Musketeers, Ten Years After?" she asked. John shook his head no. "It chronicles the civil war in England and creates a conspiracy in which the musketeers attempt to save Charles I from execution. At one point, Athos is actually hidden beneath the scaffolding, as the King is being executed. Their attempts to rescue the king are of course stalled, but you are left wondering if they were actually there. There is also the way in which Dumas portrays the human condition, the human journey, as something that is always connected to and directed by a sovereign God."

"Yes, I do remember that," John agreed. "I remember how Edmund Dantes was always wrestling in prison over why he had fallen into the hands of evil men and that he felt abandoned to a fate worse than death. And how the priest was always trying to encourage him by saying God was still in control and that there was always hope."

"That's right," it's one of the things I love about *Monte Cristo*, faith and hope," Abby paused reflecting. "Wow, listen to me, I have been rambling on. What about you, what are you reading?" pointing to the book in John's lap.

"*Kenilworth,* by Sir Walter Scott; I suppose I too am a fan of the historical novel. Actually, that's not true; I think I can admit I am a bigger fan of the swashbuckling adventure, like *Ivanhoe* and *Rob Roy*." He smiled as he said it, "in fact it was *Ivanhoe* that first got me interested in the legend of Robin Hood. I must admit though I have not read Dumas' rendition."

"It is a bit different, I am not sure you would like it as much," Abby cautioned. "So is that what you do, research the novels of Scott?"

"Well, not exactly," John sometimes wondered himself where is research was leading. "It is not the novels themselves that interest me, but instead what Scott used for inspiration. I have discovered a number of notes by Scott concerning various ancient ballads and poems. Most of them seemed to describe real events. However, I am still trying to find whether they are authentic or just myth and legend. At the same time, I am hoping to find evidence of other traditional ballads that may have influenced the story line in Scott's novels, or even his poetry."

"So, is there a particular ballad you are researching in Northumberland?" she asked.

"Yes, as a matter fact there is. Scott quotes it in *Marmion*. It caught my attention only because some of the characters in the ballad are named Ridley. It concerns the death of Sir Albany Featherstone. Are you familiar with the name or of Featherstone Castle? I believe it is fairly close to Haltwhistle."

Abby kind of bit her bottom lip, as if unsure how to answer, "Yes, I know of Featherstone Castle. And I have heard of Sir Albany, but I don't really know much about his death. As for the castle itself, it is still there and in reasonable condition. You might be able to get a tour if you like. I'm sure you will find the present owners quite hospitable. What about your visit to Hexham, what do you hope to find?" she was hoping that this was a subtle enough attempt to change the subject.

"I hope to visit it St. John Lee Church. My three times great grandfather was christened there. Have you ever been there?"

"Yes, I have. It is fairly easy to find. Do you know where you are staying in Hexham?" Abby asked.

"No, I was hoping to find a bed and breakfast or maybe a youth hostel," John answered.

"May I make a suggestion," she said. John nodded yes, he was not about to turn down good advice. "You might try the Armstrong Guest House. It is a small bed and breakfast, walking distance from the train station. It is right near the Hexham Abbey and the Old Gael. I believe there is a place where you can rent a bicycle nearby, the proprietor of the Armstrong could help you with that. You would certainly be able to get to St. John Lee Parish by bicycle. It can't be more than two or three kilometers from the guest house."

132

John was elated. He couldn't have been more fortunate, having sat next to Abby. She took out a notepad and began sketching out a map of the Hexham area. She appeared to know it very well.

"What do you do in Haltwhistle?" John asked, when she had finished the map. "I'm a waitress at a one of the local pubs."

"A waitress, really I would have never guessed that," John realized too late that he had just put his foot in his mouth again.

"It's okay, it pays the bills for now," Abby said looking a little hurt.

"Uh, sure, it's fine, I just meant, someone who is reading Dumas in French...I would expect...I mean I thought you might be a student or something," he was fumbling for the words.

"I was a student, I attended University of Edinburgh for two years, but then the money ran out and I had to stop."

"I'm sorry," John tried to move in another direction. "Are you married or do you have a boyfriend or something?"

"You get right to the point, don't you," Abby teased a bit. John blushed. "No, I'm not married, and no boyfriend." She was rubbing her ring finger a little nervously.

He noticed there was no ring, but there was a little discoloration indicating there may have been one. Was it possible she had been engaged or something? He decided not to press any further.

"What about you?" Abby took the offensive. "Are you married, or a do you have a girl friend?"

"No, neither," John thought of Annie for a brief moment, but the thought disappeared as quickly as it came.

"Where in America are you from?" She kept on the offensive.

"I'm going to graduate school at University of Illinois. It is about 100 miles south of Chicago. But I was born and raised in a small town just outside of Pittsburgh, Pennsylvania. Have you heard of it?"

"Pittsburgh, home of American steel, right," she smiled again. John wasn't sure if she was making fun of him. "What about your family, any siblings?"

Abby had the upper hand in the conversation and she kept pounding John with questions about his family and past. He felt obligated to tell her everything; everything except the part about Annie. It went on for at least an hour. It took a while before he realized that he was doing most of the talking and Abby was asking all the questions. He was surprised to find that he had talked away most of the trip and they were drawing close to Newcastle.

Just as John was relating his story about his visit to his great grandmother, Abby cut him short, "I'm sorry, I am going to have to interrupt. I need to make a trip to the loo-I think you Americans call it the rest room-before we get to Newcastle. We won't have very much time to make our connecting train."

"Oh, sure, good idea." He said, somewhat apologetically.

Abby got up from her seat and walked to the back of the coach. He remained in his seat, looking out the window and reflecting on their conversation. Besides being very attractive, she was a very pleasant girl, kind and polite. He felt very comfortable talking to her; he thought it kind of strange. They had grown up thousands of miles from each other and here they were thrown together on this train. They would more than likely never see each other again. He couldn't help thinking of the phrase 'trains passing in the night,' cliché or not. He was kind of wishing it wouldn't end, but he realized that was ridiculous. They were two people from completely different worlds. There was no reason for it to be anything other than a momentary chance meeting.

Just as Abby returned to her seat, a message came over the intercom system stating they were just fifteen minutes from Newcastle.

"I hope you don't mind me tagging along, Abby," John said. "I sort of got lost at Paddington and nearly missed the train. If it's okay, that is since we are going in the same direction and all."

"Sure, it's fine. I don't mind giving a tourist a helping hand," she was teasing again. Noticing that he was blushing again, she softened her tone slightly, and smiled, "No, really, I have enjoyed the company."

134

They disembarked from the train together and made their way to the platform where the train for Hexham, Hatlwhistle and Carlisle was waiting. They had plenty of time to board the train and get settled before it started on its way.

Abby turned to John, "This is a pretty short trip. We stop at Corbridge and then Hexham. Your's is the second stop. Not much more than half an hour."

"Thanks," John said. "I appreciate your help. You have been very kind." He was trying to get up the courage to say more, but he didn't know how to start.

"It's been my pleasure John, I have thoroughly enjoyed getting to know you and to hear a little of your story. I wish you the best of luck; finding whatever it is you're looking for," she smiled sincerely.

He looked into her eyes as she spoke and for the first time realized how vibrant they were. They were penetrating. It reminded him of something in the far reaches of his mind, but he couldn't put his finger on it. He looked away and took a deep breath.

"Ah…I don't suppose you would mind if I looked you up when I get to Haltwhistle? I mean, I don't want to be too forward. I thought maybe I could come by the pub where you work. It might be nice to see a friendly face after stumbling around in the dark by myself for a couple of days." He knew he sounded a little nervous, but he couldn't help it. He wanted to see her again, if only one more time.

"I don't know…," she hesitated, and his heart sank.

"You know, just stop off for a brief visit, on Tuesday or Wednesday; just to say hello, nothing more," he was sounding pathetic.

A brief silence hung in the air as Abby looked away for a moment, "Sure, I guess it would be all right. I'm working the afternoon shifts on both days, from lunch on. It's the Cat and Owl Pub, downtown Haltwhistle. You can't miss it." She bit her bottom lip, as if she was wondering if she should have accepted his invitation.

Just then the train pulled into Hexham station. John stood up and grabbed his suitcase from the shelf above. He held out his hand to Abby, "Thanks again, Abby, I'm delighted to have met you. Perhaps we'll see each other in a couple of days."

"It has been my pleasure as well. Remember what I said about the Armstrong Guest house. It is right down town, ask anyone you see, and they can direct you. Good luck."

Abby shook his hand and John paused just a moment and smiled, holding her hand just a little longer than normal. He then turned and walked to the coach exit, stepping down the stairs onto the platform. He walked back toward the window where they had been sitting. She was there looking down at him, biting her bottom lip slightly. She gave a brief wave and smiled. John smiled back and then turned away. He wondered if he would ever see her again. He knew he was being a little overly romantic. What was he thinking? Even if he did see her again, what did he think was going to come of it? Was he just being friendly, or was he hoping for something else? How could he be that naïve? They had just met. He really didn't know anything about her. Maybe she was just being nice and polite. Did she really want to see him again? He couldn't be sure, but one thing he did know, he just had to see her again.

He turned and looked for a way to exit the train station. He walked down the steps to the street below, stopped at the bottom and looked south toward the town of Hexham. He could see what looked like the tower of an old church. That had to be Hexham Abbey. She had said that the guest house was near the Abbey right down town. He knew where he was headed. He lifted his bag and set off for town.

It only took him a quarter of hour to find the Armstrong's guesthouse. He had only had to ask for directions once. As he approached the front door, he was pleased to see a vacancy sign in the front window. He entered and was greeted by what he guessed to be the proprietor, a middle aged man, tall and thin, with graying hair combed back.

"Can I help you young man?" he asked.

"I was wondering if I can have a room for the night," John replied.

"Of course, I assume it will be just yourself?"

"Yes."

"And is that for just the one night?"

"I think so, but could we keep it open ended?"

"Sure, no problem. I have a nice room for you right at the top of the stairs, overlooking the street out front. Breakfast is served at 7:30 AM, and we do serve dinner tonight at 18:30 if you desire, for a nominal price," he was pleasant, but very business like.

"Yes, dinner would be nice. I wonder if you know of a place where I might rent a bicycle? I was hoping to take a ride out to St. John Lee Parish Church," John asked.

"Well, of course. Just out onto the street here in front and down to your left, not more than fifty meters, is a bicycle shop. They will be glad to help you."

"And the church, is it easy to find?"

"Oh my yes, here, let me draw you a little map."

The proprietor took out a pad and pencil and sketched out a map directing him to the church. He then gave John his room key and a few more instructions concerning the room. John paid for his room and dinner in advance and then thanked him and went up the stairs to his room. He took a few moments to freshen up a bit and then made sure he had all his notes and things in his back pack and went to the bicycle shop to see about a rental.

After securing the bike, John decided to stop at a local market just down the street a bit and pick up something for a snack. He stuffed it all in his back pack, took a second look at the map he was given by the proprietor of the guest house and then started up the road toward St. John Lee Parish.

It took John a moment to remember to ride with traffic on the left. Hexham was a fairly busy town and there was plenty of traffic to navigate. He ended up going by the train station on his way out town, retracing his steps from when he had walked into town earlier. Once past the train station he crossed a bridge over the Tyne River. The map showed that he had to pass through a round-about that sent most of the traffic onto a highway going along the river east and west. Fortunately, he was going north and after he passed through the round-about he found himself all by himself on a country road with high hedges growing on either side. Through the hedge he caught glimpses of farmland in all directions with an occasional flock of grazing sheep. It was partly sunny, and there was very little traffic on the country road, so he took his time, and enjoyed the leisurely ride. The road took him past a few farms and then down an unpaved drive lined with trees on either side that ended at St. John Lee Church. As he drew close to the church, he tried to think of what he was going to say to the local rector.

At the front of the church was a cemetery with some rather ancient looking headstones. He left his bicycle leaning against a fence and walked into the cemetery to check it out. Although many were difficult to read, John was able to decipher some of the names on the headstones. There were actually a couple different headstones that had the name Ridley inscribed on the top. One was a J Ridley, but he couldn't really make out the dates. Another was a George Ridley, but again the dates were too worn away to decipher.

He walked down a path that led to the front entrance of the church. It was about half past three, he figured there probably wouldn't be a service at this time of day. He passed through the front doors, through the foyer and into the chapel. There didn't seem to be anybody there. He walked down the aisle to the front of the church. It was a very old chapel, but the large windows on either side provided plenty of natural light, making it pleasantly bright. There were long wooden pews on either side, with only enough room for the one main aisle down the middle. The walls were of stone with oak paneling extending from the floor to the height of the pews, running the entire length. The twenty foot high ceiling was supported by huge oaken beams that were occasionally separated by hanging chandeliers. Above the altar was a large stained glass window, and to the right a pipe organ with its pipes extending nearly to the ceiling. It was not as imposing as Christ's Church in Oxford, but it was not without its own charm and grace. He sat down in a front pew and waited, taking a moment to rest and enjoying the quiet contemplation. He really didn't know where to find the local rector, and even if he did, he was not exactly sure how he was going to begin. He tried to gather his thoughts.

"May I help you young man," a voice came from the darkness of a side alcove.

It startled him. "Yes...I'm sorry, I didn't mean to intrude. I am looking for the rector."

"I'm he," a priest emerged into the light. "Reverend Thomas Miller, and your name?"

"John Ridley, Father, a pleasure to meet you."

"Ah, an American...and please, you may call me Thomas. What can I do for you?"

"Yes, I'm an American. I have rather a strange request, I fear. I believe that my ancestors may have once been a part of this parish and I am trying to confirm it. I visited the graveyard outside, but I had difficulty reading the stones. Do you know if there were any other records kept, of say births or even deaths here in the church?"

"As a matter of fact, we have an extensive record of christenings and marriages in the parish and in the case of those in the graveyard, burials as well."

"Is it possible to look at them?" John asked.

"Perhaps, how far back are you looking? Do you know the names and birth years of your ancestors?" Rev. Miller seemed to be genuinely interested and willing to be of help.

"Yes, I have notes here. I am looking as far back as the early 1700s, I'm afraid. Do your records go back that far?"

Rev. Miller chuckled, "Yes, young man. I think you forget you are in England. Follow me."

The rector led John to a hallway off the chapel. This led to a staircase that went downstairs to another hallway and into what appeared to be a small library. He reached up and pulled on a string that was connected to a single light bulb hanging from the ceiling. There were a number of old books on the shelves, whose covers were worn and frayed. They seemed to have dates written on the bindings, sometimes spanning decades.

"Sit down here. John, wasn't it?" the rector directed.

"Yes, John Ridley," he sat down at a table in the middle of the room.

"What is the oldest date you have? Let's begin there?"

John looked at his notes. "A Joseph Ridley, born 1831, christened here at St. John Lee. I don't have his father."

Rev. Miller walked to the book shelf and pulled three volumes that appeared to be sequential, from the shelf. "Let's start with these." He opened the first one and gently turned the yellowed pages until he came to the entries for 1831. His finger scrolled down the list of names and then came to a stop.

"Here it is, Joseph Ridley, born March 31, 1831," and then his finger went across the page to the columns on the right. "And here are his parents, James and Margaret Ridley, of St John Lee. Here is a date for his father's birth, 1790."

John was quickly copying down everything, while Rev. Miller opened the second book he had chosen from the shelf. Once again he turned to the appropriate year, 1790 and scanned down the page.

"Here is the record for James Ridley, born June 24th, 1790. His parents were George and Isabella Ridley of Hexham. This means that his father was probably born or christened here as well. Look here, there is a notation for their marriage." He moved back several pages in the journal. "Here it is; George Ridley married Isabella Stephenson, here at St. John Lee, May 22, 1783. George was born in 1751, and his parents were Thomas Ridley and Hannah Armstrong of Bywell. Isabella was born in Acomb, just up the road a bit."

John felt his heart pounding, the adrenaline was starting to surge. It was astonishing to discover that he was actually able to step back in time generation by generation. He had known about James Ridley, but George and Isabella Ridley were from a completely new generation and now he had a new lead, they were from Bywell.

"Where is Bywell?" John asked. "Is it near here?"

"Not far, it's a small village between here and Newcastle," Rev. Miller replied.

John must have passed by it on the train. "Would there be a church that would have records for Thomas and Hannah Ridley?"

"I don't know. We're starting to get far enough back in time that it gets a little more difficult. I can't be sure the records

140

have survived. I tell you what, rather than have you travel all the way to Bywell, I will ring over to the rector at St. Peter's and see if he can do some digging for us. You wait here, I won't be long."

The priest left John to copy down the details of the records for George and Isabella Ridley and disappeared up the steps. John felt a little strange sitting alone in this dimly lit room in the basement of a church that was probably several hundred years old. He feverishly wrote everything down, as if it was about to disappear of the pages of the register.

Moments later, Rev. Miller returned. "The rector said he would see what he could find. He is going to look into it tonight, but with services tomorrow he won't be able to call back until about noon. I hope you aren't in any hurry and will be able to stay until tomorrow."

"That will be great, thanks so much. I can't begin to tell you how much I appreciate it. What time should I come back tomorrow?"

"Well, the rector said he would call about noon. However, we do have services at half past nine, if you would like to join us. You would be more than welcome."

"Thank you, I think I will," John promised.

John said his goodbyes and then walked through the graveyard to where he had left his bike. It had been sunny when he had entered the church, but he noticed the sky was beginning to turn gray. A storm was coming. He figured he didn't have long before the sky was going to let loose and he would be drenched. Riding a bike through a rain storm didn't seem very appealing, so he put a little extra effort into the pedals and raced for town. Just after he crossed over the Tyne he began to feel a few rain drops. He pedaled faster, as fast as the traffic in town would allow him. When he arrived at the guest house he stowed the bicycle in a side yard and made for the front door. Just as he rounded the corner of the building onto the porch it started to pour. He had to shake off a few raindrops, but for the most part he had managed to stay dry.

It was only five o'clock so he decided to retire to his room until dinner. He sat on his bed and reviewed over his notes. He could hardly contain his enthusiasm. He not only confirmed the origins of the Ridley family of Canada, but he had also been able to go back another generation, and who knows what else he might find out tomorrow. He read through the notes a second time and then lay back on the bed staring up at the ceiling. He began to wonder what Abby was doing right now. Was she thinking about him at all? What would she be thinking? Was he being ridiculous? She had probably forgotten all about him by now. As he lay on his bed he could hear the rhythmic pounding of the rain on the roof above. It was not long before his eyes became heavy and he drifted off to sleep.

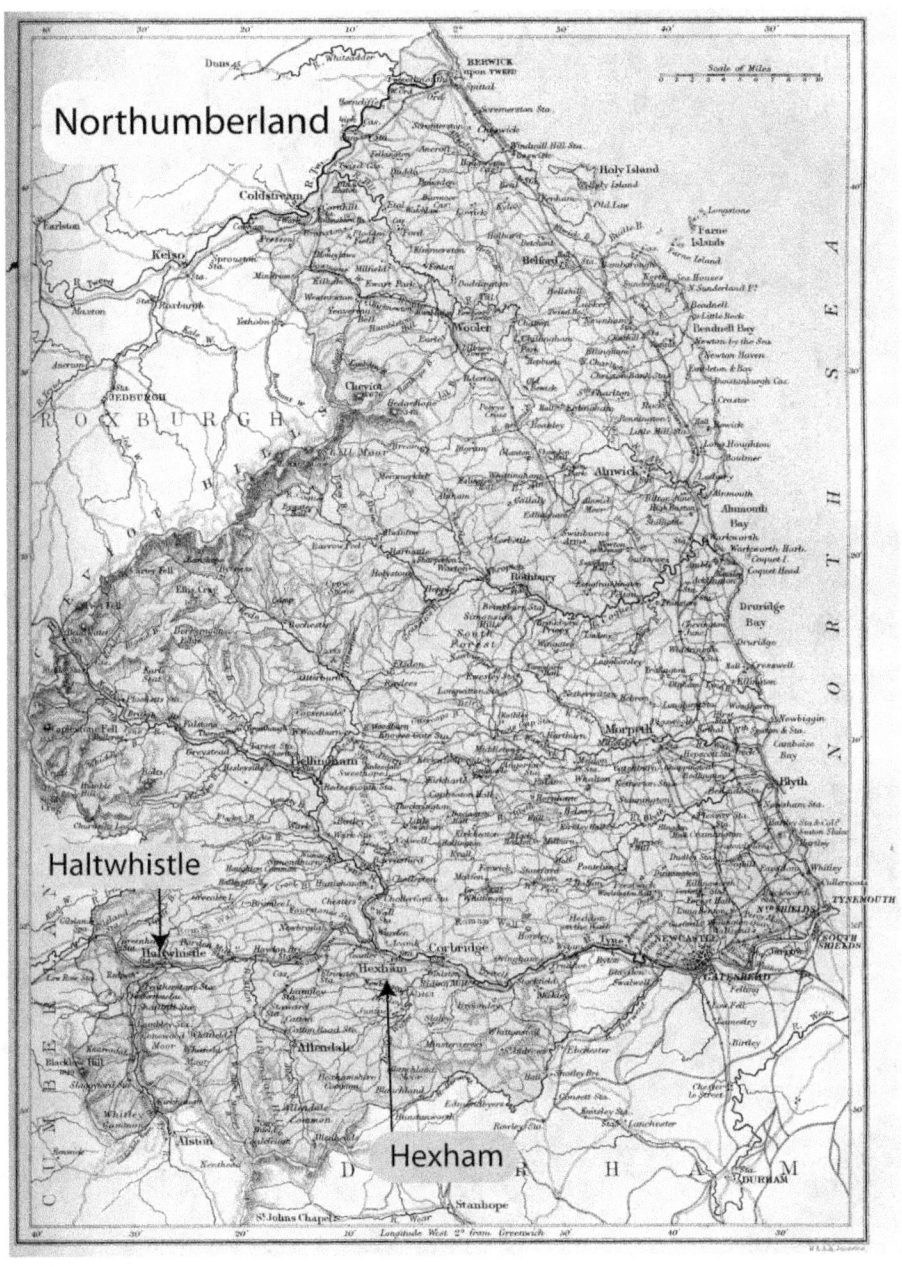

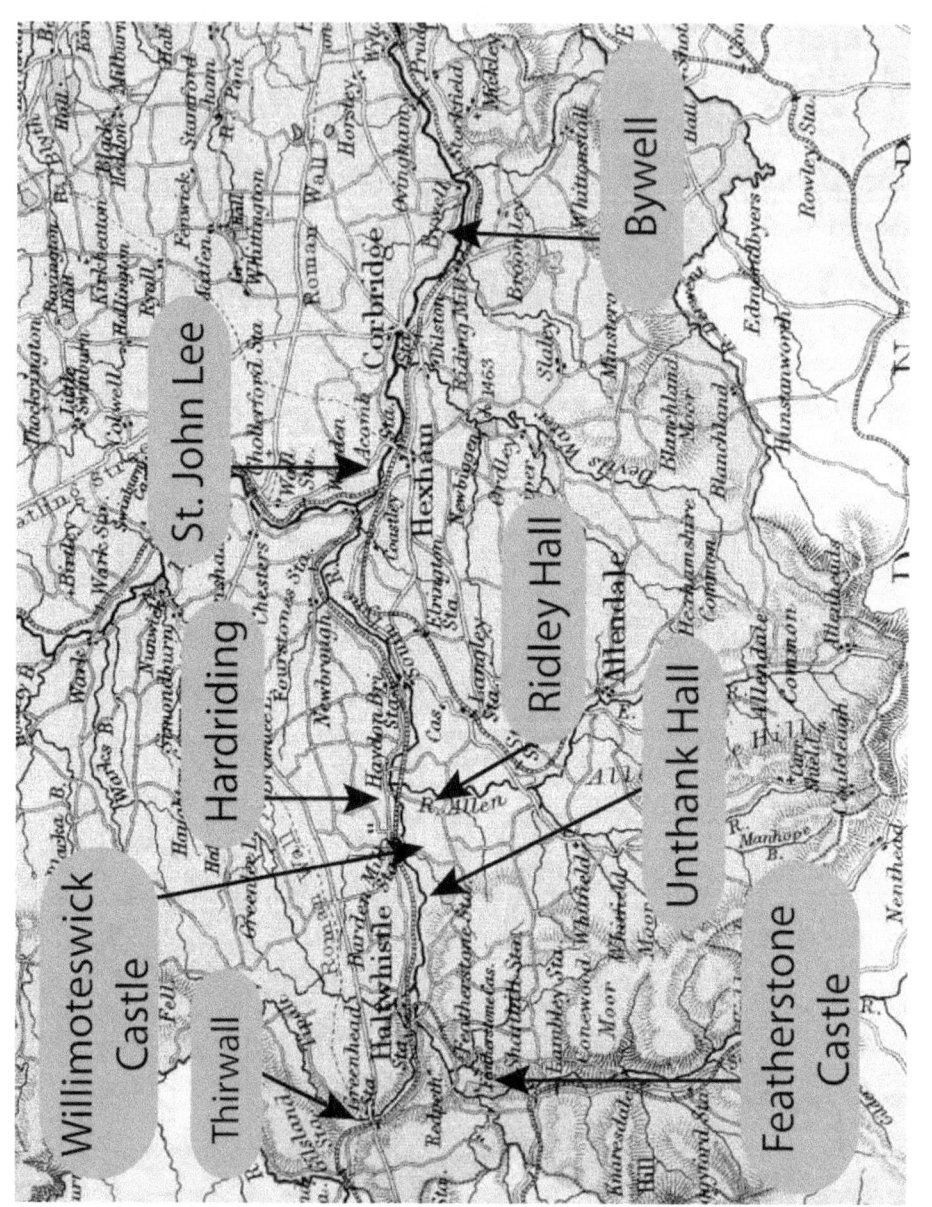

144

Chapter Seven

*The sky grew dark, there was a bright flash of lightening
and then an ear piercing crash of thunder almost immediately
after. The rain was pouring down in sheets. The trees offered very
little refuge from the torrent. He stood up and looked to the place
where he had last seen the rider, he was gone. He bent down to
look at the rock face again, but it was much too dark to make out
anything. When the lightening flashed a second time, he could see
the words, but then they were gone in an instant. The rock was of
unusual shape. It almost looked like a large stuffed chair. The
highest point was nearly four feet high and covered in moss.
About halfway down it broadened out and made what almost
appeared to be a bowl; it was collecting the rain water. He looked
down into the water. Wait it wasn't water at all. There was
another flash of lightening. It was red...it was blood...*

There was a knock at the door, "Mr. Ridley, are you in?
...Mr. Ridley, dinner is about to be served."

John opened his eyes, and then realized he had fallen
asleep, "Yes...yes, I'm here. I will be right down." He jumped up
from the bed, went into the bathroom and splashed some water
on his face. As he emerged from the bathroom and passed back
through his bedroom there was a flash of lightening outside
that lit up the entire room; it was still raining pretty hard. He
skipped down the steps and into the dining room. There was a
large dining table in the center that looked as if it could hold
eight or ten. At one end of the room, there were two smaller

tables that could seat two at a time. At the center table four of the seats were already occupied.

"Sorry I'm late, I must have dozed off," John apologized.

"It's quite alright Mr. Ridley, we understand," the owner of the guest house then proceeded to make introductions. "Everyone, this is Mr. John Ridley, from America. Mr. Ridley this is my wife, Mrs. Armstrong," pointing to a middle-aged red headed woman to his right. "And this, is Mr. and Mrs. George Crabb, up visiting us from Cornwall."

"Nice to meet you," John gave a slight bow. He was not sure what he was supposed to do. Mr. Crabb reached out his hand to shake John's and he obliged.

"Nice to meet you, Mr. Ridley, all the way from America," greeted Mrs. Crabb. "Well, well, what a treat, a treat indeed."

John was getting the feeling that this was not going to be a nice quiet dinner. It was becoming exceedingly clear that he was going to have to make small talk with this group; while still trying to get the cobwebs out from his little nap.

Mrs. Crabb began to pepper John with questions about where he was from and what he was doing in England. He felt obliged to answer the questions, even though his mind was drifting, and he kept wishing he could be somewhere else at that moment. Just as dessert arrived, he was able to get in a few questions of his own.

"Excuse me, Mr. and Mrs. Armstrong, would you know anything about Featherstone Castle?"

"Hmph," Mrs. Armstrong responded. "Now don't you go hanging about that old castle, young man. It's haunted, you know. You'll only be getting yourself into trouble if you go there. You mind me, you best stay away."

"Now Betsy, don't frighten the young man," Mr. Armstrong cut in. "It's an old wives tale, don't you pay her no heed. She has always been a bit too superstitious."

"It's no wives tale, Mr. Armstrong and you know it. My brother Tommy heard the ghosts, just as plain as day. You mind me Mr. Ridley, they're real."

"Sounds utterly intriguing," Mr. Crabb joined in. "What's this about ghosts? Tell me more."

"Yes do tell," Mrs. Crabb agreed. "Why do you think we came all the way up here, if not to explore the old castles, ghosts and all?" She smiled whimsically.

Just then a loud crack of thunder resounded through the house. The ladies both jumped. "Wow, that was close," Mr. Crabb said as he grabbed his wife's hand. "It looks like were in for quite a storm tonight. A perfect night for ghost stories, come on fill us in."

John had to admit that even he was beginning to get curious. He had not heard anything about ghosts at Featherstone Castle. He wondered if it was in anyway connected to the murder of Sir Albany. "Go ahead Mrs. Armstrong, I would love to hear it as well."

"Well mind you, I don't actually know all the particulars. I have only heard bits and pieces. It seems it had to do with some young lovers who were not allowed to be together, a sort of Romeo and Juliet, you know. Well any way the young girl, I believe the daughter of the Lord of the castle or something, was being forced to marry someone she didn't want to, so she tried to run off. When her lover tried to rescue her, there was a battle that ensued and some how the young girl came between her lover and her intended and she was actually killed. Her lover was so distraught that he ended up taking his own life. As a result, every year on the anniversary of their death, their ghosts can be seen wandering Pynkenscleugh Glen."

"Fascinating," Mr. Crabb said, excitedly. "And when is this anniversary?"

"Actually, I think it is sometime in July, this month," Mrs. Armstrong answered. "Isn't that right, Mr. Armstrong?"

"I do believe that's right, Mrs. Armstrong," her husband agreed.

"What do you think about that, Mrs. Crabb?" Mr. Crabb said with glee, "we could actually run into some ghosts when we visit Featherstone."

"Lovely," Mrs Crabb uttered, as she smiled from ear to ear. "Simply lovely."

"So, you're going to visit Featherstone," John asked.

"Yes, we are," replied Mr. Crabb. "We thought we would take in the Abbey tomorrow and maybe the Old Gaol. Then the next day we hope to visit Langley Castle, and then Thirwall Castle and maybe Featherstone on Wednesday."

John had a sinking feeling. It sounded as if the Crabbs had an itinerary that was similar to his own. It was not as though they were that disagreeable, but he sure didn't want to spend the next three or four days running into them at every turn.

As he finished his dessert, he made some excuse about having to do some studying and left the two couples still jabbering away as he made his way back upstairs to his room. When he entered the room, he turned out the lights and stood at the window, looking out at the street outside. He could see the lights of the Abbey across the market square. It was still raining pretty hard, but the thunder had seemed to move off. He could occasionally see lightening in the distant clouds and hear the soft roll of distant thunder moments later.

He reflected on the events of the day. Meeting Abby had to be the highlight. He wondered if he would ever see her again. He reached down into his pocket to make sure he still had the note paper on which she had scribbled the name of the pub where she worked, the *Cat and the Owl*. He could see her face, her eyes; those penetrating eyes. What was he going to say to her when he saw her again?

Although the dinner conversation had been a little invasive, he was fascinated by the ghost story. It was strange. On the surface it seemed to be a bit absurd, especially given Mrs. Armstrong's obvious eccentric bent, but it still left John wondering. Could it be true? Were there ghosts at Featherstone? He lay back onto the bed and stared up at the ceiling. There was another flash, and a low rumble in the distance. The rain danced against the window sill outside, pitter patter. He started to drift. He thought once more of Abby...pitter patter...the ghosts...those eyes...

*****

He rose early the next morning. It had been a rather uneventful night considering the thunder and the ghost stories and all. Although the ground was still wet, the rain had stopped; and it looked as if the sun was trying to peak through the clouds. He decided to chance it and go for a jog. It was Sunday morning, so most of the shops would remain closed and there were very few cars on the road. In fact, it was early enough that he didn't see much of anybody out and about. He went toward the Abbey and down what was called Church Row. It ran alongside a bit of a park that sat behind the Abbey. He made a circuit that took him completely around the park and Abbey and back toward the guest house. The air was cool and clean, as a result of the storm, and he was refreshed.

Upon returning to the guest house, he dashed upstairs and took a quick shower before going to breakfast. As he entered the dining room, he found Mr. and Mrs. Crabb already engaged in conversation with the other guests. There were two new members in the dining room. One was a middle aged man with dark hair and pencil mustache. The other was a young woman, perhaps in her early 30s. Mr. Armstrong introduced them both to John.

"Mr. Ridley, this is Miss Carey, from Edinburgh and Mr. Allen, from Chelsea," turning to the other guests, "Miss Carey, Mr. Allen, this is Mr. John Ridley."

"He's from America," Mrs. Crabb added.

John bowed his head slightly as he pulled his chair out from the table. "Nice to meet you," he mumbled under his breath.

"Miss Carey was telling us that she is not only unmarried, but she is completely unattached," Mrs. Crabb said somewhat triumphantly. She was clearly lacking in proper decorum. "Can you believe it, a beautiful young lady like this, unattached, and traveling all by herself? It doesn't seem right."

Miss Carey started to blush. John didn't know how to respond, but he knew if he didn't say something, Mrs. Crabb would likely continue down this very undesirable path. "So Miss Carey, you're from Edinburgh?" he asked.

"Yes I am," she replied, giving a slight sigh of relief. "And you're from America, I understand."

"He's some sort of English professor or something," Mrs. Crabb would not be left out of the conversation.

"A graduate student in English Literature, actually," John corrected.

"And what are you doing here in England young man," Mr. Allen joined in.

"I am here for a conference at Oxford, but I thought I would take advantage of some free time and do a little touring," he really didn't want to get into the details of why he was really in Northumberland.

"If you will excuse me, thank you for breakfast," Miss Carey took the change in conversation as an opportunity to escape.

"Surely your not leaving now, Mr. Ridley just got here." Mrs. Crabb was clearly disappointed.

Taking advantage of this momentary distraction and turning back to the proprietor John asked, "Mr. Armstrong, do you know anyone here in town who could help answer some questions concerning local legends, perhaps a library?"

"Well, yes, we do have a library, but might I suggest another idea. Just down the street there is the Old Gaol (the old English form of jail). A few years ago it was restored and converted into a Museum. The curator, a Mr. Forster, is a bit of an expert on local history and lore. You might try there, but I am afraid it would not be open today. Of course Mr. Forster loves to talk to anybody who will listen. He is quite passionate about history and such. If you would like, I could call him up to see if he might be available to meet you this afternoon."

"That would be wonderful. Thanks so much. If you could ask if he would be available sometime after one; I have to return to St. John Lee this morning, but I should be back by then."

"My pleasure, Mr. Ridley, I only hope that I am able to reach him."

John had to endure a little more of Mr. and Mrs. Crabb's trivial ramblings before he was able to excuse himself under

150

the pretext of not wanting to be late for church. He went upstairs to his room, grabbed his Bible and note pad and stuffed them in his back pack. He then went down to the side yard where the bicycle was still reclining against the fence, just as he had left it the night before. Fortunately, the weather looked as if it was going to remain fair. He hopped onto the bike and headed off for St. John Lee Church.

He arrived at the church just a few minutes before the service started. He was surprised to see that the congregation was not very large. It appeared that there were no more than thirty or forty parishioners spread out amongst the pews of the nave, which could easily hold a couple hundred. He attempted to be as quiet as possible as he sat down in one of the pews near the back. Unfortunately, his foot caught one of the legs of the pew in front of him and made a loud thud causing those present to turn and look over their shoulders at him. He had failed to go unnoticed.

He sat quietly and listened as the liturgy of the service unfolded. Once again he enjoyed a service that was rich in practiced liturgy and traditional music all supported by the beautiful harmonies of the pipe organ. He wanted to participate, and not merely be an observer, but he didn't know any of the appropriate responses, and although familiar, he didn't know any of the hymns that were sung. Every part of the service was reverent and orderly, following a scripted regiment of music and verse...

*****

...Abby looked up at the cross above the front altar. Rev. Simpkins was preaching a sermon on the Beatitudes, but she was not really listening. She couldn't seem to keep focused on much of anything since returning home. Her mind kept drifting to the previous day when she had first met him. She couldn't understand what was happening to her. It wasn't like her, to start day dreaming about some guy, and certainly not some guy that she had very little chance of ever seeing again the rest of her life. What was she thinking? After all he was an American, and even if he did happen to run into her here in Haltwhistle, he would be going home soon and that would be the end of it. She was acting like a stupid school girl...

What was it about him? He wasn't particularly handsome, not that he was bad looking. It's just that he wouldn't stand out in the crowd. His hair was kind of long, but well kept. He was very pleasant to talk to. He was obviously very intelligent, but he also had a certain kind of diplomacy about him. He was genuinely empathetic, and made her feel good, not just good, but comfortable, she was at ease with him. It was as if when they were talking, the whole world around them just stood still, and she was at home.

But this was stupid, there was no way anything good could come of it. She lived here in Haltwhistle and he was from some town half-way around the world. Why did she tell him where she worked? Why did she say it was okay for him to visit her? Was she out of her mind?

It was the way he got all nervous when he first started talking to her. As if she intimidated him. The way he stammered, it was so ridiculously cute! Why should he be intimidated by her? It made her feel...well it made her feel... important, meaningful. She had not felt that way for some time.

Now what was she going to do? She was not going to fall in love with this... this American! If he shows up, she will just have to be polite and say she is not interested. Of course, that is if he is interested. She may have it all wrong. Maybe he was just being nice. Maybe he was just being polite. Agh! ...Why did she have to be on that train at that moment? Men!

*****

When the service ended, John just remained in the pew. Rev. Miller greeted the parishioners as they left the church. John waited patiently until the last one had paid their respects and Rev. Miller was left alone.

"Have you heard from the rector at St. Peter's?" he asked, as Rev. Miller approached him.

"No, not yet, it might be a little while yet, services at St. Peters would have just now ended. Perhaps you would like to take a walk with me while we wait. He said he would call around noon."

Before they had left the nave, John turned to the rector, "What are the figures depicted in the stained glass windows?" He pointed to them.

There were three different windows showing a triad of individuals. "Here," the rector began pointing to the closest one, "are three kings of Northumbria, Edwin, Oswin, and Oswald. Edwin was the first Christian king of Northumbria, baptized in 627 AD by Paulinus. Over here," pointing to another, "we have three saints of Northumbria, St. Aidan, St. Cuthbert and St. Wilfrid," John remembered a Cuthbert Ridley in the family history, he had always thought it a strange name, but now he understood its origins. "And here, there are three other saints," the rector continued, "St. Benedict Biscop, St. John Beverly, our Patron saint and Bishop of Hexham, and the Venerable Bede, who you might remember wrote the first history of the English people. Finally over here we have the three apostles Peter, James and John."

"What about this window," John pointed, "the one with the birds?"

"Ah yes, those are symbols of Christ. The first is a Pelican feeding her chicks with her own blood, symbolizing Christ's sacrifice, and the other a Phoenix, symbolizing Christ's resurrection."

At this point, they were at a door that opened out to the cemetery. John followed Rev. Miller outside. They walked through the cemetery, occasionally stopping beside different gravestones, while the rector shared a story about the deceased.

"I went back through the cemetery records and found as many Ridley's as I could. I made notes for you and they are in my office. Don't let me forget to give them to you."

"Thank you, you are very kind. I deeply appreciate all of your help. I wish I knew how to repay you."

"Think nothing of it, I was glad to do it," the rector paused in front of a stone. "This one here is the marker for George Ridley, the very one we discovered the birth record for earlier." It was the same gravestone that John had seen the day before. "Have you thought much about why you are so interested in your family history John?" It sounded a bit like a leading question, John's mind immediately flashed to the Professor.

"I'm not sure," John tried to think why it was *so* important to him. "I suppose it makes me feel connected to the past. It tells me a little about who I am and where I came from. No…, it's more than that. I think it makes me feel a little closer to God. I mean, when you look at the past and you consider the people and events that brought you to this moment in time, it is hard to think of it as a chance phenomenon. It affirms that we are not alone in the universe, and there is something outside of ourselves; something independent of our choices that is directing our journey."

"Very insightful John, to discover that our history is some how connected to our present. Of course the logical outcome of this is that our present must also be connected to our future, for our present will be our history when our future becomes our present."

John had to stop and think about this for a moment. The events of yesterday are connected to the events that are to come tomorrow. The events are connected not because of random chance, but because of predetermined outcomes.

Rev. Miller could see that John was still thinking. "The connection of past, present and future, are clearly revealed in scripture. The sole aim of scripture was to unveil the predetermined plan of the Creator by revealing it through history, through prophecy and through the incarnation. When we consider this, we begin to understand the significance of Matthew chapter one."

John couldn't remember what was in Matthew chapter one, he would have to look it up later. At this point they had passed through the cemetery toward what was a little forest that sat behind the church.

"Do you know the name of this church, John," Rev. Miller asked.

"Yes, St. John Lee," John answered. "But I am not sure what the Lee means."

"It means St. John of the clearing, because the church was built here at the edge of the woods. The forest is alive, but it can be a place of confusion and even darkness. The church was built here and stands as a symbol of stepping out of the darkness and confusion and into the light. So it could just as easily be called St. John of the Light."

The two continued their stroll on down a path that wound down into the forest. Rev. Miller continued to share a little of the history of the church and the surrounding area. John listened attentively, hanging on every word. It seemed a little strange to him, unexpected, finding spiritual nourishment in this place. John had always thought that Europeans had become too secularized and no longer revered the traditions and teachings of the Christian church. He assumed that this was due to a complacency that was present even among the clergy. But here was a minister who clearly was living out a deep and personal faith. He enjoyed the time they had together.

As they returned to the church it was just turning noon. Rev. Miller led John to his office and then proceeded to call the rector at the church in Bywell. Rev. Miller was on the phone for several minutes, jotting down notes as the conversation continued. John was attempting to look over Rev. Miller's shoulder, but he was not able to make out most of what he was writing. He was excited, hopeful that he would be able to unravel a little more of the mystery of his heritage. The phone conversation finally came to an end, and the rector looked up at John with a bit of a smile.

"Well it looks as if Rev. Andrews was able to locate some additional information for you. It turns out that he had a birth record for Thomas Ridley born at Bywell in 1712. His father and mother were John and Mary Ridley. John Ridley was also born in Bywell in 1682. His father was shown to be Cuthbert Ridley, who was styled of Gatehouse and Hardriding."

John's draw dropped. "Of Hardriding, are you sure?"

"That's what he said," the Rector confirmed. "Are you familiar with Hardriding?"

"Well the name has come up in couple of different references, most notably a history of the Ridley family that I came across," John acknowledged. "However, I am not exactly sure where it is, somewhere here in Northumberland, I think."

"Yes, I have heard of it," the rector said. "I believe it is located near Bardon Mill, a small village just north of the Tyne between here and Haltwhistle."

John was writing in his notepad as fast as he could. Once again his heart was racing with rush of adrenaline. He could hardly contain his elation. The rector, realizing this, passed a sheet of paper to him. "Here John, take my notes. And here is a list of those from the Ridley family buried in the cemetery. I hope it will be helpful.

"Thanks again Rev. Miller, I can't begin to tell you how much I appreciate your help."

"It has been my pleasure, John. I will pray that the rest of your journey shall be just as fruitful. May the sovereign Lord continue to make Himself known to you through and by the events of the past."

It was a strange blessing, but John accepted it as appropriate to the moment. He looked at his watch. He had just enough time to get back to the guest house before his meeting with Mr. Forster. He said his goodbyes to the rector, jumped on his bike and rode back to Hexham. During the ride back, his head was racing. Could it be that he was actually a direct descendent of those responsible for the death of Sir Albany Featherstone? It was inconceivable that he was directly connected to the ballad from *Marmion*.

*****

On his way back, John decided to stop by the bus station. It turned out there was a 4:15 PM bus leaving for Bardon Mill. If he timed it right, he could be on it. He stopped and returned the bicycle to the shop where he had rented it; he would not be needing it any more. As he stepped through the front door of

156

the guest house he saw Mr. Armstrong and an elderly gentleman sitting in the parlor. He stepped toward them.

"Hello John," Mr. Armstrong greeted. "I want to introduce you to Mr. Forster, the curator of the Old Gaol museum."

"Hello Mr. Forster. I am very pleased to meet you. Thank you for taking time out of your Sunday afternoon to talk with me. I hope that I am not imposing."

"No, not at all, Mr. Ridley, I am happy to be of service," Mr. Forster rose and shook John's hand. He was an older gentleman who must have been approaching seventy. What was left of his hair had completely turned white. He was dressed in a tweed jacket and tie, and his clothes looked somewhat worn. "When Mr. Armstrong here told me about your research and that you would only be here a brief time, I felt I had to come. It gives me some pleasure to talk about the history of this region, so don't consider it as any kind of imposition. I have been told that you are interested in learning something of local folklore and legends."

"That's right," John answered. "Anything you could provide would be helpful."

"Well there are many stories that have been passed down locally. Is there anything in particular you are interested in?"

"Well yes. Are you familiar with the story of the death of Sir Albany Featherstone, at the hands of the Ridley clan?" He figured he would get right to it. No use beating around the bush, he didn't have a lot of time to waste.

"Yes, I have heard the story. What would you like to know?"

"Do you know anything about the feud that existed between the two families, what got it all started?"

"Well, I suppose most people assume that it goes all the way back to the Norman Conquest. The Featherstones had established themselves in Northumberland long before the Ridleys, they were Saxon. And the Ridleys were thought to be of Norman ancestry and had arrived in Northumberland by way of Cheshire. However, I once heard that it had to do more with land rights. The Featherstones believed that they were the rightful heir to Willimoteswick Castle and its lands, and that the

157

Ridleys stole the castle through marriage to a female heir, or something of the sort." This, of course, was partly confirmed by what John already knew.

"Is this the only theory?" John asked.

"There is one other. Both families were prominent in the area and historically there were members of each family who vied for the favor of the king and with it the benefit of being appointed the High Sheriff of Northumberland. This competition would have no doubt caused tension between the families as well. I believe both Featherstones and Ridleys were High Sheriffs at one time or another."

"Do you think this is why the Ridleys killed Albany Featherstone, to gain some sort of political control of the region?"

"Not likely. Despite the rivalry, I think it would have taken a little more than that for them to murder Sir Albany. At least, that is my opinion. Of course, it was a different time, a more violent time. I suppose anything could have prompted it."

"Have you ever heard that it might have involved Sir Albany's son in some way?"

"Funny you should ask that, I do remember hearing something about that, now that I think about it. Back in 1965 they were remodeling Unthank Hall and I paid a visit. The owners of the house at the time were very interested in the history of the manor, especially since it was likely that Bishop Nicholas Ridley had once lived there. Somehow they had come across a story that the Bishop's cousin and namesake had once been saved from death at the hands of the Lord of Featherstonhaugh, because of some sort of mishap between Nicholas Ridley and the youngest son of Sir Albany Featherstone. I have never been able to confirm the story or that the younger Nicholas Ridley even existed."

"That's interesting," John said as he scribbled in his notebook, nodding his head, and murmuring to himself. This would seem to confirm the account described in the letter written by the Bishop to his brother. He was looking forward to visiting Unthank Hall. It seemed to hold the keys.

"Mr. Forster, have you ever heard about the ghosts of Featherstone Castle?"

"I think it would be fair to say that just about everybody around here has heard stories of ghosts at Featherstonhaugh and every other Castle in the region. Ghosts and castles seem to be natural co-conspirators in legend. I would imagine you are most likely referring to the ghosts of the wedding party."

"Wedding party?"

"Yes, wedding party. The story goes something like this. The daughter of the Lord of the Castle was in love with a young man, whom her father forbade her to have anything to do with. In an attempt to discourage his daughter's infatuation, Featherstone arranged for her to be married to another young man, I believe a member of the Blenkinsop family. On the night of the wedding, the young girl's lover tried to intercept the wedding party as they went out for the traditional evening hunt. There was a battle that ensued and the bride was accidently killed. Her lover was so distraught over her death that he took his own life. The tradition is that on the anniversary of the wedding the ghosts can be heard in the forest near Pynkinscleugh Glen."

"Do you know anybody who has actually heard these voices?"

"Oh sure, but I can't say that they are anyone whose credibility I would trust, if you know what I mean. You know, old wives tales and such."

"What did Featherstone have against his daughter's desire for this young man?"

"Coincidently, the young man the girl was in love with was a member of the Ridley clan."

"Really, so this incident was also connected to the feud between the two families. When was this supposed to have taken place?"

"I'm not sure," Mr. Forster kind of stroked his short goatee. "I think it was about a hundred years after the death of Sir Albany."

"My notes say that Sir Albany was killed in 1530. That would put it sometime in the middle of the 1600s."

"Or maybe a little later, perhaps late 1600s," Mr. Forster corrected.

The two of them continued their conversation for over an hour, John asking questions and the old man doing his best to provide detailed accounts. Mr. Forster was a wealth of information about the Tyne Valley. He related a great deal of history intermixed with legends and traditions. John took down as much as he could in his notebook. He was surprised to discover how the families of Northumberland were connected to the royal lines of both England and Scotland. He was also fascinated by stories of the border wars, the conflicts between the clans of Northumberland and Scotland. In the end he wished that he had more time, but he had to move on.

"Thank you for your time, Mr. Forster," John brought closure to the conversation. "You have been very helpful."

"My pleasure young man, it's not often that an old man such as myself, can find someone from your generation who will sit and listen to such ramblings."

John had one more thought, as Mr. Forster began to rise from his chair. "One additional question, if you don't mind. Have you ever heard the name Beardie Grey?"

"Why do you ask?" Mr. Forster seemed intrigued.

"Just something I came across in the margin of a book," John explained.

"I am familiar with the name. Legend has it that Beardie Grey was a witch, and that she had a little cottage, right near the bridge over the Tyne that connects the forests surrounding Featherstone Castle with Pykinscleugh Glen. There used to be an old broken down cottage on the edge of the Forest that was locally referred to as the Witch's Cot. Some people still refer to the area near the bridge by the same name."

"Pynkinscleugh Glen, the same place where the wedding party met their fate?"

"Exactly. It was rumored that she was very eccentric, a recluse. Legends say she would cast spells on passers by. One such story claimed that a farmer lost his entire season of crops because he failed to provide her with some food and she cursed him. They also say that she was ageless, that she lived to be well over a hundred years old. No one knows for sure, because there was no record of her birth, probably because Beardie was not actually her Christian name. She disappeared sometime in the early 1800s. That's really all I know."

"Fascinating, thanks. Again you have been very helpful. Good bye."

"Good bye Mr. Ridley."

The bus trip from Hexham to Bardon Mill took less than half an hour. John stared out the window, following the line of the Tyne River running parallel to the bus route. Once again, his mind began drifting to thoughts of Abby. Had he been a little forward suggesting that he would look her up in Haltwhistle? Maybe he should wait until Wednesday to visit the pub where she worked. That should give the impression that his interest was nothing more than friendly. He wouldn't want her to get the wrong idea, that he was forward, or that he had any preconceived notions about their acquaintance. There was no way he could even consider not going to see her at all. To think that he may never see her again was unacceptable, even unthinkable. He was thinking crazy, how could he feel this way when he had only spent a few hours with her? What did he think was going to come of it? What could she possibly see in him? She was probably just being polite.

When he stepped off the bus in Bardon Mill he noticed the Mill House B&B immediately opposite the bus stop. It had a vacancy sign in the window, so he crossed the street and stepped through the front door. Standing behind the desk was a short, rather round lady with fiery red hair. When she looked up at him, a smile spread across her face from one ear to the other, displaying teeth that they were badly in need of a visit to an orthodontist.

"Good afternoon, young man, have you come to pay a visit to our humble establishment?"

"Yes ma'am. Would you have a room for the night or maybe two?"

"Yes we do," she said, a little enthusiastically. "Just two nights, would you mind signing in here?" she pointed to the registration book sitting on a small podium on top of the desk. "You're not from around here are you, an American I think?"

"That's right. I guess it's a bit obvious. If you wouldn't mind, I would like to leave it open ended, just tonight and then tomorrow I'll let you know."

"That'll be fine, but you won't find a nicer place than this one," she smiled bigger. "What brings you to Bardon Mill?"

"I am looking into some local history, visiting some of your local sites, Willimoteswick Castle, Ridley Hall and a few others. Are you familiar with any of these places?"

"Oh sure. Who isn't? They are just across the river. You can walk to them, or bicycle if you prefer. Very easy to get to, I can provide directions, if you like."

"Do you know of a place called Hardriding?"

"Sure, it's right here in Bardon Mill. It's not a residence anymore. It has been converted into a home for the elderly. I suppose they might let you look around a bit."

"What about Unthank Hall?"

"Unthank, a beautiful place, with a beautiful garden, just down the way toward Haltwhistle. Here is your key... uh" at this point she turned the registration book to face her, "Mr. Ridley. Mr. Ridley! Well doesn't that beat all! You're a Ridley."

"That's right," John almost wished he had used an alias. "John Ridley."

"But, I'm a Ridley also. I mean I was. My name is Joanna Willis. But that's my married name, my maiden name is Ridley. Why, we're practically family, cousins or something? And you, all the way from America."

"Nice to meet you, Mrs. Willis," John didn't know quite what to say or think.

"Please call me Joanna. We don't go for formality around here. George, George! Get out here. I want you to meet this young man." A man appeared through a doorway behind the desk.

"What is it dear?" He was a tall, thin man, balding, with a long face that seemed to end without any real chin. His shirt was only half tucked, and his trousers were held up by well worn suspenders. The sleeves of his shirt were rolled up to his

162

elbows. He looked as if he had been engaged in some kind of domestic labor.

"George, this is John Ridley, from America," Mrs. Willis introduced them. "John this is my husband, George Willis."

"Nice to meet you," John greeted.

"Yeah, yeah, nice to meet you," he didn't seem as enthused over John's name as his wife and she let him know it.

"George, did you hear what I said, John RIDLEY. He is practically part of the family."

"That's nice, now can I get back to what I was doing," he turned and walked back through the doorway.

"Oh, don't you mind him, John. He's like that. Anyway, we are pleased to have you stay with us. Here is your key, and your room is upstairs on the right. Breakfast is at eight, will you be joining us?"

At first John thought he should decline, but the look of anticipation on Mrs. Willis' face suggested that he really should not disappoint her. Besides, she was a Ridley and might actually be able to help him. She could prove to be informative. "Sure I'll be here for breakfast, wouldn't miss it." He tried to sound sincere.

"That's great. If you're looking for a place to have dinner the Two Bridge Tavern is just up the road a bit. And just a little further on is the Bardon Mill Market. Now you go ahead and get yourself settled and if you need anything, you just let me know."

*****

John went upstairs and took a moment to freshen up. It was still a couple hours before dinner so he thought he would take a walk and explore Bardon Mill. He soon realized it was nothing more than a village. Just as Mrs. Willis had suggested, he passed the tavern a short way down the street. A hundred yards further down the road was a little village market and post office. As he passed the market he realized that he was actually leaving the village, there were only a few scattered homes beyond. The countryside was beautiful. He was surrounded by gently rolling hills that were partitioned by hedges and country roads. Most of the buildings that dotted the landscape were constructed of stone and brick. Like everything else, they appeared to have a significant history. He wondered as he walked back toward the village, just how old the homes were. Did any of them date back to the 19th century or even before?

On the return trip he stopped at the Two Bridges Tavern to have some dinner. There was a young couple sitting in one corner, other than that the place was empty. It was kind of nice to just be able to sit quietly and enjoy his dinner without interruption. It was hard to believe it was only Sunday night and he had left Oxford on Saturday morning. It had already been a full trip, very rewarding and it was just getting started. He pulled his notepad and the book on the Ridleys out of his back pack. Folded in the inside cover of the book was the tracing of the map he had made back at the U of I Library. It seemed a lifetime ago.

Tomorrow, John would visit Ridley Hall, Willimoteswick and if possible, Unthank Hall. He didn't know what he expected to find. The castle was at least 600 years old and there was no telling what its present state of repair would be. Ridley Hall and Unthank Hall had probably been remodeled several times over and were not really as they had been when his ancestors had occupied them. All the same, he would enjoy seeing them.

By the time he finished eating, the young couple had already departed, and there was an older gentleman at the bar. The bartender cleared his plate and it didn't appear there was any need for John to be in any hurry to leave, so he opened up the history of the Ridleys and began to read. He scanned through the pages to see if he could find any clues to the connection between the Ridleys of Bywell and Hardriding. He went back to the place where he first noticed Hardriding mentioned in the genealogy. Thomas Ridley, who was the grandson of Hugh Ridley of Willimoteswick, was styled of Hardriding. His fourth youngest son, George was of Hardriding and Gatehouse. George had a son named John Ridley of Gatehouse. This must have been the connection he was looking for. John Ridley must have been the father of Cuthbert Ridley of Gatehouse and Bywell. It then followed that John was not only a descendent of the Ridleys of Hardridng, but he was also the descendent of Hugh Ridley, Unthank Hall, the cousin of Bishop Ridley and he was also the descendent of Sir Nicholas Ridley "The Broad Knight" of Willimoteswick, who was responsible for the death of Sir Albany Featherstone.

So here it was. Not only did he feel a connection to the Ridley clan mentioned in the ballad, but he was in actuality a direct descendent of the "Broad Knight". He had never allowed himself to dream of this possibility. How could he have ever imagined where this journey would end up leading him? And yet here he sat in a pub, in a tiny little village, a million miles from anywhere. Once again the adrenaline was starting to flow. With each new discovery, his excitement grew, anticipating the next part of the journey. Tomorrow couldn't come soon enough.

Chapter Eight

...the mist began to rise. There was something or someone in the glen. He moved closer, slowly. Through the mist, he could barely make out a horse standing in the glen, its head hanging low. Just in front, was a man, dressed in armor that glistened in the moonlight; he was kneeling on the ground, with his head bowed. Rising from the ground just in front of the man, a sword, its handle and pommel forming a cross, like the headstone of a grave. The man appeared to be praying. As he drew close, the knight turned to face him, and spoke 'she waits and she is alone. Who will she turn to? She cries in the darkness. Who will save her'...

John woke up early. A ray of sunlight peaked through the curtains and fell directly across his face. He rose and looked out the window to where there were sheep grazing in the field on the opposite side of the street. He remained standing there, looking out at the landscape, lost in thought. He could hear a bird singing in a neighboring tree. There were drops of dew dangling from the leaves, glistening in the sun. It was a beautiful morning.

He glanced at his watch. It was time to face the music. He knew he would have to endure a breakfast conversation with Mrs. Willis. There was no way of avoiding it. He could only hope that she was not a morning person and that she would be moving a little slowly. He showered, dressed and went downstairs to the breakfast room.

"Good morning John," Mrs. Willis was waiting. "How are you this beautiful morning?" she sang out. She was a morning person.

"Good morning Mrs. Willis, I'm fine thank you."

"Did you sleep alright?"

"Yes, a very pleasant room, thank you again."

"Would you like some coffee?"

"No thank you, tea would be great," John much preferred tea, and besides, it seemed the English thing to do. "No milk, just a little sugar, if you please."

"Coming right up, I hope you're hungry," she proceeded to uncover some muffins in a basket on the table, and then set a plate of eggs and sausages in front him. After pouring his tea, she sat in the chair opposite John. It didn't appear that there was anyone else staying at the Mill House. "Is there anything else I can get you dear?"

"No, thanks this looks like plenty," John tried to remain polite.

"So do you know where you are going today? Do you need any directions?" she asked.

"No, I have a map, thanks. I may need some help securing some transportation. Do you know where I might rent a bicycle?"

"Oh, no need, John. We have a bicycle here that you can borrow."

"That is excellent, thanks," John paused to think carefully about his next question. After a moment he convinced himself that it would not do any harm to ask. "Mrs. Willis, I wonder if you might tell me a little of your family history?"

"Sure dear, what would you like to know?"

"Where are you from, do you know who any of your ancestors were?"

"Well, let me see," she began, "when I was a little girl my grandfather would tell me all sorts of stories about my ancestors. He said that we were descended from the Ridleys of Hardriding, which is just down the way, just beyond Henshaw. There is a farm still there, but I don't think it is the same house."

"Hardriding huh...I don't suppose your grandfather ever talked about the ghosts of Featherstone Castle?"

"Of course, many times, it was one of my favorite stories," she stopped herself. "I mean it was so tragic."

"Do you know any of the details? Who were in the wedding party and how did they die?"

"Well mind you, this story has been passed down for hundreds of years, but I will try and remember everything I know. There had always been a feud between the Ridleys and the Featherstones, most people thought it had to do with wealth and power. Who was going to retain control of the Tyne Valley; that sort of thing. I suppose no one really knows for sure, but for whatever reason, the two families hated each other. But just as fate would have it, two young people, one a Featherstone and the other a Ridley, fell in love. The young man was said to be John Ridley, of Hardriding, the son of Thomas Ridley, of Hardriding, perhaps a distant relative of mine. The young lady was Abigail Featherstone, the daughter of the Lord of Featherstone Castle.

When John Ridley approached Lord Featherstone for the purposes of obtaining Abigail's hand in marriage, the Lord erupted in anger. You see, he had no male heir, which meant if his daughter married a Ridley, well then Featherstone Castle would come into the possession of the Ridley clan. This was more than he could tolerate. He would prefer that the castle fall to any family other than the Ridleys. It was believed that Willimoteswick Castle had also been secured by the Ridleys in the same manner, through the marriage of a daughter.

Despite the pleadings of his daughter, Lord Featherstone made arrangements for her to marry one Thomas Blenkinsop. Some believe that the Blenkinsops were so determined to gain possession of Featherstone Castle, that they actually paid a ransom to finalize the marriage contract.

John and Abigail, however, were still very much in love, and not about to give up. They plotted to escape on the night of the nuptials, before the marriage could be consummated. As was the tradition, after the marriage ceremony, the wedding party left the castle and went for a hunt in the twilight. Abigail

168

had decided to sneak away in the dim light to meet her lover at Pynkinscleugh Glen. Unfortunately, one of her bridal maids saw her leaving the party and alerted the others. A chase ensued and just as she arrived at the rendezvous, the wedding party caught up with her.

In anticipation that their plan would not come off smoothly, John Ridley had brought a few of his friends for support. Swords were drawn and a battle began. While the groom and the bride's lover were engaged in a fierce mortal battle, a member of the wedding party, thinking he was coming to the aid of the bride and groom, raised a bow and sent an arrow towards young Ridley. The young lady, witnessing this action, threw herself and her horse into the arrows path. As fate would have it, the arrow struck the bride directly in the heart and she was thrown to the ground, mortally wounded.

The young lover, John Ridley, having seen the result, took his sword by the pommel and threw it at his combatant, striking him in the chest and killing him. He then dropped from his horse to kneel by his lover's side. He gently lifted her body and leaned her against a nearby rock. As he knelt over her, with her last breath he could hear her whisper, "another time, another place...it was never meant to be, I love you my dearest..." and with that she expired.

The young man's grief was so great that he immediately drew his side dagger and thrust it into his own chest. He fell across the body of his beloved and died. Those who were still left alive, immediately stopped and looked upon the two lovers with shock and horror. Looking around, most of the wedding party lay dying, as for the friends of John Ridley, half had also been slain.

Meanwhile, back at the castle the Lord of the house waited in the dining chamber for the return of the wedding party. After several hours the doors flew open and the members of the party entered. But it was only a short moment before the Lord realized their clothes were torn and bloodied. In the same moment, the party disappeared entirely. It had only been ghostly apparitions of the wedding party. One member of the wedding party did survive and later returned to reveal the horrible events that had transpired. The Lord of Featherstone went mad in his grief.

To this day, it is believed that the ghosts of the wedding party can still be seen wandering in the forest near Pynkinscleugh Glen, on the anniversary of the event. Others have claimed to have seen the two star crossed lovers walking hand in hand in the woods at the edge of the glen."

"Amazing story," John said at the story's close. "That is the first time I have ever heard an account with so much detail."

"Well like I said, my grandfather told it to me over and over again when I was a little girl. It is possible that he embellished it a bit."

John wondered if it was much of an embellishment. So far everything he had heard or read about the story showed surprising consistency. He wondered if it could all be true, or if it was like most oral traditions, the embellishment had grown so great, that there was very little truth in any of it. He would have to keep looking for answers.

"Mrs. Willis, have you ever heard of a Beardie Grey who lived near Pynkinscleugh, a witch, I think."

"Yes, I have," she replied. "It's funny you should ask, because some people think that she actually witnessed the battle between the wedding party and the Ridleys. She was supposed to have had a cottage near Pynkinscleugh Glen. Others think that she was the one that actually made up the ghost story to keep people away. And others believed that she didn't live until a hundred years after the event and therefore could not have witnessed it, but could have easily made the whole thing up. She was thought to be deranged. It was probably why people called her a witch."

"Yeah, that certainly make sense," John agreed. "Well you have been a great help, but I really should be going. I have a full day ahead of me."

"You are more than welcome, John," she looked a little disappointed that he was leaving. "You go on ahead. If you have anymore questions, I will be glad to help you later when you return."

John got up from the table, went upstairs and gathered a few things and placed them into his back pack. He then found Mr. Willis in the car park on the west side of the guest house, wiping off a bicycle with a rag.

"Here you go young man," Mr. Willis greeted. "I have it all cleaned up for you. It shouldn't give you any trouble. Do you know where you are headed?"

"Yes, thank you, I have a map," John answered.

He gave the bicycle a once over, concluding that it was in suitable working order. He then hopped onto the seat and with his pack strapped to his back, took off down the road. After stopping at the Bardon Mill market, he briefly glanced at his map to get his bearings and then started off toward his first stop of the day, Ridley Hall.

As he left town going east, there was nothing but rolling farmland as far as the eye could see. On either side he passed sheep and cows grazing in the morning sun. Just a mile down the road he came to a sign pointing to the right, to Ridley Hall. He turned right and crossed a bridge that passed over the Tyne River. A little further on, he passed through an underpass beneath the train tracks. As he came out on the other side, immediately in front of him was a sign indicating Ridley Hall. There was a gate house, but the gate was open so he continued on up the drive.

The drive was lined with trees, so John could not get a clear view of the house until he emerged from the trees as the way passed along the front of the house. He was immediately in awe when he first saw the house. He hadn't expected it to be so big. It didn't exactly look like a castle, but more like a mansion, three to four stories high, with a huge tower on the left front corner. He leaned his bike against a stone fence and walked into the large garden in front of the house. Beyond the garden was a huge green and he stepped back into it so he could get a better look. It was an impressive structure. It sort of had a Tudor style to it, with the tower having what looked like battlements across the top. He guessed that it might have been built in the 18th or 19th century, but the tower looked to be older, probably a part of the original house.

He decided to go to the door and ask if there was any chance of seeing the inside. The house was no longer a place of residence. It had been used for a prep school in the 1960s and now was being used as a conference center and guest house. The front door was open, so he walked into the entryway. He stood in the center of the foyer looking around to see if there was anyone there.

"May I help you," greeted a voice from above at the top of the stairs. It was a young woman.

"I'm sorry if I am intruding, I was wondering if there was any way that I might take a look around, or perhaps get a tour of the interior of the house."

"You're an American aren't you?"

John was getting a little tired of being immediately recognized as a tourist. "Yes, my name is John Ridley, I'm a visiting student at Oxford," he thought that the mention of Oxford might give him some credibility.

"Ridley, I see, so you're here to trace your roots?" she sounded a bit patronizing.

"No, not really, well, yes maybe I am... I just thought it would be nice to see the interior of the house since I was here," he was no doubt blushing by now.

"No need to be embarrassed, we get visitors from all over. I would be glad to show you around, but I am afraid we will be limited to the ground floor. My name is Julia, Julia Sutton," she had come down the stairs and was now extending her hand to his.

John shook her hand, "Hello, Julia. Thank you ever so much. I don't mean to impose."

"No, it's quite alright, I'm glad to be of service, follow me."

With that John followed her as she led him through some public rooms on the first floor. She also took him down the hallway and showed him a library. While they walked, she shared what little history she knew about the house. It had been originally built in the 16th century and inhabited by the Ridley family. It was possible that Bishop Ridley might have even spent time here in his youth. She asked John if he knew of the Bishop and he nodded his head in the affirmative. In the

18th century, the house was damaged by fire and rebuilt. The cellars were the only thing that remained of the original house. The house had changed hands in the 17th century. It was believed that the Ridleys had lost all of their lands during the civil war due to their undying loyalty to King Charles. As a result the house passed into the hands of the Lowes family. The Lowes were best known for having been ancestors of the present Queen Elizabeth. In the 19th century, the house was remodeled again in the present neo-Tudor style.

So, although called Ridley Hall, the house had really only been in the possession of the Ridley family for only 150 years of its 500 years of existence. After the tour, Julia invited John to spend some time in the gardens and the woods to the west of the house. John thanked her and left the way he had come in.

Once outside again, John wandered in the gardens for awhile. He found a quiet spot where a bench had been placed that had a view of the house. He sat and had a little lunch in solitude. As he sat looking at the house, he tried to imagine how many had spent their lives in this mansion over the past 500 years. What kind of stories would they tell?

He took out his history of the Ridleys and began looking over the names once again. Mrs. Willis said that it was a John Ridley who was in love with Abigail Featherstone. He went back to the place where he had first noticed the Ridleys of Hardriding. There was a Thomas Ridley of Hardriding who had four sons. The oldest was John Ridley and the notes beside his name stated that he had died without issue. This would be mean that he died before being married. This fit; it must be the John Ridley from the legend. It had to be. And then he noticed something else, this John Ridley was the brother of George Ridley of Hardriding and Gatehouse, his ancestor. How could it be, that these stories were all somehow connected to him? How was this possible?

After having something to eat, John went back to where he had left the bike and then continued his journey down the road. Not more than half mile away was the ruins of the ancient Willimoteswick. This old castle, which was first constructed in the 12th century, sat on top of a rise looking out over the Tyne valley. It was no longer used as a residence, instead the heavy stone walls and tower and been incorporated into a modern farm building. The tower sitting on the front corner was four stories high, with very small windows, a reminder of its defensive purpose. This old fortress had once been the ancient seat of the Ridleys of Northumberland.

John leaned the bicycle up against the stone wall, and walked up the drive to the tower. There was a large arched passageway and there was no gate or other impediment, so he decided to enter. It opened into a large court yard surrounded on all sides by the walls of the original castle. There didn't seem to be anybody around.

At the base of the tower, there was a door ajar and so he decided to look inside. Inside he found that it was a storage room for a variety of farm implements and in one corner there were stone stairs leading upward. He realized he was trespassing, but his curiosity got the best of him. He quietly crept up the stairs, not knowing what to expect. The second floor was much the same as the first, so he continued on up to the third. There were small narrow windows opening on the west and east wall, with nothing but bare stone on the south. On the north wall was a fire place and chimney, it looked to be original. Looking through windows on the west wall, he could see nothing but farmland as far as the eye could see. To the east, at the bottom of the hill, was a small wood and flowing out of it to the north, toward the River Tyne, was a small stream. The wood made it difficult to track the source of the stream to the south.

He walked over to the fireplace and ran his hands along the mantle. The stone was worn smooth by years of use; the bottom edges colored black by soot and smoke. His eyes followed the line of stone all around the perimeter, then back again, and then he noticed something. On the far right edge there was a stone which had been etched with the name Ridley. He traced over the edges of each letter with the point of his finger and then around the edge of the stone. As he looked closer he noticed that the mortar around the stone had a threadlike crack that circumscribed the entire stone. He pressed his hand on the stone and noticed a nearly imperceptible movement. Reaching into his back pack he pulled out his pocket knife. Carefully, he slid the point of the knife into the crack at the bottom and then lifted slightly, using the knife blade as lever. The stone moved, no more than an eighth of an inch. He repeated the procedure, again a slight movement, and then again and again. After several attempts he realized he had moved the stone just enough to actually be able to get his finger tips around the edges. He grasped the stone both top and bottom and pulled outward. It moved again, this time another inch, then another, and finally he had it all the way out.

He looked into the opening he had created. Inside, tucked neatly into the cavity, was a small wooden box. He reached in and carefully removed it. Opening the lid, he found some parchment, folded and wrapped in leather. He stepped closer to the window and held the contents up to the light, then very gently unfolded the parchment. It was a letter of sorts, written in old English script. Although difficult to decipher, he was able to read most of the contents.

1649, February 23, 24th Year of Charles Stuart,
King of England,

Willymonteswyke, my home since birth,
Faithfully thou hath served,
the bastion of Northumberland.
Thou mighty fortress, resisting all enemies,
standing steady and true,
Never hath thou known defeat,
nor hath thy walls been breeched,

Willymonteswyke, protector of the Tyne,
Great see of Ridley, both sanctuary and dwelling.
When the hordes of the north surround thee
and all seems lost,
None need despair,
for thou have kept secret a way below and to the east.

Willymonteswyke, both birthright and legacy,
My enemies now press in about me,
thy walls protect me not.
Thou defender of the Lord's anointed,
turned plunder for a Charlatan.
For to love thy King, a virtue,
hast now been deemed a crime.

Willymonteswyke, never to know defeat in battle,
No arrow, lance or catapult do thee now face,
Yet surrender thee must to political intrigue and writ,
The Lord's anointed hath passed this world and we are left alone.

Willymonteswyke, Oh Willymonteswyke,
My heart is heavy laden, my soul can know no peace.
Shall I never more sleep within thy walls,
nor walk thy halls at ease,
Willymonteswyke, My Willymonteswyke, no more.
M. Ridley

The room was empty, the quiet resounding, all that John could hear was the beat of his own heart. He dared not tarry in the room much longer, for fear of discovery. Without thinking, he folded the parchment back into the box and slid it into his pack. After replacing the stone in the fire place wall, he quietly descended the stairs and stepped out into the courtyard. There was still no one to be seen. He passed back through the archway and found the bicycle where he had left it. Instead of climbing into the seat, he simply walked with it at his side until he had reached the bottom of the hill. Seeing what he believed to be the source of the stream through the trees, he left the bicycle once again and climbed over the roadside wall. He found a path that led down into the trees and he followed it to the streams edge. To the north the stream passed beneath a bridge and then continued on toward the Tyne. To the south it disappeared into the thick forest beyond. It was difficult to see very far upstream due to the overhanging trees. He decided to investigate further. Not more than forty yards into the trees, completely hidden from the road, was a small opening in the embankment, just to the right of the stream. It was covered with ivy, but he could make out the rods of an iron grating through the foliage. He picked up a stone and tossed it through the opening. It made a clicking sound as it deflected off the stone walls inside. It seemed to be a small tunnel of some sort, a passage. Could it be some sort of underground passage that lead back to the castle. He looked at his watch, and felt a twinge of disappointment. He didn't have the time to investigate any further. It was already mid afternoon. If he left now, he would just be able to make it to Unthank Hall before he would have to return to Bardon Mill.

He returned to the bicycle, glanced at his map to get his bearings and then set off again. The road to Unthank was not direct, and at least part of the way he had to travel by unpaved roads. At one point a dirt path took him through a heavily wooded area, during which time he completely lost his sense of direction. Fortunately, as he emerged from the trees he came upon Unthank Road.

Unthank Hall was an imposing house, not like Ridley Hall, but still impressive in its own right. The house faced the river and there was a beautiful garden out front, just as Mrs. Willis had said. John stepped off the bike and leaned it against an old oak tree. There was an older gentleman who seemed to be pulling some weeds in the garden. He decided it wouldn't hurt to make some inquiries, so he walked directly toward him.

"Good afternoon, I wonder if you might help me?" John greeted.

"Oh hello, what can I do for you son?" The old man looked up from his gardening. "Are you lost?"

"No, I don't think so, not if this is Unthank Hall. I was just wondering if I might ask you a few questions, that is, as long as I am not disturbing you. I mean, I don't want to keep you from what you're doing. I was just wondering if you live here."

"This is Unthank Hall, and yes I do live here. Even worse, I own this place. My name is Charles Brown, and you are?"

"John Ridley, it is a pleasure to meet you, sir. Brown, say, you wouldn't be related to an Abby Brown?"

"I might be," the old man seemed cautious. "Why do you ask?"

John thought it better to leave it alone for now. He wasn't here to ask about Abby. "Oh nothing, just someone I met." Changing the subject, "the reason I am here is that I was sent by a Mr. Forster, at the Old Gaol in Hexham. He said that someone here might know something about the feud between the Ridleys and the Featherstones, most specifically, about the death of Sir Albany Featherstone. You see, I am a graduate student visiting Oxford and I am doing research into ancient legends and folklore. I wonder if you could help me?"

"What exactly do you want to know?" Mr. Brown's expression suggested that he was agreeable, at least for the moment.

"I have been trying to determine if the events surrounding Sir Albany's death were merely legend or if they were true. I am also trying to find out if there was any evidence of why Sir Albany Featherstone was killed."

"Hmm...it has been a long time since anybody has asked me about that old story, but I suppose I know why Mr. Forster suggested that you visit here. Twenty years ago, when we decided to remodel Unthank we came across something of a surprise. One day we unearthed a hidden vault in the cellar that no one had opened in years. It contained several different old artifacts, but the most interesting was a journal that had been owned by Hugh Ridley, the brother of Bishop Ridley. It had been carefully wrapped and kept for safe keeping, presumably by his wife, after Mr. Ridley had passed on. In it we found several entries from around the time Sir Albany Featherstone died.

It seems that a Nicholas Ridley, a cousin, once removed, of the Bishop and his brother, had befriended the youngest son, William by name, of Sir Albany Featherstone, against both their fathers' wishes. The two boys would often secretly plan to rendezvous and gallivant all over the country side without either of their father's knowledge. One day they decided to go deer hunting together. The two boys were stalking a large buck, when the deer bolted. In attempt to gain their quarry the boys gave chase, and then tragedy struck. They were running blindly through the trees when the young William tripped and fell head long into a ravine. The fall broke his neck and he was killed instantly.

When the boy's body was brought to Sir Albany, he flew out of the castle in a fit of rage. Despite the fact that all evidence indicated it was merely an accident, Sir Albany blamed the young Nicholas for his son's death. He called for the men of the Featherstone clan to join him, including his oldest son, Thomas. They raced off toward Willimoteswick in order to gain revenge on the death of poor William. When Sir Nicholas Ridley, "the Broad Knight", and leader of the Ridley clan, heard of Sir Albany's intent, he rode out to meet him, along with a few others of the Ridley family. Having had to wait on some of his entourage to arrive, Sir Albany had barely gotten beyond the edge of his own estates before he was met by Sir Nicholas.

The Broad Knight pleaded with Sir Albany to calm himself. He insisted that there was no need for any more bloodshed. The young Nicholas was beside himself with grief, and in fact loved the poor lad, William, and would have never wanted any harm to come to him. It was an accident and nothing more. They debated for some time, until it became clear Sir Albany would have none of it. Without warning he charged forward, clearly intending to kill the young Nicholas. The Broad Knight stood his ground in defense of his grandson and as Sir Albany approached, the brazen Sir Nicholas struck with one fierce blow of his sword, throwing Sir Albany from his horse and wounding him mortally.

Sir Nicholas slowly dismounted his own steed and stood over the dying Sir Albany. Hugh Ridley who was present at the event, overheard the knight say, 'Here dies a brave and yet foolish man. Remember his valor, but also remember that no man is the judge, it is only God who is just, and in this moment His truth and justice has prevailed.' With that, Sir Albany expired.

As his father lay dying, Thomas Featherstone fled the scene, possibly because he feared for his life, or possibly because he felt the shame of his father's foolishness in defeat."

"Fascinating" was all that John could think to say. He now was convinced that the events of the ballad were real, but the manner in which oral tradition had portrayed them was much different than the actual events themselves. This also confirmed what was written by Bishop Ridley to his brother. "Do you still have the journal?"

"No, I am afraid not. Because Hugh Ridley was the brother of the eminent Bishop Ridley and since many of the other entries made reference to their relationship, we thought it best to present the journal to the Museum of Antiquities in Newcastle."

John was a little disappointed that he wouldn't be able to see it in person, but he was satisfied that he'd succeeded in finding a more definitive explanation of the events surrounding the death of Sir Albany Featherstone.

"Thank you Mr. Brown, you've been more than helpful. I appreciate you taking the time away from your gardening to share with me the entire story."

"It has been my pleasure, John Ridley...given your surname, I imagine that your interest in this ballad is more than academic. Do you have a personal connection, as well?"

"Yes, I suppose I do. Just recently I discovered that I am a descendent of the Nicholas Ridleys, both the grandfather and the grandson."

"Well then I guess this means that if the grandfather had not intervened, the grandson might have met his end and you would not be here today."

John was kind of caught off guard by this statement. Everything was happening so fast, and he'd not had time to reflect and consider the implications of this new revelation. "Yes...I suppose you're right. I hadn't even thought of that." He stood motionless, staring into the distance, momentarily stunned by the reality of the statement.

"Don't fret young man, we all have a connection to the past, but we can not change it. All that matters is what we do with the time we have now, and how this impacts the future."

The familiarity of these words rang in John's ears. "Thanks again, Mr. Brown," extending his hand. "I won't forget you."

"Your welcome," as he turned and walked away he could hear the old man whisper, "Seems like a nice young man, I hope he finds what he is looking for."

Abby couldn't believe her eyes, as she stood looking out the window of the sitting room of Unthank Hall. What was *he* doing here? Why was he talking to grandfather? It seemed incomprehensible. She had come to make her biweekly visit to Unthank. It was important to her. She came because it brought her peace, it was sort of therapeutic.

She stood practically motionless, wondering what she should do. Should she go out and speak to him? She wanted to, but not here, not now. Why did he have to come here? He couldn't possibly know she would be here. What were they talking about? Why was it taking so long? 'Wait it looks like he's leaving,' she thought to herself. 'He wasn't here looking for her after all.'

When John was far enough down the road that she could no longer see him, she went outside and walked to where her grandfather was still working.

"Who was that grandfather?" she asked.

"Don't you know? He seemed to know you."

"Well, we may have met," she replied, hesitant to divulge too much information. "But, what was he doing *here*? He wasn't asking about me, was he?" Although she was giving the impression of being irritated, down deep there was this nagging thought, a sort of hopeful thought, that he might actually be there looking for her.

"No, no, I'm not sure he knew you had any connection to the place. He was simply here asking questions about Unthank Hall and the Ridley family."

"Oh, yes, of course, I should have known. After all he's a Ridley."

"So you do know him after all," her grandfather was beginning to sense there was something else going on here.

"You seem a little disappointed that he left without inquiring after you."

"Who me?" she tried to play innocent. He was not buying it. She could see him smile slightly as he turned away. This was crazy. How did he end up here, right at this moment while she was visiting? She stood staring down the road in the direction in which John had departed. She was trying to sort out her own feelings. Was she disappointed that he had left without seeing her? Did he still want to see her? Why did she care at all? She did not even really know him. He was just some guy she had met on a train. It didn't mean anything. It couldn't mean anything. Nothing was going to happen. He was from half way around the world, after all. It was just a chance meeting, two ships passing in the night. Why was she thinking about him at all? It was all so ridiculous.

"I think he's gone," Mr. Brown said after a few moments, following her eyes with his own.

"Of course he is. What do I care?" again she tried to hide what she was really thinking.

"It just looked as if you were about to follow him. He couldn't have traveled far. It's probably not too late."

"Don't be silly," and with that she turned and marched toward the house. Still, there was this nagging urge to turn around and chase down the road after him. She tried to put it aside.

*****

It was a longer ride back to Bardon Mill than John had realized. He'd been following the Tyne westward and his journey took him to the very outskirts of Haltwhistle. To go back toward Bardon Mill he had to pass over the river, then through the edge of town, and then connect with the road traveling east.

He wondered what Abby was doing right now. He wasn't sure if she had to work on Monday or not, but it really didn't matter. He wasn't going to visit her today. It was too soon. Still, he did feel a little tempted to try and find the pub where she worked, since he was so close. It was possible that she might be getting off work right about now. He wanted to see her again, he couldn't help himself. He knew it was kind of silly, she might have already forgotten about him. She was probably just being polite. He tried to put out of his mind.

As he continued toward Bardon Mill he passed through a couple small villages. It was a beautiful day and it was still early, he had no reason to be in a hurry. He decided to take his time and enjoy the trip. When he arrived in the second village he stopped and checked the time, it was just a little before five and he was only a few miles or so from Bardon Mill. He noticed a sign pointing north that said 'Roman Wall'. He had noticed the Roman Wall on his map and curiosity got the best of him, he decided to take a detour. When else would he have this opportunity? The road intersected with a main road traveling east and west. He turned east toward Bardon Mill, a little further on and he found a road that led north to the wall.

The road began to climb. When he reached the top of the ridge he came to the stone wall that ran both east and west along the ridge. Just a short distance off the road, there was a small car park set amongst some trees; it was clearly a stepping off point for those who wanted to hike along the wall. He leaned his bike against the fence and walked back toward the wall. He paused for a moment when he reached the wall, wondering which direction he should take. For no particular reason, he decided to go west, walking along the north side of the wall.

From atop the ridge, he could see for miles in all directions. The stone wall only stood three to four feet high in most places, but it had been placed on the top of huge mounds of earth which stretched for miles in both directions, east and west, and at times it was difficult to know if these mounds of earth were completely of natural origin or if they had been man made. The centuries of history since the time of the construction of the wall had erased all evidence. After having walked a quarter of mile, he stopped and looked back in the direction from which he had come. There was a huge craggy cliff in the distance and he could just make out the line of the wall ascending to the top of and tracing out the line of the ridge. Beneath this cliff was narrow lake. To the west there were rolling hills, with the line of the wall disappearing in the distance. To the south, there were miles of farmland stretching as far as the eye could see. He climbed up onto the wall and sat for a moment, enjoying the restful quiet.

It was still difficult to come to grips with where he was. It seemed as only a few moments ago he'd arrived in England. Everything was moving so quickly, he barely had the time to pause and reflect. He wanted to slow the clock down, to be able to enjoy the moment, before rushing off to the next thing. He was in a place so rich in history and tradition, so foreign and yet so familiar. He didn't want to miss out on any part of the experience. As he thought back over the events of the previous two weeks, he found it all a little blurry, almost dreamlike or surreal. He wanted it to feel real. He wanted to be able to remember each moment, to somehow keep it close. He smiled as he remembered how resistant he'd been about coming in the first place. He had been wrong. Now that he was here, he found it difficult to think about having to leave.

He reflected on what Mr. Brown had said about how, if "The Broad Knight" had not intervened, John would not be alive today. He could've never imagined that when he first began doing research on the works of Sir Walter Scott, specifically the ballad from *Marmion*, that it would've had anything to do with him. He'd always seen himself as an observer, not a participant in the story line of his research.

Was it possibly true that his very existence had been determined some 500 years ago, when two knights faced each other in battle, just there to the south, beyond the Tyne, a few miles from where he now sat? Is that the way it worked? Were the events of human history connected to every birth and every death? Logically, there were only two possibilities. Either every human birth is a completely random event without any meaning or real purpose. Or every human birth is predetermined by a purposeful, all knowing, all powerful Creator; One who has the ability to determine human events, even the birth of child, because the Creator exists outside of space-time and has the ability to alter any event. Of course, this requires that the former would mean there was absolutely no real meaning behind any human event and that human history has no significance whatsoever, while the latter would mean that every human birth and death had real purpose and meaning and in the big picture, some may have greater purpose than others. Ultimately, it means we are either alone, or we are not alone, either there is purpose and meaning or there is not.

He had always believed that the latter was true-that everything has a purpose and meaning-and now he was becoming more convinced that it was true; that there is a plan and purpose for all things and all people. What about now? Was there a purpose or reason behind him being here right now, at this particular moment? He realized that some events had to be more important than others, that there was the big picture plan and a lot of small picture plans. This would allow for some events to have variable outcomes without the big picture plans being interfered with. Was this one of those moments? Was his being here in England a part of a path that was allowed to have variable outcomes, or was it a part of something more significant? How could he know for sure?

It seemed to him, the only reasonable approach, would be to believe that every decision, every moment, was significant, and one should act and think accordingly. If one treated every moment as insignificant, then nothing would have purpose or meaning. The problem rested with the fact that a man is incapable of knowing what moments or what decisions were more important than the others, only the All-knowing could know these things. Therefore, a man would have to treat each moment with the same sense of purpose and meaning and then trust that the All-Everything would intervene when necessary.

It began to dawn on him what "The Broad Knight" had meant. He was not the judge and executioner of Sir Albany Featherstone. Instead, he believed that had the Almighty Judge wished to intervene and preserve the life of Sir Albany, he would have. "The Broad Knight" did not believe he had won a victory because of his greater skill or strength, but that the only possible outcome was that which had already been determined by the Sovereign Judge.

John's head was spinning, and his stomach was starting to growl. He had noticed a little village and an Inn just at the bottom of the hill at the crossroads. It might be a good idea to get something to eat and then head back. If he left now, he should still be able to make Bardon Mill before dark.

Chapter Nine

...it was dark in the forest and cold. The moisture in the air from the recent rain brought a chill to her bone. Someone was following her, she didn't know who. She could hear his steps behind her. It was too dark to be able to see him. The moon provided a little light through the trees, just enough to see the path in front of her. She began to run. She didn't know why. What was she afraid of? Was she in danger? Perhaps it was a friend.

She kept running. It was difficult for her to run, her gown was long and dragged against the wet ground. Why was she dressed like this? Without warning she stumbled over something in the dark and fell to the ground. She turned to face her pursuer. She could feel her heart pounding in her chest. What was she going to do? She trembled with fear. "Who's there?" she cried out. "What do you want? Won't you please leave me alone!"...

Abby woke with a start. 'That was weird," she thought to herself. She couldn't remember the last time she'd had a nightmare. She was perspiring. She sat up in bed and let her legs fall over the side. She rubbed the sleep from her eyes. She could see the sun just starting to peak over the distant hills through her bedroom window. It must be about six thirty. She had to clear the cobwebs from her mind for just a minute. She wasn't immediately sure where she was.

She looked around the room to get her bearings. She was still at Unthank Hall. Now she remembered, she had decided to stay over. She wasn't due at work until eleven. She had plenty of time. She slid off the bed onto the cool wood floor and made her way to bathroom. She cringed a little, the floor was icy cold and she tiptoed, trying to minimize the discomfort. She took a shower-it was at times like these that she was most pleased that Grandfather Brown had modernized the bathroom- and then went down stairs to see if she could scrounge up some breakfast. She figured Grandfather would already be up and out, probably taking his normal morning stroll.

There was a pot of water, still hot, on the stove. On the counter were some scones with a note instructing her to go ahead and help herself. She made herself some tea, and made quick work of a scone before taking off out the back door to the stable.

When she got to the stable, she saw that Grandfather had already fed Clover. Clover was her four year old bay mare. She had ridden Clover to Unthank Hall the day before from the farm where she was boarding her.

She had grown up on a farm and she had always had a horse. When her father passed away last year, her mom could no longer keep the farm and they had to sell it. As a result, her mom had moved into town to share a two bedroom flat with Abby. One of their neighbors, who had a farm just on the south edge of town, had offered to board Clover. She would go riding whenever she had the opportunity. One of her favorite rides was to come here to Unthank and visit Grandfather Brown. He lived here all alone, and she felt responsible to check in on him from time to time.

She prepared Clover for the ride back, and then before leaving, she looked around for Grandfather. He was nowhere to be found. He must be on one of his walks. He knew that she had to work today, so he would not expect her to wait around for him to return. She mounted Clover and started down the road to Haltwhistle.

She didn't like to stay on the road with her horse because of the vehicle traffic, so she cut across country. She headed west cutting through the pasture land. It was still early enough in the day so she didn't really need to be in a hurry. As she came to the top of a rise she stopped for a moment to let Clover rest. She sat looking out over the Tyne River Valley. She could see Halwhistle to the north. In front of her was the tree lined bank of the Tyne, and immediately below her was the road that ran parallel to the river, going south to Rowfoot, a village just east of Featherstone Castle. There was a solitary man walking south on the road. She watched him for a moment before she realized it was him, John Ridley. She could not be mistaken. She could tell by the way he walked. She couldn't see his face, he was too far away, but it was him, she was convinced of it. What was he doing here? He was going away from Haltwhistle. Wasn't he coming to see her today? She caught herself. What did she care if he was coming to see her or not? She was simply not interested. It was too complicated. She didn't really know him at all. Why was she even thinking about it? She needed to get to work.

*****

John saw what appeared to be a fairly flat place on top of the stone wall on the edge of the road. It was just beneath a large oak tree that was casting a bit of shadow from the morning sun. He thought it was as good a place as any to stop for a brief rest. He pulled out the juice bottle in his back pack and sat down on the wall, surveying the country side. There were sheep grazing in the field next to where he was sitting. Across the road on top of the hill there was a person on horseback. It appeared to be a woman and it seemed as if she was looking at him, but he couldn't be sure, she was too far away. Just then she turned her horse and disappeared down the other side of the hill.

He had risen early that morning, had a very quick breakfast and caught a bus for Haltwhistle. He had told Mrs. Willis that he intended to visit Featherstone Castle and wondered if she knew of any place to stay nearby. She had suggested the Whitfield Arms Bed and Breakfast in Rowfoot.

She explained that it was a comfortable and quiet place and that the proprietor would be able to tell him anything he needed to know about the local area. As he was leaving she cautioned, "you watch out for those ghosts, John Ridley, don't say I didn't give you fair warning."

The bus dropped him at Bellister Road which ran south to Rowfoot. He figured he could walk to the B&B. It wasn't more than a couple of miles, and the weather was supposed to remain nice. It was only ten now, he should be able to check in and spend most of the afternoon exploring Featherstone Castle and the surrounding area. Mrs. Willis had called ahead so he was assured of getting a room for the night.

Although he was looking forward to seeing Abby again, it was probably best to wait until tomorrow. It wasn't as if she would be expecting him today anyway. By now she may have forgotten about him entirely. Was he really thinking anything could come of it? He was 10,000 miles away from home, he met a girl on a train, and then he set a date to see her again. He must be out of his mind.

After a brief rest, he started down the road again. The B&B was only another mile or so. As he walked, he kept trying to convince himself that he needed to stop thinking about Abby. If he were able to see her tomorrow, great, but if not, well, that was that. He occupied himself with planning what he was going to do when he finally got to Featherstone Castle. He wondered if he would be able to locate Pynkinscleugh Glen or Deadmanshaugh.

When he arrived at the Whitfield Arms, the proprietor already had his room ready. He took his bags to his room, cleaned himself up a little and went down stairs. There was a nice little pub connected to the B&B and he was able to have a leisurely lunch before heading for Featherstone. He figured he was in no hurry, since the castle was just a half mile down the road and he had all afternoon to explore.

Just as John's lunch was delivered to the table he heard an all too familiar voice. He couldn't believe his ears. A shiver passed down his spine as he looked over his shoulder.

"Well, what do we have here? Look George, it's Mr. Ridley." It was Mr. and Mrs. Crabb.

"Hello, young man," Mr. Crabb echoed. "Fancy meeting you here. What a surprise to see you again."

"A lovely surprise, George," Mrs. Crabb agreeing. "Do you mind if we join you? Of course you don't," not allowing John to reply. "Are you sitting here all by your lonesome? It's a mighty fine thing we happened here at this moment. It's a terrible thing, you eating lunch all by yourself. We won't have it, eh George?"

"Absolutely not," Mr. Crabb barely got his two cents worth in.

Up to this point, John had not even been able to get a word out. He was completely dumbfounded. What were they doing here? "Good afternoon Mr. and Mrs. Crabb. This *is* a surprise."

"An absolute delight, that's what it is. I was just saying to George here, wouldn't it be nice if we ran into that fine young man again, and here you are."

"Whatever brings you to the Whitfield Arms, my boy?" Mr. Crabb asked.

"I wanted to visit Featherstone Castle, part of my..." John realized he had just made a horrible mistake. There was no going back on it now.

"Well what a bit of fortune. We are here to see Featherstone as well. We shall go together, as soon as we've finished our lunch."

"I wouldn't want to intrude," John was not looking forward to spending a whole afternoon with these two.

"Don't be silly. It's not an intrusion. We would love for the company. We have a car right outside. Please say you'll join us," Mrs. Crabb was not about to give up.

"Okay, if you're sure," he was trapped now.

"You missed a treat yesterday John," Mr. Crabb began. "We visited Langley Castle. Beautiful old place, 14th Century I believe..."

"...they've turned it into a hotel," Mrs. Crabb interrupted. "The rooms were just lovely, decorated in medieval style..."

"...it was like walking back in time," Mr Crabb continued. "It was all I could do to keep from putting on a suit of armor, climbing upon my faithful steed and challenging the locals to battle, ya know..."

"...Oh George stop being silly. Don't you listen to him John, he is just spouting off some boyhood fantasy. Langley was amazing just the same, the woods and garden surrounding the castle, a beautiful setting," Mrs. Crabb wasn't about to let her husband get the upper hand in the conversation."

This exchange between Mr. and Mrs. Crabb continued on through the rest of lunch. Back and forth, as if they were volleying a tennis ball, they took turns telling John about every detail of their experience at Langley. While the one talked the other ate and in the end they made quick work of their lunch.

While John listened, he tried to think of some sort of excuse to avoid having to spend the entire afternoon with them, but no matter how hard he thought he could not come up with anything. He was condemned to this unfortunate fate. He would have to make the best of it. When lunch was over, the three of them got into the car and headed for Featherstone. He could at least find some satisfaction in knowing he was getting a free ride out of the deal. The trip by car was not more than five minutes. The road passed through some trees and then they came to the top of a hill, from which they could get a clear view of the castle sitting in the valley below. As they reached the bottom of the hill, they turned off the road onto the drive leading up to the castle. Mr. Crabb pulled over to the side and parked at the edge of the drive.

"Let's walk from here, what'd you say, Emma?" Mr. Crabb suggested.

"Good idea George," then she turned back to John, "Hope you don't mind John, we like to enjoy the walk."

"No, not at all, I feel the same way," John thought the open spaces might minimize the conversation.

As they walked up the lane he could see a gate tower, with a stone arch connecting it to the main castle. It looked familiar to John, but he couldn't think why. In all of his research he couldn't remember ever seeing a picture of the castle, and yet it seemed as if he'd been here before. The trees along the drive shielded a portion of the castle from his sight, but as they walked up the drive, they were afforded an unobstructed view of the entire structure. He stopped in the lane to admire it. It was far better preserved than Willimoteswick and it genuinely gave one the sense of walking back in time. As they passed through the arch of the gate, they entered what at one time must have served as some sort of court yard, but now served as a small car park. John walked over to the low wall that surrounded this courtyard and ran his hand along the weathered stone. It was inspiring to him that these stones had been put into place hundreds of years before. He turned and faced the castle, looking east. It had two large towers with battlements rimming each tower and stretching across the length of the roof line. It was entirely made of stone and mortar. Although it had probably been rebuilt or had additions constructed over time, there was no indication of the relative age of any portion. It all looked very old.

The three of them walked through the courtyard toward the south end and through an arch to a small garden on the south side. Here there was an old fountain in the middle of the green, but it appeared to have been inoperable for sometime. One of the unique features of the south end of the castle was a round peripatetic extending from the face of the building. This curved projection, broke up the symmetry of the otherwise rectangular elements of the castle's construction. To the right of it was an arched opening that seemed to be the entrance of some sort of workshop.

As they rounded the building on the west side there were more gardens and what appeared to be an entrance. The Crabbs had been surprisingly quiet during this tour of the grounds surrounding the castle. Finally, Mr. Crabb broke the silence, "Let's see if we can get a look inside, shall we?"

"By all means," Mrs. Crabb was right behind him. "She's a beauty, isn't she George?"

"Very impressive, very impressive indeed," he agreed. "Not like Langley, but very impressive in her own right."

John thought it strange that they were referring to the castle as a she, but it seemed somewhat fitting. He followed his companions to the front door. He was anxious to see inside as well, and in this case he might benefit from their boldness.

The castle was no longer a residence, but instead was used as a prep school. The students were off for the summer, so the place was relatively empty. When they knocked on the door, they were greeted by the caretaker, who agreed to take them on a tour. Although there had been some attempt to preserve the history and charm of the castle, the interior had been somewhat modernized. This was probably necessary for its present use. Electricity had been brought to the castle and the lamps lighting the interior seemed anything but medieval.

They were pleased to discover that the caretaker had at least some knowledge of the history of the castle. The Featherstones were of an Anglo-Saxon line and there were claims that they could be traced all the way back to the 11th century. There was a second branch of the family who had settled at Stanhope (John later learned that this was a village to the south, in Durham County). The family see was actually first built on the rise just to the west, however, it was later moved to this location in the valley, closer to the river.

After their tour of the interior of the castle, they took a stroll through the gardens on the east side. The gardens afforded a nice view of the hills above. There was a stone wall that surrounded the entire castle grounds, probably built for defensive purposes.

John wandered away from the castle and found a gate through the wall on the south end. It was an opportunity to distance himself a little from the Crabbs and to get a slightly different point of view. The fields surrounding the castle were still occupied by grazing sheep, probably much as they had been for centuries. John found a huge oak tree to sit under, providing beneficial shade. He found a comfortable place to lean up against the tree and then pulled his note pad from his back pack and began jotting down some notes.

As he sat looking at the castle, he began to imagine how many families had occupied it during its history. How many children must have played in the garden, perhaps even in this very tree he now reclined against, or rode their horses in the field. He only knew a small portion of the history of the proud family who once occupied this land and he realized that there were probably hundreds of interesting stories left undiscovered.

He closed his eyes and tried to imagine what it must have been like living here 300 years ago. As his mind began to drift to another place and time he could hear the gentle breeze rustling the leaves in the branches above. He could feel it brush across the skin of his cheeks and hands. It was cool and soothing, refreshment from the warmth of the summer day...

> *In his minds eye, he could see a man on horse back, clothed in a warrior's garb, plates of armor interspersed with mail and leather. He brandished a sword that gleamed brilliantly in the summer sun. His horse snorted and pranced as if anticipating the impending conflict, the muscles in his legs and shoulders rippling with tension and his body shiny with perspiration...*

*****

John was awakened from his dream, "Hello, John!" Mr. and Mrs. Crabb were approaching the tree where he was reclined. They had noticed him missing and had decided to look for him. He rose to his feet, brushed off his pants, stuck his pad in his back pack and started walking towards them.

"Sorry," he apologized, "I was just enjoying the day and this seemed like such a restful spot. I suppose I must've dozed off."

"Oh, don't be sorry," Mrs. Crabb assured him. "We can appreciate the need for a little solitude. We just thought we should let you know that we are about to call it an afternoon. We were going to head back to the car, and return to the Whitfield Arms. What do you say? Have you seen all you wish to see?"

195

"You go on ahead," John saw a chance to be alone. "It's still early yet and I thought I might explore a little down by the river. Besides, it's really not that far back to the Whitfield Arms and I think I might enjoy the walk."

"Suit your self," Mr. Crabb said. "Perhaps we will see you at tea then."

"That'll be fine. I'll see you both then." He wasn't really promising anything, but he thought he should at least be polite about it.

Just as they were walking away, Mr. Crabb turned back to John, "Don't be too long John, it looks as if there might be a little bit of a storm brewing in the distance." He pointed southeast to where it looked as if some clouds were creeping up over the horizon. They did look somewhat dark, but still a good distance away.

"Don't worry, I'll be fine. A little rain never hurt anyone. Besides, I have been through my share of summer thunderstorms." Even as he said it, he was hoping this would not have to be another one of those times.

*****

The Crabbs turned and walked north toward the drive where their car was parked and John walked toward the river where he came upon a dirt road that ran along its edge. He still had hopes of finding Pynkinscleugh Glen, and perhaps some evidence of the Witch's Cot. He remembered that the glen was somewhere on the other side of the river, just beyond a bridge. Eventually the road intersected with the road that he and the Crabbs had traveled on from Rowfoot. As he continued a little further down the road, he came upon a foot bridge that crossed over the river. On the other side of the river was a heavily wooded area that blocked any view of the land beyond. He crossed over the bridge and found a path that passed through the trees and then appeared to open into a field beyond.

He paused a moment, standing on the path, looking along the bank of the river in both directions. There didn't seem to be any other choice, this was the only path to take. It was possible that this was exactly what he was looking for. The field ahead could be Pynkinscleugh Glen. But how could he be sure? After all, it had been more than three hundred years since that fateful night. There was no telling how much change had taken place in the landscape since that time. Although there was a bridge here now, it was clearly modern and there was no way of knowing if this was the location of the bridge back then. He decided to begin by exploring the field ahead.

As he emerged from the trees there was a large pasture to the south and west. It climbed to a rise, on top of which there was a small farm house. Like the field in front of Featherstone, it was dotted with sheep. To his right was a thick forest, it ran all the way to the top of the rise creating a northern boundary for the field that lay in front of him. There was also a bit of forest to his left, lining the western bank of the river. The woods to his right were too thick to be able to know how far it was to the other side. It appeared that there was a path that passed through, just ahead.

He decided to take the path to try and pass through to the other side. As he walked down the path, the trees formed a canopy above that nearly blocked out the sky entirely. It was dark and quiet. A bit of a chill went down his spine. He had the strangest feeling, as if he had been on this path before. He brushed the feeling aside. He used go to hiking in the forest near his home in Pennsylvania, this was not much different. He was just feeling a little déjà vu.

He was surprised to discover that after only about a quarter of a mile he emerged from the trees on the other side. It was not exactly what he expected, but then again, he was not sure what to expect. There was another huge glen on the other side, similar to the one he had just left. It too was dotted with sheep. To his right the forest continued northward following the edge of the river. It was possible that this could be Pynkinscleugh Glen, or it was the field he had just left, there was really no way of knowing for sure. He decided to walk north along the edge of the forest on his right to see where it might take him. Perhaps there was another bridge ahead.

As he approached the north end of the field, he came upon a narrow road that came from the hills on the west and headed toward the river. There were trees lining the road and so he took a moment to rest in the shadow of one. As he looked back in the direction of which he had come, he noticed the sky to the south was getting darker as the clouds continued to gather. He looked up into the trees and could see that the wind was blowing slightly north which meant the clouds were heading in his direction. He was confronted with a difficult problem. The road might in fact cross the river at a bridge just ahead or it might go northward for awhile still. It certainly seemed that he was about to get caught in a storm and he should start to make his way back. He knew what he would face if he went back the way he came. If he went on, there was no telling how far out of his way it would take him. There seemed only one thing to do.

He got to his feet and started back through the field the way he had come. He quickened his pace just a little to see if he could beat the storm that seemed to be headed right for him. The sky continued to get darker as the clouds slowly began to move overhead. He had covered about half the distance to the south edge of the field when he began to feel the first rain drops. It was just a sprinkle, nothing to worry about for the moment, but he was sure that it was going to get worse. The sky was now so dark that it almost had the feel of twilight. He had gone nearly three fourths of the distance when he noticed what looked to be a different path winding its way into the forest toward the river. He hadn't seen it coming the other way because the entrance was slightly blocked by a small tree. It appeared to angle toward the bridge area. Perhaps it was a more direct route. It was starting to rain just a little harder so John decided to chance it. If nothing else, the tree cover would provide a little protection from the storm.

The forest was very dark here, compounded by the dark stormy sky above. Suddenly there was a flash of lightening. Everything on the forest floor was brilliantly lit for just an instant. Within moments the thunder began to echo through the trees. The storm was now directly overhead. With the thunder came the rain, a steady down pour, sounding like a million tiny drums beating against the leaves of the trees overhead.

For the moment, John was staying relatively dry, but he knew he should find a little extra protection. Just ahead, on the edge of the path was the huge trunk of an ancient oak tree. He found a dry spot beneath a large limb near the base, and sat down, in hopes that he could wait out the storm as it passed. The rain was echoing in the trees above, but for the moment he was dry and comfortable and he was in no hurry to be anywhere else. If he were delayed enough, it could work to his advantage. He would now have a reasonable excuse for missing tea with the Crabbs.

Every few minutes there was a flash of lightening, and for just an instant John could see into the depths of the wood. Standing timeless were the aged trunks of oak and elm, clad in ivy, ascending upward, supporting huge leafy boughs that were presently providing both shadow and shelter. Huge ferns grew up from the forest floor, intermingled with an occasional rock, worn and weathered, covered in patches of moss and lichen. He pulled out a package of crackers he had stowed away in his back pack for just such a moment. He sat back, leaning against the ancient oak, nibbling crackers and listening to the constant pitter patter of rain drops all around him. In the distance he could hear the croak of a frog, suggesting that the river was not too far away.

Pitter-patter, croak, pitter-patter, rumble...John closed his eyes.

Pitter-patter...croak. Wait there was a different sound, what was it? It was ahead, deep into the trees, it sounded like voices. John opened his eyes. It was so dark now he could barely see. He looked at his watch. It was nearly seven o'clock. It was approaching dusk. He must have fallen asleep. There it was again, despite the constant croaking of the frogs nearby, he thought he could here voices. The rain had nearly stopped. He rose to his feet. Was there someone else here? It was so dark he could hardly see anything. He stepped out from under the oak tree and onto the path. He wished he had thought to pack a flashlight. He could just barely see the path through the trees ahead. He started forward. There it was again, more voices.

"Hello!" He figured it would not hurt to call out. "Is anybody there?"

Nothing, the only thing that could be heard was the constant croaking of the frogs. Maybe he was imagining it. He continued to walk on. It shouldn't be far now, he had to be approaching the river. The ground was wet beneath his feet and he had to be careful of the occasional patches of mud created from the water that was draining from the higher ground. Before long the trees began to thin overhead and he could see the grayness of the twilight between the leaves and branches. The path opened up ahead as well, and as he looked down the path he could see some movement. He couldn't be sure, but he thought he saw some people walk across the path. He started walking faster and then just as he began to jog, he came to the end of the path. It opened up into the field to his right. The foot bridge was just to his left, a little ways down the path. The rain had completely stopped, but it was twilight and the heavy humidity and cool air were creating a mist on the glen. Instead of going toward the bridge, something urged him to walk out into the field. The sheep were no longer there. They had probably found a refuge from the rain. At the top of the rise he could see some people walking. Through the mist he could barely make them out, the colors were all muted in the twilight. They looked gray and ghostly. Just then he noticed the woman at the rear of the party stopped, turned and looked directly at him. He couldn't see her features, she was too far away, but he was certain she was looking at him. A patch of fog passed between them and she was lost from sight.

John rubbed his eyes and looked again. There was no one there. Was he imagining things? The mist can play tricks on your eyes, he was well aware of it. He stood gazing for a moment. There had been someone there, he was sure of it. When he was sure they were gone, he turned and walked away, debating with himself whether he had seen anything at all. He crossed over the bridge and began walking up the road toward Rowfoot. During the entire walk he tried to convince himself

200

that he was just been seeing things, or maybe there had really been some people out walking and like him had been caught in the storm. He didn't need to let his imagination run wild.

*****

John finally arrived back to the Whitfield Arms a little before eight. He went directly into the pub and ordered some hot tea and a sandwich from the kitchen. The Crabbs were no where to be seen. It seemed as if his timing was good after all. The waitress noticed he was a little worse for the wear.

"Looks as if you got caught in the storm mister," she said as she delivered his tea. He was the only one in the restaurant and so she was making an effort to be friendly through conversation.

"I suppose it is noticeable, isn't it," he replied. "I was on the other side of the river when the storm hit, and I had to take shelter under a tree."

"This is not a good night for you to be out and about, and I don't just mean the weather. What were you doing over there anyway?"

"Just exploring, what do you mean it's not a good night?"

"This is the night the ghosts come out. Surely you know about the ghosts of Featherstone Castle, the wedding party?"

"Yes, I have heard the story, but I didn't know that was tonight."

"Tonight, yes, the anniversary of the death of the wedding party," she continued. "I don't suppose you were anywhere near the Raven's Stone? You know, that is where it is said that the ghosts appear each anniversary of their death."

"What is this Raven's Stone, I have never heard of it," John asked with anticipation. "Where is it?"

"Just across the bridge to the north, hidden in the trees, a large rock that flattens out on one side with a slight hollow on top. I can't believe you've heard of the wedding party, but not the stone." As she was about to tell him, the cook announced that his sandwich was ready. She went to get the sandwich, placed it in front of him and then sat down in the chair opposite him. She began to talk in a low voice as if she didn't want anyone else to hear, even though they were completely alone.

"You know how the wedding party was attacked by the Ridleys and how the bride was accidently struck by an errant lance intended for her lover?"

"Uh huh," John acknowledged, leaning close to hear every word.

"Well, when she fell down dead, her lover, John Ridley, from Hardriding was so distraught he laid her against a stone at the edge of the glen and then stabbed himself in the heart with his own dagger. When he fell down dead, it is said that he fell across her body and together their blood mingled and flowed into the hollow of the stone. When the bodies were removed, it was said that ravens came down and drank the blood that remained in the stone and as they did so they let out a horrible scream. Thus the name given to the stone was Raven's Stone. It's believed that on the anniversary of the death of the two lovers their ghosts, along with the ghosts of the others who died, that night, can be seen near the Raven's Stone."

"Interesting, I'd never heard that part of the story before," John couldn't help but wonder about the apparitions he had seen earlier. There was no way that he was about to believe in ghosts, but it was a very strange coincidence.

"That's not all," the waitress continued. "It's said that a hundred years later a witch built a cottage near the Raven's Stone and each year when the ghosts would appear she would go to the place and she would actually talk with the ghosts, and they with her. This was said to have gone on for years, and all of sudden one day the witch was gone, up and disappeared. No one ever heard from her again and no one ever knew what happened to her."

"Was this witch, by chance, named Beardie Grey?" John asked. "That's right, Beardie Grey, so you've heard of her?"

John smiled, "yeah, I've heard of her..."

"Well, in any case, you ought to know better than to be out on this night in the future," the waitress cautioned.

"You're absolutely right, I should be a little more careful. By the way, we haven't met, what was your name."

202

"Janie Kendall. And yours?"

"John, John Ridley," he said hesitantly.

"John Ridley, just like in the story," she laughed. "Oh that beats all. Well you be careful tonight, John Ridley, you don't want to run into any ghosts out there."

John finished his sandwich and his tea and went upstairs to his room. He took a hot shower, got ready for bed, and then wrote a little in his journal and did a little light reading before he drifted off to sleep.

Chapter Ten

...the rain had stopped. It was shortly after midnight, when he entered the woody defile of Pynkinscleugh where he found the path shaded by a dense wood; it overhung and interlaced so as to almost exclude the beams of moonlight which now broke from behind a thick bank of clouds, and created an eerie softness to the surrounding scene. The moonlight glinted off natural objects of fallen logs and gnarled misshapen roots that created a silvery ghastly relief. Amidst this gloom, there shown one brilliant orb, luminescent, as if the source and not the reflection of the lunar glow. It was her, whom he had seen so many times before, her, who he longed to be near, whose hand he longed to hold in his. She was there in the glen, all dressed in white, beckoning for him to come to her.

She spoke. Her voice was soft and melodic, rising amidst her ethereal surroundings. 'You have come to me at last. I have been here waiting, alone, but hopeful. And you have come.' It was then he noticed something. There was a spot of red on her dress, just between her breasts. It was growing, getting larger, she was bleeding. He looked in her eyes. 'Do not be deterred,' she said, 'it is not too late, you might still save me, it is not too late...'

John awoke to a brilliant beam of sunshine coming in through the window of his room. It was so bright he immediately closed his eyes and turned away. Gradually, he opened them again, just a slit at first, allowing his pupils to adjust to the morning light. He slowly allowed his legs to slide over the side of the bed and he let his bare feet get used to the cold wooden floor. He stood up and walked over to the window. Everything always looked so fresh and green after a rain storm, and this morning was no exception.

He had another one of those dreams last night. Although now it was beginning to be difficult to discern what was the dream and what was reality. Had he actually been in the woods last night, claiming shelter from a rain storm? And had he actually seen ghostly images in Pynkinscleugh Glen? Or was it all a dream, right up to the moment he saw the bride in white. But wait, he remembered talking to the waitress somewhere in between. She was not part of the dream, was she? Was it real or dream? He wondered, waiting for the last bit fog to clear from his mind.

It seemed strange that the bride in white was all of sudden speaking to him. And what did she mean when she said she could still be saved. Was this just his subconscious playing tricks on him? He needed a break from all this; the ghost stories, ancient ballads, legends and his family history. It was all occupying too much of his thoughts and that had to be the reason for all these dreams. There was a perfectly reasonable explanation. He was going to leave castle exploring behind. Today he was going to Haltwhistle to see Abby. She would be a pleasant distraction. She would take his mind off things, that is, if she was willing to see him at all.

He got dressed and went down stairs to get some breakfast. As he entered the restaurant, Mr. and Mrs. Crabb looked in his direction and began waving frantically, offering an invitation for him to join them at their table.

"Over here, John," Mrs. Crabb yelled across the room, "come and join us. We want to hear all about your adventures last evening."

"Good morning," John greeted, realizing he wouldn't be able to avoid them this morning. "I trust you slept well. What do you mean by adventures?"

"Tell us about your walk, we heard you were caught in a rainstorm," Mrs. Crabb insisted. "And that you may have run into some ghosts."

"How do you know about that...?" Out of the corner of his eye he caught a glimpse of Janie at the bar, looking a little sheepish. So at least she was real. "Oh, I don't know that I would call them ghosts. It was too dark and misty to see much of anything. It was probably just some people out walking, they were really too far away for me to see clearly."

He was trying to act nonchalant about it, but he wasn't sure it was working. Mrs. Crabb continued to prod him with questions, so he obliged by recounting his entire walk, including every detail, since she would obviously not be content with anything less.

"Sounds mysterious," Mrs. Crabb finally interjected. "Voices in the dark, ghostly apparitions, oh I wish we would have been there."

"Yes sir, John, Mrs. Crabb would have got to the bottom of it," Mr. Crabb joined in. "She would have rooted out those ghosts." He chuckled as he said it.

"Oh, you be quiet George. I'm just sorry that we returned so early that's all. It would've been worth braving a little thunder shower for a chance meeting with ghosts."

"Well anyway, where are you off to today, John," Mr. Crabb tried to change the subject.

"I was going to meet a friend for lunch in Haltwhistle." He was glad that he had some legitimate plans.

"A girl?" Mrs. Crabb asked, while giving him a little wink.

"Well, yes, as a matter a fact, she is a girl. Someone I met on the train on the way up here."

"Good for you John, a fine looking young man like you, should be meeting a girl for lunch," again she winked, causing John to blush a little.

"Were headed toward Haltwhistle this morning ourselves," said Mr. Crabb. "Perhaps we can give you a lift."

"That would be fine," John figured getting a ride from them would not cause any harm. "Let me get my things from my room and I'll be ready to go."

"Take your time," Mr. Crabb assured him. "There's no hurry. Let's say we meet back down here around ten."

"Fine, ten it is." That was perfect. John could actually use a little time to gather his thoughts from the previous night. He took advantage of the time and went for a stroll around Rowfoot.

It was a beautiful morning, the grassy slopes of the surrounding hillside sparkled in the light, still damp from the previous night's shower. There were gay flowers of a variety of herbs bedecking the green grass, and throwing up their bright glances to the sun. And in the leafy shade of the ancient oak and elm trees, he could see slumbering sheep, lazily taking a morning nap, while the winged occupants of the wood, ceaselessly sang out their constant melody, as they fluttered from tree to tree.

It was a peaceful moment and for John it seemed as if time stood still. He was full of mixed emotions, excited that he would have an opportunity to see Abby again, while at the same time fearful that she had already forgotten all about him. He couldn't understand what was happening, how could he already have these attachments to a young woman who he'd only met once, who he really knew very little about? Why did he find himself constantly thinking about her? What was it about her? She was beautiful, to be sure, but he'd known other beautiful girls. What was it about her that was so captivating?

He continued to ponder these things as he returned to his room and packed his bag. He figured he would take a room at an Inn in Haltwhistle, tonight. He'd already planned to take a day trip to Edinburgh by train the next day, and Haltwhistle seemed a good place to call home for the next couple of days. Maybe he could even convince Abby to show him around. If he was to see Featherstone Castle again, to find the Raven's Stone, it would have to be at a later date.

*****

The car ride to Haltwhistle only took a few minutes so John decided to look for lodgings before looking for the Cat and Owl Pub. He found the Laidlaw House Inn right down town on Westgate Road. It was a little early for check in, but the proprietor allowed him to leave his bag at the front desk and then gave him directions to the Owl and Cat Pub. It turned out that it was only a couple blocks away.

He had a little time before lunch so he decided to explore Haltwhistle a little. The village had a quaint charm about it, a lot like Hexham, but a little smaller and not as busy. Not far up the street he found the train station. He stopped in to find out what time he could catch a train for Edinburgh the next day. There was one leaving at nine in the morning and he could catch a return that would get him back to Haltwhistle at ten in the evening. That would give him a full day of exploring at the Univesity of Edinburgh library, more than enough time.

He walked back through town until he came to the Owl and Cat Pub. He stood across the street for a moment just staring at the front of the pub. There were a couple of tables and chairs outside, but they were unoccupied. He stood there trying to summon up his courage. What was he going to say? Maybe he should just forget the whole thing. No, he had to at least see her one more time. Whatever was to happen, he would have to be content knowing he had made the effort. After what seemed like several minutes, he finally crossed the street, opened the door to the pub and stepped in. A bell tingled as he let the door close.

"Go ahead and help yourself to a table, I will be right with you," it was Abby's voice from across the room. She was serving a couple who were sitting at a table at the other end of the room. She hadn't looked up to see who it was.

He sat down at a table just past the entrance, near one of the front windows. He watched her as she had her back to him. Then she turned and began to walk toward his table. When she saw him, she hesitated just slightly, then smiled, and continued toward the table. He took the smile as a positive sign. At least she recognized him.

"Well, hello there," she said pleasantly. "Welcome to Haltwhistle. I'd begun to think you weren't coming." She handed him a menu.

"Hi Abby," he was a little nervous and his voice quivered. "Sorry, I was a bit tied up yesterday." He was pleased to know that she had missed him. It meant that she was at least thinking of him. "How have you been?"

"Fine, thank you. How have you been enjoying Northumberland? Have you seen Featherstone yet?"

"Yesterday, got caught in a bit of a thunderstorm I'm afraid. But otherwise had a wonderful day," John really hated small talk, but he didn't know what else to say. "Can you recommend anything?" he glanced down at the menu, but he really couldn't get his eyes to focus. He looked up and met Abby's eyes. Just for a moment he saw something, something familiar, something warm and inviting. Then she looked down, as if she were a little embarrassed, he was staring.

"The fish is good, and people seem to like the turkey sandwich," she answered.

"I'll have the fish and chips then."

"And what would you like to drink?"

"Do you have coca cola?"

She smiled, as if it were kind of a silly question, "Okay, one fish and chips and one coke. I'll have those for you in just a few minutes."

She turned and walked back to the kitchen. John followed her with his eyes. He then looked over at the couple on the other side of the room. They quickly averted their eyes and pretended to be occupied by their lunch. They'd been watching John and Abby, he could sense it. He turned and looked out the window, trying to look calm and casual.

A few moments later Abby returned to the couple and asked if they needed anything else. She then came to his table, pulled out the chair opposite him and sat down.

"We're kind of slow for now, so I think I can sit for a moment. They should be fine for now," indicating the couple. "So, you visited Featherstone. What did you think?"

"Very impressive, I think more impressive than Willimoteswick," John replied.

"So you were there as well, and Ridley Hall?"

"Yes, and I was able to see Unthank Hall, as well," John noticed a slight smile when he said this. "They were all very intriguing. Everyone I met was extremely helpful, and were not

209

hesitant to share stories. I have gathered I great deal of notes for my research."

"And have you learned more of your family history?" she asked.

"Yes, in fact the vicar at St. John Lee was very helpful. It turns out that I may be a direct descendent of Sir Nicholas Ridley, the one who killed Sir Albany Featherstone."

"Oh, I see, a bit of a black sheep in your past," she said with a smile, indicating she was just teasing, or at least he thought she was.

"Actually, it turns out that Nicholas Ridley tried to avoid the conflict with Sir Albany, but it seems he was left no choice."

The other couple stood up from their table, and they were now preparing to leave. Abby came to her feet and went to see if they needed anything else. She took the payment for their bill and then walked them to the door. She then went back to the kitchen. When she returned she was holding John's lunch. She placed it in front of him and then sat down again. They now had the place to themselves.

"I hope you enjoy this," she said.

"I'm sure I will, although I feel a bit funny eating it in front of you."

"Oh, go on, don't worry about me. I'm fine. Just make sure you leave me a big tip," again she smiled.

John was beginning to appreciate her sense of humor. "Is it always this slow?"

"No, it will probably pick up in a little while. It's a little early for our normal lunch crowd. So you never did say what impressed you about Featherstone."

"It was so well preserved. It was like stepping back in time. The only thing missing was the moat and drawbridge."

"Some think there might have been one once, but it has been filled in. The low fence about the castle may have marked the outer boundary of the moat. Moats became a bit passé by the 18th and 19th century. Did you cross over to the other side of the river?"

"Yes I took a walk through the trees and along the edge of the field on the other side, Pynkinscleugh Glen I think they call it."

"And did you see any ghosts?"

Clearly, she was kidding. "As a matter of fact, I think I did. In fact, I think one of them looked surprisingly like you. Any chance you're related?" He could play at this game as well.

At first she turned just a little serious, but then she laughed. "You never know, my ancestors tend to show up at the craziest times." She laughed again and he joined in.

Just then the door opened and several people walked in. Abby jumped to her feet, grabbed a couple menus and showed them to a table. John continued eating his lunch while he watched her work. Just as she finished taking their order, another couple entered and she had to show them to their table, as well. She was the only one working the room so she also had to bus the table from earlier. Clearly it was getting a little busier. By the time Abby returned to the table, John had finished eating and she was handing him his bill.

"Sorry, John, it sometimes gets like this in the afternoon."

"That's okay Abby, I understand. Say, when do you get off?"

"At four, why do you ask?" Abby was a little pensive.

"I was wondering if you wouldn't mind showing me around Haltwhistle, you know, Abby's special tour, and then maybe later I could buy you dinner in return, what d'ya say?"

"Uh, okay, I suppose that would be alright." There was some hesitancy in her voice.

"Why don't I meet you here at four then?" John was going to stay on the offensive.

"Well, wait, you have to give a girl a chance to get cleaned up. Where are you staying?"

"The Laidlaw House Inn, do you know it?"

"Yes, why don't we meet in front, say at five," she smiled nervously. "That will give me a chance to stop at home, and let my mum know I won't be home for dinner."

"Sounds great, five it is." With that John handed her enough to cover his bill, and provide a handsome tip, and then left her to her work.

As he left, Abby stood staring out the door for just a moment. What just happened? This was going beyond just being polite. This looked very much like a date. She couldn't remember the last time she had gone on a date, and now here she was about to go to dinner with someone she hardly knew, who was from half a world away.

"Hey Miss, could we get some service here," it was one of the customers who had just come in.

"I'm so sorry, what can I do for you?" Abby snapped out of her trance and went back to work. From that point on the afternoon was just a blur. She was barely able to stay focused on work, and was fortunate to not have any mishaps.

*****

All afternoon she kept thinking about John and their chance meeting. It was so random and unexpected; it had completely caught her unaware. She hadn't been looking to get involved with anyone. It was the last thing on her mind. Even so, she did feel attracted to him, at least intrigued. It was hard for her to put her finger on it. It was the way in which he acted a little nervous when talking to her. It was not as if she felt sorry for him. It was just so cute, to have him fumbling over his words; to think that he felt she was worth getting nervous over. She liked him, he was kind, and he laughed at her jokes. It was not as if she felt all flustered around him, it was just the opposite. He made her feel good, he made her feel at ease, and he made her feel right. Something she had not felt since...well, for a long time.

John was on cloud nine as he walked down the street toward the Inn. He invited her to dinner and she said yes. Okay maybe she was a little hesitant, but in the end, she said yes. He was not exactly sure why he felt so giddy. It was only dinner after all. Did he remember where he was? What did he think was going to come of this? He had no expectations, none, at least that's what he kept telling himself. It was just dinner, nothing more.

As he turned the corner, he noticed that the Haltwhistle Library was just across the street. He glanced at his watch. It was quite a while before he would be meeting Abby. He needed something to pass the time. He crossed over the street and entered the front door. The librarian was at the front desk.

"Good afternoon," the librarian greeted, "may I help you?"

"Yes, thank you. I was wondering if you have anything on local history? Maybe something about some of the local castles, like Featherstone, for instance?"

"Oh, my yes, we have a nice collection of local histories. Perhaps we can find something to your liking. Is there anything in particular you are looking for Mr...?"

"Ridley, John Ridley. Anything about the local castles or other places of interest would be helpful. Thank you."

"Mr. Ridley, very nice to meet you, my name is Ms. Thomlinson. I think I have what you need right over here." She then led John to a bookshelf labeled 'Local Interests'. She pulled a book from the shelves entitled *Northumberland Castles: Legend and Myth.* She handed it to John and showed him to a table where he could sit and read in quiet.

John perused the table of contents. There were several entries for local castles, including Featherstone, Thirwall, and Blenkinsopp Castles. He turned to the description of Featherstone Castle and began reading. A part of the entry gave explanation for how the Featherstone family had been divided into two parts.

> *The family has been at several times subdivided into several branches particularly two, viz, of Fetherston<u>haugh</u> and Fetherston<u>halgh</u>. The tradition of the family is that many hundred years ago, Albany Fetherstonhaugh married two wives and had a son by each of them. The first succeeding to his father's estate in Northumberland. The second inherited that of his mother. He was descended from William de Monte*

*who lived in the time of King Stephen, and was
called de Monte from his house situated on Craig-
hill near Stanhope in the county of Durham. She
was the last heiress of her family. And it was to her
estate, which was considerable, that her son
succeeded. The two brothers thought it proper, in
case their families should grow numerous, to
distinguish them by the words "haugh" and
"halgh", the former meaning a "low" place; the
latter a "high" one.*

A little further on, he found a description of the events
concerning the ghostly wedding party. One detail he'd not
heard before, was that the intended groom was one Thomas
Blenkinsopp, of Blenkinsopp Castle, just to the north. Another,
even more striking detail, was the description of the bride's
father waiting for the return of the wedding party.

*Midnight had passed. A deep sleep composed
the baron's harassed frame. Suddenly the sound of
many hoofs broke upon the stillness of the night.
The noise became more distinct. They neared. They
came beneath the frowning gateway. They halted
and again all was silent as the tomb. There was no
challenge of warden, no sound of falling
drawbridge, or jar of opening gates. But all of a
sudden, the door at the foot of the great hall
opened noiselessly and there appeared the bridal
party. Foremost came the bridal and his bride,
then, followed the rest of his troop. All took their
seats in silence, and never a word passed between
them and the host. The baron aroused from his
stupification, now turned towards his guests and
soon found that no earthly company graced the
board. The visage of each was distorted with the
throes of death, and the ashy pallor of many a one
was relieved by a streak of blood. A fearful icy*

shudder ran through his frame, and he arose and crossed himself in agony and affright. A sound, as of a mighty rushing wind chilling the very life sprung, passed through the hall & the unearthly bridal party disappeared. The menials when they awoke from the trance, into which they had fallen, found their master swooning on the floor of the hall. The baron was paralyzed and was to never again utter a single phrase. (William Pattison)

Once he had read the entry for Featherstone a couple different times, he scratched down some notes in his journal and turned to the entry for Blenkinsopp Castle. Much to his surprise he discovered another ghost story, complete with similar mystery and intrigue.

Bryan de Blenkinsopp held the castle some six centuries ago and although a brave and distinguished man on the battlefield, his one weakness was an inordinate greed for wealth. At a wedding feast, he was teased about his own marriage plans but replied, "Never, never shall that be until I meet with a lady possessed of a chest of gold heavier than ten of my strongest men can carry into my castle." Subsequently feeling ashamed of this outburst, Sir Bryan quit the castle and the country. After many years he returned with a wife and a box of gold that took 12 strong men to carry into the castle. But the marriage was not happy because Sir Bryan's wife would not tell him where she and her servants had hidden the chest. Eventually Sir Bryan left the castle and no-one knew where he had gone. For more than a year his bride was grief-stricken and filled the castle with inconsolable shrieks. She sent out servants to try to find him, but they failed, so she went out herself to look for him, neither of them were to be heard of again. It is averred that the

*lady, tortured by remorse for her undutiful
conduct, cannot rest in her grave. She is doomed to
wander back to the old castle, mourning over the
chest of gold, until somebody shall follow her to
the mysterious vaults where it lies buried, remove
it and thus give her unquiet spirit rest.*

As John continued to read, he discovered that just about every castle he came across had some sort of ghost story or some other mystery. He was beginning to wonder if it was more the rule, than not. Somehow medieval castles and ghosts just seem to naturally go together. After reading several other entries, he gave the book back to the librarian. He then asked her if she knew where Blenkinsopp Castle was located. She took out a map and pointed out that is was located a couple miles outside of town, to the north and west.

"Thank you, you have been most helpful."

"You're more than welcome, Mr. Ridley. Is there any thing I can do for you?"

"No, I think I have enough here," he replied as he looked back over his notes. "Wait, maybe I could use your help with one more thing. Do you happen to know when King Stephen reigned?"

"Well, yes, I do," she answered. "He was the grandson of William the Conqueror. His reign was during the middle of the 12th century. Is that all?"

"Yes, thank you," he made a note. "Goodbye, thanks again."

John left the library and walked back to the Laidlaw house. He took his bag to his room and took a moment to freshen up. He went back over his notes from his research at the library to make sure he had not forgotten anything. He then removed the parchment he had found at Willimoteswick. He noted the signature at the bottom and then returned to his genealogy of the Ridleys. He found a reference to a Musgrave Ridley, great great grandson of "The Broad Knight", and named after his great great grandmother, Mary Musgrave, his wife. He was styled the last of the lords of Willimoteswick, having to surrender it to the Nevilles in 1652, after the execution of Charles I. In looking back at the descendents of Sir Nicholas Ridley, he also noticed that his second son Christopher, of whom John was descended, had married Anne Blenkinsop, and thus there had been established a relationship between the Blenkinsops and Ridleys through marriage.

*****

It was starting to approach five o'clock and so John decided to go downstairs and wait for Abby at the front of the Inn. As he stepped onto the sidewalk, he looked down the street in both directions. No sign of her yet. A car pulled up in front of him.

"Get in!" It was Abby.

John was caught by surprise. For just a moment he didn't know what to think or say. He just stood frozen, unable to react.

"Come on, what are you waiting for? I can't wait here forever."

John opened the door and slid into the front seat. "Sorry, I wasn't expecting a car."

"We do have cars you know." She was teasing again, as she pulled away from the curb and started down the road.

"I know you have cars. I just meant I thought we were going to walk."

"That's the advantage of being the tour guide, you get to decide the mode of transportation, as well as the destination."

"Where are you taking me?" John was a little nervous and Abby seemed to be in complete control.

"I figure you have already seen the best parts of town. I thought I would take you to one of my favorite places. Sit back and enjoy."

Within minutes they were leaving the village of Haltwhistle and headed along a narrow country road that was lined by trees on one side and a low stone wall on the other. The further they went, the thicker the woods grew until the over hanging trees were nearly blocking out the sky. As they approached a bend in the road, Abby pulled to the side and parked. Right at the bend was a gate that protected the entrance of what looked like a path for hikers.

"Are you ready to work for your dinner?" Abby asked as she stepped out of the car.

John followed her example, "I suppose so. What is this place?"

"It's called the Burn. There is a stream that flows through the woods here, headed for the Tyne. There are hiking trails that follow the stream to the north, all the way to Hadrian's Wall. I think you will enjoy it. That is, if you like hiking."

"I love to hike, especially in a setting such as this. Lead the way."

They started down the path with Abby leading. She was very much in her element. Every once in a while she would stop and point out some of the interesting features on the trail. She explained that coal used to be mined locally and burned in woolen mills, lime kilns and brickworks that had one time operated along the burn. There were still remnants of these mills, including a lone brick chimney, a testimony to the industry that once flourished here. Much of stone used in the construction of the buildings in Haltwhistle was pulled from the banks of the burn. It was a beautiful setting, completely sheltered from the outside world by huge elm trees. After they had walked for what must have been nearly a mile, Abby stopped and suggested they sit for moment.

It was perfectly tranquil. The only thing to be heard was the soft gurgling of the stream as it gently tumbled over rocks on its way southward, the occasional bird chirping in rhythm, and the slight rustling of the leaves as a gentle breeze passed through the trees overhead. They each seemed content to sit quietly, just enjoying the moment, both waiting for the other to break the silence, neither in a hurry for the silence to come to an end. It was as if neither knew where to begin, what to say.

"This is a beautiful place Abby, thanks for bringing me here." John broke the silence first.

"It is beautiful, isn't it? So peaceful, I find I can become completely lost in the serenity. I think it is important to appreciate beauty, especially the beauty of nature, so simple, yet so glorious. Don't you think?"

"Yes, I do, as well. It's important that we never take for granted what we've been given. It's also important to see the goodness and beauty and to celebrate it…", he paused. "Do you come here often?"

"Whenever I need to be alone, to stop and think. This is a place where I can shut out the world. It's a place I can seek for answers without diversion, where I can be alone with God."

"And now I am disturbing the tranquility," he sounded apologetic.

"No, it's okay. I don't mind. Sometimes, it's important to share it with others. I am glad you are here…" Abby hesitated as if she was sorry that she said it.

John noticed her embarrassment, but tried to carry on as if he was unaware. "I find that I enjoy being alone with my thoughts as well. However, since coming to England I've discovered something new about myself. The quiet can be loud. Too much alone time, can be wearing. I've had many wonderful moments the past few weeks. But not being able to share these experiences with someone else has left me feeling in want. You can't imagine what it is like to go for weeks without having a conversation beyond the superficial.

"I think I can," Abby interjected. "One doesn't have to *leave* home to feel alone."

"No, I suppose not. I guess in my bumbling sort of way, I'm just trying to say how much I appreciate you agreeing to spend this time with me. I realize how strange it must be to have a complete stranger, someone you barely know, let alone from another country half way around to world, ask you to dinner. It had to seem a little forward."

"I must admit, at first I had my reservations. I kept trying to talk myself out of it. However, I consider myself a pretty good judge of character. You didn't seem like a deranged stalker."

"Thanks for that. I do try to make a good first impression," he was trying to make a joke.

"What I meant to say is that there was something about you that made me comfortable. I felt I could trust you. The fact that you were even concerned that you might have been a little forward just confirms it. I was hesitant, and I'm not sure why, but I'm not sorry I said yes. I suppose that I just wanted to find out who you were, I was curious. Or maybe I should say you were intriguing."

"Intriguing, huh, I suppose I will take that as a compliment. As far as finding out who I am, that might be a little more difficult than you realize. Right now, I'm not sure who I am. I mean, I thought I did, but being here, right now, sitting here talking with you, I'm no longer sure. How did I even get here? I don't really know, but I do know I wouldn't want to be anywhere else..."

Abby didn't respond right away. It was as if she didn't know what to say or perhaps she was simply reflecting. The dead air grew a little uncomfortable. "Have you always lived here in Haltwhistle?" He finally broke the silence.

"Yes, I grew up on a farm just on the west side of town. For most of my life it's been my whole world. When I left for school, it was a huge change for me. Even though Edinburgh is not that far away, it seemed half a world away to me."

"Have you ever traveled outside of the British Isles?" John asked.

"Once, just after high school, my parents took me to Paris. They knew how much I enjoyed French literature. We visited the Louvre and Notre Dame and Sacre Coeur. We took a boat trip on the Seine and ate dinner near the Eifel tower. It was a very special time for me. How about you, have you ever been to Europe before now?"

"No, this is my first trip. I have traveled some in Canada, and my parents used to take my brother and I on camping trips in the Blue Ridge Mountains-that's in North Carolina-but I had never left North America until now."

"And how do you like England?"

"Oh, I have enjoyed it a great deal. I think what has been a little surprising is the people. Americans tend to think of the

British as being a little cold and reserved, you know, stuffed shirts and all."

Abby giggled, "Kind of the way we British think of the Americans as being a bit arrogant and petty."

"Yeah, I suppose so," John agreed. "Abby, what were you studying when you were at the University of Edinburgh, I mean, what were you hoping to do?'

"Well, French literature has always been my interest, however, what I really wanted to do was teach, you know, grammar school. I really enjoy children. What about you, do you enjoy children...?" Abby stumbled over the words again, and her cheeks became flushed. "...er, I mean did you ever think about teaching something other than college, maybe high school?"

"Well, I suppose so. The truth is, I don't really see myself as a college professor. I sort of fell into the graduate program without really thinking it through, where it was taking me and all. I think teaching high school could be good if it were the right situation. The trouble is, I'm afraid I would grow impatient with students who don't seem to care enough to invest themselves. I'm sure that I would find it frustrating."

"Yeah, I know what you mean," She said. "I would be disappointed if my students did not care, as well. I suppose that is why it's important to teach the things we are truly passionate about. Perhaps you will find a way to encourage that passion in your students." She jumped to her feet. "Well I think we better keep going, or you will never get a chance to buy me dinner tonight." She smiled as she said it and then began walking up the path, leaving John still sitting, looking at her in bewilderment.

He jumped to his feet and quickened is stride in an attempt to catch up. The trail began to descend slightly. Abby looked over her shoulder, smiled a bit and then began to run. John was caught off guard and had to sprint to catch up. Reaching the bottom, the trail changed and started to climb. The going was a little more difficult, but that was not enough to deter Abby, she continued to run, until he finally caught up to her. She then slowed to a leisurely stroll, and as she looked over at him, she gave him a wink. He was out of breath and unable to make any comment.

They walked on in silence for a few minutes, and before long emerged from the trees. There was nothing but rolling hills in all direction. Not far ahead was a road, but Abby kept leading on the path that ran along the stream as it flowed parallel to the road. Eventually the source of the stream turned to the north and went beneath the road. Here they stepped out onto the edge of the road and walked east. Just a hundred yards down the road, where it intersected with a road running north and south, there was a country inn. It was their destination for dinner. The restaurant had several tables outdoors, and since it was still early they figured they had plenty of daylight, so they decided to eat au fresco.

As the waitress handed them their menus, John asked, "Is there something you could recommend, Abby?"

"The flat iron steak sautéed in mushroom sauce, is very good."

"Sounds good, I'll have that," he said.

"Make it two," Abby added.

"Do you think you will ever go back to school?" he asked after the waitress had left.

"Oh, I don't know. It doesn't seem likely…I don't know how I could afford it, especially now that my dad is gone."

"How old was your father…when he passed away?"

"He was fifty three; he had a heart attack, completely unexpected. My Mum, was completely devastated. That is why I asked her to come live with me. I thought it might be easier, you know."

"Wow, it must have been hard. Do you have any siblings?"

"Yes, my older sister Jane, she's married. She lives with her husband over in Carlisle, not too far away. We get to see each other often. What about you? You haven't told me anything about your family."

He proceeded to tell her everything about his parents and his brother, his home town of Beaver Falls and how he ended up in Illinois. He told her how his advisor had encouraged him to take the fellowship and go to Oxford (leaving out the part of breaking up with Annie). He even told of his trip to visit his great grandmother in Canada and how she had given him the book about his family history.

"Have you always been interested in your family history, the Ridleys that is?"

"No, not really, I mean, I suppose I liked to hear stories about my relatives and ancestors, but it was never that meaningful to me until now. I feel more connected to it, maybe because it has been driven partly by my research, but mostly because it says something about how I came to be, maybe why I am here."

"You mean here in England?"

"No, that's not exactly what I meant. I meant here on earth, but maybe in some ways it might have something to do with why I am here in England as well. I don't know. I guess that's what I am trying to figure out. It's not just the family history. It's history in general. Why are we concerned with the past? Why did ancient people sing ballads and write poetry, chronicling the events of their lives and then pass it on to their children? Why was this important? I mean, have you ever thought of how you got where you are? What about your own family history, do you know who you are?"

Abby blushed, she hesitated just a moment before responding, "I think I know who I am, but I sometimes wonder where I am going. I also wonder why things are the way they are?"

John sensed he must have touched a nerve, "like your father dying?" Abby nodded. "I'm sorry Abby. I don't mean to drudge up the pain."

"No it's okay, I don't mind. I loved my dad, I'm grateful for the time we had. I'm not bitter or anything, it's just that I don't totally understand why? It's not that I need to understand why, it's just that I don't."

"It must have been really hard, for you, losing him so unexpectedly."

"Yes...I guess it was. I wasn't really able to grieve, not at first. I was just numb. Then as the feeling came back, the pain came with it. It wasn't as if I was crying all the time or anything like that. There were moments of grief interspersed with moments of peace. But every once in awhile, I would find myself really missing him, you know, at special moments..." A tear started well up in Abby's eye.

He stayed silent for a moment. He needed to change the subject.

"What are you going to be doing tomorrow?" he asked.

"...uh, I don't know, I hadn't really thought about it," she seemed caught off guard. "I'm not working, if that's what you're wondering. Why, what did you have in mind?"

"I'm going up to Edinburgh tomorrow, to the University, I could really use a guide. What do you say, would you be willing to put up with me for the day."

"I...I don't know John. I am not sure that is a good idea."

"Come on, I could really use the company. Besides, I will cover the whole trip, train ticket, meals and all. You would really be helping me out."

"When will you be leaving?"

"There's a train leaving at nine tomorrow morning and if everything goes well, we'll catch a train that will get us back around ten tomorrow night."

"I don't know, I think I'm going to have to think about it."

The sun was just about down to the horizon as they were finishing their meal. "We'd better get started back. We don't want to get caught walking in the Burn in the dark."

John agreed, he paid the check and they headed back the way they came. The walk back was fairly quiet. He was hoping he hadn't put a damper on the evening. He probably shouldn't have pushed so hard for Abby to go with him the next day. She was obviously a little nervous about the whole idea. Maybe he was expecting too much.

Abby was alone with her thoughts as they walked back along the path. John seemed content to remain quiet. She knew that he was disappointed that she was hesitant about going to Edinburgh with him. It was written all over his face. What was she going to do? She really enjoyed being with him, but could she seriously consider spending tomorrow with him. What was she thinking? Where was this going?

224

As they entered the trees lining the burn, the sun had already disappeared behind the hills. It would be dark soon. She quickened her pace. As she walked, she became riddled with guilt. She wasn't being fair to John. She was holding back. She hadn't told him everything. Did she need to tell him everything? After all in a couple of weeks he would be going back home to America. Nothing would come of it. Of course, if nothing would come of it, then what difference did it make what she told him. Still it wasn't fair, he should know the truth. He's a really decent guy. The truth was she really liked him. The truth was, down deep, she really wanted something to come of it.

Is that how she really felt? What was she thinking? It was impossible. He was from half way around the world. What if he did know the truth, what then? He might just turn tail and run and she would never see him again. Maybe that was for the best. Oh! What was she going to do?

She spent the entire walk back to the car, playing mental ping pong. Just about the time she had herself convinced it would be okay to go, she would completely reverse her position and argue that it was inconceivable that she would even consider going. In the mean time John was being extremely patient. He seemed perfectly content to remain quiet. Was he upset? He didn't seem upset. Just ahead was the car.

The drive back was just as quiet. As they pulled up to the front of the Laidlaw house, John finally broke the silence.

"Thanks, for a wonderful time Abby. I can't begin to tell you how much I enjoyed your company. It was a beautiful hike, and I appreciated you showing it to me. I would never have known the Burn was there."

"It was my pleasure, John, I too had a wonderful time," She tried to think of something else to say.

"Look, about tomorrow," John began as he was getting out of the car. "I don't want you to feel any pressure about it. Really, I just thought it would be nice for you to come along, a stranger in a foreign land and all that. But, I wouldn't, in any way, want you to feel uncomfortable about it. I tell you what, I will be at the station at 8:45, if you decide you want to come, I would love for you to meet me then, but if you decide not to, don't worry, I will completely understand. I'll be here for a few more days. Perhaps we can see each other again, in any case."

"Thank you John," Abby was still wrestling with what to do, what to say. "Good night."

"Good night, Abby."

Chapter Eleven

...she was standing alone in the shelter of an ancient, now dead, oak. The dead branches cast dark eerie shadows over the night landscape and the brilliance of the full moon illuminated everything within its reach as it peaked between the receding clouds. The ground was still wet from the recent thunderstorms and the air was still heavy and damp. She could feel her heart beating beneath her breast. She was content to stand her ground. She had stopped running, whatever was coming, she was prepared to face it, with courage and resolve.

In the branches, she could see the dark silhouettes of ravens. They sat motionless, staring at her with iridescent eyes. Why were they watching her? It was unsettling.

Across the glen, emerging from the shadow of the forest was a rider on a silver horse. He was a warrior, dressed in armor and mail that shimmered in the moonlight. In his right hand he held a sword; it glistened brilliantly as he turned slightly and looked over his shoulder. Without warning he applied his heals to his charger with a sudden thrust, causing his battle weathered companion to bolt forward in a gallop. Together they flew across the glen in a direct line for where she now stood.

She stood her ground, frozen in time. It would do no good to run, he had already seen her. She was completely vulnerable and in submission to whatever fate this moment held. As the warrior and his mount drew close, the steed suddenly rose upon its haunches coming to an abrupt halt. The knight sheathed his sword in a flash, and did something quite unexpected. He leaned forward extending his hand to her.

'Take my hand, milady, before it is too late. Fear not, I am not here to harm you. I am here to save you. You may trust in me, my life is yours...'

Abby jumped up in bed. Her room was bright with the morning sun. She turned quickly to examine her bedstand clock. It was 7:45. She had no time to waste. She must hurry if she was going to make it to the train station. She clamored out of bed and ran to the bathroom. She turned on the shower, and then ran back to her closet, where she proceeded to lay out the clothes she wanted to wear. After a quick shower, and even quicker dress, she bounded down the stairs into the kitchen. Fortunately her mother was up and had already put the tea on.

"Good morning, Mum," She greeted, as she popped a slice of bread in the toaster on the counter.

"Good morning, Abby," her mother greeted back, with a sort of sly smile, as if her daughter was up to some sort of mischief. "It looks as if you have made up your mind to go."

Abby had wrestled with it all night. Her mother was waiting up for her when she got home and the two of them talked about it late into the evening. As always, her mother was slow to offer any kind advice. She was comfortable with her daughter living her own life, making her own decisions. She was more of a sounding board, and although Abby appreciated her mother's lack of interference, there were times she wished for an opinion.

"Yeah, I've decided to go," she bit her lip as she said it. "Why, don't you think I should, do you think I'm making a mistake?"

"It's not for me to say, Abby," her mother smiled; consistently non-committal. "You have to find your own path. I have known that for a long time now. I just want you to be happy, and don't want you to get hurt."

"You think I am going to get hurt?" Abby was still wrestling were decision.

Her mother just stood there smiling, and shaking her head. "If you're going to go, you'd better hurry, or you're going to be late. Maybe when you get back from Edinburgh, you might bring this young man around so we can meet him."

Abby downed the last bite of her toast, took a final sip of tea, grabbed her bag and was out the front door. Before the door had a chance to close behind her, Abby came back through the door and skipped back up the stairs. She had nearly forgotten something.

As she arrived at the train station, she could see John waiting in front of the ticket counter. She stopped for just a second, weighing her uncertainty. He turned to face her. Their eyes met and she knew there was no going back now. She continued walking toward him.

He smiled. "Good morning, Abby, thanks for coming."

"Well, I couldn't let you go wandering around Edinburgh by yourself. If tomorrow's paper had a report of some tourist getting lost and mugged in the big city, I would never have been able to forgive myself," she smiled. She didn't want him to read anything into this. As far as he was concerned, she was just a tour guide, nothing more, well maybe a friend and tour guide, but nothing more.

"Thanks, I feel much safer, now that you are here," John smiled, indicating he wasn't buying it. He turned to the counter and requested a second ticket from the agent.

Abby felt a little awkward letting John pay for her ticket, but she decided to let it go. As he paid for the ticket, she gave a quick look around the station. She was hoping there was no one there that recognized her. The last thing she wanted was for someone she knew to see her getting on a train with some stranger. The local gossips would have field day.

As she settled into her seat, she leaned back and closed her eyes. It was the first moment she had to think about the dream she had last night. She didn't understand what was going on. She typically never remembered her dreams at all, and now in the past week she had three very vivid dreams that she not only remembered, but had to convince herself were not real. Could it mean something?

"Someone didn't get enough sleep last night," John kidded.

She opened her eyes and smiled. "Why is there something wrong with the way I look?"

"No, I didn't mean..."

"Relax, I know what you meant. I must admit, I'm a little tired, a bit of a bad dream. Actually bad, is not the right word, just a strange dream."

"Do you want to talk about it?"

"No. Not especially; maybe later. What are we hoping to see today? What mysteries are we going to unravel?"

"I don't know if we will be doing any unraveling today. We're just on an information gathering expedition. I do want to see a bit of the city, but the main objective is to go to the University of Edinburgh Library. I have been told that they have an exceptional collection of Sir Walter Scott's notes and such. Although my research is into ancient oral traditions, it seems as if Scott's name comes up the most when talking about authors who made the greatest use of these traditional sources."

"Is there anything specific you are looking for?" Abby was not just making conversation, she was genuinely interested. Although Scott was not one of her favorite authors, she couldn't help wonder about the connections Dumas may have had to oral histories as well.

"In Oxford, I came across a footnote in an older edition of one of Scott's works that made reference to Beardie Grey. It makes me wonder if Scott knew anything of the history of Pynkinscleugh Glen, you know the ghost story and all.

Abby hesitated before commenting, carefully selecting her words. "This ghost story seems to be of particular importance to you. What are you hoping to find?"

"It's not just this story. In the case of the ballad about the death of Sir Albany Featherstone, it seems there was more to the story than what first meets the eye. It's possible the same is true for the story concerning the death of these two lovers. I have a suspicion that there is something more to it. It seems unlikely to me that the girl's father would have been so adamant about his daughter not marrying a Ridley because of something that had happened a hundred years before, long before he had ever been born. What kept the feud going for so long? Or is it possible it wasn't about the feud at all? Who was this groom and why was the father so insistent on this marriage?"

"Or maybe it was just what it was. He just didn't like the Ridleys. After all, not all the Ridleys are as likeable as you," Abby was teasing again. "My theory is that it's your American upbringing that makes you a little more bearable." She laughed as she said it.

"Okay, very funny," John laughed with her. "Maybe you're right. Lord Featherstone merely disliked the young Ridley. But if there is a chance there was more to it, then I think it is worth pursuing. Either way, the more evidence I gather about these legends, the more likely they end up becoming authentic historical accounts, regardless of the details."

"Do you remember me telling you about Dumas' book, *Ten Years After?*" Abby asked. John nodded yes. "Remember how I said that it left me believing that the musketeers had actually been a part of a failed plot to save King Charles. I wonder if Dumas used any oral traditions or legends to establish his story line. For example, were there legends about musketeers who had actually lived that formed the basis for his characters? I think I heard once that his father might have been the source for the character, Athos."

"That's exactly what I am talking about," John interjected. You see, my belief is, if there are enough separate sources making reference to a legend, then the legend starts become less of a legend and more of a historical account. After all, what is history, but the stories that have been passed down from generation to generation? And, how far removed is historical fiction, from history textbooks? Take, for example, Charles Dicken's *A Child's History of England*. It reads like historical fiction, however, it is collaborated by other sources, other histories, even though Dickens had given it his little twist. This makes it more likely to be credible."

Their conversation continued until they reached Carlilse, at which point they had to change trains. Before long, they were on their way again, headed north and east toward Edinburgh.

Knowing that it would be more than an hour to Edinburgh, Abby decided to take advantage, so she leaned back in her chair to catch a short, but needed, late morning nap. John let her sleep and was content to sit back and enjoy the scenery of southern Scotland.

He could barely hide his excitement when he first saw Abby at the train station that morning. He laid awake part of the night worrying that he might have pushed her away the night before. He looked over at her, admiring her angelic continence as she slept in the seat next to him. She was beatiful, and the more time he spent with her, the more they talked, the more he realized that he was starting to fall for her. He knew that he shouldn't even be contemplating such thoughts, but it was a little too late for that now. It was so unexpected. They had only met five days ago. How, in such a short time, could he possibly let himself get emotionally attached? He knew he was setting himself up for disappointment. There was nothing that could come of it.

The rolling hills of the countryside flew by the window outside and he tried to think of something other than Abby, with very little success. No matter where his mind drifted it kept coming back to her. As he stared out the window, the rhythmic sound of the train wheels clicking over the seams of the rails beneath caused him to grow sleepy, until he could no longer resist and he let his eyes close.

He was not sure how much time had passed when he opened his eyes again. Abby was still sleeping in the seat next to him, but now her head was resting on his shoulder. Her hair smelled a bit like lilac-probably her shampoo-sweet and tantalizing. He remained as still as he could, he didn't want to wake her. He could feel her breathing, rhythmic and easy. In that moment he felt as peaceful as he could ever remember feeling. He would have been perfectly content for the moment to go on forever. A message came over the intercom that they were approaching Edinburgh and it was only fifteen minutes until they arrived.

Abby stirred and then opened her eyes. At first she seemed to be unsure of her surroundings. Then all of sudden she realized that she had her head on his shoulder and she jumped up with a start.

"Sorry, I guess I must have fallen asleep. I didn't mean to be so presumptuous as to use you for a pillow."

"Think nothing of it," John assured her. "It wasn't entirely unpleasant. Besides, it seems I drifted off as well."

As they pulled into the station, Abby explained that they were within walking distance from the University and the Library at George Square. Fortunately, the train station was centrally located and they could see plenty, without having to make use of any buses or cabs. John suggested that the first order of business might be to find a place to eat lunch. She suggested a favorite place she had frequented when she was a student.

After John and Abby disembarked from the train, they exited the station and walked across the North Bridge, which afforded a beautiful view of the city. They continued down South Bridge Street toward the University. Just a few blocks down the street, she grabbed his arm and pointed to the place where she thought they should get some lunch.

As they ate, he asked her where she had lived while a student. She attempted to draw a map of the campus with her fingers on the top of the table, pointing out some of the major landmarks, and then describing where her flat had been and its proximity to the various buildings making up the campus. Realizing that John was having a hard time following her invisible map, she laid a napkin out on the table and began creating a rough sketch of a map of campus, showing the major buildings. She included George Square, showing its location relative to where they were now eating.

After lunch, Abby took them on a direct route to George Square. On the far end of the square was the main library. John was immediately impressed with the modern architecture, it seemed a bit out of place in such an old city. It was nothing like the Bod at Oxford. Together, they walked around the square to the entrance of the Library. As they entered the front lobby, he began to wonder how he should proceed. Where should he start? He walked up to the front desk at the main entrance; Abby trailing behind.

"Excuse me," he tried to get the attention of the person behind the desk. "I was wondering if you could help me?"

A young man not much older that John looked up from whatever he was reading and smiled, "Aye, what can I do for ye?"

It was the first time he had heard such a strong Scottish accent, "I am a visiting student, from the United States..."

"Aye, an American are ye?"

"I've been doing some research on the work of Sir Walter Scott, and I understand that you might have a collection of his notes and journals as a part of the library collection."

"Ye might try the sixth floor, Research and Collections. Ask for Mr. McNeal. He should be able to help ye. The elevator is just there to your left."

John and Abby took the elevator up to the sixth floor. Mr. McNeal was on duty at the research desk. John explained that he was a visiting graduate student from America and doing research on the life and work of Sir Walter Scott.

"Yes, we do have a number of items in our Scott collection, but I am afraid you might have to be a little more specific. Is there something in particular you are interested in?"

"I'm looking for any reference that Scott may have made to the area in Northumberland around Haltwhistle and Featherstonhaugh Castle. Including any mention he might have made in regard to Pykinscleugh Glen or a witch living in the area by the name of Beardie Grey."

"I see, Northumberland, the Border Wars and such. I am sure we can find something that will be of help. Perhaps some of Scott's personal notes and journals might provide you with something."

"That's right, exactly."

"Hmm, let me think," Mr. McNeal stroked his chin lightly as he thought about where to begin. "Give me a moment. I will be right back." With that, he disappeared, leaving John and Abby standing alone at the desk. With nowhere else to go, they decided to sit at a table in a nearby study area, and wait.

Mr. McNeal had been gone for several minutes when Abby stood up from her chair. "John, if you don't mind, I think I will take a walk. I imagine you'll be tied up here for some time, and there is no use me getting in the way. It's a nice day out. I might as well take advantage and get some fresh air."

"Sure Abby, you go on ahead. I'll be fine. And you're right, I have no idea how long this is going to take."

Abby smiled, gave a little wink, and then made her way to the elevator. Just as the elevator doors closed and she had disappeared from sight, Mr. McNeal returned carrying several items in his arms. He carefully laid everything out before John on the table.

"I did find a few things. Are you familiar with Marmion, and the reference to the ancient ballad concerning the death of Sir Albany of Featherstone Castle?"

"Yes, I am. I suppose I should have explained. I have been researching this ballad and I am looking for evidence which would support its authenticity. At the same time I have come across other legends from the same region that may have had some connection to this ballad," John was hoping that the librarian was not going to provide him with the same sources he had already acquired. His only reason for coming to Scotland was the hope of finding something new.

"You are no doubt familiar with the notes in Marmion then?" Mr. McNeal asked.

"Yes, very familiar."

"Perhaps this might help. This is a transcription of Scott's actual journal and contains his original notes on this entry in *Marmion*. It is possible that there might be something here that was not included in the published version. There is also a collection of his notes on the *Border Minstrely,* which you may find helpful. I thought you might be interested in these as well," he pointed to two more works: *A Bibliography of Sir Walter Scott: A Classified and Annotated List of Books and Articles Relating to his Life and Works 1797-1840*, published by a James Campbell, and a copy of *Sir Herbert Grierson's Edition of the Letters of Sir Walter Scott,* just recently published. He then pointed out a table nearby where John could sit and work quietly without interruption.

"This Bibliography was published by a Librarian who used to work here and is now retired. If you come across anything in this list that would be of interest to you, I'm sure I can procure it for you. Just say the word."

John felt his optimism growing. He was hopeful of finding what he looking for. "Thank you," he said as he spread everything in front of him on the table. "This looks like a really good start. I will let you know if I need anything else."

*****

Abby stepped outside and paused a moment to catch her bearings. It was sunny and pleasant outside, not always a common thing in Edinburgh, so she decided to take a stroll through Meadow Park, just south of the library. It was nice to be back in Edinburgh. She had loved her time as a student at the University. She missed it. There was something about the academia that had always excited her. She always had felt as if she was headed somewhere, moving forward. It made her feel alive. Not like the past year, when she had felt as if the world was standing still, and she was fixed in time and space, unable to look past each day.

How did she come to be here again? It seemed incomprehensible. What was she doing? It was not like her, to do something so brash, so spontaneous. She had always lived her life cautiously, keeping her ducks in a row. What had made her throw caution to the wind?

As she walked, she thought of what she needed to say to John. She was starting to feel a little ashamed that she hadn't told him everything from the start. She was torn. At first it didn't seem important to tell him her whole life story, but something was happening she couldn't quite explain. Was she reading more into this than she should? Did she really need to say anything to him at all? What difference did it make if he was leaving in a couple days and she would never see him again? The truth was, she didn't want him to leave, not now. She really wanted to see him again. The thought that he may leave and she would never see him again, made her distressed. But how was that possible, how could she possibly feel this way? She had only known him a short time.

*****

John's enthusiasm waned slightly as he began scanning the pages of the volumes that Mr. McNeal had given him. It didn't take long for him to realize that the task before him was a little more difficult that he had first imagined. There was far too much material for him to be able to read and disseminate in the short time that he had.

He started with the notes on *Marmion*. Despite being more detailed than the footnotes in the published poem, John didn't find anything substantial that would shed additional light on his research. There were a few more details of the circumstance in which Scott had first heard the ballad concerning the death of Sir Albany. His source had been a woman who was very advanced in age and who had first heard it when she was a little girl. Scott described the setting in which he met the woman and her own recollection of the origins of the ballad, which was clearly nothing more than supposition. The woman had insisted that the events and persons in the ballad were real and accurate, but she was relating an oral tradition more than 180 years after the events had actually taken place. Although an interesting account, it didn't provide any new revelation.

The collection of Scott's personal correspondence, proved to be far more rewarding. It provided a special insight into the life and even personality of the author. John was particularly fascinated by the correspondence between Scott and his bride to be, Charlotte Spencer, during the months leading up to their nuptials in December of 1797. At one point Scott tried to justify their all too brief courtship and insisted that the suddenness of their romance should not be cause to consider it less real.

*You seem to doubt the strength or at least
the stability of my Affection. I can only protest to
you most solemnly that a truer (love) never
warmed a mortals breast and that tho' it may
appear sudden it is not rashly adopted.*

*You yourself must allow that from the nature
of our acquaintance we are entitled to judge more
absolutely of each other than from a much longer
one trammelled with the usual forms of Life-and
tho' I have been repeatedly in similar situations
with amiable and accomplishd women the feelings
I entertain for you have ever been strangers to my
bosom except during a period I have often alluded
to.*

It seemed that Scott was as much a romantic in life as were the characters in his novels.

As John continued to read and take notes he felt a gentle tap on his shoulder. "Excuse me Mr. Ridley, I don't mean to disturb you, but I may have something else that would interest you." John looked up from his work. "I took the liberty to make a phone call to James Campbell, the editor of the work there in front of you and who, although retired, still resides here in Edinburgh, and nearby, at that. He is sort of the local expert on Scott, and in fact compiled a rather large collection of artifacts and even correspondence from the life of Scott, all of which he donated to the Library when he retired five years ago. I thought he might be able to provide some other sources for your research. He was very interested in your mention of Pynkinscleugh Glen. So much so, that he would very much like to meet you. If you would be of a mind to see him, I could direct you to his residence. I explained that you were from America and would only be here for a short time, and so he suggested that you visit him this afternoon."

John could hardly believe his ears. "I would love to meet him, thank you..."

"Fine then, he has a flat on Lutton Place. Here I will draw you a map," he pulled out pen and paper and proceeded to draw a map, complete with directions.

Abby had returned from her walk a little earlier and was in earshot of their conversation. "Oh, I know where that is. It's not far from here."

"That's right," Mr. McNeal confirmed. "Mr. Campbell said he would make himself available to receive you any time this afternoon, at your convenience."

John felt he was not going to get much further with his present task, and talking to Mr. Campbell might prove to be far more profitable. Anyone who had dedicated himself to becoming an expert on Scott, would have far more to offer in the way of directing John to the right sources to look for credible information. If nothing else, once he talked with Mr. Campbell, he could always come back to the library. Besides Abby and been particularly patient waiting for him, and it would probably be prudent to provide her with a change in setting. He had been so engrossed in what he was reading, that he had not even noticed that she had returned.

"Sorry Abby, I didn't know that I would be so long. I sort of lost track of the time. I hope you haven't been too bored."

"No, not at all, I completely understand. Besides, I'm quite capable of occupying myself. I had a very pleasant walk, and I still have not finished Robin Hood," Abby held up the book so John could see. "Did you find anything of interest?"

"It hasn't been a total waste of time, but I was hoping for something a little more substantial. I kept holding out, hoping that I would come across something, but there was nothing new. Perhaps this Mr. Campbell might provide us with some help. Are you ready to go?"

Abby stood up from her chair, "lead on."

"Actually, I think you'd better do the leading."

She smiled, "Of course, follow me. Don't give up, it sounded to me as if Mr. Campbell may already have something for you. After all, why would he invite you to meet with him?"

"That does sound reasonable. I can only hope your right." John had been thinking the same thing. He'd been pleasantly surprised on more than one occasion by British hospitality, but it seemed as if Mr. Campbell was going a bit out of his way, since he had no idea who John was. Just being American couldn't be enough to warrant an audience."

Abby took the lead and they walked eastward toward Lutton Place. According to the map that Mr. McNeal had scrawled out, it was not more than a few blocks away. In less than a quarter of an hour they were standing in front of Mr. Campbell's residence. It was a two story complex, divided into personal apartments.

Mr. Campbell had a flat on the bottom floor. As John knocked on the door he could feel a slight twitch of nervousness. As the door opened he scrambled for the words to say. "Hello. Are your Mr. Campbell? My name is John Ridley, this is my friend Abby, Mr. McNeal from the University Library said you would be expecting us."

"Yes, I'm Mr. Campbell. Welcome, come right in Mr. Ridley and Miss…"

"Brown," Abby added.

"I'm happy to meet you both, please, come in, make your self at home. I have just put some tea on, would you like some," Mr. Campbell turned and walked toward what must have been the kitchen.

John and Abby found themselves standing alone in a sitting room. Four comfortable chairs, none of which matched the others, sat at the corners of a low coffee table in the center of the room. Abby chose to sit in one of the two facing toward the kitchen door, John sat in the other.

A few moments later, Mr. Campbell returned with a serving tray holding tea service for three. He gingerly laid it down upon the table and poured tea into each of the cups.

He was an elderly man with wavy silver gray hair. He was wearing a blue oxford shirt and beige slacks. He had round wire rimmed spectacles that sat a little low on his nose, so as he served them their tea he had to peer over the top rim to look at them.

"Help yourselves to milk or sugar," he offered, as he sat in one of the chairs opposite them. "Is there anything else I can get you," they both shook their heads no, "no, well then if you are both comfortable, then perhaps we should get started."

"Mr. Campbell, I want to thank you for taking the time to see us, I can't begin to tell you how much I appreciate it...

"Please, call me James; there's no need for any formality here. I must admit, I don't normally invite students to come and see me, however, when Mr. McNeal called, I was intrigued by your requests. I've spent a lifetime collecting documents and artifacts from the life of Sir Walter Scott. I've had numerous requests from researchers all over the world, but you were the first person who has every tried to make a connection between Scott and Pynkinscleugh Glen. I have to ask, what prompted you to ask about this particular place. I have never seen any mention of Pynkinscleugh in reference to the murder of Sir Albany Featherstone."

"It wasn't a direct connection," John explained. "While researching Featherstone Castle, I came across several references to a ghost story that had its beginnings more than a hundred years after the death of Sir Albany. It was concerning a sort of Romeo and Juliet saga in which the two lovers died at the edge of Pynkinscleugh Glen. However, I have been trying to find an explanation for the tragedy, and to see if their forbidden love was in any way connected to the feud between Sir Albany and the Ridleys a hundred years earlier. What is your interest in Pynkinscleugh?'

Mr. Campbell smiled and then reached down to pick up a binder in front of him. "Early in my career, just after the war, I was at an auction and ran across a letter in Scott's hand that he had sent to his friend and publisher early on. Since I had just begun my collection, it was a special find for me, and fortunately I was able to purchase the letter at a fairly reasonable price. When I donated my collection to the University Library, I decided to keep this one item back. I think, once you have a chance to examine it you will understand why. It has a mystery to it that I was never able to decipher. Now it's possible, together, we might be able to unravel the riddle."

He opened the binder revealing a hand written letter on yellowed paper preserved in a plastic sheave. As John looked closer, he could make out the date at the top, September 18, 1797. The ink on the page had turned brown and faded with time. The script was difficult for John to read. "This is incredible, Mr. Campbell, I mean James. It's a little difficult for me to decipher. What exactly does it say?" John asked.

"Look here," Mr. Campbell turned the page revealing a typewritten transcription of the letter. He handed it to John, who in turn began to read it aloud.

Wednesday, December 28, 1797

Dear James,

I trust that this letter finds you in good health and pleasant demeanor. Thank you for your recent correspondence and congratulatory remarks regarding our recent nuptials. Charoltte sends her love, and although disappointed at your absence at our marital union, she conveys her understanding, recognizing that circumstances are not always within our control. It was most appropriate for us to stay our honeymoon at Gisland Spa, considering it is the location of our fateful first meeting. We had a wonderful time and were blessed to enjoy beautiful weather the entire time.

I can not help but to tell you of a most unusual event that occurred while my dear Charlotte and I were exploring the local countryside. On one of those unusual winter mornings when the sun was bright and the air was crisp, bright and warm enough that even a few song birds ventured to leave their nest, we decided that it would be a nice day for a ride. We had heard about the splendid condition of Featherstonehaugh Castle of that ancient family of the same name. Taking advantage of the surprising atmospheric conditions we decided to set out early on horseback in hopes of reaching the castle before noon.

As we neared the southern portion of the Tyne River we had to pass through a wood before arriving at the bridge that would allow us access to the boundaries of the Featherstonehaugh estate. The path through the wood was heavily traveled and easy to follow, although the environs were of a mysterious and foreboding nature. The ancient elm and oak of the forest nearly blocked out the sun, creating an appearance of night at midday. You can be sure that my bride was feeling uneasy, even though her Lord and protector never left her side.

As we approached the end of this tunnel through the shadowy foliage we found ourselves both surprised and alarmed to come upon an old women sitting before us on an immense moss covered stone. Her hair was completely white and unkempt, falling in length to her shoulders and back. Her clothes were soiled and tattered and it was quite clear that it had been a great deal of time since her last bathing. Her face was weathered and wrinkled and her eyes were dark, no doubt dilated from the continual darkness of the forest. As she smiled at us she revealed teeth that were yellowed and decayed. In all, she was a frightening sight, even for one who has seen many unnerving images in even so short a life span.

As we reined in our mounts, motionless before her, she suddenly spoke with a whiny, scratchy voice. "So you have come to see the witch have you. You have come to find answers to that which is hidden. The wise will listen, the wise will hear what the witch has known."

I of course responded that I did not have the least idea of which she spoke, that we were merely travelers looking for Featherstonehaugh.

"Oh so it is Featherstonhaugh you seek. Then you will hear what the witch has to say, you will listen carefully, if you seek what is true." She then began to speak the following poem. I am now able to repeat it to you in its entirety only because she repeated it twice, perhaps thrice, during our encounter with her.

At Pynkinscleugh there was much

gentil blood spilt that day,
For the father of an only daughter
had lost his way,
To trade for gilt and glitter that eternal gleam,
And realize the loss in the twilight of the horrid
dream,
But wait not all is lost, for love knows no time,
There is another who will come,
With cautious heart and anxious mind,
She does not know what ransom waits,
But she must follow the ravens from the gate,
Follow the ravens from the gate.

At the end of this recitation she laughed an eerie laugh that chilled Charlotte's heart, and perhaps mine as well. She then ran off into the trees. When she was out of our sight, we turned our horses down the path and almost immediately emerged from the trees onto a little stone bridge that crossed the river.

Later as we visited the castle we asked the house steward if he knew anything of a witch living in the forest beyond. He responded that there was a legend of a witch by the name of Beardie Grey who had a cottage near the bridge, however, she had not been seen in many years and was presumed to be dead. This of course was somewhat unsettling to both my new bride and I.

I was confident that you would find this story most amusing. Perhaps I will one day be able to make use of this character, Beardie Grey, in my writing.

Until we see each other again, God bless you.

Your friend,
Walter

John looked up from what he was reading, not really sure what to say. "Amazing," he uttered. "This is one of the most fascinating discoveries yet. It connects Beardie Grey, Sir Walter Scott and the ghost story."

"It is rather fantastic, isn't it," Mr. Campbell said, smiling. All this time I have had it in my possession, but I was never able to connect it to anything. Scott never mentions it again. So you can see why I was particularly interested in any light you might shed."

At this point John began to relate to Mr. Campbell everything he had discovered up to this point. He described how he had come across the note about Beardie Grey and then how he kept hearing stories of the ghosts of Featherstonhaugh from the local inhabitants of the Tyne River valley. Meanwhile, Abby didn't say a word. She simply sat musing, while John and Mr. Campbell traded stories.

When John was finally finished relating everything he knew, Mr. Campbell posed one more question, "But what do you think about this poem. Do you have any idea what it might mean?"

John thought for a moment. "I'm not sure, but I can't help but think it is making reference to the father of Abigail Featherstone. The blood spilt was obviously a reference to the death of the wedding party. But, I'm just not sure of its entire meaning. Like any poem, it is not immediately obvious. This part about 'another one will come' might be a reference to another member of the family. I don't know, it is very strange." He then took out his note pad and quickly copied the entire poem.

The two spent another hour talking, while Abby sat quietly, sipping her tea. She was caught up in her own thoughts, trying to come to her own conclusion about the poem. It was a strange poem and the more she thought about it, the more it disturbed her.

"I'm sorry Abby," John finally remembered she was also present. "We've been completely ignoring you. I imagine all this talk of Scott is little mundane for you."

"No, no that's alright," she really wasn't feeling left out. "I totally understand. In fact I have enjoyed listening. You are both obviously passionate about this topic."

"In any case, we have taken up too much of your time already, James," John turned to Mr. Campbell. "We probably should be getting along. I wonder if I might impose upon you a little further. Would it be okay if I write to you on occasion if I have any more questions?"

"Only if you promise to let me know if you are ever able to decipher this poem," Mr. Campbell returned.

"It's a deal." John stood to his feet, followed by Abby and Mr. Campbell. They were escorted to the door and as John and Abby stepped out onto the street, he turned to face her, "Thanks, this was very profitable. Thank you, for bringing me, and for waiting patiently while the two of us rambled."

Abby smiled, "I'm glad I came, really. It's all rather exciting. I wouldn't have missed it." She meant it, sincerely.

They spent the remainder of the afternoon and early evening touring Edinburgh, with Abby playing the part of guide. She wanted to be sure that John was able to enjoy a close up view of the Edinburgh Castle. While they were passing through Greyfriars Kirkyard they came across the statue of Greyfriars Bobby. Abby proceeded to tell John the story of the Yorkshire terrier that refused to leave the graveside of his master. As she was telling the story she reached over and took his hand in hers. It was not a conscious act, just something that felt natural. They continued their walk to the castle, hand in hand.

The evening train back to Carlilse and Haltwhistle didn't leave until just before seven. That gave them time to have dinner before the trip back. During the entire dinner, John could talk of nothing, but the letter that Mr. Campbell had shown them. Like everything else, one new revelation led to another mystery. He was intent on unraveling the mystery of the poem.

As he was looking back over his notes, he drawn back to the beginning of Scott's letter, "This place, Gilsland Spa, does it still exist? Do you know where it might be?"

"Yes, as a matter of fact, it's still a resort, even after all this time," Abby said.

"Do you think you could show it to me?"

"I suppose so, if you think you have time." Abby replied.

"Great!" he said.

Abby realized that her role as tour guide had just been expanded. She had been hoping to talk to John on the train trip back, but it was clear that he was a little distracted. She didn't mind. She was happy for him, and it gave some time to think through what she was going to say.

Overall, it had been a successful trip. The connection John had made with Mr. Campbell was clearly a relationship that would pay many dividends in the future. She was glad that she had come.

By the time they arrived back in Haltwhistle it was nearing eleven. John insisted on walking Abby to her door, she tried to resist, but he would have none of it. As they walked up the street toward her apartment, he reached down and took her hand in his. She looked up at him and smiled. They didn't say anything as they walked.

When they arrived at Abby's front door, John broke the silence first. "Good night Abby, thanks again. I had a wonderful day. It wouldn't have been the same without you."

"Good night, John, I enjoyed it as well. I'm really glad I came."

They were standing close, face to face, their hands still touching. John hesitated slightly and then he leaned toward her in an attempt to kiss her goodnight. To his surprise Abby raise her hand and gently placed her fingers on his lips.

"I don't think we should," she said, biting her lip as if she was nervous. "I mean, it's not that I don't want to. I do. But not yet, there is something I must tell you, something really important."

"Go ahead I'm listening," John's countenance grew serious.

"No, not now, tomorrow," Abby was not sure why she kept putting it off, but she knew she was vulnerable right now, and it was not the right time.

"You promised to show me Gilsland Spa, how 'bout then," John was not going to let her off the hook.

"Okay, tomorrow, but I have something I have to do in the morning. Come around noon and we will go on a bit of picnic."

"Sounds great!" John smiled.

Abby turned and went to the door. She paused and turned back, "Goodnight John, I really did enjoy our day together, until tomorrow then."

"Goodnight Abby, until tomorrow."

Chapter Twelve

...he emerged through the trees and stopped for a moment, trying to catch his breath as he looked out over the meadow in front of him. There she was, standing at the top of the rise, not more than fifty yards away; the moonlight creating a halo at the edges of her white gown and veil. She was turned toward him, facing him, as if beckoning him to come forward.

He started forward, slowly, carefully, so as not to startle or frighten her. He had been close before, but each time she would escape into the mist. This time seemed different, he was now only twenty yards away and still, she remained. He could see glimpses of her features beneath her veil; her eyes were dark and penetrating. Another step, and then another, and still she remained where she was. Ten yards, then only five, and then he was standing immediately in front of her; so close he could hear her breathing, so close he could reach out and touch her. He could sense the tension in her frame, she wanted to flee, but could not. This time there was something forcing her to stay. What was it? What was different this time?

Slowly, her hands rose from her side and felt for the edges of the veil draped across her breast. With one slight movement she took hold of the veil and lifted it straight up, pulling it aside, revealing her face.

Undefinable emotions welled up inside of him to the point of eruption, he was excited, confused, and awed, all in the same moment. She was beautiful, but she was not a stranger. She was familiar, he knew this face. How did he know her? Why did he know her? How was it possible?

John rose and enjoyed a leisurely breakfast in the dining room of the Laidlaw House, after which he took a morning walk. It was another beautiful morning and it was nice to be able to be alone with his thoughts. His emotions had been strung tight from the events of the previous day. He was still very excited that he'd had the opportunity to meet Mr. Campbell. He would obviously be a tremendous resource in his research of Sir Walter Scott. John couldn't have been more fortunate.

He still didn't know what to make of Abby. At times she was warm and sincere and then, all of a sudden she would be a little distant, as if she didn't want to get to close. He understood, he didn't really know where their relationship was going either. It seemed unlikely that they could form any real attachment in so short a time. However, he could sense that down deep, he was falling in love with her. He didn't see how that was really possible. None the less, it was happening and he no longer felt in control of the situation. He realized that it was highly improbable that anything could come of it, but he couldn't ignore his feelings. He had tried to resist his emotions, to persuade himself that he was being foolish and impetuous. Despite this ongoing internal debate, he continued to cling to the hope that what he felt was real, and that there was more to it.

Just when he thought Abby felt the same way, right as he was about to kiss her, she put up a brick wall. Could he possibly have misread her entirely? Was she just being nice, and could it be that she didn't really have feelings for him? What did she mean when she said that she had something she needed to tell him? What was she hiding? Why couldn't she just tell him? Maybe she was just afraid, like he was. Maybe she was unable to see any real potential in their relationship. Maybe she just needed time to find the right words to tell him to get lost; after all she was nice, and probably didn't want to hurt his feelings.

The more John thought about it, the more it drove him crazy. Abby said she would come by at noon, which was too far off. He needed to occupy himself. He decided to go back to his room and do a little writing in his journal. Maybe if he thought through his conversation with Mr. Campbell and reviewed his notes, it would be enough of a distraction to get his mind off of her. That was it, he needed a diversion; to think about something besides Abby.

It was so quiet in his room, that John could actually hear the tick of the clock as the second hand moved in its never ending circle. He was able to do a little writing, but as he reread it, he realized that it was nearly incoherent. Tic, tic, tic... He was beginning to worry about his lunch meeting with Abby. He couldn't help but think about it. He believed he was about to get some bad news. Why else would she have been so hesitant? She was going to tell him that she couldn't see him anymore. That had to be it. But why do it over lunch, why not just have told him last night. She did promise to take him to Gilsland Spa, but that couldn't be the only reason she was seeing him again, or was it?

At a quarter of twelve, John was standing on the sidewalk in front of the Laidlaw House. He figured it would be better to wait there, rather than pace in his room. He kept staring at the pavement, occasionally kicking at a pebble with his shoe. He felt a sense of relief when Abby's car pulled up. At least the waiting was over. He opened the door and slid into the passenger seat.

"Hello, John," she greeted. "I hope you're ready for traditional English picnic. I know of an excellent place out by Gilsland Spa."

"Sounds great," before he could even get the words out, the car lurched forward and they were on their way. Once they left Haltwhistle, all that John could see, was endless miles of rolling hills, sheep pastures, bordered by stone walls and hedges. For several miles the landscape barely changed. If he hadn't known better he would have thought they were traveling in circles.

Eventually they passed through the little village of Greenhead and then turned north. A little further on they passed through the village of Gilsland and John assumed they must be getting close. All the time, Abby remained quiet. She didn't even take the opportunity to play the part of tour guide and describe any of the places they were driving past.

"Are we almost there?" John asked, breaking the silence.

At that very moment, they pulled over to the side of the road and stopped. They were parked in front of an old country church. It was constructed of stone and had a small steeple and bell tower. Abby jumped out of the car, and then turning to look back through the door, "Well, what are you waiting for, we're here."

He opened the door and joined Abby as she opened the boot, as she called it, and helped her unload a blanket and a picnic basket. She led the way to where there was a small gate that opened into a small cemetery on the side of the church. He followed, right on her heels. He was a little perplexed. She proceeded to open the blanket out on the grass at the edge of the cemetery. Despite being a little confused, he went along with it and provided what a assistance he could.

Finally, he could contain himself no longer, "Where are we? Do you mean for us to have our lunch in a cemetery?"

"Why not, I don't think they will mind," she was indicating the gravestones. "If you look over there," she was pointing toward a distant hill, "That is Gilsland Spa. I don't think you can find a better view than from here. This has always been one of my favorite spots. I love this little church, and although it may seem a bit strange to be sitting in a cemetery, I doubt that we could find a more private place to enjoy our lunch." This she said while opening the basket, and proceeding to spread the faire out onto the blanket. Meanwhile John remained standing, dumbfounded and unable to think of how to respond.

"Oh, come on and sit down," Abby instructed. "It's not as if there are any ghosts here to be worried about. Where is your sense of adventure?"

"It's not that I am afraid, exactly, after all it's broad daylight. It just seems a bit weird, that's all. I mean, I don't really know the etiquette of cemeteries. Is it considered appropriate to have lunch in a cemetery? I don't want to show any disrespect."

"Once again, I don't think they'll mind. After all, they're dead. I assure you, I have sat and eaten lunch here on more than one occasion and I have yet to have any problems with any angry apparitions," she smiled as she said it.

Even though John was feeling a bit unsettled, he didn't want to make a fuss. At least Abby had not lost her sense of humor. He gradually warmed to the idea, and without any further objections, he sat down and took the plate that she was holding out to him. As they were about to begin eating, Abby bowed her head. Without hesitation, he followed her lead. There was a moment of silence, followed by "Lord bless what we are about to partake." He thought it kind of funny. They had already had two or three meals together, and it was the first time he had seen her offer a blessing. It was nice, but it made him wonder, why now, what was different?

As they started eating, Abby looked back toward Gilsland Spa, "that is essentially the same place that Sir Walter Scott and his wife would have visited in 1797. The buildings have been remodeled a few times since, of course."

"And how far is it from Featherstone?" John asked.

"Eight to ten kilometers, I should think. It would have taken the better part of the morning to go there by horseback, although they would have been able to take a fairly direct route."

They sat eating in silence. John looked out over the landscape. He could see what appeared to be the western extension of the Roman wall. In the distance, on the northern horizon, there were clouds gathering, otherwise it was a beautiful afternoon, and although they were sitting in a cemetery, it was a very pleasant setting.

Abby finally broke the silence, "I'm sorry about yesterday...I mean last night." Her calm exterior and turned anxious and she was reaching for the words.

"It's okay," John tried to ease the tension and give her some assurance that he was fine. "I understand..."

"No, you don't understand…I don't understand, I mean…" she paused again. John let the silence hang in the air. She was obviously trying to get something off her chest, and he thought it better not to interrupt.

"I'm sorry, this is just so confusing. We have only known each other for a week. Clearly something is happening that is more than just a casual acquaintance or chance friendship. It's not that I didn't want to kiss you last night. It's just that I don't know what to expect. I don't know where this is going…"

"I know, and I do understand," He tried again to reassure her. "I am just as confused. This just doesn't happen…"

"No, you don't understand, not entirely. Please, let me try and explain."

"Okay, I'm listening."

"It's not just that we have only known each other a short time," Abby began again. "You see, I'm married, I mean I was married… I'm a widow. I lost my husband, Mark, a year ago. I know I should have told you sooner. When we first met it didn't seem that important, after all, I didn't ever expect to see you again. Then later, it seemed like there was never the right moment. Well that's not exactly true, I think down deep I didn't want to scare you off. For the past year, I haven't even as much as looked at another man. I've not even been on a date. I must admit, that when I met you it was different. When you first asked me to dinner, it seemed safe, after all you were going to be leaving and I would never see you again. You were so nice, it seemed harmless. I had no idea that it would go this far. Not that it's really gone anywhere, at least not yet."

"How did he die, your husband?" John's first was of shock when he heard the word married. Watching Abby, as she tried to explain, his shock soon turned to empathy.

"His name was Mark, Mark Brown, he was in the military. He was killed in the Falklands…stupid war."

"I'm sorry, Abby. It must have been horrible for you."

"Mark and I had practically grown up together. His parents live in Newcastle, but every summer he would come to visit his grandparents at Unthank Hall. We met one summer when we were about thirteen and became friends, then later fell in love, and were married the summer before he joined the army. I didn't want him to join, but his father had been in the RAF during the war, and it was sort of a family thing to do."

"I think I met his grandfather at Unthank," John interrupted.

"That's right. He's there all alone now. I still go and check in on him from time to time."

"We were very much in love. I was devastated when I heard the news. For several months, I could hardly breathe. I had lost a part of myself and I didn't know who I was anymore. I didn't think I could go on, but down deep I knew I had to."

"I am sorry, Abby. No one should ever have to go through something like that. It sounds as if you loved him a great deal. I wish I knew the right words to bring you comfort. I don't always know the right thing to say or the right thing to do, but I do know that I have to...well, say...Abby, I have fallen in love with you. I don't understand it entirely. I know we have only known each other a very short time. It doesn't make sense, but maybe it doesn't need to. The fact that you were married and are now widowed doesn't change a thing. If anything, your devotion to Mark only makes me love you more. I realize this makes you conflicted, and for that I'm sorry, the last thing I ever wanted to do, or ever want to do is to cause you any pain, to make you feel uncomfortable. I love you, it's real and it's true. I know it, I can't explain it. I just know it."

Abby was silent, she looked away, toward the rolling hills beyond. John sat watching her and waiting, wondering if he had said too much. After a lengthy silence, she turned back to face him. She looked strained, worried.

"John, I just don't know how to feel. A year ago I was in love with Mark. Then I lost him. Now I may be falling in love with you. How can that be? We have only known each other a few days. A few days, it's incomprehensible. Every time I think of walking away, something draws me back. I don't understand what is happening. You're from half way around the world. How could anything come of this?"

John thought for a moment. "Look, I know we are from two different worlds. It's not immediately obvious how anything could happen between us. However, is it possible we were brought together right now, at this very time and place, for a reason? Is it possible that it was just meant to be?"

"Wait. Let's not get ahead of ourselves. Before you go any further, there is something else you need to know...Once again, I should have told you this before. I don't know why I didn't. I wish there was an easier way to say this." Abby started rummaging around in her purse. She then pulled out a photo and showed it to John. "Here," she said as she handed it to him.

"I have a daughter, her name is Maggie, she's almost three, and she is my whole life."

He looked at the picture and then looked at Abby. She was nervously biting her lower lip. He smiled, "she's beautiful. Why didn't you tell me? Do you think this would change the way I feel. It doesn't. I love kids. If you let me love you, I'm sure I will love her as well. It doesn't change anything."

Abby took the picture back and looked at it. "I don't know why I didn't tell you. I think it was because I was afraid. Afraid that you would run away and I would never see you again. But that doesn't make sense. The only reason I would be afraid is if I was falling in love with you. But, that can't be. This just doesn't happen."

"Who's to say that it doesn't happen? Who's to say that two people can't meet and in a few days know that they were meant for each other, that it was just meant to be? After all, time was not on our sides. If we didn't fall in love at first sight, so to say, then it would never happen. So, maybe it had to happen just as it has."

"I don't know, this whole 'it was meant to be' thing is a little hard for me to get my mind around," Abby was still putting up a fight. "After all, what you're saying is that it is a part of God's plan. But how does that work? Was it a part of God's plan for me to fall in love with Mark and the two of us marry? Was it a part of God's plan for him to die in the Falklands? Was it a part of God's plan for Maggie to be born and then to be left without a father?"

John paused a moment to reflect... "Look I don't claim to have all the answers, but I do believe that our lives have purpose and that in some way our lives are intertwined with the plan and purpose of our Creator. There are times when some individuals are more important to God's purpose than others, such as Abraham, or Luther, while others are of less significance. I don't know whether our lives are of particular importance to God's purpose, but we can never know that. Regardless, we are still a part of the plan and the events of our lives are not random, but are determined.

It's like this. God may have known all along that Mark was going to die in the Falklands. We don't understand the why or how of this, it's far too complex for us to have that kind of understanding. But, just because Mark was going to die, does that mean he should have never known you, that he should have never loved you. Would you have denied him the opportunity to have loved you just so that you would have been spared the pain of his loss? Is it possible that God brought you together for the expressed purpose of being able to share your love together, because he knew that in the end Mark's life would be cut short? And what's more, if you had not fallen in love, you would not have had Maggie. Is it possible God brought you together just so that Maggie could be born? Would you have given up Maggie to avoid the pain of losing her father?"

Abby looked at him as he spoke. There were tears forming at the edges of her eyes. She knew in her heart that he was right, she had always known. The tears were not of sorrow, they were of joy. It was at that moment, she knew she loved him.

John waited for a reply, but none came. "Is it possible that the first moment we met on the train, was a moment intended. We were meant to meet. And although we have only had a few days together, it was enough. It was enough for us to start down the journey to this moment."

"And so where do we go from here?"

"I don't know. It's not always for us to know where we are going, just where we have been and where we are now. What I do know is that right now, right here, I am in love with you. I can tell you how we arrived here, or at least how I arrived at this moment, but I can't tell you why. I am not sure that I will ever know why."

"It seems a little less than romantic." Even though Abby believed what John was saying was true, she was still resisting it. There was something that wouldn't let her give in. "What I mean is, wouldn't it be more romantic if you loved me, well just for me, not because it was meant to be, that it was predetermined."

"Call it fate or call it destiny, whatever you want. Just because the events of our lives are not entirely in our control does not mean that it is less romantic. Did Jacob love Rebecca less just because their coming together was a part of God's plan?"

Abby paused for a moment before responding, "So it all goes back to that moment on the train. Somehow I knew it then, when you first introduced yourself and I winced at the mention of your name."

"My name, what does my name have to do with anything."

"John, my last name is Brown. That is my married name, not my maiden name."

"What's your maiden name?"

"Featherstone," Abby paused and allowed it to sink in. "My name is Abby Featherstone, Abigail Featherstone to be exact. Don't you see, from the very first moment I was afraid to tell you my real name; to tell you who I really was. I was afraid that you would read into it or something. Maybe you would think something ridiculous, like we were the reincarnated souls of John Ridley and Abigail Featherstone. That we were meant to be together, and here you are telling me exactly that."

This caught John a little off guard, but he plodded ahead. There was no use going back now. "Look, I don't believe in reincarnation any more than you do. We are not the reincarnation of two souls that lived four hundred years ago. But you have to ask yourself why you didn't want to tell me your last name, your maiden name. Why were you so afraid of what might happen? All you had to do was say goodbye to me on the train, and never look back. Why did you agree to see me again? Especially given the prospects were not good, that is, me being from half way around the world, and all."

"I don't know. I was afraid of..." Here Abby stopped. It was as if she was afraid of what the next words out her mouth would be.

"Afraid of what? You still had a choice to make. You could've still said no when I asked you to meet me. But, you didn't. I don't know how our choice and God's plan works together. Most of the time it doesn't make sense to me either, but then again I realize that I'm rarely, if ever, the one in control. Whether it works for my good, is not dependent upon my understanding. There is very little I understand about love. But right now I know that I love you, it's not just a feeling, but a certainty. I can't imagine having not known you. If it's God's plan and purpose for us, then that brings with it a confidence that it is right and true. I don't think you can get more romantic than that."

"I was afraid of you. Don't you see, I'm afraid of falling in love with you. What happens if I fall in love with you and then you up and leave and return home? Okay, it's not the same as losing Mark, but I really don't want to go through that again. Once is enough. I'm not even sure I'm ready to love again, even if it were someone from around here, I would be afraid."

"But that is the way love is. You give, you love, and then at some point it can be taken away. Mark's death was a tragedy, and I can't begin to tell you how much it grieves me to know that you had to endure it. However, everyone dies. I will die, you are going to die. This means that when we love, we always are under this cloud of knowing that someone could die. But you have to ask yourself, would you have chosen to have never known Mark, to have never shared the years you had together, just so you would not have had to experience the pain of his death? Hearing you now, I can tell how much you loved him. Would you go back and do it differently, if you could?"

"No, you're right. I wouldn't have given it all up, knowing Mark, having Maggie, just to avoid the pain of this past year. I loved him, and it was right and it was good. But now, I don't know. Is it right for me to love you? Is it right to give away my heart again? I'm so confused. I need more time, but that's just it; time, there's not enough. Time brings growth, it allows for healing, it allows for love to blossom and flourish. Where is the time?"

"Right now, I wish I could stop time, but I can't. We can't. I don't want to lose this moment, or the next moment to come. I know there are circumstances here that are creating what appear to be insurmountable obstacles. I don't know what tomorrow holds, anymore than I understand the events of the past."

Abby didn't say anything. John allowed the silence to continue a moment before adding, "I don't know why the Abigail Featherstone and John Ridley of the past were unable to be together. I don't know the mind of God. But I also don't think it has anything to do with us. In other words, I don't think we are here in this moment, because we were destined to reclaim the love that they lost. It's possible that the tragedy of their lost love was used to bring us together. Not that they had to lose their lives for our sake. However, it was their story as well as the story of Sir Albany that brought me to England. What was destined for them is exactly what happened, but that doesn't mean that the circumstances of their lives, of history, could not be used to bring us together now. It is at least possible."

Again it was silent. And then Abby spoke, "time, if only there was more time." Abby sat looking toward the distant hills.

John turned away and looked in the same direction. In the distance, clouds were gathering. It was clear that a storm was gathering, although it was still some distance away. The tops of the clouds were like stubby fingers reaching for the sky, with the tops brilliantly lit by the afternoon sun. Beneath the clouds, descending all the way to the horizon, it was dark, a mixture of grays and purples. They sat quietly for several minutes. He knew that it was best to give Abby some space; realizing that he had just unloaded a great deal. He had no intention to attempt to persuade her to his own convictions. She would need to discover on her own the nature of her own heart. He would have it no other way. Finally, Abby broke the silence, again.

O though here fair blows the rose,
and the woodbine waves on high,
And oak, and elm,
and bracken fronds enrich the rolling lea,
And winds, as if in Arcady, breathe joy as they go
by,
Yet I yearn and I pine for my North Countrie!

I leave the drowsing South,
and in thought I northward fly,
And walk the stretching moors
that fringe the ever-calling sea,
And am gladdened as the gales
that are so bitter-sweet rush by.
While grey clouds sweetly darken
o'er my North Countrie.

For there's music in the storms,
and there's colour in the shades,
And joy e'en in the grief so widely brooding
o'er the sea;
And larger thoughts have birth amid
the moors and lonely glades
And reedy mounds and sands
of my North Countrie!

"That's beautiful," John nearly whispered. "What is it from?"

"I'm not sure I remember. It is something I memorized in school. Some English poet I presume. I just have always liked it...I just need a little more time. Is that okay?"

"Of course, not just okay, but absolutely reasonable. I'm not trying to convince you of anything, please know that. I just want you to know how I feel and I want to know how you feel, what you think." John said this while still looking out at the impending storm.

Abby leaned over and gave John a kiss on the cheek. She then whispered in his ear, "What I feel and think is that I am very glad I have met you John Ridley."

Before John could respond, Abby jumped to her feet. "Now we had better get moving. That storm is headed our way and I still have one more place to show you before it gets here."

Together they quickly packed up the remnants of their lunch, folded up the blanket and headed back to the car. John had wished that they had the time to explore the inside of the little stone church, but it looked as if he would have to wait for another time.

As they drove through the country side, they were both quiet. At one point John asked, "Where are you taking me?" Only to have Abby respond with the very brief, "It's a secret, be patient."

They were on the road for only a few minutes before Abby turned off the main road onto a small single lane road that was lined by a post and wire fence that then turned into a stone wall. At the end of the road, John began to discern what appeared to be the remnants of an old castle. It seemed to be a little out of place, for it stood less than fifty yards from the barn and house of a working farm. It was almost as if the farm had simply been built around the ruins, as if they weren't even there.

Abby parked the car near the wall got out, indicating that John should do likewise. They walked across the road and stood in front of a placard. "These are the ruins of Thirwall castle," Abby explained. "It was believed to have been first built in the 12th Century, very old, and in great need of repair."

The castle no longer had a roof, and in fact the walls were crumbling and in various forms of decay and disrepair. In some places there were no walls at all. Still, one could discern that it had been a fortress at one time. Entirely made of stone a couple of the walls still reached a height of twenty or twenty five feet. In the walls were very narrow windows, indicating that the need for defense was greater than the need for light from the outside.

Abby took John up to the top of the rise on which the castle sat. She then took him around one side to a place where the wall was completely gone. She then took him by the hand and led him into the interior.

"Now here you have real history. You can feel it in the stone," as she reached out and touched the stone wall. He did the same. "Thirwall means, near the wall. This would have been one of the first castles encountered by invading marauders from the north as they passed over Hadrian's Wall. The Thirwalls were an ancient and prominent family. It is said that Sir Percival Thirwall was the standard bearer for Richard the Lionheart. Like most ancient castles of this land, it too has its own fantastic story.

It was told that a Thirwall once returned from the wars, perhaps Sir Percival himself, laden with treasure including a large gold tablet. Furthermore, it was described that a hideous dwarf was set to the task of guarding the tablet. Upon hearing of this treasure a Scottish chief invaded the castle, slaying the Lord and all of its inhabitants. However, the dwarf and the golden tablet were never found. Tradition has it that the dwarf threw himself and the tablet into a draw-well. It has never been seen since, and so it is believed that somewhere around here, hidden beneath the surface, is a draw-well which contains the treasure."

"Very interesting," John smiled. "I wonder, have you ever tried to look for it?"

"Once, when I was just a young girl; you know, the fantasies of a young romantic."

"Yes, I can just see you rummaging all through the pasture land hereabouts, the whole time believing that you were destined to find the treasure."

"Something like that," Abby laughed. Whatever melancholy spirit had possessed her was now gone. She was almost giddy. "I love coming here. I used to sit for hours, right here," as she plopped down on the grass that now occupied the floor of the castle. "I would fantasize about all sorts of wonderful adventures that may have happened within and without the walls of this castle. I would become completely lost in my dreams until my mother or father would wake me from my day sleep. I suppose it all came from reading too much Dumas."

"I'm not sure. I don't know of any young boy or girl who does not have a fantastical imagination. I, for one, had my share of living out adventures in my daydreams. But unlike you, I didn't have the advantage of being able to daydream while surrounded by these ancient walls, or any other castle, for that matter."

Abby lay back in the grass. John lay down beside her, the two of them looking up into the sky. They remained there quietly, staring at the blue sky that showed through the non-existent roof. After a few moments he felt her hand take hold of his. He closed his fingers lightly around hers and then gave a gentle squeeze. Nothing needed to be said. They lay there for sometime before John noticed clouds moving across the top edge of one of the walls. He turned his head slightly and looked over at Abby. Her eyes were closed. He wondered if she was dreaming now, and if so what was she dreaming? She seemed so content, so peaceful. Just then a raindrop hit his cheek.

"Hey, Abby are you asleep? I think I just felt a raindrop. I think we'd better get out of here."

Abby opened her eyes, just as a large drop landed on her nose. The splatter caused her to blink. "I think you're right." She jumped to her feet. "Come on, I think it is going to let loose."

Together, they emerged from the castle only to find the sky had grown very dark. They ran, hand in hand toward the car, but it was too late. Just as they were halfway there, the sky let loose. No longer a sprinkle, the rain came down in a torrent. By the time they hit the bottom of the hill the grass had already become slippery and it took every bit of coordination they had to keep from falling into the mud that was already gathering at the edge. The fact that they were still hand in hand was probably what prevented them both from falling on their backside. As they each jumped into their respective seats, they slammed their doors simultaneously. They turned to face each other, only to break out in laughter. They looked like a couple of drowned rats.

"I could go for a spot of tea," Abby said while giggling. "What do you think?"

"Sounds great," John agreed. Something hot in a cup would take a little of the chill out.

"Fine, I know just the place."

Despite the pouring rain splashing against the windshield, resulting in very poor visibility, Abby was able to navigate the narrow, now muddy roads without too much difficulty. They were soon back on the main road headed back toward Haltwhistle. A few miles more and she turned off onto a side road, and then pulled into a car park that was along side what sort of looked like an old pub adjacent to the ruins of another castle.

"I think you'll like this place. This is the Blenkinsopp Castle Inn. It is a restaurant that has been built next to the ruins of Blenkinsopp Castle."

"As in Thomas Blenkinsopp?" John asked.

"The very one. Thomas Blenkinsopp, who was to marry, the now infamous, Abby Featherstone, or maybe I should say, the original Abby Featherstone." She smiled as she said it.

Braving the rain, the two dashed from the car to the entrance of the pub. As they entered, they each tried to shake off as much of the water as they could. The place was nearly empty so they took a table that was near the fire place. Fortunately, a small fire had already been lit, and they would be able to take advantage of its warmth.

A waitress came to take their order. "Tea, please," Abby said without hesitation.

"For two," John added. "And do you have any thing sweet on the menu?"

"We have some fresh baked apple tarts," the waitress replied.

John looked to Abby, she nodded her head yes, as she was still trying to straighten her disheveled hair and clothes. "Two please, thank you."

Even soaking wet, Abby looked beautiful and graceful. Despite this, she excused herself to the W.C. He sat alone with his thoughts, gazing into the flames of the fire. Just as Abby returned, the waitress arrived with their tea and tarts.

"Well look who's here! George, look!"

John couldn't believe his ears. He turned to look. Sure enough, it was the Crabbs. They had just entered the pub, and Mr. Crabb was having difficulty folding an umbrella in his hands. John looked back at Abby. She had a sort of playful and curious look on her face. He rolled his eyes. She just smiled back. He turned and looked again at the Crabbs. They were already making their way to the table. There was no escaping. He rose to his feet as they arrived.

"Abby, this is Mr. and Mrs. Crabb. We met at a B&B in Hexham. Mr. and Mrs. Crabb, this is Abby Brown." John almost stumbled over the name Brown. He nearly said Featherstone, and was glad he managed to catch himself.

"Please call me Emma, and this is George," Mrs. Crabb jumped right ahead. "Aren't you the sweetest thing? Abby, was it? My, don't you make the cutest couple? Don't they make the cutest couple George?"

"Yes dear, very cute," by this time the two had already pulled up two chairs to the table where John and Abby were sitting, without invitation, as this was their habit. John was showing the signs of a nervous fidget. Abby just smiled and took it all in.

"John, what a fantastic chance that we should run into you here," Mrs. Crabb continued. "And this must be the girl you told us about, the one you were going to meet in Haltwhistle. But you never told us how adorable she is, simply adorable. Isn't she adorable, isn't she George?"

"Yes, adorable," George was merely being agreeable. It was clear he had something else on his mind. "My, that apple tart sure looks good. Waitress, could we see a couple menus? I'm starved, how about you Em?"

"Oh George, you're always thinking about your stomach. I want to hear more about this young lady."

At this point, Mrs. Crabb, in her usual non-tactful way, began to grill Abby with questions about her personal history; where she lived, what she did for work, etc. Fortunately, she didn't inquire about her marital status, probably because she assumed that Abby was unmarried. John didn't want to have a discussion with the Crabb's concerning Abby being a widow, with a child.

Once done inquiring after Abby, Mrs. Crabb went on to give the personal history of her and Mr. Crabb, much of which John had already heard. Abby played the role of interested party admirably, and John patiently waited for the awkwardness of the moment to go away. Of course, he wasn't sure that he could count on the awkwardness ever going away as long as the Crabbs were present. As much as he wanted to be alone with Abby, he was not about to be rude and send them away. Abby seemed to sense his apprehension and nonchalantly reached under the table, grabbed his hand and gave it a squeeze. This was accompanied by a slight wink, unnoticed by either Crabbs, giving John the assurance that she understood, and she was quite comfortable playing along and enduring the two curious newcomers.

At some point, the conversation came around to why the Crabbs were there. "We came to visit the ruins of Blenkinsopp Castle, of course. John, don't you remember, the whole reason, we came to Northumberland was to visit castles. We were wandering around the ruins when the whole sky let loose. Fortunately, Mr. Crabb is never without his umbrella or we would have been drenched. Clearly the two of you were not so fortunate." Although drying nicely, John and Abby still had the look of a good drenching.

"So, John, did you hear about the White Lady?"

John had no idea what she was talking about. "What white lady?"

"The ghost that inhabits Blenkinsopp castle," this time it was Mr. Crabb taking the lead. "It seems that hundreds of years ago the Lord of the castle boasted that he would only marry a wife who brought with her a dowry of gold so large that it would require a dozen men to carry it. Eventually, he was able to secure such a wife, only to have her become enraged and jealous to the point of taking the gold and hiding it in the dungeons beneath the castle. The Baron was so irate that he left the castle, never to return. The lady then wandered the castle in grief until she too disappeared without a trace. It is said that her ghost still wanders the castle crooning for her lost husband. Furthermore, the gold was never found and it is believed that it is hidden somewhere beneath the castle."

"Never found, huh," John said. "It sounds a bit like an old wives tale. Certainly men would have been digging for centuries until they found it. No one would leave a treasure of that kind buried all this time."

"I'm just telling you what we have heard," Mr. Crabb insisted. At that moment the waitress arrived with their food. "Waitress, Miss ..., have you ever heard of the treasure of Blenkinsopp Castle?"

"Sure, who hasn't," the waitress replied.

"Was it ever found?"

"Well, no, I don't think so. Although some people say that the Blenkisopp family spent it over the years. Evidently they were very extravagant. One story I heard stated that they had given a part of it away."

"Gave it away?" Mrs. Crabb was now asking the questions. "Why would someone give away a chest of gold?"

"Something about making a contract or some kind of ransom, I think, I'm not sure. In any case, most everyone still believes that it is still buried somewhere. But nobody really knows where to start looking." With that, the waitress returned to her duties.

George and Emma Crabb began their own dialogue concerning the whereabouts of the treasure, each of them having their own theories. John and Abby stayed out of the conversation, perfectly content to let them argue it out for themselves. Having finished their tart and tea, it seemed an opportune time for the two of them to politely excuse themselves.

"Mr. and Mrs. Crabb, George and Emma," John caught himself, "I'm afraid it's time for me to get Abby home."

"Oh, so soon? We were just getting to know you," Mrs. Crabb speaking to Abby.

"I'm afraid so. It has been a pretty long day, and I'm afraid I'm a little beat," Abby replied. She understood John's intention and played along. The two rose from their chairs, shook the Crabbs' hands and said their goodbyes.

"Goodbye John, goodbye Abby, it was very nice meeting you. Perhaps we will bump into each other again," Mrs. Crabb was clearly disappointed to have their visit cut short.

John and Abby stepped out into the parking lot. The rain had stopped, but the sky was still very dark. Although there were still a couple hours of daylight left, it already looked as if it was night.

"Sorry, about that," John apologized, even though it was completely out of his control. "They are bit overbearing, but relatively harmless. This is the third time we have literally bumped into each other."

"It was fine. I actually enjoyed them. To be precise, I enjoyed watching you squirm a little. It was clear from the start that you were worried they were going to do something embarrassing. But you remained polite and courteous. It was nice to see. It gave me a chance to see you under pressure; you maintained your kindness and dignity. I didn't mind at all, it was quite educational."

"For me too, it seems that in the most awkward moments, you can act with patience and kindness as well, and after all, you're so *adorable*." John said with a smirk.

There was a slight pause and then they both looked at each other and laughed out loud. Despite the complete lack of tact that the Crabbs managed to display, it had been a perfectly entertaining, although somewhat anxious moment.

The drive back to Haltwhistle took only a few minutes. John was a little disappointed, he realized it meant their time was soon coming to an end. As they pulled up in front of the Laidlaw house, his heart sank. He would have liked to spend a little more of the evening together.

"I'm afraid this is it for now, John. I must get back. My Mum and Maggie will both be waiting for me. I would like you to have invited you home, but like I said, I need a little more time. I'm not sure if I am ready to introduce you to Maggie just yet."

"What about tomorrow?"

"I have to work all day tomorrow."

"Dinner tomorrow? Remember I have to go back to Oxford on Sunday."

"Okay dinner tomorrow." Abby then looked at John, hesitating as if she wasn't sure what to do next.

He knew that she was waiting for him to leave, but he instead he just sat there staring at her. Then he began to lean a little toward her, not really thinking, just reacting. She did the same. Their faces were close enough to touch, and for just a moment it was if time stood still, the two of them looking into each other's eyes, their breathing so light it was nearly imperceptible. And then they kissed. When their lips parted, Abby sat back, as if surprised, her eyes wide. "I don't know what to do with you John Ridley. I think I am falling in love with you and it is as if there is nothing I can do about it. Now, get out of my car, I need some time to think."

John, smiled, then opened the door and stepped out of the car onto the wet sidewalk. He closed the door and bent over to look through the window at Abby one more time. He thought he caught a glimpse of a smile just as the car pulled away from the curb and headed down the street. He stood there watching it as it turned the next corner. And then he just stood there watching nothing, thinking, trying to understand what just happened. Was it really possible? Could something so unlikely really happen?

Chapter Thirteen

...he was standing beneath a very large oak tree. Across the path was a rock, and on top of the rock was a haggard old woman. She was frightening, not because of her age, or worn and soiled appearance, but because of her eyes. They were dark and eerie, with a touch of craziness. She spoke...

> *'At Pynkinscleugh*
> *there was much gentil blood spilt that day,*
> *For the father of an only daughter had lost his way,*
> *To trade for gilt and glitter that eternal gleam,*
> *And realize the loss in the twilight of the horrid dream,*
> *But wait not all is lost, for love knows no time,*
> *There is another who will come,*
> *   with cautious heart and anxious mind,*
> *She does not know what ransom waits,*
> *For she must follow the ravens from the gate,*
> *   Follow the ravens from the gate.'*

John awoke and went to the window. The clouds had moved on, and it was another beautiful, sunny morning. He took a shower, got dressed and went downstairs, where he did quick work of his breakfast and departed for town. There was a market just down the street and he was hoping it was open. He was in a bit of hurry, not really knowing how much time he had.

As he walked down the street, he thought about his previous night's dream. This one was particularly weird. It wasn't a dream at all, it was a memory. He was remembering the story that Scott had written about in his letter. He was remembering the letter, but he had taken the place of Scott in the story. He had already come to the conclusion that all the dreams had some sort of connection. His subconscious was playing some kind of game with him. However, this time it wasn't purely subconscious, it was connected to a real event. Was it possible that the other dreams were some sort of weird premonition? He didn't really believe in premonitions, but he couldn't help being a little open to the possibility.

He found the market, and to his delight they did sell flowers. He picked out a single daffodil. He paid for it and then made for the Cat and the Owl. He was hoping to catch Abby before she started work. As he arrived at the pub, he noticed that it was not going to open for another half an hour. He sat down at one of the outdoor tables. A few minutes later Abby came around the corner. She saw him immediately, hesitated slightly, smiled and then continued walking toward him.

"What are you doing here?" she asked gently and with a smile.

"I couldn't let your day start without a little sunshine," he then handed her the daffodil, and gave her a kiss on the cheek.

"Well, aren't you full of surprises," she kissed him on the cheek in return.

"You didn't tell me when you're getting off tonight."

"Six o'clock. I told my mum to expect a guest for dinner. She will be expecting you at six-thirty, not a second before. You must give a girl a chance to get cleaned up from a long day of spilled ale and fish and chips."

"Sounds great, I will see you then."

Abby then turned and went inside the pub. He stood there for a moment, thinking about what he should do with his day. Then a thought came to him. He turned and walked in the direction from which Abby had just come.

He paced back and forth on the sidewalk. He was contemplating what he should do, or what he should say. Every once in awhile he would stop and look at the building across the street, the flat where Abby lived with her mother and daughter. He had fully intended to walk right up to the door, knock, and introduce himself. He was not really sure what Abby had told her mother, or if Maggie would be frightened by this strange man coming to the door. He wanted to get to know them. This seemed like a good opportunity, he didn't want to wait until dinner that night, he had to leave tomorrow. What was he supposed to do?

As he stood staring at the door, it opened. He stepped back around the corner, just out of sight. Abby's mother came through the door, holding the hand of her granddaughter, carefully supporting her as she gingerly descended the front steps. They turned and walked up the street in the direction opposite from where he was peering around the corner of the building. He watched them as they slowly made their way down the block and then turned the corner at the next street. He stepped out from the building he was standing next to and began to follow them.

Turning the corner where they had disappeared from sight, he hesitated for a moment. He didn't want to get too close. They were just fifty yards ahead of him. They were moving very slowly, which was to be expected given Maggie's short little legs. He tried to match their pace, although it was very difficult to maintain the distance between them. After a couple of blocks they turned into what looked like a little park. When he came to the edge of the park, he stopped and followed them with his eyes as they walked to the other end. There were a couple of children, about Maggie's age, playing in one corner of the grassy field. As Maggie and her grandmother approached them, they seemed to recognize each other. Not far away, were two mothers sitting on a bench watching the children. Maggie sat down on the grass next to the other children. Abby's mother sat down on an empty bench near by.

The field seemed to be some sort of athletic field. There was a group of elderly people on the field playing what appeared to be lawn bowling. Several spectators lined the edges of the field. John had never actually seen a lawn bowling match, so he couldn't be sure what he was watching. He remained standing at a distance, watching, pretending to be interested in the game, while occasionally looking in the direction of Maggie and her grandmother. Eventually, he worked up enough courage to walk toward the benches. He sat down on the opposite end of the bench from Abby's mother, all the time appearing to be interested in the match.

"What's the name of this game?" John asked looking directly at the competitors.

"Lawn bowls," Mrs. Featherstone answered. "You've never seen it before?"

"No, it's my first time. If you don't mind, could you explain the object?"

"See that little ball, the yellow one, it's called the Jack. The object is to get your ball as close to it as possible. The team with the bowl which is closest to the jack at the end, scores a shot. First team to 21 shots wins. Are you really interested in lawn bowls or are you just making conversation, John Ridley?" She smiled slightly.

"You know who I am...what gave me away...er, Mrs. Featherstone?"

"Please call me Lillian. You're American accent for one. Why would a young American be sitting here, mid morning, watching lawn bowls, especially, when he has no idea what he is watching?"

"I guess I am sort of out of place. So Abby told you about me."

"Yes, she told me about you."

"I didn't mean to intrude, I wanted to meet you and Maggie, and when I saw you leaving the flat this morning, I thought I would follow you. I hope it's alright."

"It's perfectly alright with me, but I think Abby was hoping to make the introductions tonight. I suppose you are hoping for some sort of acquiescence or perhaps blessing."

"I don't know, I mean, I had not really thought about it...of course I...I would like your...blessing," he was stumbling, and had no idea how to get back on his feet. "I really just wanted to get to know you a little, to get to know Maggie. I don't really have any other expectations... I mean, well I'm not really sure

274

what I mean." He wanted to crawl in a hole. He had not expected to be completely disarmed so easily.

Mrs. Featherstone chuckled. "It's okay, young man. Abby has always known her own mind. She doesn't need any help from me, least of all my approval. She's a grown woman and I trust her judgment. To be perfectly honest, I'm kind of glad to see her getting out. She's been hiding from the world, ever since she lost Mark. If it wasn't for Maggie, I may have lost her entirely."

"How so?" He asked.

"When Abby got news of Mark, she fell into a dark depression. She could hardly get herself out of bed. Eventually Maggie brought her out of it. It was as if her motherly instincts kicked in and she knew she had to be there for Maggie. She snapped out of it, out of the depression that is, but then she just withdrew herself from the world. She went to work, came home, spent whatever time she had with Maggie and that was the extent of her day. As far as I know, you are the first person of any kind that she has given as much as the time day."

"She is a very special girl, Lillian. I have never known anybody quite like her. I know it seems a bit unlikely, but in the very short time we have known each other, she has come to mean a great deal to me. Believe me, I would not do anything to hurt her."

"I believe you. What's more I think she cares for you a great deal as well. She has been acting very strangely, confused, unsure of herself. You have definitely stirred her up, but she is still uncertain." At that moment Maggie toddled over to her grandmother and grabbed her knee.

"Who's that Granmum?" she asked.

"That's John, Maggie. Can you say hello John?"

"Hello John," Maggie greeted. She had her mother's eyes and curly blonde hair. She was wearing a little pink jumper over a white blouse. She smiled brightly as she looked at John.

"Hello, Maggie, it's nice to meet you." He held out his hand to her.

"Go ahead, shake his hand Maggie," her grandmother encouraged. Maggie reached out her tiny little hand to John. He took hold of it, gingerly giving it a slight shake.

"How old are you Maggie?'

She held up her fingers to indicate three, although she had to use her left hand to hold down the little finger of her right hand. "I'm three," she said with pride.

"Three years old. My, aren't you a big girl."

"Who are you?" Three year olds tend to get right to the point, no beating around the bush.

"I'm a friend of your Mommy," he explained.

"Mommy's at work," she said with a little emphasis on the word work, as if she had heard it many, many times.

"Yes, I know."

Maggie turned to her grandmother. "Granmum, I'm hungry."

Her grandmother proceeded to reach into her purse and pull out what looked something like crackers. She handed one to Maggie, who then turned around and walked back to where her two little friends were still playing.

"She's a beautiful little girl. You must be very proud."

"She's my delight. She reminds me of Abby when she was her age; quite precocious, always getting into everything; a real bundle of energy. She keeps me young."

"Abby says that you have to leave tomorrow, something about going back to Oxford."

"That's right. I am participating in a symposium on medieval literature. It continues for two more weeks, then, I hope to return here to Northumberland. That is, if it is okay with you, and Abby."

"It's not up to me. As for Abby, well I guess we will leave it to her. What then? What happens after you come back to Haltwhistle?"

"I wish I knew. I'm not suggesting that I have it all figured out. Right now I'm just taking it one step at a time. For right now, I want to spend as much time with her and Maggie as I can."

276

Mrs. Featherstone paused before proceeding. "John, there is something you must know about Abby. When she gives her heart to someone, she gives it fully. Once done, it can not be undone. If you love her, then you better start thinking about where this is going. Once she gives her heart to you, there is no going back. If you are unprepared for this, then it is probably best that you don't return to Haltwhistle."

"I understand, Lillian. The thing is, I think she already has my heart. Perhaps for me, it already too late, and there is no going back."

"And what about Maggie?" looking over at her granddaughter.

"I fully realize this is a package deal. I'm only asking for an opportunity to get to know both your daughter and granddaughter. The one already has my heart, I think it's only a matter of time before the other does as well."

"You seem very sure of yourself."

"No, that's not exactly right. I'm just as confused and unsettled as Abby. I can assure you that I am not usually so impulsive. However, circumstances require that I put aside convention and even rational thought, to give us a chance. I don't know what happens from here, I do not presume to know the future. The best that I can do is to take each moment one at time. I have fallen in love with your daughter, don't ask me to explain how such a thing can happen, I don't understand it myself. I believe in my heart that it's real, that it is not just some fantasy or infatuation. Something inside of me tells me that it is more, much more, and I am willing to listen, to understand. Is this something supernatural, is this God speaking to me? I don't know, but I want to find out."

"So you think God may have something to do with this?" Mrs. Featherstone looked a little skeptical.

"I think that God has something to do with everything. Did He determine that Abby and I should meet, that we should fall in love? I'm not sure, but I am open to the possibility. It's not that it makes perfect sense, at least not now."

"Abby has endured much pain, but she is strong. She may not fully realize it, but she is. She knows her own mind and heart, but it is difficult for her to think beyond anybody's needs but Maggie's, and perhaps mine."

"And that's why I love her. I don't want to cause her any more pain, nor would I want to hurt you or Maggie in any way, you have my promise of that." John turned and looked at Maggie playing with her two little friends. They sat silently for a moment, the two of them watching the children play. He couldn't help but wonder what was going through Mrs. Featherstone's mind. Did she trust him at all? Could she trust him at all? Was she afraid of him, afraid that he would take her daughter away?

After several moments of just sitting and watching Maggie, he noticed that the mothers were gathering their belonging as if preparing to leave. They called to their daughters and let them know that it was time to go home. Mrs. Featherstone stirred as well.

"It's time for us to go," she said softly. "You seem like a very nice young man, John. I'm sure you would never do anything to hurt Abby or Maggie, at least not intentionally. Just be careful. Don't start down a journey you're not willing to complete." Then she hesitated, turning to John she asked him one last question, "Tell me, how do you know… how do you know when that little voice that you hear is God, and not just your own little voice? How do you know when it is right, or when it is just wishful, or just selfish?"

"I have to admit, I am not sure," he answered and then thoughtfully added, "but just the fact that I'm not sure, that I'm asking the question, is this God or is this just me, tells me that it may be something outside of myself that is working in my heart and mind. It's my experience, that when we listen only to our self, the voice is so loud that we can't hear anything else. My own uncertainty causes me to stop and listen more carefully."

She looked him in the eyes, and smiled. "Then I will pray that you are listening." Turning to her granddaughter, she said a little louder, "Come on little one, it is time to go home." Maggie ran to her grandmother and grabbed her hand that was extended.

"Say goodbye to John, Maggie," she instructed.

278

"Goodbye, Maggie, it was very nice meeting you."

Mrs. Featherstone turned and faced him one more time. "This was very educational, young man. I will look forward to dinner tonight."

"As will I", he returned. "See you then."

Hand in hand Maggie and her grandmother started off down the street in the direction they had come from. John sat back down on the bench, watching them as they departed. After they turned the corner out of sight, he turned and faced those who were playing lawn bowls. He wasn't really paying any attention to the match at all. His mind was somewhere else, not far away, just a few blocks, to be sure. He was wondering what Abby was doing, what she was thinking at that moment. Then he had another thought. How was he ever going to explain this to his parents? He was pretty sure that the last thing that would have entered their minds was that he would have met a girl in England and had fallen in love. After all, it was the last thing that had ever entered his mind.

*****

That afternoon he went back to the Laidlaw house and tried to find things to occupy his mind. He tried a little reading, but his mind kept drifting. He did a little writing, but it was no better. He just couldn't focus. The clock seemed to move at a snail's pace. Finally, mercifully, the clock struck six. He cleaned himself up a bit and when he thought he had timed it right, he started for Abby's.

When he knocked at the door, it was opened immediately as if someone was anticipating his arrival. Abby was standing on the other side. She smiled and then leaned forward and gave him a kiss on the cheek. "Welcome, come on in. Make yourselves at home."

Abby directed him to a sitting room. It was a room at the front of the house with a nice large window looking out onto the street. In the corner of the room, near the window was an upright piano with its back against the wall. In the other corner next to the window was a comfortable chair. In the middle of the room was a round coffee table that looked as if it had seen years of use. On the other side of the table sat a small couch. The room was not very large and the few furnishings were spread apart enough to allow some space on the floor, where, at the moment he entered, Maggie was playing with some of her toys. She looked up at him and smiled. "Hi John!" she shouted.

A look of surprise spread across Abby's face. "You two know each other?" she blurted out, "but, how?"

At that moment, Lillian entered the room. "We ran into Mr. Ridley a little earlier, at the lawn. We had a nice long talk."

John blushed a little. "I guess they didn't tell you, huh?"

"No, they didn't," She gave a scolding look in the direction of her mother. "What do you mean you had a nice long talk? Have you been sharing secrets? I mean, what did the two of you talk about?"

"No secrets," John assured her. "We just got to know each other a little."

"Now Abby, stop getting your ire up. It's a mother's prerogative to tell or ask whatever she sees fit," Mrs. Featherstone was obviously teasing. Now, John understood where Abby got it. "Enough chit chat, we can discuss it over dinner. Come on, the food is getting cold. Right this way John." Lillian turned and led the way to the kitchen.

John waited while Abby bent down and swept up Maggie into her arms. "Come on little one, it is time to eat." Maggie giggled as her mother swung her up into the air and let her fall back down into her arms. The three of them followed Lillian into the kitchen where she had prepared a generous meal of bangers and mash.

Maggie was placed in a chair equipped with a booster seat that was between her grandmother and mother. John was directed to a chair that was on the other side of Abby. After they were all comfortably in place, Mrs. Featherstone turned to John and asked, "Perhaps you would do us the pleasure of saying grace, John." As she said this, she took her granddaughter's hand, as Abby did the same on the other side.

John took Abby's hand, "Sure, I would be glad to." They all bowed their heads, even Maggie. "Dear Lord, thank you for this home. Thank you for bringing me to this place. Bless this family and bless this food that you have provided for us, and the hand's which have prepared it. In the name of your Son, Amen"

For the next several minutes Mrs. Featherstone asked John questions about his family in America. He was pleased to provide an entire family history. It was safe, nothing pretentious. As he talked about his family, he tried to give them a mental picture of the places he had lived. When he got around to the part of talking about his great grandmother, Mrs. Featherstone seemed even more intrigued. She asked a number of questions about the family in Ontario, as well as the ancestors who had emigrated from England. He obliged her by giving the entire history he had learned while in Northumberland, at least, what he could remember of it.

Eventually, it was John's turn to ask the questions. He wanted to know more about their farm. Where it had been located and what it was like growing up for Abby. Mrs. Featherstone took the lead answering most of the questions, with Abby jumping in on occasion. Like most of the farms in the area, they raised sheep. By the time Abby was a teenager she gave very little attention to the sheep, and instead was fully occupied by her horse. The way her mother described it, it was as if the two, Abby and her horse, were joined at the hip.

"Do you like horses?" Mrs. Featherstone asked.

"I did a little riding when I was growing up. Our cousins had horses in Ontario, so I would get a chance to ride when we would visit them, you know, at family reunions and such."

"Well, perhaps, while you're here, we will have to have you revisit your youth. I think I could arrange for a little ride if you're up to it," Abby teased. Or at least, John thought she was teasing, he wasn't exactly sure.

"Yeah...sure, maybe we can do that when I return in a couple weeks."

"So you're leaving?" Mrs. Featherstone asked.

"Yes, unfortunately I am scheduled to leave on the train tomorrow morning. I have to return to the symposium at Oxford. But I will be back as soon as it is over."

Attempting to change the subject, Abby interjected, "maybe we could have dessert in the sitting room. What do you think?"

"You two run along. I will get Maggie cleaned up and bring the dessert in just a few moments," Mrs. Featherstone offered. "I hope you like strawberries and cream, John."

"Yes ma'am, but are you sure I can't help you with the dishes."

"No, you two go on ahead. Maggie and I will be fine."

Abby and John went into the sitting room and sat together on the couch. Only a few moments had passed when Maggie came running and climbed onto the couch between them. "What do you think about my little princess?" Abby said as she reached out and pulled Maggie close, giving her a little tickle as she did.

"She's beautiful, just like her mother." He reached out and poked Maggie in the ribs in an attempt to tickle her. "And I see she is ticklish as well." Maggie fell backward into her mother's lap as she giggled.

"What d'ya say, Maggie? Do you think John might be ticklish." Maggie stood up on the couch and with her finger poised to attack, she slowly stepped toward John. John remained still. All of sudden Maggie jumped onto his lap and attempted to tickle his ribs. Just as Maggie thought she had the upper hand, John grabbed her by both legs and lifted her into the air so that she was dangling upside down. She had a look of shock and pleaded "let me down!" John obliged only to have Maggie attempt to tickle him again, in which case John lifted her into the air again. This process repeated several times as Maggie giggled and screamed the entire time.

Mrs. Featherstone entered the room, carrying dessert on a tray. "What's all this laughing and carrying on?" she asked.

"I'm tickling John, grandmum," Maggie shouted with glee between giggles.

"From what I'm hearing, it's hard to tell who's ticklin' who. In any case, it is time to stop. That is, if you want any dessert, young lady."

John stopped lifting Maggie into the air and Maggie quieted down, recognizing the prospects of having strawberries and cream and not wanting to forfeit her privilege. Mrs. Featherstone served everyone and then took her seat in the large comfortable chair.

"I noticed you have a piano, Mrs. Featherstone, do you play?" John asked.

"No, that's Abby's piano. Don't tell me she didn't tell you. She's a wonderful pianist." Then she turned and looked at Abby. What other secrets have you kept hidden, daughter?"

"Yes, what other secrets have you kept hidden?" John smiled. He liked having a little of the upper hand.

"It wasn't a secret, it just never came up," Abby glared at her mother as she said it.

"Play for us mummy," Maggie jumped in.

"Yes, play for us mummy," John said teasingly.

"Oh no, you don't need to hear me play."

"Come on Abby, don't be shy. The young man wants to hear you play," her mother half scolded.

"Yeah, come on, I would love to hear you play," John echoed.

"Play mummy," Maggie added.

"Oh, alright, but don't expect too much, I don't get to practice as much as I used to."

Abby got up off the couch and made her way to the piano. Maggie followed her and climbed up on the bench next to her mother in anticipation. As Abby started playing, John surprised at her ease. As he sat back and listened, he soon found himself in awe. He recognized the melody, but he couldn't remember where it was from. It was beautiful and Abby's talent was immediately obvious. As he watched her, he sensed that she was not only playing the notes, but that she was feeling the music. It was as if the music was an extension of her soul.

About half way through the piece, Maggie slipped down off the bench and began dancing around as if she were a miniature ballerina. She was whirling and twirling all around the room, much to the delight of her grandmother, who was clearly enjoying the moment. She was relishing in the talent of her daughter, and the innocent enthusiasm of her granddaughter. It was in that moment of watching the three of them, enjoying each other, that John realized that the events unfolding before him had some far reaching implications.

He was falling in love with Abby, or more accurately had fallen in love with her. But what did that mean? What was going to happen? Did he think it possible that Abby would want to marry him? Or for that matter, was he thinking of marriage? Just a few months ago he had been engaged to someone else. Was it even reasonable to think of starting a new life with Abby? Would he take her and Maggie back to the United States? What about Abby's mother? Would Abby be willing to leave her home? On the other hand was he willing to stay here, in England? Suddenly he began to feel afraid. He loved Abby, but there were too many uncertainties, too many unknowns. How could this ever work?

There had to be a way. He couldn't begin to contemplate the alternative; of leaving and never seeing her again. It was unthinkable. But what was he going to do? It was all so unexpected. How did he get here?

The music faded, bringing John back to the reality of the present. Maggie made her last twirl, before collapsing onto the floor. Mrs. Featherstone clapped, praising her granddaughter's performance. He gave a little applause as well.

"That was beautiful Maggie, you are a wonderful dancer," her grandmother congratulated.

"Did you like it mummy?" Maggie directed toward Abby.

"Yes, it was beautiful. However, I think it is about time for someone to go to bed. Perhaps you should find a book to read. Who do you think should read to you tonight, grandmum, or mummy?"

"I want John to read to me," Maggie said, smiling up at her mother.

"Really, well don't you think you should ask him first," Abby suggested.

284

"Would you read to me John?" Maggie pleaded.

"Sure, I would be honored. What would you like me to read?"

"This one," Maggie handed John a book and then proceeded to climb onto the couch and then onto John's lap. He made sure she was comfortable, opened the book and began to read aloud.

Lillian got up from her chair and began to gather the dessert dishes. Abby stayed at the piano bench as he began reading. Then, after the first few pages had been read, she slowly got up from the bench and without causing any distraction, she slid into her seat next to the two of them on the couch. She sat quietly as he read, captivated not by the story, but by the ease at which John and Maggie had already grown comfortable with one another. Maggie was attentively listening to every word as John attempted to use different voices in playing out the characters of *Peter Rabbit*. As he read, Maggie leaned her head back against his chest. Her eyes were starting to get heavy, but they would snap open each time he turned the page and pointed out the next scene. Abby pulled her legs up on the couch and tucked them beneath her as she leaned back against the arm. She listened and watched as Maggie slowly fell asleep.

As John finished the story, he looked up at Abby. She smiled at him and reached out to take the book from his hands, carefully, so as not to wake Maggie up. She then whispered, "It looks as if you have made a new friend."

He nodded his head. "Would you like me to carry her to her bedroom?"

Abby nodded and stood up. He gently leaned forward and stood to his feet, still holding Maggie in his arms. She then led him up the stairs and into the bedroom that was shared by mother and daughter. She walked over to Maggie's bed and pulled the covers down. John carefully laid the little girl onto her pillow. Abby then proceeded to unbutton her jumper and pull it over her head, all the time trying carefully not to awaken her. The two carefully and quietly backed out into the hall. As they descended the stairs, they could hear Lillian rattling the dishes in the kitchen.

"Let's go out on the porch," Abby whispered.

As they stepped outside Abby sat down on the top step. John followed and sat down next to her. It was a pleasant summer evening; a slight breeze was easing the warmth of the day. The sun had just peaked beneath the horizon and a waning gibbous moon could already be seen in the twilight.

"Maggie is a wonderful little girl," John broke the silence first.

"Thank you. She is everything to me. When we lost Mark, it was all I could do to get out of bed in morning. It was Maggie that finally brought me out of it. She has the best parts of Mark. In a way she helped me to know that he was not really gone."

"You loved him very much, didn't you?"

"Yes, I did. How does one explain it? He was my best friend. When he told me he was being sent overseas I was crushed. I was supportive, but in my heart I was scared. I couldn't have imagined him not being a part of my life. I didn't think it possible that I could ever love any one like that again...not until now."

Abby paused for a moment in contemplation, while John remained silent. "It's funny how things work. A week ago, I didn't even know who you were. Four days ago, I was scared to death, afraid even to see you, afraid of what I might feel. I sat right here on these steps, debating with myself as to whether I should get on the train with you to Edinburgh. And now here I sit, wishing that you didn't have to leave tomorrow, wondering how I will feel tomorrow when you're gone."

"I know exactly what you mean. The last thing I was thinking when I boarded the train in London, was if I would meet anybody during my venture into Northumberland. If I remember right, I was just worried I wasn't even going to make the train and I was simply feeling relieved when I sat down in my seat on the train, nothing else." He smiled at Abby. She understood that he was trying to make her feel at ease.

"It seems so long ago now," She said. "I barely remember what I was thinking. Something like, who is this strange stammering man, this silly American." She couldn't help taking the opportunity to tease him again.

"Was I really stammering, was it really that noticeable?" He could feel that he was blushing slightly, but he was hoping it was barely noticeable in the dim twilight. "I guess I was a little nervous. Perhaps I was disarmed by your beauty and confidence."

"Don't get me wrong, it was kind of endearing. I thought it was cute."

"It wasn't as if you didn't have your own little awkward moments. Don't think I didn't notice that you bite your lower lip when you get a little nervous."

She giggled. "Okay, okay, we were both a little nervous. But how did we ever get from there to where we are now?" She took hold of his arm and then laid her head onto his shoulder. "I wish you didn't have to leave tomorrow."

"It will be okay. Remember, absence makes the heart grow fonder."

"I know that's what they say, but I'm still afraid that absence may cause the heart to forget. It's almost inconceivable that in so short a time I could feel this way. I don't want to lose you."

"You won't lose me. If the way we feel now were to change during so brief an absence, it would only mean that it was never real. I believe it's real, and therefore we have nothing to fear. I promise you this, regardless of what happens, I will be back here, two weeks from today."

"You're right of course. I know you're right. I don't need to be afraid. But promise me this; in two weeks when you return, if anything has changed I don't want you to hesitate. You look me straight in the eyes and just say to me, I'm sorry, but it was all a mistake. Don't try and string me a long to soften the blow, give it to me straight, no regrets."

"Nothing is going to change. The way I feel now isn't going to change. You don't need to worry."

"I know how you feel now, but I need you to promise me this. I don't want to be left wondering, even for a moment."

"Okay, I promise, but only if you promise to do the same."

"I promise…I love you, John Ridley, with all of my heart."
John smiled. "I love you too, Abby."

For the first time, Abby was genuinely afraid. For the first time, she realized how she had fallen deeply and madly in love with John. She had thought it impossible that she could ever feel like this again. Now that she had succumbed to her feelings, she was afraid that she was going to lose him. As she sat quietly with her head on his shoulder, she held tight to the moment, she didn't want it to end. For the first time in a long time she felt at peace.

They remained there for some time, not speaking, each one lost in their thoughts; thoughts about the day, thoughts about the future. At some point, the door opened behind them and Mrs. Featherstone stepped onto the porch. "How are the two of you getting on?" she asked.

Abby lifted her head and turned toward her mother. "I'm sorry Mum, we didn't mean to leave you all alone."

"Don't be silly, Abby, you don't need me playing the third wheel. The two of you need your alone time. I just wanted to make sure you don't need anything else. Perhaps John would like something to drink, tea maybe."

"No thanks, Mrs. Featherstone, I'm fine. You have been the perfect hostess. Thank you so much for dinner. And thank you for making me feel so welcome in your home."

"Yes, thanks Mum, you've been a peach. I'll be in, in a bit."

"Don't worry about me Abby. I am going to do a little reading before I go to bed. You two enjoy yourself. I'm going to say goodnight, John. I look forward to seeing you again, real soon."

"Good night, Lillian, thanks again. See you in a couple of weeks."

"Good night, Mum."

John and Abby were left alone again. "What time does your train leave tomorrow?"

"Nine AM," John replied.

"I won't be able to see you off John. Tomorrow is Sunday, and we will be in church at that time."

"Probably for the best, I don't need a bunch of tears as I board the train," he half smiled. "Don't worry Abby, its not goodbye, I'll be back."

The time came for John to say goodnight. Abby walked him down the sidewalk to the end of the street. He turned to face her. They kissed and then she wrapped her arms around his waste and buried her head into his chest. She held on for what seemed several minutes. "Good night John, have a safe trip."

"Good night Abby, sleep well."

Abby turned and walked back toward home. She didn't know if he was still standing there, watching her. She never turned to look. She didn't want him to see that she was crying.

The Meeting Place

Abigail stood on the rise overlooking Featherstonhaugh, looking to the east for any sign of a rider. Her own horse was tied to a bramble bush just a few yards away. She looked back toward the west; the sun was just now descending beneath the horizon. She could see the castle in the valley below, the lights already coming to life in the east windows. Her father would still be in the great hall, finishing his dinner and musing about his personal wealth. It would be another two hours before he would make his nightly visit to her bedroom to check on her before he retired for the night.

How much longer must she wait? There was so little time and she did not want to waste a moment. This was not the first time she had stood waiting. For more than a year they had made appointments to meet every fortnight, at sunset. He had never failed to show.

Just then she could see the last glimmer of sunlight reflect off the unmistakable white stallion of her conspirator. He was just on the rise opposite and he would be with her in just a few minutes more. Despite the regular occurrence of the meeting, she still found a surge of excitement coursing through her veins. She stopped her pacing and sat upon the stone from which the castle derived its name.

The horse and rider approached at a gallop and then reared suddenly upon drawing close. Abigail remained seated, almost appearing to give no notice. The rider remained in the saddle leaning forward slightly.

"Is this the proper greeting for your beloved?" the rider spoke, smiling slightly as he said it.

"You've kept me waiting. Is this anyway to treat the lady of the castle?" she said looking hurt.

"I beg your pardon milady, but the appointed time is sunset, which has only happened this moment. It is you who are early, not I who was late, but I shall forgive this slight misjudgment."

"Forgive me? I think not, there is nothing to forgive. If my arrival was premature it was only due to a fortnight of anticipation. I would think that your own anticipation might

have the same affect. Or am I to take it that you have better things to do on such an evening as this. I am beginning to think that this appointment has become more a chore than a pleasure. In fact, I am of a mind that I should return to the castle and leave you to your own devices."

"Very well, milady, if you wish it, I shall leave you and return to Willimoteswick." As he said this he began to turn his steed.

"No, wait!" Abigail was not about to lose the moment. "Don't leave. John, why must we quarrel when we have so little time as it is?"

John Ridley jumped down from his horse, strode up to where Abigail was sitting and pulled her from her perch. They embraced for a moment, just holding each other, not wanting to let go.

"Oh, John, how long must we keep up these pretenses? How long must we keep our love for one another a secret?"

"Say the word and I will speak to your father tomorrow." John replied.

"It's all so impossible. You know that my father shall never give his consent. He cannot. He will not. His hatred for the Ridley clan runs too deep within his veins. He could never consent to his only daughter marrying a Ridley."

"If this be true, then how will we ever be together?"

"Take me away with you. We can ride to Hexham this very evening and be married in the Abbey. We shall elope."

"Abigail, you know this is impossible. If I take you by force, it will surely mean war between the Ridleys and Featherstones, and much loss of life. We cannot let this thing happen. The only way, is to secure your father's blessing. "

"Then we are doomed to be apart, for I cannot believe that he will ever have a change of heart."

"We must convince him that this feud is meaningless. He must realize that the offenses of the past are long since gone and should be forgotten. How can we continue to be bound by mistakes that were made by our ancestors; actions taken long before we were even born?"

At that moment they heard a strange laugh behind them. Emerging from behind an old oak tree was an old woman. Her hair was all white and her clothes were badly soiled. She was ill-kept and haggard looking.

"It is the witch," Abigail whispered through clenched teeth.

"Beardie Grey," John nodded. "What do you want witch?" He shouted. "Be off with you. Leave us be. We want nothing of your bewitching, you're strange ways. Be off with you, I say."

The old woman did not move. Instead she smiled and began to speak. Her voice was kind of eerie, scratchy, with a sharp whine at the beginning of every phrase.

> Two lovers in secret meet,
> Trusting their rendezvous is made discrete.
> Hidden in twilight beneath oak and sky,
> Avoiding chance discov'ry of prying eyes.

"Be still witch," John shouted once more. "What is this nonsense you speak?"

"Yes, why must you taunt us so?" Abigail added.

The witch laughed again and then continued ignoring their demands for privacy and silence.

> Two lovers kept separate by chance of birth,
> Two families at war, o'r a small patch of earth,
> Holding to all hope, their hearts e'r entwined.
> They seek to find answers, a word or a sign.

> Listen Miss Abigail, if you will,

> Tis time to act, before it's too late,
> Your own father, about to seal your fate,
> He cannot forget, he will not concede,
> Instead, plots to commit an evil deed .

> Give ear to these words, or forever regret,

> To claim you his own, another will come,
> If you look in his heart, love there is none,
> Blinded by wealth, a father's great sin,

His foolish resolve, twill be your ruin.

You might ask yourself, how can this be?
Beardie Grey should come and speak of thee,
How can she know, what fate awaits these two?
Strange and true, The White Lady told me of you.

Just as secretly as she came, the witch turned and stole in to the darkness, leaving John and Abigail standing alone, silent and confused. Neither knew how to react or what to say. It was so strange. Why had she come at that moment? How could she know anything about them?

"I don't understand, what does she mean? Who is the White Lady?" Abigail broke the silence.

"None of it makes any sense; just the ramblings of a crazy old lady, nothing more."

"But how did she know we would be here? And what did she mean about my father, that he has already sealed my fate? John, could she be right. Is it already too late?"

"It will never be too late, Abigail. I will not give you up. Upon my life, I will not give up. We will find a way."

Chapter Fourteen

...she was standing in the field, just to the west of the castle. It was night, pitch black, the moonlight unable to break through the clouds. She could just make out the battlements of Featherstone rising to meet the sky. There was a soft glow emanating from the front windows.

She had been here many times before. It was all too familiar. But, why was she here now, like this, at night? She was afraid, but of what? What was the cause of this fear? She felt it down deep, things were changing and she was no longer in control. Something was about to happen, but what?

In the opening of the front gate there was a woman, all dressed in white, holding a candle in her right hand. She was just standing there, waiting, peering out into the darkness. She held out her left hand in front of her. The woman in white was beckoning, inviting her to approach? Or was she? Out of the night, a winged hellion descended and landed, taking hold of the lady's wrist. But it was not a spirit, it was flesh and blood. It was a raven...

Abby could barely keep her mind focused on the minister's sermon. She had had a hard time falling asleep the previous night. She couldn't stop thinking about John and all that had transpired in the past week. Once she did fall asleep, she had another one of those strange dreams. She didn't know what to make of it. None of it made any sense.

Rev. Hopkins was teaching on faith. Abby tried to listen to the sermon, but it was no use. It was all she could do to keep her eyes open. They were sitting fairly close to the front and the last thing she wanted was for Rev. Hopkins to catch her sleeping in church. She would never hear the end of it. She looked down at Maggie, who had already fallen asleep, with her head on her mother's lap. Abby gently stroked her blonde curls.

When Rev. Hopkins finally finished with a prayer and the congregation rose to sing the closing hymn, Abby felt a little relieved. She remained seated with Maggie asleep across her lap. The sound of the organ caused Maggie to open her eyes. She sat up and looked around, still rubbing the sleep out of her eyes. By the time the hymn had reached the final stanza, she was standing on the pew, with her mother holding on to make sure she didn't fall. She tried to mouth the words, as if she knew the words to the hymn.

When the service ended, Abby remained seated, waiting for the congregation to clear out behind her. When the majority had left, she stood up and helped Maggie to the floor, all the time keeping a grip on her hand. Mrs. Featherstone led the way back down the aisle to the rear doors. As they exited the church and descended the steps down the sidewalk, Maggie all of sudden released her grip on her mother's hand and started to run down the walk. Before Abby could even call out to her, she heard Maggie cry out, "John!"

Maggie ran down the walk to a waiting John Ridley. As she drew close, John bent down and let her embrace him with a hug. "Good morning, Maggie," he stood up, while grasping Maggie by the hand.

Abby stepped toward the two of them, "I don't understand. What are you doing here? Did you miss your train?"

John sort of shrugged his shoulders, "when I got to the train station this morning, I noticed there was a train leaving for London tonight at seven. It will mean catching a late night train or early bus to Oxford. I may have to spend the night in Paddington, but it would be worth it if I could spend the afternoon with the three of you; that is if you don't have any other plans."

"As a matter of fact, it's such a nice day, we thought we might go for a picnic lunch," Mrs. Featherstone said.

"Sounds great!" John exclaimed. "Where are we going?"

"Well, believe it or not we were thinking of going to Featherstone Castle," Abby said. "There's a nice little grassy area over looking the river, right at the footbridge. It looks like a beautiful day, and if it gets too warm, we can always do a little wading in the river."

The four of them started walking back toward the flat, Mrs. Featherstone leading, with Abby and John trailing, each holding one of Maggie's hands as she walked between them. Abby didn't know what to say, she just looked at John and smiled.

It didn't take long for Abby and her mother to pack a lunch into a basket, while John played with Maggie in the sitting room. Before long, they had all piled in the car and were off, headed south toward Featherstone. The trip didn't take long, and as the road began to run along the river, John felt in familiar surroundings. Abby parked the car at the entrance to the drive that opened into the pasture on the west side of the castle. John carried the basket and a blanket as the others lead the way to the bridge.

It was a perfectly summer day, bright and sunny, with no hint of clouds on the horizon. Between the road and river was a nice grassy bank, perfect for a picnic. They picked a spot underneath a young elm tree. While Abby and her mother got everything ready for lunch, John did a little exploring with Maggie. They discovered a butterfly in the grass and Maggie started to chase it, running in circles, as it stayed just out of her reach. Round and round it spiraled. She ran, trying for all she was worth to catch her prey, to no avail. After several minutes she collapsed in the grass, worn out from the effort. John sat down beside her.

"I thought you almost had it Maggie."

"I almost did," she was still breathing hard from the exertion, "but it was too fast...Look!" Maggie was pointing at John.

Just at that moment, the butterfly landed on John's shoulder. Slowly and very carefully, he cupped his hand over it, trapping it against his arm. He then held it up to Maggie, so she could touch its wings.

"Isn't it beautiful, Maggie?"

She simply nodded her head and giggled with glee. After a few moments he opened his hand and the butterfly resumed its flight. In the distance, they could hear Abby announce that it was time for lunch.

As they ate their lunch, John asked if they knew any of the history of the Castle. He was particularly interested in its more recent past. Abby explained that the castle had passed out of possession of the Featherstone family some time toward the end of the 17th century. Some believed it was just after the tragic death of Abigail Featherstone. The Baron of Featherstone had no sons, so there was no one to inherit the castle. She also explained that Abby's father, therefore, Abby as well, was the descendent of a younger son of a different branch of the family.

"Have you ever heard of the Raven Stone?" John asked.

"You mean the stone on which John and Abigail bled, where the ravens came and drank the blood of the two poor unfortunate lovers, after their death?" She smiled, "everyone knows that story."

"Have you ever seen the Raven Stone?"

"Yes, I have. Why, would you like to see it?"

"Yes. I tried to find it the first time I visited the castle, but I couldn't find it. The legend suggested it is somewhere near the bridge, where the conflict took place and the unfortunates lost their lives."

"But not this bridge," she said pointing to the foot bridge nearby. "The bridge in the legend was further north. I can show you, if you want."

"Great, lead on."

"Mum will you watch Maggie, while John and I take a walk? Don't let her wander too near the river."

"You two go ahead, don't worry about us, we will be fine."

Abby took John by the hand and they walked to the foot bridge. On the other side of the bridge, she started down the path where John had emerged from the trees during his previous visit. Not more than fifty feet up the path, she turned onto a path that led toward the river. The path was much narrower and more difficult to follow. He realized he would've never noticed it at night. They continued on the path, the river on their right, the dense wood to their left. The trees seemed to close in about them, Abby pressed on, with John trailing behind. Just as he was beginning to wonder if they had lost the path altogether, they stepped into a little clearing. It was not much of clearing, just a small space that was surrounded by several large elm trees. The canopy overhead nearly blocked out the sky entirely. At the edge of this clearing was a large moss covered rock.

John could hardly believe his eyes. He knew this place. The trees and underbrush were different, but there was no mistaking the rock. He had seen it before. Not that he had ever been here before, not really. This was the rock in his dreams. But, how was this possible? How could he have possibly dreamed this? Had it been a premonition? No, that wasn't possible. He didn't believe in premonitions.

"Well, here it is," Abby turned and looked at John, noticing the confusion on his face. "...something wrong?"

He caught himself, "No, I'm fine. It's just that it's exactly what I would have expected, moss and all."

He walked over to it and touched it, moving his hand across the mossy surface.

"This is where it is believed that the blood gathered," Abby said, pointing to the low portion of the stone.

"Yes, that makes sense, he said as he walked around to the back of the rock. He lifted a portion of the moss up so that he could look underneath, then a little more, and a little more. "Look here Abby, there is something underneath the moss; something carved into the stone."

Abby and John both knelt down, as he continued to pull moss off the surface of the stone. "I don't think I've ever noticed

298

that before; it seems to be some sort of inscription," Abby whispered, as if someone else might be watching.

He had a pen in his pocket and he used it to clean the moss from each of the characters. The inscription had been scratched directly on the stone. It was clearly very old, perhaps preserved by the moss covering protecting it from the weather. After several minutes of scraping and brushing, they had completely cleaned the area immediately around the inscription. It seemed to be a poem of some sort. Abby read it aloud.

> *Wandering alone, as in a spell,*
> *A wayward shaft and here She fell.*
> *Taken, deceived, to gain a chest,*
> *Given in greed, she cannot rest.*
> *Lady in white, who began this quest,*
> *Girl in white, lies beneath the crest.*

"What do you think it means?" John asked. He was looking for something in his pocket to use to copy it down.

"It must be about Abigail Featherstone. See here, the second line, 'A wayward shaft' must be in reference to the way she died. 'Lady in white' must be a reference to her wedding dress. But the rest of it, 'chest, crest', I'm not sure what those mean."

John had placed the receipt from his stay at the Laidlaw house in his pocket. He proceeded to copy the poem down, double checked it, and then placed it back in his pocket.

"I wonder who carved this into the stone?" Abby asked.

"My guess would be Beardie Grey," John surmised.

"The witch?"

"Yes, the witch. It makes sense. Remember the letter from Sir Walter Scott. He said, when he came to the river he found her sitting on a rock, this rock, the Raven Stone. I think it's possible that the poem she spoke to him is related to this poem as well."

"But I don't understand. Beardie Grey lived a hundred years after Abigail Featherstone. What's the connection?"

"I'm not sure…" He paused, "But I would sure like to find out."

"We should be getting back," Abby said. "My mum will be wondering where we are."

"Yeah, you're right," he turned to look at the Raven Stone one more time as Abby started for the trail. It was kind of strange being here. It was so familiar, while at the same time so mystical. He turned and followed Abby into the trees.

As they arrived back to the bridge, Abby stopped before crossing. She turned to John, "how did you know to look under the moss, John?"

"Just had a hunch, something I read." He was not about to tell her about the dreams. There was no way she would believe him. He was not sure he believed it himself.

*****

When they returned to the picnic spot, they found that Maggie and fallen asleep. She was lying on the blanket, while Abby's mother was leaning up against the tree, reading a book. "Did you have a nice walk?" She asked.

"Yes, Mum, thanks. I see our princess has decided to take a little nap."

"She just fell asleep a few moments ago."

"I think she might have the right idea," John said as he sat down on the grass next to where Maggie lay. "It seems a perfect Sunday afternoon for napping." He lay back in the grass, closing his eyes.

Abby stood shaking her head at this sight, "I see, well I'm not about to waste a moment of this beautiful day lying around dozing. Mum, will you keep an eye on these two while I take another stroll?"

"Sure, Abby, you go ahead, I have everything under control. I won't let them out of my sight."

Without opening his eyes, John raised his hand and gave a slight wave. "Don't get lost Abby, I don't want to have to come looking for you."

300

She smiled as she turned and walked toward Featherstone. She had just started to cross the pasture that lead to the front gate, when all of sudden she stopped, staring at the castle. She was experiencing a bit of déjà vu. She was overwhelmed by the memory of her dream the previous night. Standing there, looking at the castle gate, it was as if she was reliving it. She could see the woman in white, standing at the gate, holding the candle in one hand and supporting the raven in the other. What did it all mean? Did it mean something, or was it merely her subconscious playing games. She had never believed that dreams were anything more than just that, dreams, but the events of this past week were beginning to change the way she looked at everything. Was it possible that what she dreamt meant something more? If so, were the candle, the woman, and the raven symbols of some kind?

She continued to walk toward the castle and the open gate in front of her. She stopped at the entrance and turned in the direction of the pasture, as if taking the same view of the woman in white. What was she looking for? Who was she waiting for? She looked around at the ground, the arch above the stone bricks that had been used to construct it, ancient stone, weathered and etched. She walked to one side of the gate, reaching out to touch the stone, feeling its coolness in the shadow of the arch. She allowed her hand to glide across the stone moving from the inner wall to the exterior where the stone felt warm from the sun. She looked down to the ground, her eyes examining each crack and edge. There, near the base there was something unusual in the color of the stone. She knelt down and pushed back the grass at the base to get a better look. There was definitely something there, something that had been carved into to the stone. It was barely visible after years of weathering. She could hardly believe her eyes. She reached down and ran her hand across it...

*****

John was not actually sleeping. He had closed his eyes, but his mind was still racing from the discovery of the Raven Stone.

It was just like in his dream. The writing on the stone was actually there. It was as if he had already been there, had already seen it in his mind. But how was this possible? How could he have dreamed something, days before he actually experienced it? He did not believe in premonitions, at least he never had before. Now he wasn't sure. If it was a premonition, then it must have a purpose, there must be a reason. It couldn't simply be random chance. But what did it all mean?

There was a slight breeze blowing, just enough to provide a cool respite from the heat of the afternoon sun. It was soothing, and he found himself dozing. He began to think about the past week, the chance meeting with Abby, the visits to Edinburgh, Featherstone, and Thirwall, along with the chance encounters with the Crabbs. It all seemed like a dream. Pennsylvania, and U of I, seemed a million miles away. It was as if he had experienced a lifetime of events in a very short time. He liked it here, in Northumberland, and he was not in any hurry to go back to Oxford.

He wondered what the Professor would say about all of this. After all, it was his fault. He was the one that talked John into this excursion to begin with. What would he say if he knew that John was contemplating remaining in England? That was what he was thinking. Now that he had met Abby, he was not about to let her go. There was no way he could ask her to go to the states; to pick up her life, uproot her daughter and leave her home. Perhaps there was a way he could complete his studies here in England. Admittedly, his education was the least of his worries. Completing his Ph.D. seemed like such a small thing at the moment.

Just as he was about to drift off, he felt something poking him in the side. He reached for it only to discover a small little hand. He opened his eyes to discover Maggie leaning over him with her face near his. "Are you asleep, John?" she whispered, as if she was trying not to disturb him, while at the same time hopeful that he would awaken.

He smiled, "No, I'm not asleep, Maggie, at least not now. What are you up to?" He grabbed her around the waist with both hands and lifted her so she was hanging in midair directly above him.

She giggled with glee, "Let me down. Let me down!"

"Not until you tell me what you want."

"Grandma said we could go to the river when you wake up." She giggled again as he moved her side to side, as if he were about to drop her.

"The river, huh, you want to go down to the river?"

"Yes, please put me down." Maggie insisted.

"Sorry, John, I didn't mean for her to wake you," Mrs. Featherstone, said from her perch beneath the tree.

"Oh, don't worry I wasn't really asleep." He looked around. "Hasn't Abby come back yet?"

"No, I saw her walking over by the castle. She is probably still walking in the garden."

He sat up, gently setting Maggie back to earth. "I tell you what Maggie, why don't we go find your mother and then we will go down to the river together."

"Okay," Maggie agreed.

"Would you like to come with us Lillian?" he asked.

"No, you two go ahead. I am going to pick up here a bit and then I will join you later."

John stood up and took Maggie by the hand and they started off for the castle. As they were crossing the pasture, Maggie noticed the sheep not far off. John lifted her up and placed her on his shoulders so she could get a better view. As they approached the front wall of the castle, Abby came through the front gate.

"Hey you two, what are you up to?" she asked.

"We were looking for you mommy," Maggie was quick to respond, as John lifted her down off his shoulders and set her on the ground. "We're going to the river. Want to come?"

"Absolutely, it sounds like a wonderful idea." Abby took Maggie by the hand.

Maggie reached out with her other hand and took hold of John's. Together they walked hand in hand back through the pasture to the river. They spent the remainder of the afternoon wading at the river's edge, exploring for anything living in the water and skipping rocks. It wasn't long before the activity became somewhat mischievous as Maggie would occasionally splash the others with water. Maggie thought it was all great fun, which made it all the more enjoyable for John and Abby. Mrs. Featherstone joined them, and sat on the bank, watching safely from a distance. She seemed quite pleased to see her daughter and granddaughter fully enjoying the moment.

When it came time to leave, it was disappointing for all, but especially for Maggie. Mrs. Featherstone was the one who had to deliver the sad news. They would have to leave soon, if John was going to make his train. The walk back to the car and ride back into town was fairly quiet.

When they arrived at the train station, Mrs. Featherstone was the first to speak, "it was a wonderful day, and I'm very glad you were able to spend it with us John." John could sense that this was her way of showing him her approval.

"Thank you Lillian, I had a wonderful time as well. Thank you again, for letting me share it with you. You have been a gracious host."

As they stepped out of the car, Mrs. Featherstone remained still, holding Maggie's hand in hers, "Maggie and I will say our goodbyes. Abby, you go ahead and walk John to the train. We will wait for you here." She reached out her hand to John, "Goodbye, John Ridley, I'm sure we will see you again, soon."

"Goodbye, Lillian, two weeks." John then bent down to Maggie's level, "Do you think I can get a hug Maggie?"

"Say goodbye Maggie," her grandmother instructed.

She put her arms around John's neck and squeezed, "Goodbye, John."

"Goodbye, Maggie, see you again real soon."

Abby took John by the hand and walked to the train platform. As they stood waiting for the conductor to signal boarding, they remained quiet. When it was time for him to leave, Abby leaned forward and kissed him. "Remember, when you come back, no false pretenses between us. We remain honest and truthful with each other."

"Agreed," he shook his head. "I do love you. Don't fret Abby, I will be back soon."

*****

The train trip back to Oxford was all a blur. He tried to sleep on the train between Carlisle and London, but it was not a restful slumber. He had to wait around in Paddington, before he was able to catch an early morning train to Oxford. When he walked out of the station, he decided to forgo the morning seminar and instead return to his room to try and get some sleep. He passed Ian as he entered the dorm. They chatted briefly and promised to get together for lunch, to catch up.

John tried to settle into a normal routine, attending classes in the morning, sitting in on discussion groups in the afternoon, and chatting with fellow participants over dinner. He attempted to stay engaged, and contribute to discussions, but the reality was that he often found his mind wandering, thinking of Abby and Northumberland.

In midweek, he got up the nerve to call the Professor and tell him about his desire to stay in England. "Don't do anything rash," was the Professor's first response. "Maybe you just need to extend the summer a little longer. There's no real reason to rush back, especially since you have a wonderful opportunity to continue your research."

John was not about to argue with him; he couldn't remember having ever won an argument with the Professor, and there was not a reason to think he would now. At least he had broken the ice; there was plenty of time for further discussion. His real concern was how he was going to tell his parents. He did not even know where to begin. Did he start right off by telling them about Abby? Every time he ran over the conversation in his mind, he started to panic. He couldn't seem to organize his words into anything that made any sense. As a result he kept putting it off.

It wasn't until Thursday evening that he was able to return to the Bod to do some follow up research on some of the stories he had run across when in Northumberland. He was intrigued by the story of Blenkinsopp Castle, especially since Thomas Blenkinsopp was Abigail Featherstone's intended. He came across a description of the legend in an 18th century publication *The Tyne and its Tributaries* by James Palmer.

> *Bryan de Blenkinsopp was gallant and brave, and his praises were sung by the minstrels, but he had an inordinate love of wealth, and declared he would never marry until he met a lady possessed of a chest of gold heavier than ten of his strongest men could carry into his castle. After the lapse of some years he brought home a wife and the box of gold, but the lady caused the gold to be secreted, and would not give it up, and at length the young lord suddenly left the castle, and went no one knows whither. His lady was inconsolable, and at last with her attendants went forth in search. The fate was enveloped in mystery; they returned not to Blenkinsopp, but tradition tells us that the lady, filled with remorse, cannot rest in her grave, but must needs wander back to the old castle, and mourn over the chest of wealth, the cause of all their woe. Here she must continue to wander until some one shall follow her to the vault, and, by the removing of the treasure, lay her spirit to rest.*

The same legend was repeated in several other sources, always under the title of *The White Lady*. John was immediately struck by the use of the word "chest" of gold. He went back to his notes, the third line of the poem, *Taken, Deceived, to gain a Chest.* Was there a connection between the legend of Blenkinsopp Castle and that of the Featherstone?

In another source, *English Border Ballads* by Peter Burns, he came across a reference to Thirwall Castle. It, at first, seemed far afield from his research, but since he had visited the castle, it caught his attention. It seemed there was a legend of a "golden table". It was told that one of the Barons of Thirwall had returned from the wars (perhaps the Crusades) laden with a great treasure, that included a table made out of solid gold. It had such great value to the Baron that he installed a guard, in the form a hideous dwarf, to keep watch over the table at all times. Thirwall Castle, being north of Blenkinsopp and so close to the Roman wall, was at considerable risk to the marauding hordes from the north. On one such occasion, a rather bold Scot invaded Thirwall, killing the Baron and his supporters. However, the table and dwarf were not to be found. Tradition has it that the dwarf threw the golden table into a well, and jumped in after, to preserve it and himself from the Scots. He, nor the table, were ever seen again.

John was particularly curious about the way the table of gold had been hidden in a well. He traced his steps back to the story of the White Lady. She had hidden the gold in a vault that Bryan de Blenkinsopp had never been able to find. Was it possible that this vault was not necessarily, immediately beneath the manor, but may have been in some other underground location, a well, a sewer, or something of the sort? He made additional notes for himself and continued on with the research.

John used every free moment to continue his investigation into the myth and lore of Northumberland. The story of the White Lady and the Golden Table were in several different sources, none of which revealed anything new. It was difficult to determine whether there was any basis in truth in any of it. It appeared that each legend was the product of oral and not written traditions. This made it difficult to identify the original source and therefore the validity of any of it. It was quite possible that none of the legends or ballads had any basis in fact. Or, it might be the case that there was always some element of truth and the final result was merely an embellishment. If it was embellishment, then it made for a good story, and it was no wonder that authors, such as Sir Walter Scott, would take advantage.

On Saturday, John was surprised to discover a letter from Abby left for him in his box at the dorm. He had not intended to write her, and he was a bit surprised by her correspondence.

Thursday, July 14, 1983

Dear John,

The days seem empty without you here. It seems so strange to suggest this, since we have only known each other less than a fortnight. I suppose the days were empty before we met, but I was ignorant of how much. It is now, in making the comparison to the days we spent together, the days which you made full, that I now fully understand my previous condition. Although I have my mother and Maggie, I realize now that I am alone. I miss you and I long for the day of your return.

I visited Mark's grandfather yesterday. It is something I do regularly, but I suppose in this instance, I needed to tell him about you. Despite the joy you have brought back into my life, there is still a feeling of guilt and remorse. Have I betrayed Mark? I needed to hear from someone else and he was the best choice.

To my surprise, he asked to see you. I suppose, see you again would be more appropriate since you have already met once. He has invited you, me and Maggie, to come and visit him, to stay with him for a few days, when you return. I have made arrangements at work, so if you are comfortable with the idea, we will visit him straight away when you return.

I realize this seems strange, however, my father is not here, and I respect his wisdom. Please say yes, it would mean a great deal to me.

I can not wait for your return. I have something to show you, a surprise.

Maggie says hello.
Love,

Abby

John immediately took out pen and paper to compose a response. He was not at all uncomfortable with meeting Mr. Brown again. He had thoroughly enjoyed their first encounter, and now knowing of his relationship to Abby, he looked forward to a second meeting. Besides, the thought of staying at Unthank Hall was very appealing; after all, it was the residence of his ancestors.

Saturday, July 16, 1983

Dear Abby,

Of course I would love to see Mr. Brown again. No worries, I do not feel any awkwardness at all. I am not asking you to forget Mark. I am not here to replace him. I realize this would be too difficult a task.

I respect your loyalty to Mark. It is part of what I love about you. It helps me to know your level of commitment, that the depth of your love was not frivolous or haphazard, but instead unselfish and enduring. If I can experience this same commitment, to know this same love, if I can fill your life with joy and companionship again, it would be enough.

I also miss you. It has been very difficult to concentrate on my work here. You and Maggie fill my every thought. Say hello to her for me. I look forward to the day we will be together again.

I shall not stop loving you.

See you in a week.
John

He put it in an envelope, put a stamp on it and then delivered it to the mail slot at the front desk.

*****

That afternoon John decided to return to the Bod. He was sure he had not exhausted all the library's resources. He could spend every day of his time in Oxford at the library and only scratch the surface.

As he arrived at the reference desk, the librarian who had helped him before recognized him in greeting.

"Hello Mr. Ridley, good to see you again, I suppose you're here to follow up on your previous visit," the librarian was cordial.

"Yes, as a matter of fact, I am."

"I have something here that I thought you might enjoy. I know you have been researching Scott's works, but I came across an obscure ballad from a lesser know work that you might be interested in. It struck me as peculiar since it actually mentions your family name in it, Ridley."

John took the book from the librarian and began scanning the page. The *Fray of Hautwessel*, was the title of the ballad. "What is this Hautwessel?" he asked.

"That is the ancient name of the village of Haltwhistle, are you familiar with it."

"Yes as a matter fact, I have just recently returned from a visit there, and the word fray?"

"It is the same as foray, or battle," again, the librarian answered.

John whispered a "thank you" and then sat down at the nearest table and began reading.

The Fray of Hautwessel

The limmer thieves o'Liddesdale
Wadna leave a kye in the hail countrie.
But an' we gie them the caud steel

Our gear they'll reive it a'awaye;
Sae pert they stealis I you say:
O'late they came to Hautwessel,
And thowt they there wad drive a fray,
But Alec Ridley shot too well.

Twas some time gane, they took our naigs,
And left us eke an empty byre:
I wd the deil had had their craigs,
And a'things in a bleeze o'fire;
Eh! But it was raised the warden's ire,
Sir Robert Carey was his name;
But an John Ridley thrust his spear
Right through Sim o' the Cathill's wame.

For he cam riding o'er the brae,
As gin he could na steal a cow;
And when we'd got our gear awa'
Says - 'Wha this day's work will avow?'
I wot he got reply enow,
As ken the Armstrongs to their grief.
For to tine the gear and Simmy too,
The ane to the tither's nae relief

Then cam Wat Armstrong to the town,
Wi' some three hundred chiels or mair,
An' swore that they wad burn it down;
A' clad in jack, wi' bow and spear.
Harnessed right weel, I trow they were;
But we were aye prepared at need,
And dropt ere lang upon the rear
Amangst them, like an angry gleed.

Then Alec Ridley he let flee
A clothyard shaft, ahint the wa';
It struck Wat Armstrong in the ee',
Went through his steel cap, heid and a'.
I wot it made him quickly fa',

He could na rise, thourgh he essayed;
  The best at thief-craft or the ba'
  He ne'er again shall ride a raid.

Gin should the Armstrongs promise keep
And seek our gear to do us wrang;
  Or rob us of our kye or sheep,
I trow but some o' them will hang;
Sharp is the sturdy sleuth dog's fang,
At Craweragge watchers will be set,
At Linthaugh ford too, a' neet lang,
Wow! But the meeting will be het.

He read over the ballad several times. The fact that it was concerning Haltwhistle and that at least two different Ridleys were mentioned made it very intriguing. He began to write down notes, scribbling in his journal words that he did not understand, that he would have to look up. He went back to the librarian and asked if he had any type of old English dictionary. The librarian obliged.

It turned out that Liddlesdale was a river valley just across the border into Scotland. Evidently it was common practice for reivers (the old English for thieves) to cross over the border and raid the villages of Northumberland. This ballad was chronicling just such an event. Evidently, they were attempting to steal cows (kyes) and horses (naigs), but were confronted by the townsfolk. Alec and John Ridley happened to kill two of the Armstrongs, Wat and Sim, which gave explanation for why the Armstrongs and Ridleys were always at odds.

Overall, the afternoon proved to be very fruitful. John couldn't wait until he had an opportunity to talk to Abby and others to see if they were aware of this legend, and if there were any other variations.

*****

As church ended on Sunday, Abby stayed behind after the service. She sent Maggie ahead with her grandmother, promising to follow in short order. As the sanctuary emptied, she sat quietly in the pew, looking up at the image of the cross on the wall behind the altar. After everyone had left, she stepped out into the aisle and went to the front of the church where she knelt down, placing her arms on top of the railing of the altar.

> *Dear Lord,*
> *Thank you for the blessings of my life, for my parents, for the gift of my dear little girl. I cried out to you in my despair when you took from me the love of my life, my husband, Mark. I wept before you in my pain and in my grief, and yet, I did not hear your voice. I did not understand. Now I cry out to you once again, not in pain, but in confusion. Let me hear your voice, let me know your mind. What would you have me do? Do I dare to love again? Is it right, is it good? What am I to do?*
>
> *You are the Lord God, the God of Jacob and Rebecca, the God of Boaz and Ruth. Let me hear your voice. In thee and thee only shall I trust. Teach me thy will.*
> *Amen*

Abby stayed at the altar a little longer, looking up at the cross and then she stood to her feet and left the church. She had her answer. After so many days of silence, she finally knew what to do. It was not that God had been silent, she had failed to listen. It was just as John had said, she was not in control. God was. As she was about to the leave the church, she turned one more time to look at the table of the altar. Inscribed across the front edge of the table were written the following words: *Trust in the Lord with All Thy Heart and He will direct Thy Path.* She smiled. It had always been about *Trust.*

The following Wednesday proved to be a very strange and important day for John. Early in the day he had a most unexpected letter in the mail. The return address was a Dr. Reginald McIntire of University of Edinburgh. As he opened the envelope, he could not imagine who Dr. McIntire was, and how he even knew who John was. He took a second look at the front of the envelope to be sure that it was in fact addressed to him.

Saturday, July 16, 1983

Dear Mr. Ridley,

Let me introduce myself. I am Dr. Reginald McIntire, Professor of English Literature at University of Edinburgh. I am a friend and colleague of one Dr. Robert Winslow, with whom you are no doubt acquainted. Dr. Winslow gave me a call last week and presumed to ask of me a favor, which he claimed was payment for an old debt. It turns out that due to an unexpected illness of one of my students, I have an opening in my department for a teaching assistant, of which I am prepared to make an offer to you, with the belief that my department will approve of your appointment as a visiting fellow. This fellowship comes with it, a large enough stipend to provide for your housing and board with perhaps a little left over.

As a visiting fellow, I am prepared to act as your advisor and counselor in the absence of Dr. Winslow, allowing you to continue your research here. This would enable you to take advantage of the wealth of resources available here in the University Library and more. Dr. Winslow would be able to continue his role as your primary adviser for the completion of your degree at the University of Illinois. In short, you would be here on loan in what might be termed as a study abroad.

Dr. Winslow suggested that I write you immediately, given that a letter from me would arrive much sooner than any correspondence he would be able to complete, in so short a time. I imagine he will be contacting you via telephone in the near future.

I look forward to meeting you. Attached is a copy of the proposed fellowship and the terms, including all dates and expectations of teaching responsibility.

Sincerely,
Dr. McIntire

John could hardly believe his eyes. He just sat staring at the letter for the longest time, reading it over and over. He looked over the terms of the Fellowship. It was unbelievable. He could not have imagined the possibility. Just when he thought he had the Professor figured out, he up and did the most unexpected. He made a note to himself to be sure to call the professor that night before he went to bed. This pretty much settled it. He was going to be staying in Great Britain.

The Foray of Haltwhistle

Located in the southernmost part of Scotland is the valley of Liddel Water, the river which forms the border with Northumberland. This valley was the home to a number of border reivers who would often fly down from the north and raid villages and hamlets in Northumberland, robbing and pillaging as they went. The families which occupied this valley included the Elliots, Armstrongs and Parks. Members of the Ridley clan had been given the appointment of High Sheriff of Northumberland for nearly 150 years and, therefore, were responsible for the defense of Northumberland against these Scottish invaders.

***

It was nearly dusk, long shadows stretched out in the rolling landscape. The silhouette of two men on horseback could barely be seen against the gray sky as they sat atop the Roman Wall overlooking Warks Burn. They sat on their steeds motionless and quiet watching the sun settle gently over the western horizon, both at ease on their mounts and content to remain quiet.

Finally the first rider broke the silence, "well Alec, I suppose it will be dark soon, we should start for home."

"Yeah, you're right cousin, I am afraid I have waited too long, and I will have to go the long way around to reach home. The shadows are growing and I fear it will be too dark to pass through the burn."

"The moon shall be nearly full; you shall not find it too difficult," Willard assured.

Willard and Alec were cousins, both descendents of the Ridleys of Willimoteswick. Willard was from Walltown, to the north, and twice-fold a descendent of Willimoteswick, being that his paternal grandparents were both of that line. Alec, on the other hand, was from Haltwhistle, to the south. They had known each other their entire lives and now that they were fully grown men, enjoyed the opportunity to go hunting together whenever possible. From this place upon the wall, they could see many

316

miles in all directions. It was here they would meet each time and from here they would go their separate ways.

"Alec, what do you make of that movement down in the shadows of the wall there, just to the west?" he pointed in the direction, nearly a half mile to west.

"I'm not sure, it appears to be riders."

"Can you make out how many?"

"I can't be sure, they seem to be clinging to the shadows, but I would have to say a dozen or more."

"More like three dozen, if you ask me," Willard said sharply. "It seems strange that so large a number would be out for a joy ride this late at night. It gives one cause for concern."

"Reivers!" they both said in unison as they arrived at the same conclusion.

"It appears they may be waiting for dark and since they are below the Roman Wall already, one would have to assume they are headed for Haltwhistle."

"I'm afraid you're right Wil," the townsfolk must be warned.

"It is up to you, Alec, it looks as if they have a little bit of lead on you. If you are to get there in time, you must leave now. Meanwhile, I will ride north to Walltown and muster up enough riders to come to your aide."

"In order to reach Haltwhistle in time, I will have to chance the burn," with this said, Alec applied his heels to his mount and the horse bolted forward. "Don't be too long Will, tell your father to come at once or it will be too late," he shouted over his shoulder as he departed.

Willard did not delay, he turned and set off at a gallop in the other direction.

Alec had been right to be wary of the burn. The moment he descended into the trees, he was enveloped in darkness. The huge oak and elm canopy above completely blocked out any twilight. He slowed his horse slightly, allowing his eyes to adjust to the darkness. Once he was accustomed to the shadows, he once against applied his heels, and the horse leaped forward at a gallop. It was difficult to see the path ahead, but he had made this journey more than once, and he was now trusting in his instincts, and the instincts of his mount.

There was not a moment to lose. As it was, he could only hope to reach the outskirts of Haltwhistle but a few moments before the reivers. As he raced down the path that paralleled the river, he had to duck beneath the overhanging branches for fear of getting knocked off. It appeared that his mount could see more clearly than he, for it caught him completely by surprised when they became airborne as they leapt over a fallen branch. It was all he could do to keep from falling from the saddle. As they rounded the last turn and came out upon a clearing, he could see the lights of the outlying cottages.

As he drew near he began shouting, "to arms, to arms! The reivers are upon us."

As he arrived at his home, his father was already at the door, pike in hand. In the distance he could hear a commotion, voices shouting, and an unmistakable sound of alarm. He had not arrived a moment too soon, the reivers had already reached the edges of the village, and were meeting with some resistance.

"Father, reivers have descended from the north, they mean to do us harm. Wil and I spied them from atop the wall, three dozen or more."

His father was already running toward the sounds of battle heard in the distance. "Quick, Alec, ride through the village and make sure everyone is alerted. We must all stand together," he shouted over his shoulder as he ran off.

Alec followed his father's instructions, fearful that he might have arrived home too late. Once he was sure that all had been alerted, he galloped in the direction his father had gone. He arrived upon a scene that was difficult to discern in the darkness. There were men in combat all around, and it became very difficult to determine who were the defenders and who were the assailants. Looking around he realized that the reivers had already managed to separate some of the livestock from the village, including a large number of horses. Some were driving the animals back into the darkness, while others were guarding their escape.

He looked around, wondering what he could do to help. In the middle of the foray, was a man on horseback, who seemed to be holding the men from the village at bay, all by himself, as he swung his sword with broad arching sweeps that knocked aside any man who dared to get too close. The lights held by those from the village gave Alec a glimpse of this bastion. He recognized him immediately as William Armstrong, the chieftain of the Armstrong clan, from Liddesdale.

He continued to search the night for his father, when all of a sudden he caught a glimpse of him, locked in combat with a large brutish man, mounted a coal black steed. His father was clearly at a disadvantage, not only for being on the ground while his opponent was on horse, but also, because his adversary was much larger and stronger. As he watched in horror, he saw his father fall to the ground, with his assailant leaping from his mount to finish the job. Instinctively, Alec raised his hunting bow and let an arrow fly. If he had waited a moment later it would have been too late. Just as the giant of a man was about to strike the final blow upon the man laying defenseless on the ground, the arrow caught the intended target in the right eye socket, passing through his head and the steel cap upon his head, killing him instantly. He fell dead upon Alec's father lying prostrate on the ground. Imagine the surprise on his face when he looked up from beneath the corpse, to see Alec standing with bow in hand.

"Here father, let me help you," Alec offered. It took both of them to roll the dead man aside, giving freedom to a somewhat humbled Robert Ridley.

"Thank you son, I think you have saved my life," his father said as he stood to his feet.

"Who was he father?" Alec asked. "Wat Armstrong, son. It has been said that no man has ever bested him in combat, I am afraid I was sorely overmatched. It is fortunate you happened along, and that you are so proficient with the bow, or I am afraid you would have been made fatherless tonight."

As they turned to check the progress of the defense of Haltwhistle, it became clear that the Armstrong clan had the upper hand, and without any support from outside of the village they were doomed to be overrun. Just as the situation appeared most hopeless, the sound of horses could be heard in the distance.

"Look father, it is our neighbors from Walltown. They have come in our defense."

There were more than two dozen men on horseback and in the lead was John Ridley, father of Wil, and himself a formidable warrior. They thrust themselves right into the middle of the assault causing surprise and confusion amongst the reivers. Even Kinmont Willie was no match for this unexpected change in fortune.

John Ridley went directly for the leader with all his might. There was a huge clash of blades as Ridley tried to dislodge Willie from his horse. The chieftain fell back from the blow almost falling from his mount. Just as Ridley was about to strike another blow, Willie's brother directed his mount between them. There was another loud clang as the swords of John Ridley and Sim Armstrong struck each other. Although Sim showed surprising courage and skill, he was no match for John Ridley. After several parries, Ridley found his opening and struck a fatal blow to Sim Armstrong, dismounting him with the act. This seemed to send the Armstrongs into disarray. Kinmont Willie was clearly disheartened by the fall of his brother, and signaled for the others to retreat. As quickly as they came they stole out into the darkness.

The rescuers from Walltown gave chase, but it was fruitless in the dark of the night and they soon returned to inspect the damage and care for the injured.

"Are you all right, Cousin?" John Ridley asked as he dismounted from his horse at the feet of Robert Ridley.

"Yes, cousin, thank you. We have some wounded and I think that they have made off with a portion of our livestock, including the horses, but had you been delayed even a moment, I am afraid we would have been done for."

"I think the thank you goes to these two young men," John pointed to Alec and Will, who were standing near. "If not for their quick wit, I'm afraid it would have been too late. I think they have saved the lives of many, here, tonight."

Alec and Wil turned and smiled at each other.

"I find it bold that the Armstrongs would come and attack us in the middle of the night, just as James IV is calling for peace. I think we will have to send notice to our cousin the Sheriff. I am quite sure we shall be supported in seeking restitution and even *perhaps, securing Kinmont Willie's head on a stick. He will no doubt take our offense to the Baron de Scope."*

"I agree, Cousin. I am sure this is not the end of it, or the last we shall see of Kinmont Willie."

Chapter Fifteen

It was a gloomy June day, a slow but steady precipitation fell from the sky and there was a slight chill in the air. A fire burned in the fire place of the great room, but it was not enough to brighten the room, which was subject to gather only the little light that passed from the overcast day through the windows whose drapery had been cast wide open. The Baron sat alone at his table perusing the letter before him, contemplating the meaning of its contents. He was in a state of trepidation, concerned that he was about to step down a pathway that might lead him to his own destruction; a path that once begun, there would be no going back.

The butler of the manor house entered the great room, and, not wishing to disturb his master in what was obviously so great a contemplation, had no choice. "My Lord, there is a young man here to see thee."

"Send him away. I have no desire to see him or anyone else today. I am not to be disturbed," the Baron insisted rather sternly.

"But Sir, He insists that it is of the utmost importance, or I should have sent him away directly. I think thee should see him."

"Why, who is it?" the Baron asked, disturbed that he should be questioned.

The butler hesitated slightly, "John Ridley, Sir."

"John Ridley, the scoundrel. What would I have to do with him or his entire family for that matter? A bunch of thieves and liars they are. Why should I give him the time of day?"

"He insists it is of a most urgent matter, and he is quite determined. He said he is willing to wait as long as it takes, but he would not depart the premises until he has an opportunity to have an audience with my Lord."

"Oh, very well, I shall not sit here and debate the matter. Show him in. I will give him just five minutes to state his business, and not a minute more." As the butler left the room, the Baron continued to mutter to himself, "The thought, a Ridley should demand an audience with me. What utter arrogance. What impudence."

"My Lord, John Ridley of Unthank Hall, to see thee," the butler announced to the Baron, as he reentered the hall. He was followed by a young man who had not yet seen his twenty fifth birthday. He was tall and handsomely proportioned, with dark brown hair and deep blue eyes.

"My Lord Featherstone," the young man gave a slight bow, out of respect to the Baron of Featherstone. "Thank thee for seeing me. I shall come to my business without delay, not wishing to hinder thee from your present responsibilities."

"Yes, yes, young man, get on with it. What could a Ridley possibly have to see me about, let alone someone of such immaturity?" The Baron was clearly irritated, and in a foul mood. The young man was immediately put at a disadvantage.

"My Lord, I am much aware of the ongoing feud that has existed between our families for more than two hundred years. A feud that has seen blood spilt on more than one occasion. A feud which, I might state, is unclear in its beginnings. It is, in fact, propagated by each succeeding generation, not by reason, but by some insane inclination toward upholding the hatred by mere tradition.

I, for one, and there are others who would agree, see no purpose in this feud, and I would seek to bury this hatred and to make all attempts at healing the transgressions that exist between these two great houses, and to seek a peaceful resolution."

"I see, after two hundred years of bitterness, you, a young man who is barely old enough to have left the nursery, would now propose to me that thou could be the instrument by which

this feud could be dissolved. What is thy proposal?" The Baron saw no real purpose in this conversation. From his perspective, the feud existed because the Ridleys were a notorious family, who could not be trusted. After all, they were originally of Norman ancestory and therefore, not the true heirs to the land that they now occupied at Willimoteswick, Unthank Hall and Ridley Hall.

"What thou may not be aware of Sir," the young man continued, "is that from early childhood I have made acquaintance with your daughter, Abigail, and have formed a loving friendship and attachment for her." The Baron began to fidget in his seat, he did not like where this was going. "To that end Sir, I would propose to thee...I would ask of thee, thy blessing, in the joining of my hand and hers in matrimony. Let these two great halls, these two great families, once and forever set aside our differences, our petty feuds and join together as one."

The Baron could not believe his ears. He banged his broad hand upon the table, causing such a loud noise that the young man was caused to jump, both in spirit and body. He stood to his feet, "thou impudent whelp! To think, to believe, that thee could march into this hall- a hall that has been home to my family for generations, and might I add, a family of ancestors who, today, are turning over in their grave-that thou could have the audacity to ask for the hand of my only living daughter, unheard of. Thou are most fortunate that I do not strike thee where thou standest."

"Sir, I am much aware that these words would be a source of such consternation to thee that it would cause you to shudder throughout thy extremities. But I must inform thee, thy daughter, Abigail, and I have been very much in love for some time. We know the traditions of our own parentage and the feud that exists between our families, of which we have no desire to give credence to. We love each other and wish to be the bridge that will bring peace, at last, to this land, so that no Featherstone or Ridley need fear the other for generations to come."

"Thou poor naïve boy, to think that because of some fanciful and youthful amorous feeling, that thou would be a deserving husband of my beautiful Abigail. Even now I hold in my hand a second proposal, from a most prominent and respected family, *who are willing to pay not so small a sum for the privilege of being joined with this ancient see."*

Suddenly there was a shriek that came from the alcove to one side of the hall. Emerging from the shadows was a young girl of about twenty, with golden locks of hair falling down upon her shoulders and brilliant blue eyes that were supported in their vibrancy by the gown she was wearing of the same color.

"Father, what do mean?" the young woman shouted as she made her entrance. "What proposal? Who has proposed marriage to me, without my consultation?"

"Be still, daughter, this does not concern thee, this is a conversation between men, leave us."

*"Does not concern **me**! How can you suggest that a proposal of marriage to someone I do not even know, does not concern me? If it does not concern me, then pray tell, who then?"*

The Baron was growing more irritated by the minute. With each successive exchange, his ire grew and the volume of his voice with it. "It is to someone thou knowest. I hold here a proper proposal by the Baron of Bellister Manor, on behalf of his son, Thomas Blenkinsopp. And I must say, it is a highly generous proposal, indeed."

"Thomas Blenkinsopp is an arrogant, pompous imbecile. I would sooner marry the stable boy. How could thou possibly consider such an offer?"

"Sir, would you prostitute thy daughter, in this way, to hand over so precious a flower, to be crushed in the hands of an ogre, all for some shiny baubles? If it is merely gold that thou wish, then simply name thy price and I will make it good. Then thou shall not only have thy treasure, but a loving and devoted son-in-law as well." John Ridley was not about to give in.

*"Thou misunderstand me sir, it is not for the money that I would give my daughter's hand to another, but it is my desire that she marry any other, **but thee**."*

"But Father, I love John Ridley. He has never done anything to deserve such prejudice. He is the man I wish to marry, there is no other. I would die before I would consent to marrying anyone else." Abigail pleaded with her father, but there was no change in his continence, no softening of his grim exterior.

"Quiet girl, thou must know that your father loves thee and I would never do anything to harm thee. But, thou are too young and too easily given over to infatuations. Thou must trust thy father's judgments in these matters. Now, leave us, return to thy room."

"Father, please. Do not do this thing. This man here, standing before thee, is the man I love. Do not think me naïve or immature. In this one action you would sentence me to a life of unhappiness and sorrow. I beg of thee please, allow me to marry John Ridley."

"Sir," John Ridley interjected, hoping to take advantage of the emotional strain now visible on the Baron's face. Clearly, he could not withstand his daughter's pleas for long. "I love thy daughter with all of my heart. She is my breath and my all. I would seek to be her protector and would give my life to save hers. I would not now presume to take her from her father, who is alone, widowed and without other children to bring him comfort in her absence. We would reside as near to you as you would command, even here in this manor if thou so desire, so that thy daughter and thy grandchildren might bring thee satisfaction in thy waning years."

For a moment it seemed as if the Baron was beginning to soften, but then his eyes grew large, as if wakened from a dream, "Thou would presume to come and live here, anticipating that I would soon succumb to that eternal sleep, so that the name of Ridley would then fly from the ramparts of this great hall. Thou would use my daughter, to once again gain the occupation of a land which does not belong to thee or any of your kind, just as thou once did of Willimoteswick. I shall not so easily be swayed by the musings of so treacherous a stranger or the musings of a hysterical daughter. Enough of this; leave me. Thou are no longer welcome in this place, John Ridley, thee or any of thy kind."

"Father please," Abigail sank to her knees, her head turned upward to her father, tears streaming down her cheeks, "please do not do this."

"As for thee, my daughter, I am sorry for thy grief, but someday thou will understand that I do this because I love thee. I forbid thee to ever see this young man again. Next month on a *date of my choosing, thou shall marry Thomas Blenkinsopp, until then, thou will not be permitted to leave the walls of this manor unaccompanied."*

At this, Abigail let out a wail of grief that sent shivers down the spine of all who were present. She bent her head to the ground and sobbed profusely, tears wetting the skirt of her dress. Meanwhile, the Butler stepped between the Baron and the young man, making a clear indication to the young man that it was time to leave, and pointing in the direction of the door he was to exit.

As John Ridley was leaving he stopped and turned, uttering one last proclamation of his love, "I love thee Abigail Featherstone. I shall never love another. As heaven is my witness this day, I shall not give up, I shall find a way." He looked directly at the father, as if making him a promise that he would keep.

The father sat down in his chair, tears forming at the edges of his eyes. What had he done? Was this the right course of action? Of course it was. What else could he have done? He hated to see his daughter so, but it could not be helped.

A maid entered the hall and proceeded to where the young girl remained sobbing, nearly prostrate on the floor. The maid bent down and assisted the young girl to her feet, and then supported her as she walked out of the hall. Between sobs, Abigail offered one last plea to her father, "please consider this moment father, turn away from your bigoted and prejudicial mind and see the truth and honor that is to be found in John Ridley. Do not be deceived by the luster and brilliance of gold, or the false pretenses of a superficial and beguiling clan as the Blenkinsopps. If thou go forward in this manner, thou has destined me to destruction and thee as well." She turned away and left the hall.

The Baron was left staring into an empty room. The uncertainty of the moment still weighed heavily upon his shoulders, a burden much too heavy to bear. It weighed him down to the point of despair, but there was no alternative, no going back. Abigail would have to marry Thomas Blenkinsopp, for better or for worse.

The month that followed was a solemn one. Abigail was essentially under house arrest, unable to even step into the pasture surrounding the castle without an escort. There had been no sign of John Ridley, but given his testament, it was unlikely that he had given up altogether.

It had grown quiet between Abigail and her father. If it was her intent to punish him, then she had been quite successful, for to not hear his daughter's voice on a daily basis, was a torment that required great fortitude and patience. As the wedding day drew close, the Baron became more and more despondent, no longer confident in his decision to go forward with the promised nuptials. On the morning of the wedding, a coach arrived, under guard, carrying a large chest, with what must have been the wedding ransom.

This ransom could not be considered a dowry, for in Northumberland, as elsewhere, the dowry was provided by the father of the bride, not the father of the groom. The Baron of Featherstone had no male heir, and thus this ransom was a payment for the privilege of the joining of the two houses of Featherstone and Blenkinsopp. By accepting this ransom, the Baron was insuring that the descendents of his daughter would continue to hold rights to Featherstone Castle, even though those descendents would no longer carry the Featherstone name. Despite the entrepreneurial nature of this arrangement, the Baron continued to argue with himself that it was an honorable choice, based on his desire to protect the interests of his daughter and her children. Despite this internal debate that raged within his soul, he could not get past the sorrow of his beloved Abigail and thus the intense feeling of guilt that racked his soul.

The wedding was a simple affair held in the chapel of the castle and led by a local bishop. The only guests were the members of the two families, Abigail's father, some of the members of the household, Thomas' parents, and his seven siblings, five brothers and two sisters. There were no vows, no promises of love and fidelity, no spoken words between the bride and groom. It was merely a matrimonial declaration by the bishop, announcing the legal union. The Wedding Mass did not require much time and before Abigail could summon up the courage to protest, the ceremony was over and they were pronounced husband and wife.

The Northumberland tradition called for the groom and his companions to ride out into the forest before twilight came and to hunt the game to be cooked at the wedding feast. Abigail asked that she be allowed to participate in the hunt, at least from the back of her horse. Although it was unusual for the bride to participate in the hunt, it was not unheard of. It was a simple request and so her father consented. Unbeknownst to the Baron, Abigail had received communication via one of the household maids that John Ridley and his brothers intended to meet the hunting party and steal her away. Her father was completely oblivious to the change in her countenance when he gave her permission to ride, otherwise he may have succeeded in recognizing the deception.

It was not long before one of the hunters of the wedding party was able to down a young stag with an arrow from his bow. The deer was bled and then strapped across the hunter's horse, prompting the wedding party to begin the journey back to the castle, for it was twilight and soon to be night. As they passed through Pynkinscleugh Glen, John Ridley and his brothers emerged from the trees.

"What business dost thou have here, John Ridley? Be off with thee and take thy abject band with thee."

"I am here on a matter of the heart, Thomas Blenkinsopp," Ridley returned. "I am here to take possession of what is rightly mine, both soul and body. We, that is my abject band and I, are prepared to take her by force, if necessary, and I shall warn you, that we are prepared to use all means, and believe ourselves to be a formidable force."

With this announcement the other members of the wedding party, drew whatever weapons were at their disposal, whether sword or bow, as the Ridleys did likewise.

Thomas paused for a moment, considering carefully his next chosen word. "Come, come Ridley, as you can see, the bride has already taken her nuptials, and is now only preparing the celebration feast. See here, we have shot a deer, and I invite thee to come back with us and partake of this young venison and we will toast to each other's good health. We are already married and there is nothing to be done about it."

"This marriage has not been consummated and, in fact, the bride was not able to act of her own volition, and therefore it is not recognized by heaven. Why risk thy life and limb for a woman who clearly does not love thee, and all the while she is with thee, she is thinking of another? Desist and allow us to take her without violence, there is no need for blood to be spilt between us."

Again Thomas paused, looking on the countenance of his adversary and recognizing his determination. Although fearful of combat with a foe so confident and properly equipped, he felt his pride injured before his brothers, having been challenged so openly and without regard for his superior position. His humility was not sufficient to allow him to turn away, but instead he brandished his sword aloft and signaled to his companions to make themselves ready.

"I cannot let thee take her. Marriage is rarely a matter of the heart, more often a matter of convenience. I make no claims on Abigail's affection, but she has been given to me, and since it be for a price, I will not give her up without a fight. I suggest you prepare thyself to meet thy maker."

"Thou are a fool Blenkinsopp, thou may have walked away while thy blood still courses through thy veins. While I still breathe, I will not allow thee to violate this angel with so grievous a motive. But, consider, my rival, that we need not involve others in a quarrel that involves us alone. Cannot two men of honor come to resolution that does not require the loss of innocent blood? Dismount from thy charger and face me alone on this field of battle. The one who is left standing shall be declared victor, and shall claim this priceless vessel."

John Ridley dismounted and waved to his brothers to stand back, and create space. Thomas Blenkinsopp hesitated for a moment, but then also removed from his stallion and stood facing Ridley, not ten paces away, sword in hand and at the ready.

Up until this moment, Abigail had remained quiet, but she could contain herself no longer. The thought that her lover could be injured or worse, killed, regardless of how unlikely, caused her to tremble. As she slid from her horse she shouted to the combatants, "Stop! Must thou quarrel thus. John Ridley, I love thee with all my heart, but I will not stand by and see thee done injury on my behalf."

"Do you hear Blenkinsopp, she loves me? Tis music to my ears; giving endurance to my heart and strength to my right arm which now holds the instrument of thy death." As he said this, Ridley struck at Blenkinsopp, only to have his first parry blocked by the defendant's raised sword. The clang of metal against metal shattered the night air.

"Stop, please!" Abigail pleaded once more. "Thomas, there is no point to thy madness. I do not love thee, nor does thou love me. Let me go, preserve thy honor and thy life before it is too late."

"Be still, Abigail," Blenkinsopp shouted, as he stepped back from the foray. "This scoundrel before me is not disserving of so fair a prize, and I will not stand by while he steals what is rightfully mine, before my very eyes." With this, Blenkinsopp struck back at Ridley, only to have his attack easily deflected aside.

Cautiously, the two combatants dealt blow after blow upon their opponent only to have each attempt defended without injury. The specter of two skilled warriors engaged in mortal competition, completely occupied the attentions of both parties present. Abigail stood back, wincing and writhing in apprehension as her lover dealt with each offensive with skill and precision. Unnoticed by any of those watching there was one member of the wedding party who remained in the shadows, with bow drawn, waiting for an opportunity to release its deadly shaft.

The battle raged on, neither man willing to yield. However, with each thrust and parry delivered by young Blenkinsopp, it was clear that he was tiring and was facing a foe who was built of a stronger capacity and who would prevail in the end. Fear and despair became his expression and it seemed only a matter of time before Ridley would gain the upper hand. Abigail looked back at the wedding party, sensing their concern, wondering if they would act to support their champion, who would soon fall. It was then she noticed a glimmer of light reflecting from the point of the arrow which was now aimed at the body of her beloved. It was at this very moment that Ridley found his opening and struck with all his might, a blow that would prove to be

Blenkinsopp's undoing. Suddenly, Abigail shrieked and threw herself between Ridley and the projectile sent in his direction. With Blenkinsopp on the ground, his life's blood finding the earth beside him, Ridley turned in reaction to the outburst by the young girl, only to have her fall into his outstretched arms, a deadly shaft protruding from her chest.

Ridley cried out, "No! What fiend has done such an evil deed as this?" Without any need for exhortation from their leader, the Ridley band immediately threw themselves upon the remaining members of the wedding party, reeking vengeance for this horrible act, showing no mercy.

As the battle continued about them, Ridley gathered his beloved Abigail into his arms and carried her to a nearby rock, laying her carefully upon its rounded, sloping surface. "Oh Abigail, my love, what have I done?" Realizing, in his heart, there was nothing he could do for the fallen damsel.

"Fret not, my dearest John, it is not thy fault," she whispered to him. "I could not have survived thy death, and my life I freely give for thee. Farewell my love, God has not willed it that we should be together in this life." She breathed her last and expired.

John Ridley gave out a horrible cry, even as the last of the Blenkinsopp party closed their eyes for the last time. The Ridleys in unison turned to offer their brother support and comfort, only to see a most horrible display. John Ridley stood above the body of his lost love, and pronounced, "If God has deigned that we should not be together in this life, then may he be merciful and gracious and allow us the privilege to be joined in the next." He then raised his own dagger and plunged it into his own heart. He then fell down dead, his body lying across the now dead corpse of his beloved Abigail.

Those who were left, stood in shock and dismay, disbelieving what they had just observed. For several moments, no one moved, uncertain of what to do and entranced by so dreadful a scene. Finally, George Ridley gathered his brother in his arms and placed his body upon his horse. William Ridley, in turn, did the same with the body of poor Abigail. As for the others, dead and dying, they were left where they lay.

The Baron waited patiently in the great hall of Featherstone for the return of the overdue wedding party. Servants were sent to observe their return and announce their coming. As the evening waned, fatigue befell his aged frame, causing a drowsiness that he could not defy. As he sat dozing at the table, he was suddenly awakened by a chill, followed by the opening of the hall's doors with such violence and clamor that he nearly fell backward out of his chair. A great wind wailed through the hall, as the wedding party returned. But, something was wrong. From the moment the figures entered the hall, the Baron recognized their ethereal appearance; not quite real. And then without warning, they disappeared, all of them, without a trace, as if they had never been there at all. The Baron frantically fled through the doors out into the night, only to realize his greatest fear. There before him in the yard was Abigail's bay, and draped across the saddle, a body all dressed in white. Hesitantly, he approached the mare, wanting to look; not wanting to know. He gently stroked the blond tresses that hung low, and then carefully, he lifted her head, only to be racked with the horror of looking upon the lifeless face of his loving daughter, Abigail.

As if crushed beneath a load of coal, the Baron fell to the ground, giving forth a wail that caused every one in the household to come running. "My sweet Abigail," he cried, staining the ground with his tears. "What abomination has befallen thee? Who would dare harm such an innocent dove? Why has God forsaken me this night?" With this utterance, he fell into such hysterics, that all future articulation was nothing more than the ravings of a man who had completely lost all sanity.

The next day, the remaining bodies of those who expired were found in the glen, with the exception of the body of John Ridley, which had been carried home by his brothers. The stone upon which Abigail had been laid and upon which John had fell, had a natural bowl on one end that had been naturally formed by weather. As the two victims of this calamitous night gave up their vital humors, it was gathered in this slight hollow. As those living retrieved the dead for burial, ravens gathered upon the stone, drinking the blood and singing a mocking song, underscoring the abhorrent tragedy that had befallen Pynkinscleugh Glenn. One member of the wedding party miraculously survived with only superficial wounds, and was able to convey to those present the events of the previous evening. This narrative brought little comfort to the Baron, but instead brought additional grief and despair. He would not recover. He would only know sorrow for the remainder of his days.

Chapter Sixteen

...it was so dark he could barely see his own hand in front of his face. The ground beneath his feet was damp. He was in some sort of cave, or tunnel. He reached for the rock wall to his right. He kept his hand on it as he stepped forward, further into the darkness. He did not know where he was going, but he was compelled to continue. As he felt his way in the darkness, the stone wall turned to brick. He could feel the seams in the wall filled with mortar. If only he could see better. He took off his back pack and began rummaging through it. There, he found what he was looking for in the side pouch, a box of matches. He took one from the box and struck it against the emery on one side. It immediately flared to life, illuminating the entire passage. He looked from side to side and then to the floor. There was a small stream, just a trickle, running along the base of the tunnel. It was some sort of drain. The walls were hewn rock all around, except for the one closest to him. It was a brick wall, from ground to ceiling, as if it was constructed to enclose a passageway beyond. He lit another match and held it above his head. There it was at the top of the wall, a crest. He held the match close. At the bottom of the crest was a name, he could barely make it out... it was...Featherstone!

John awoke to the intercom announcing their arrival into Newcastle station. It was Saturday, the symposium at Oxford was behind him and he was returning to Northumberland. He had not slept very well the night before, but he was able to catch a little nap on the train from Paddington. He would have to change trains in Newcastle, just as before, but by now he was feeling fairly comfortable with his surroundings and the local modes of travel. He thought back to three weeks ago, his first time entering Newcastle station. It was the first time he had met Abby. Only three weeks, and yet it seemed like a lifetime ago.

He was looking forward to seeing her again. Although he had felt a little anxiety when leaving two weeks ago, he had received two letters from her, relieving all his fears. He could hardly wait to tell her about the fellowship at Edinburgh, but he would have to patient, waiting until the right moment.

Changing trains in Newcastle went like clockwork, and he was soon on the last leg of the journey; or perhaps it was the first leg of a new journey. As he sat looking out the window, following the line of the River Tyne as it ran parallel to the train, he began to think back to all that had happened over the past three weeks. The wheels of the train made a constant clicking as they passed over the seams in the track. It was somewhat hypnotic, and he was lost in his daydream. It had been quite an adventure, coming to England, and yet he couldn't help thinking that it was just the beginning.

As the train approached the Hexham station, he was reminded of his visit to St. John Lee and the discoveries he had made about his ancestry. He knew that Grandmother Ridley would be excited to hear of his successes. He felt a little ashamed that he had not written, as he had promised. He took out some paper and began composing a letter.

As the train pulled into the Haltwhistle station, John leaned against the window so that his nose was almost touching the glass. As the train slowed to a stop, he caught a glimpse of Abby and Maggie standing on the platform. They were waiting for him. Abby was looking up and down the train, and it was clear that she could not see him through the glass. He folded his completed letter and put it away; he would mail it later. He jumped up out of his seat and grabbed his bags. The train was not very full, so it was only a matter of seconds before he was stepping down onto the platform.

Abby saw him immediately, and with Maggie in tow she hurried to where he stood at the bottom of the steps, leading down from the train car. As he placed his bags onto the walk, Abby threw her arms around his neck and hugged him. As she did so, she whispered into his ear, "I was afraid, just for a tiny moment, afraid you would change your mind and that you wouldn't come, that I would never see you again."

He pulled back a little so that he could look into her eyes, there were tears forming in the corners. "I told you I would be back, and now I am here to stay. There is no need to fear, Abby, ever again." He kissed her on the forehead and they embraced.

At that moment, John felt a little tug on his pant leg. "Hey! What about me?" Maggie exclaimed.

"Hello, Maggie, I haven't forgotten you," he bent down and gathered her up in one arm, and then, for a moment, the three of them embraced in one group hug.

It was late afternoon when the three of them arrived at Unthank Hall. As the car pulled into the driveway, Mr. Brown emerged through the front door to welcome them. As John stepped out of the car, Mr. Brown extended his hand in a warm greeting. "Hello, John, it is good to see you again. Welcome to Unthank Hall, I trust you had a good trip."

"Yes, thank you, Mr. Brown, it was a very good trip. Thank you for inviting me to stay here, it means a lot to me, more than you can imagine."

"Ah, yes, you must be referring to your ancestral heritage. The Ridleys did have possession of Unthank for a time. Well you should make yourself right at home. I imagine you could use a little freshening up. I will let Abby show you to your room." With that Mr. Brown gave Abby a wink. "In the meantime, I will keep an eye on our little princess. Do I get a hug, Maggie?"

As Mr. Brown knelt down, Maggie ran into his arms. "Hello Grandfather."

"Careful Maggie, you don't want to knock your poor old grandfather over," Abby cautioned.

"And if she did, it would be my own fault," Mr. Brown chuckled.

John grabbed his bags and followed Abby inside and up the stairs to his room. She showed him where the W.C. was and she pointed out the room which she and Maggie would be sharing down the hall. Unthank was a very large house with plenty of room for all of them. He wondered how Mr. Brown was able to manage it all by himself. "You go ahead and take your time John. I am going to go downstairs to help Grandfather get dinner started. I'm sure you're hungry or soon will be."

John smiled, "I'll be fine. You go ahead. I'll just get myself situated here and then I'll be down to help in short order."

"Don't be silly, you just relax, we have everything taken care of. There will plenty of opportunity for you to pitch in later."

John wasn't exactly sure what she meant by this, but he had a feeling it had something to do with doing the dishes. He unpacked his clothes and then spent a little time getting cleaned up. By the time he came down the stairs, he could smell the makings of dinner emanating from the kitchen. Rather than disturb the cooks at work, he decided to take a walk outside in the garden. The front of the house faced north toward the River Tyne. Beyond the garden wall, was the typical pasture; separating the grounds surrounding the house from the tree lined riverbank. He walked through the gate, out into the pasture, toward the river. Once he had walked far enough, he turned to get a view of the house. It was an impressive structure, with ancient stone walls covered in ivy reaching up to the eaves. One part of the house was a three story tower, no doubt a remodeling of the original pele tower. Unthank Hall was ever bit as impressive as Featherstone, although not as ancient a structure.

As John stood standing in the field, Abby appeared at the gate. She waved and he assumed this was a signal for him to return. As he approached, she smiled and said, "You had better be careful not to wander to far off. We don't want to lose you on the first night."

"Don't worry. I am somewhat familiar with these surroundings. It was not that long ago that I was riding a bike down Unthank Road, there." He pointed back in the direction of the road. "Somehow, I managed to get myself all the way back to Bardon Mill without getting lost."

"A pretty impressive feat, for a *foreigner*," Abby put a little emphasis on the word foreigner, as a sort of jab at his cockiness. "In any case, it is just about time for dinner, and around here, if you're late for dinner, you may not get any."

"Let's go then," he stepped through gate, not waiting for a second invitation. As they walked toward the house, he began to run, and right on cue, Abby took the challenge to race to the front door. She edged him out slightly when he realized it was not gentlemanly to ease her aside with his shoulder as they reached the porch, so he backed off.

*****

At dinner, Mr. Brown obliged John by giving him a brief history of Unthank and how the Browns had come into possession of the estate. John was also somewhat curious as to how Mr. Brown was able to manage such a large place all by himself.

"Oh I have plenty of help. Most of the pasture land around is actually maintained by some of my neighbors. I don't actually raise any livestock anymore. I have a lady come in twice a week who helps with the cleaning. Then Abby checks in on me fairly often. And then, there are the relatives who keep popping in all the time. In fact, I would have to say, that I am rarely alone at all."

"What would you like to do tomorrow, John? Abby asked. Anything special?"

"I was thinking we could go exploring. Some place I haven't been yet. Perhaps another castle or something, got any ideas?"

"A few," Abby smiled.

"I was kind of wondering if you would let me drive your car? I think I would like to learn this backward way of driving," John said sheepishly.

"A little impertinent to suggest it is backward, don't you think? I mean, after all, this is the mother country," Abby kidded.

"That's true, but we did invent the automobile, and somehow the plans got reversed when they were shipped back across the ocean."

"Easy, you two," Mr. Brown cut in, "we don't need another revolution, here at the dinner table."

Abby and John looked at each other and then at Mr. Brown and then they all started laughing.

"What's so funny?" Maggie interjected. This made them all laugh even louder.

*****

After dinner, as promised, John helped Abby with the dishes, while Mr. Brown read to Maggie in the sitting room. When everything was cleaned up, Abby invited John to go with her to the barn to check on the horses. Abby had brought down her bay a few days earlier and there were two other horses that Mr. Brown allowed the neighbors to board in his barn. Abby checked their water and feed and did a little cleaning of the stalls, while John watched. As they left the barn, the sun was setting and stars were beginning to emerge. He took her hand in his as they walked around the perimeter of the house, slowly, silently, enjoying the solitude, relishing being together again.

As they entered the house, they noticed that Maggie was falling asleep in her grandfather's arms. Abby carefully lifted her from his lap. "I guess it's time to put this girl to bed."

"Do you need any help?" John asked.

"No, you stay here and keep Grandfather company. I'm sure you can think of something to talk about." Abby carried the sleeping Maggie up the stairs to her room.

"Thank you, again, for inviting me to stay with you, Mr. Brown. It was very gracious of you."

340

"Think nothing of it, John. Abby is very important to me, I love her as if she were my own granddaughter and…"

"And Maggie of course *is* your great granddaughter, I understand. Here I am, a complete stranger, having come out of nowhere, to step into their lives, and into yours. It had to come as a bit of surprise, happening so quickly and all."

"I have known Abby since she was just a young girl. She and Mark seemed destined to be together from the very start. It did an old man's heart good to see two youngsters who were so much in love. I was very happy for both of them."

"From what Abby has told me, Mark sounded like a wonderful husband and father."

"That he was, and we were all devastated when we got the news of his passing. It was such a ridiculous loss, to be killed in such a meaningless war. Of course, Abby took it hardest of all. I didn't think she would ever get over it. To be honest, I felt a bit guilty."

"Guilty. Why?"

"It was because of me that Mark had joined the military. He was following in my footsteps and in the footsteps of his father. He did it because of an unspoken family obligation. The difference is that I never saw any combat. I came of age after the Great War, the war to end all wars. The same was true of his father who came of age after World War II. It wasn't right, Mark dying; someone so young, and so much to live for."

"You could not have known. Only God knows the time, the comings and goings of man. It has always been this way. It is not for us to understand. *There is a time to live and a time to die.* It was not your doing, not your fault, nor the fault of his father."

"Yes, of course, you are right. I have always known this, but it does not ease the pain. I have seen my grandparents and my parents die, and then of course my beloved Mary. None of those moments compare to the pain of losing a child or a grandchild. We are not supposed to see our children die, and certainly not our grandchildren."

"As I told Abby, the pain reminds us of what we have lost. It should remind us to be grateful for what we had then, and what we have now."

"That is a good deal of wisdom coming from someone who is so young. It is easy to see why Abby is so fond of you."

"Good training, I suppose. I have had the benefit of learning from those who have come before me, my parents, my grandparents, and even my great grandparents. I sometimes forget how much I have been influenced by their life experience. I suppose I have, more often than not, taken it for granted. It's only during life's most meaningful moments that I realize how much I have been blessed."

"And what about Abby, are you as fond of her?"

"More than just a fondness, I believe I love her. She is an extraordinary girl. I don't believe I have ever known anyone quite like her."

"Yes, she is special. And I think she is quite fond of you as well."

"I suppose she is, but I'm trying to be cautious. Just like you, she is still holding on to Mark. It is completely understandable. In a way, she probably thinks letting go, means forgetting. And I would never ask her to do that. She needs time to heal, and I don't want to rush her."

"Abby is much too young. I would not want her to dwell on the past when she has so much of life ahead of her." Mr. Brown paused for a moment before verbalizing his next thought. "It's time for her to move on with her life. Mark would not have wanted her to pine for him. He would understand. I think she knows that already. Down deep, she is probably afraid. Perhaps, it is because when she loved Mark, she gave herself fully, and in the end she was devastated by his loss. To go through that even once, is enough for anyone. If she allows herself to love that way again, she puts herself at risk of going through it all over again. You may need to be patient with her."

John thought for a moment before responding. "I realize things have moved a little quickly for the two of us. I would like to slow the clock down and take a more leisurely approach to things. I don't really understand it all myself, how I could have fallen in love so quickly. The last thing I want to do is to hurt her or pressure her. But I don't want to lose her. I also want her to feel safe, to know that this is real and not just some kind of illusion. Most of all, I want to be honest with her."

"And Maggie? What about her?"

"I think Maggie is wonderful. I am not here to replace Mark, her father. But if Abby wants me to be a part of her life, then I realize Maggie is a part of the deal."

"You appear to be very sincere, John. I don't doubt your intentions are right and good. You have my blessing if you need it, only I have to ask one thing of you. Be very careful with Abby, she is fragile. Don't play with her emotions, and do not try and force her to be something she is not, or to make a decision before she is ready. It must be when she is ready, not before. Can you do that?"

"Yes, I think so, but how will I know?"

"From what I have heard tonight, I think you will figure it out."

John didn't know how to respond to this. He was trying to be cautious. He was concerned for where her heart was. He didn't need to pressure her, to make her feel awkward. He needed to be patient, but how could he be sure that he would know the right time?

"Don't you two think it is about time for bed?" Abby entered the room.

"You're exactly right, Abby. It's not good for this old man to burn the midnight oil."

"I'm sorry, I shouldn't have been keeping you up," John apologized. It wasn't really all that late, but he wasn't sure what kind of hours Mr. Brown kept.

"Goodnight, you two," Mr. Brown said as he got up from his chair and headed for the stairs.

"Goodnight, Grandfather," Abby said as she sat on the couch next to John. After Mr. Brown had left she asked, "What were the two of you talking about?"

"Oh, just getting to know each other a little bit. You know the same old stuff. He was asking a lot of questions and I did my best to answer." He was not really very good at even telling a little white lie and he sensed that Abby knew that there was more to it than what he was letting on. However, she didn't press him any further.

"You haven't told me if you like Unthank Hall."

"Yes, very much, it is just as impressive inside as it is out. I must admit, it gives me kind of a weird feeling. A couple of months ago I didn't even know this place existed, and yet it was once inhabited by my ancestors, hundreds of years ago. They would have sat, talking in this very room. It seems strange to be able to connect with my family history in this way."

"I suppose it would seem strange to you, having lived in a completely different part of the world. For me, it is different. I have always felt a strong connection to my past. I have never lived anywhere else, and going back twenty or more generations, my ancestors have all lived here in Northumberland. It is all familiar to me, nothing strange and nothing uncertain. I know who I am, because I know where I have come from. And yet, in another way, I do not know who I am, because I do not know what lies ahead. I had always imagined a future with Mark. Just as our pasts were intertwined, so our future would be."

"It's true, that understanding the past does give us a sense of who we are and, perhaps, where we belong. I suddenly feel as if I have two pasts, the one I left in Pennsylvania, and the new one I have just now discovered in Northumberland. They are both a part of who I am. The future is far more complicated. It is what makes us human, this uncertainty, this not knowing what tomorrow might bring. It is a part of the journey. It's what forces us to make choices, to live life. If we actually knew what tomorrow brings, we might not get out of bed in the morning, we might try to avoid it, even change it. Of course, we don't really have the power to change it, not really. If we think we are in control, it is merely an illusion…"

Abby interrupted here, "We have to learn to trust, to know that we are not alone. That there is someone else who is in control, someone who has the power to do what is right and what is good."

"That's right, but not just anyone. In this case, that someone is benevolent. He generally cares what happens to us.

It doesn't mean that every moment will be to our liking, but regardless, He will not leave us alone."

"I know, John. It was not until recently that I began to understand this. Perhaps meeting you had something to do with it, I'm not really sure. I think that when Mark died, I not only felt the pain of losing him, but I was also afraid. I was afraid that I no longer had control. I was under this illusion of thinking that I had a plan, and that I was in control of that plan. Mark's dying was not in my plan, and it shook me to my foundation. I did not want to get out of bed, because I was no longer in control of tomorrow. In a way, I stopped living."

John did not respond right away. He was beginning to fear that he was just waxing philosophically, when he was really trying to say something comforting. "And now, how are you feeling?"

Abby hesitated. "I am still afraid, but I guess I am not paralyzed by the fear. I realize that I can't stay closed off from the world. For one thing, Maggie needs me to show her the way. At the same time, I can't remain standing still, all alone, never looking forward, seeing the path ahead, but too paralyzed to take another step. This would be just as painful as stepping off a precipice from time to time, perhaps more painful. Tomorrow may not bring what I expect, or even what I desire, but that doesn't mean I should not get out of bed." She smiled, "of course neither one of us is going to get out of bed, if we don't get some sleep. I think I have kept you up to late, especially after your long day traveling."

"I don't mind," John assured her. The truth was that he could have sat and listened to her all night long. He never wanted it to end, but he realized that it was impractical and she was probably tired as well. "But you're right. We really should get some sleep. After all you're giving me a driving lesson tomorrow."

"We definitely need to be alert for that," she smiled again. "Well I guess it is goodnight, then."

"Goodnight, Abby."

John sat quietly in bed, looking at the shadows cast on the wall by the table lamp at his side. He could hear Abby's footsteps in the hall. She was probably making one last look in on Maggie's room. He reached behind his head and gently brushed the wall he was sitting against. He wondered how old this room was. Was it possible that this wall had once been touched by one of his ancestors? Or perhaps Bishop Ridley had actually occupied this room at one time. Was that possible? The phrase 'if only these walls could talk' took on a whole new meaning to him in that moment. Oh, how he wished they could talk. He wanted so much to know even a few of the stories they might tell. As he lay musing about his present surroundings, he gradually drifted off to sleep.

The next morning they all had a leisurely breakfast and then took a stroll down by the river. Maggie wanted to play in the water, but Abby thought it best that she stay dry, so they kept their distance from the edge. It had rained a little the night before, but it looked as if it was going to be a very pleasant day, perfect for a drive in the country.

In the afternoon, John began his driving lesson. Abby thought it might be fun to drive over to Carlisle. They had passed through on the train, but John had not had the opportunity to visit the castle. They drove down Unthank Road and then passed through Haltwhistle, turning onto the A69, which would take them all the way to Carlisle. The trip was just a little over thirty minutes.

As they arrived at the castle, John was immediately struck by its size and appearance. Where Featherstone Castle retained the appearance of being a residence, Carlisle Castle was definitely a fortress with high walls around and battlemounts aligning the tops of every wall. The castle sat upon a promontory, which contributed to its imposing defensive design. Sticking up from the interior was the original pele tower. Leading to the entrance was a long stone bridge which transversed what had clearly been a moat at one time, but was now a grassy ditch.

They took a walking tour of the castle, and then took a moment to sit on the grass and relax, while Maggie played nearby.

"This is a very impressive castle, much more imposing than Featherstone," John said.

"Yeah, I thought you would like it, there is a lot of history contained within these walls."

"It seems to me, this castle was mentioned in one of the ballads contained in *Marmion*," he said.

Abby began to quote:

> *They bound his legs beneath the steed,*
> *They tied his hands behind his back.*
> *They guarded him, fivesome on either side,*
> *And they led him through the Liddel-rack.*
>
> *They led him through the Liddel-rack,*
> *And also through the Carlisle sands;*
> *They took him to Carlisle Castle,*
> *To be at my Lord Scrope's commands.*

John's eyes grew wide. "You know this ballad?" he asked in surprise.

"Yes, I had completely forgotten about it until this moment. I learned it as a girl in school. I guess I had forgotten that it was from *Marmion*, or perhaps, I never knew. Every school child in Haltwhistle can quote it or at least part of it."

"Do you know anymore?" John, asked, still stunned.

"Yes, I think my favorite part is,

> *He turn'd him on the other side,*
> *And at Lord Scrope his glove flung he.*
> *"If ye na like my visit in merry England,*
> *In fair Scotland come and visit me!"*

It seems Kinmont Willie had a bit of sense of humor."

"I am not sure I understand. Every school child learns this, why?"

"Tradition, I suppose. The ballad has a special connection to those of Haltwhistle. Legend has it that Kinmont Willie had raided Haltwhistle on more than one occasion and that is why the Baron Scrope had him arrested in the first place. It is not as if he is a hero, but simply a way of remembering the past."

"Exactly, I am beginning to realize this more and more," John said. "Are you familiar with the Fray of Hautwessel, then?"

"Yes. Legend had it that Kinmont Willie actually led that raid even though he is not mentioned in the ballad. Of course Willie was an Armstrong and the deaths of some of his kinsmen are mentioned."

"Amazing, you never cease to surprise me, I think that is what I love about you most."

Abby just smiled in return.

John hesitated slightly, considering his next words carefully. "Abby, before I left for Oxford, you said that when I returned, there would be no pretenses, that we should be perfectly honest with each other. We should say it like it is, so to speak."

"Yes, I did."

"Well I don't know how else to do this, so I am just going to jump in with both feet. Abby, I have fallen totally and completely in love with you. I don't understand it, I still can't comprehend how something could happen in so short a time, but it did. Going back to Oxford, changed nothing. If anything it only caused me to be more certain of how I felt about you. As it stands now, I can not imagine my life without you.

I have so much to tell you, so much to say to you, I hardly know where to begin." He was starting to stumble a bit. Abby tried to interrupt, but he was a train rolling down hill and there was no going back now. "Last week, I found out that my adviser had arranged for me to receive a fellowship at University of Edinburgh, so that I can now stay here and complete my schooling in Britain. It means that I don't have to return to the U.S.... that is, if it's okay with you. What I mean to say is that I am here to stay. I am not going anywhere. What I really mean to say...or what I mean to ask is... will you marry me?" John held out a box containing an engagement ring.

Abby had tried to say something, but then had decided it was best to just sit patiently, waiting for John to complete his thought. He was obviously nervous, and she didn't want to interrupt him. As she listened, her heart began to beat harder. She knew what was coming, but she didn't really know why. Even so, once she heard it aloud, it seemed unbelievable to her. How was she supposed to respond, what was she suppose to think? She looked at Maggie. She knew that this was a defining moment for her as well. Whatever, they decided, whatever she decided; it would be a life changing moment for the both of them.

She looked into John's eyes. Even though she had only known him a short time, she knew in her heart that he was a man of integrity, a man of kindness and compassion. He was not irrational, and he was not acting on a whim. He was honest and speaking from his heart. That was one of the many things she had grown to appreciate about him in such a short time. He was not showy, nor did he have a false pride. He was real and sincere. He was not merely being impulsive, it just wasn't his nature.

John interrupted the silence, "Have I acted too rashly? Is it too soon? I don't want to make you feel uncomfortable, to cause you stress, or to pressure you. Take your time."

Even as he said it, Abby could see the anxiety in his face. She could not leave him there, hanging on a limb. "No, John it's not too soon. Don't take my hesitation as an answer. I'm just trying to act with the same care and thought, as you have, clearly, already done. I have been falling in love with you from the very start, that is no secret, but I have also been fighting my own feelings. Unsure of whether I could completely give my heart to someone again. I wanted to, but I found myself wrestling with myself, uncertain, afraid. It was not until a couple of days ago that I finally realized what I was feeling. It was not that I was feeling guilty about Mark, and it was not that I was afraid of being hurt again, it was coming to the realization that I was not completely in control. It was not until I realized that I could let go, and trust again, trust in Him, that I finally could be honest with how I felt. The truth is, I love you John. I can not imagine my life without you. I'm no longer afraid of giving my heart to you, I'm far more afraid of losing you. Yes, I will marry you." She bit her lower lip. "Of course I will marry you." And then she leaned forward and kissed him, and they held each other.

Both of them turned and looked at Maggie as she was playing in the grass, realizing that she was as much a part of this as they were. She had been spinning around and had become so dizzy, that she promptly fell to ground right at their feet. They both started to laugh.

"What's so funny? What are you laughing at?"

"You, silly," Abby answered. "She leaned over and picked her daughter up and set her in her lap. "Maggie, do you remember what we talked about last night," she continued. "Do you think it would be okay for Mummy to marry John, and for him to become your new daddy?"

"Okay," Maggie said, "I think that would be okay. Do you want to marry my Mummy?" She asked, turning to John.

John smiled at Maggie and then picked her up in his arms and gave her a hug. "Yes I do. I love her very much, and I love you too. And if it is okay with you, I would love to be your daddy." He felt kind of funny. It was the first time he had said it out loud. He was about to become Maggie's father. Not her real father, of course, but Maggie was too young to really remember much about her father. She was less than two years old when Mark had left for the Falklands. In a real sense, John was about to become the only father she would ever really know. He smiled at Abby and she smiled back. Then he remembered she had not taken her ring yet, he was still holding the box in his hand.

"I suppose we should make this official," he said, reaching out his hand that contained the ring.

Abby looked at the ring, looking almost as if she was afraid to touch it. John took the ring out of the box and then took her left hand in his and placed the ring on her finger. She held it up to allow it to catch the light of the sun. "It's beautiful," she said and then she kissed him again. Then, without warning, she backed away with a bit of concerned look on her face.

"Oh no! What is my mum going to think?" she said. "We are going to have to tell her right away."

"I wouldn't worry," John assured her. "I have a feeling that your *Mum* saw the writing on the wall. I don't think she will be that surprised."

"Well we will find out soon enough," Abby said. "She and my aunt are going to join us for breakfast at Unthank tomorrow morning. Oh, my aunt! I had not even thought about her. She is going to think I am nuts. She hasn't even met you yet."

"Don't you think she'll like me?" John asked.

"No, it's not that, it's just how sudden it is and all. You know what I mean."

"Yes, I am afraid I do, I haven't even breathed a hint of this to my parents yet. I have no idea how they're going to react."

They spent the next several minutes talking through how they were going to tell the members of their respective families. Talking it through put them both a little more at ease and instilled a new confidence. While their conversation continued, they grabbed Maggie by the hands and started walking toward the car. As they walked, Abby inquired further about John's appointment at Edinburgh University.

By the time they had walked back to the car and were on the road again it was beginning to approach dinner time. Abby knew of a pub in downtown Carlisle, so they decided to stop, before heading back to Unthank.

While waiting for their meal to come, they kept talking about their family and how they might react to the news. Then John decided to change the subject. "Abby, I know this has been a bit of an overwhelming afternoon, but I was wondering if I could ask you about the poem we saw on the Raven Stone?"

"Sure, go ahead."

"Do you think it is possible that the poem was not referring to Abigail Featherstone alone, but, that it, in fact, was referring to two different people?"

"What do you mean?"

"I mean, is it possible that the 'Girl in White' refers to Abigail, but the 'Lady in White' is actually the 'White Lady' of Blenkinsopp Castle lore, and that there is a connection between her story and the story of the wedding party? Look here, I have separated the first, third and fifth line of the poem from the second, fourth and sixth."

Wandering alone, as in a spell,
Taken, deceived, to gain a chest,
Lady in White, who began this quest,

A wayward shaft and here She fell.
Given in greed, She cannot rest.
Girl in White, lies beneath the crest.

"Notice how the odd numbered lines seem to go together, as do the even numbered lines. One group refers to the Lady in White, the other, the Girl in White. There has to be a connection."

"What kind of connection?"

"Is it possible that the mention of the 'chest' is actually a reference to the chest of gold? That somehow this was connected to the marriage contract between Abigail and Thomas Blenkinsopp. Let me ask you, who would have inherited Featherstone if Abigail and Blenkinsopp were married and the Baron of Featherstone were to die?"

Abby thought for a moment. "Since the Baron did not have a son, if there were no other suitable male heirs, the inheritance would revert to his son-in-law."

"Then, is it possible," John continued, "that the Blenkinsopps, in an attempt to gain ownership and control of Featherstone, paid some sort of ransom to the Baron and that this ransom could even have been the very chest of gold that was believed to be buried somewhere beneath Blenkinsopp Castle? Don't you see, people have been trying to find this gold for sometime, but maybe they have been looking in the wrong place?"

"You mean that it is buried at Featherstone?"

"Yes, that is exactly what I mean, but I have no way of proving it, nor do I have anyway of knowing where."

Abby smiled, "maybe I do. While you have been unraveling the poem on the Raven Stone, I have been thinking about the poem quoted by Beardie Grey to Sir Walter Scott. I have discovered something that I think may shed some light. But I have to show you, at the castle itself."

"I haven't forgotten that poem, as well. Remember the words, 'a father traded his daughter's love for something that glitters.' It all fits. Do you think we could make a trip back to the castle tomorrow?"

"Sure, once we have breakfast with my aunt and my Mum, then we can leave Maggie with them. Perhaps it would be a good opportunity for you to revisit your youth and take a little ride on horseback."

"Sounds good," he said this, even though he was not exactly thrilled about the prospects of getting on a horse.

"Its sort of sad, don't you think?" Abby asked. "I mean about Abigail. It would be horribly sad to think that her father denied her happiness because of his own personal greed."

"He probably had convinced himself that he was doing it for her, providing her with security and wealth. Imagine the guilt he must have felt when he first became aware of Abigail's tragic end. I wonder if he ever got over it. In the end, it was still about his greed, and it lead to her destruction."

"*He who is greedy is always in want,*" Abby reiterated.

"Who said that?" John asked.

"Horace, I think. Something I remember from school."

"You're just full of bits of wisdom," he smiled as he said it, being a little sarcastic. Not to be outdone, he offered up his own proverb. "*If you're not greedy, then you will go far, and you will live in happiness too...*"

"I don't believe I have ever heard that one," Abby said.

"The Oompa Loompas, *Charlie and the Chocolate Factory.*"

They both laughed.

Kinmont Willie

Sir Nicholas Ridley was the high sheriff of Northumberland in the 28th year of Elizabeth I, the same year Kinmont Willie and the Armstrong clan raided the village of Haltwhistle. He was the third Sir Nicholas Ridley to serve as high sheriff, being the three times great-grandson of "the Broad Knight" of Willimoteswick, and the son of Nicholas Ridley and Mabel Dacre, his mother being descendent from the kings and queens of England.

Kinmont Willie had already escaped back to Liddesdale by the time Sir Nicholas received word from his cousin Robert concerning the foray of Haltwhistle. He, in turn, sent word to Sir Thomas Scope the 10th Baron of Bolton and the Warden of West March, pleading that he lend his support in apprehending William Armstrong.

Sir Nicholas, along with his three brothers, William, Lancelot and Thomas, joined Thomas Scrope and two hundred riders as they marched toward Liddesdale. A truce was held at Kershopefoot, a short distance from the Liddel Water. Two hundred riders also came across the river from Scotland, Kinmont Willie among them. A truce was established to settle debts and compensation for those who had been robbed. The Ridleys were standing in the background, as Sir Thomas negotiated with the Scottish Nobles who were represented by Walter Scott, the first Lord of Buccleuch.

"...at a time when James and Elizabeth have resolved to live in peace, I find it reprehensible that these scoundrels and rogues would chose to break the peace and come into Northumberland, robbing and destroying as they went...", Sir Thomas was speaking.

"Who are you calling a scoundrel?" Willie shot back, as his hand went to the hilt of his sword.

"Be silent Willie. This is neither the time nor the place," Walter Scott intervened. "Let the Baron have his say."

"As I was saying," Sir Thomas gave a wary look at Kinmont Willie, "If we are to continue to maintain the peace along the border, it seems that restitution must be made. We can not continue to have one act of violence returned for another;

354

revenge upon revenge. Where will it end? I have here a list of the livestock that was taken and the damage, as well."

'The Bold Buccleuch' remained contemplative for a moment. "It is true that this marauding must come to an end. If I have your word of honor that you will keep the men of Northumberland at home, I will do my part to do the same in Scotland. The livestock, including all the horses, will be returned here, and I personally will cover the cost of all damages, if I can have your word that it will end here."

"But what about the lives of my kinsmen Wat and Sim? Who will make restitution for them? Give back the bounty that was claimed by their lives, how can this be?"

"Yes, Willie, it is unfortunate, the death of your kinsmen. But the people of Haltwhistle were merely acting in defense of their own. It was you who was the aggressor and must carry the burden of their loss," Scott defended.

"You are all fools and cowards to parlay with the English, and I will not be a part of this," as Willie said this he turned and stormed off.

"He is ill of temper, that one, and it will be his ruin," Sir Thomas whispered to his aide, "have the Ridleys bring him to me." Then, turning back to Scott, "I accept your terms, Lord Buccleuch, and my party will wait here to receive the restitution." The two shook hands as he spoke.

"Brother, Kinmont Willie has left," Lancelot whispered to his oldest brother, Nicholas. "I am afraid he is not of a mind to let this stand as it is."

"Yes, Lance, I believe he is headed home, but I doubt that he will stay there long." Sir Nicholas responded.

"I am afraid he will be up to some kind of mischief before too long," William added.

The brothers all shook their heads in unison. As they were making these observations, the Baron's aid came over to Nicholas and slid him a note. The elder brother unfolded the paper in his hand and glanced at the message.

"What is it, brother?" Thomas asked.

"It seems that the Baron is of the same mind. He wants us to bring Kinmont Willie to him," Nicholas replied.

"I don't think we should tarry, Nicholas," Lancelot suggested. "I do not think Willie plans to stay in this place. Even now, I am afraid he may have flown."

The four brothers stepped aside from the negotiations and followed in the direction they had seen Willie depart. When they saw him climb upon his horse and ride off with two of his companions, they decided to return to their own mounts and follow. Rather than follow, they chose to increase their pace, and circle around in order to intercept him on the road.

Kinmont Willie was completely unaware that he was being followed. He was still deep in thought concerning what had just transpired and how he would find his revenge. It was not of his nature to give up and turn tail. Regardless of what agreement had been arrived at, he was of no mind to be a part of it and he would find a way to make the Ridleys pay. He was so entrenched in his own thoughts that he was completely caught off guard when he rounded the bend in the road, only to find four horseman standing in his path.

"What is this, thieves on the road? How bold! I have just had everything taken from me, and now I find the vultures have come to pick the bones," he said wryly, watching for the smallest sign of weakness in the countenance of his opponents.

"We are not thieves, Willie, as you well know. Just a simple sheriff, doing the bidding of his Lord," Sir Nicholas responded.

"What business do you have with me?" Willie asked. "I am but a weary traveler, longing for the warmth and comfort of his own home. Now step aside and let me pass."

"I'm afraid we cannot. I believe Baron Scrope would like to have a word with you before you leave. He is more than aware that you are the one responsible for the attack on Haltwhistle, and he wants some assurance that you will not continue your raids across the border."

"He has already had his dealings with The Bold Buccleuch. I don't see how I have anything to add. Let the nobles parlay if they wish, but it has nothing to do with me."

"Come now, Willie," Nicholas continued, "for many years there has been bad blood between the Ridleys and Armstrongs, but I think it is time to lay down the sword. We cannot repair the *damage of the past, but we can set it right for the future...for our children."*

"Easily said, coming from the mouth of a relation of those who spilled the blood of my two kinsmen," Willie was never known to have a short memory and it was clear that he was still out for revenge.

"It is unfortunate that your brothers now lay dead, but my cousins were only defending their land and family. They were left little choice. Now put away your vengeful heart and return with us. Have your say with the Baron and then be done with it."

"Clearly, I have nowhere to turn. You block my passage and at odds of four to one, I have little chance of overpowering you. I will go with you peacefully, if you will pledge me your word that I will have safe passage."

"You have my word," Nicholas granted.

The five riders returned to Kershopefoot. There was little more said between them as they rode. It was clear that Kinmont Willie had little affection for his escort. Had he been given the opportunity, he surely would have bolted, but he was alone and had no chance of escaping.

As they arrived at the tent of Thomas Scrope, Nicholas and Lancelot escorted Willie to the entrance, where he was promptly disarmed by the Baron's guards. Willie began to protest, but then thought better of it. It was clear that he was in no position to resist. The three of them stepped inside the tent. Willie stepped forward to meet the Baron who was sitting at a table; the two Ridleys remained at a distance.

Before the Baron had a chance to greet his guest, Willie began, "I am here, Baron, speak your mind and be done with it. I have little desire to remain here any longer than I must."

"You have a strange way about you Willie. It occurs to me that you could learn a little diplomacy. We are not of equal station, and it would be good of you to learn you place," as the Baron spoke the color rose in Willie's cheeks, it was clear that he was not about to give his host the upper hand.

"Your position means very little to me since I am not English and you are my enemy. As for diplomacy, the only diplomacy I know comes at the end of a sword," Willie was clearly not looking

357

to make a good impression. "Now have your say and I will be on my way."

"It is true, we have been enemies in the past, and you have always been a valiant warrior," this was clearly an attempt by the Baron to appeal to Willie's ego. "However, the time has come to put aside our differences, and if we cannot become friends, then at least we must become peaceful neighbors. It is what my Queen and your King wish, and that should be enough. I have brought you here to ask that you reconsider your position. We must have peace, and I need to know that you will honor it. I need your word on it that you will cease making raids into Northumbria from this day forward."

"And if I refuse?" Willie was still in a fit of anger, and ready for a violent conclusion to the matter.

"There are always consequences to every decision, but I think you need to pause and consider these. Come now, you must realize that there is nothing to be gained by remaining obstinate."

There was silence as Willie considered his next words. In that brief moment it appeared his prudence would win out over his temper, but that was not to be the case. "I cannot relent. I cannot give you my word, because I do not believe there can be peace between us. The minute my Scottish brothers relax their defenses, we will be overrun. The only way we can protect what is ours is to continue to keep at bay those who live along the border. I cannot give you what you ask."

"I was afraid this would be your answer. This being the case, I have no other choice. Guards, seize this man and place him under arrest." Before Willie could react, and before Nicholas and Lancelot realized what was happening, two guards rushed to the side of Kinmont Willie and secured his arms, not allowing him to move.

"What treachery is this?" Willie protested. "You cannot arrest me. We are under a flag of truce. I was granted safe passage by this one," indicating Sir Nicholas.

"It is true, Baron, I gave him my word..." Nicholas added.

"I am sorry, Sheriff, but you misspoke. You did not have any authority to grant safe passage. This man has robbed and *pillaged the poor people of Northumbria for long enough, and he shall now go to prison."*

"But, my Lord, what about Lord Buccleuch? He cannot possibly support this decision. This could eliminate any chance of peace between us," Lancelot interjected.

"Silence gentlemen, I will have no more of this. Let me worry about 'The Bold Buccleuch'. Thank you for delivering your charge, but your task is now completed; be off with you. Guards, take this man away from my sight."

As Willie was ushered from the tent he turned toward Nicholas, "you shall rue this day, Sir Nicholas. You have deceived me and it will not be soon forgotten."

Sir Nicholas was clearly disturbed by this chain of events. He could not have imagined that the Baron had all along intended to arrest Kinmont Willie. To do so under a flag of truce was unfathomable. His brothers were unable to cure his melancholy demeanor as they left for home. They all recognized that his honor had been compromised and the hurt would not be easily healed.

The Baron had acted somewhat hastily in his arrest of Kinmont Willie, with little consideration of the place of incarceration. It was finally determined that the reiver would be imprisoned at Carlisle Castle, where he would be tried and sentenced. The trial was of little consequence, since Willie did not recognize the authority of the English Baron and therefore would not offer any defense. As a result, he was sentenced to death by hanging, one fortnight from the day of his arrest.

When Walter Scott heard of this chain of events he became furious. He exclaimed, "Now Christ's curse upon my head, but avenged of Lord Scrope I'll be."

Even though he was not particularly fond of Kinmont Willie, The Bold Buccleuch could not allow this false arrest, under the flag of truce, to be excused. Gathering around him as many men as could be mustered he set out for Carlisle Castle, on the eve of the execution. He had studied the defenses of castle and had determined the postern gate was the weakest point of defense. He sent a spy ahead who was able to bribe the gate keeper, thus giving the men from the north the advantage.

The Scottish reivers approached the castle in the dead of night, counting on the element of surprise. A small party of men, led by Will Eliot and Willie "Red Cloak" Bell entered the castle by the compromised gate, while the majority of the riders remained back with Scott to protect their line of escape. The guards inside the gate were dispatched by Eliot and Bell with little resistance and almost no sound. By the time the occupants of the castle were alerted to the invaders they had already liberated Willie from his cell and were making their escape.

"Good to see you Will," Willie shouted as he jumped atop the horse he was provided.

"Good to see you as well, cousin. Now let's make our way, before the entire castle is upon us," Eliot returned.

The sounds of alarm could be heard over the walls as the escapee and his companions stole out into the dark of night. It was only moments before they rejoined the rest of the liberating party led by Scott. Without hesitation, they turned and headed for home, just as the light of dawn was beginning to emerge in the distance.

Scott was well aware that they would not be safe until they were back in Scotland. He left two small parties in ambush to cover their retreat. The darkness covered their approached, but with the imminent sunrise, they would be left completely exposed to their pursuers.

Nicholas had not been completely aware of Walter Scott's anger, and had been wary of the possible attempt of an escape. Although he had felt that Kinmont Willie had been imprisoned wrongfully, he was now fully aware that if he were freed, there would be little peace in Northumbria. Anticipating that an escape may take place, he had gathered together the best men of Northumbria to guard the passage back to Scotland. In the night one of the local farmers had alerted him that he had heard the commotion of riders passing on the road to Carlisle. Nicholas, his brothers, and fifty or so men were lying in wait as the escaped prisoner and his escort crossed the Esk River.

When Scott realized their path to freedom was blocked he hesitated for moment. However, Kinmont Willie recognizing Nicholas Ridley at the lead of the riders from Northumberland, charged ahead plunging into the midst of their would-be captors. A huge clash of men and horses ensued, as the men of Northumberland held their ground, not allowing the Scottish reivers to pass. The battle was evenly matched and the outcome undetermined. In the middle of the foray, Kinmont Willie was fighting like a mad man trying to gain an advantage over the larger Sir Nicholas. The clash of metal against metal rang out as sword met sword up and down the line. Just as it appeared that the men of Northumberland were gaining the upper hand, the Scottish parties that had been covering their retreat arrived upon the scene giving the Scotts greater numbers.

With this advantage, the reivers broke through the line of the Northumbrians. At this very moment, Kinmont Willie found a vulnerability in Sir Nicholas' defense, and was able to strike a deadly blow with his sword to his opponents neck. Sir Nicholas fell to ground, Lancelot, nearest to the High Sherrif, jumped from his own mount to come to the aid of his brother. Willie did not hesitate, taking his opportunity for escape, he joined his brothers in arms, who were already on their way to Scotland. A few of the men of Northumbria started to give chase, but it was quickly realized that it was futile.

William and Thomas knelt beside Lancelot who was now holding his brother in his arms. Nicholas looked at his brothers, aware that he was mortally wounded and that he would not recover.

"It would seem that Willie had his revenge in the end...," he was struggling to speak. "I am afraid I am not long for this world...," taking William's hand in his, "You are now the elder brother Wil, it is your responsibility to watch out for the rest...I shall leave you to the office of Sheriff of Northumberland...until such a time as the Queen chooses another."

"Continue to live a life of honor, brothers...let no man take this from you...farewell...," He breathed his last.

"Farewell, brother," William whispered, "go with God."

"Farewell, brother," the other two whispered in unison.

Chapter Seventeen

..."Abigail, wake up." She opened her eyes, and then closed them again, it was too bright. "Abigail, its time," she opened them again this time, a little more slowly. She was lying on her back in a field of grass. She sat up. Standing before her was the Lady in White, the sun directly behind her so that she could not see her face. As she stood to her feet, the Lady in White turned and walked away. She followed.

'Where are we going?' she asked.

"There," the Lady in White pointed down into the valley, to the castle. "It is there that the quest is ended."

"What do you mean?" she asked.

A stranger in a foreign land, afraid,
alone, and far from home,
My heart sought love, but there was none.
His eyes were true, His soul not won,
Why forsake such love? To possess a chest,
And now I wander, never more to rest.

But not all is lost, for there is one,
Who found love once, its joy and pain.
And when twice it came, courage did not wane.
Can one so true, so good, so pure,
Escape temptation's spell, and strong allure?

Wisdom guides her mind, justice leads her heart,
Strong is her virtue, unyielding her resolve,
Through her courage, I shall know peace,
And by her love, I shall find rest.

The next morning came much too soon. Maggie was up early and began poking and prodding Abby, to wake her up. At first, Abby was slow to respond. Slowly, but surely, she opened her eyes. And then like a flash, she remembered what day it was. She jumped out of bed and bounded down the stairs, with Maggie trailing. When she arrived to the kitchen, she found Grandfather was a step ahead and had already started on breakfast.

Realizing that she was not actually needed, she left Maggie in the care of her grandfather and returned upstairs to shower and dress. She was surprisingly calm, given that her aunt and mother would soon arrive and she was about to share what should prove to be surprising news. Her composure was more than likely due to her resolution, a confidence she had not felt for a very long time. Even though she had known of John's feelings from nearly the first, she had never really dared to believe that a proposal was forthcoming. When it came, she was all of a sudden confronted with the realization that she could not imagine going forward in life without him. Strangely, it was the same thing she had felt when she had first been given the news that Mark had been killed. The difference being, that she did not have to go on without John, she had a choice. And in the end, there was only one choice to be made.

As Abby emerged from her bedroom, John appeared in the hallway at the same moment. She smiled, walked toward him and gave him a kiss on the lips. "Good morning," she said softly. She then took his hand and led him down the stairs.

As they were descending the stairs, he was able to blurt out a greeting, "good morning. Did you sleep well?"

"Very well," she returned. "Full of pleasant dreams." She didn't really remember if she dreamed at all, but at least she hadn't had one of those curious, disturbing dreams.

Together, they entered the kitchen to find Abby's mother and aunt had already arrived. The table was set and breakfast was ready to be served. Abby's mother turned and looked at her aunt and smiled as they saw the young couple arrive, hand in hand.

"Good morning, Abby, good morning, John," Mrs. Featherstone greeted. "John, let me introduce you to my sister, Emily Miller."

"Nice to meet you," he greeted, shaking her hand."

"Nice to meet you as well, John," she returned. "I have heard a great deal about you, from my sister. Not that I have heard anything from this young lady," pointing to Abby. "When were you going to come around and see me, Abby?"

"Sorry, Auntie, I've been meaning to come by. I've been a little preoccupied lately."

Everyone sat down at the table and the conversation began to flow freely. Abby's aunt was somewhat forward and didn't hesitate to interrogate John, asking all kinds of questions about his personal history. On occasion, Abby would answer on John's behalf, trying to deflect her aunt's inquisition. John didn't seem bothered in the least. He even seemed to enjoy the banter. For just a brief moment, Abby started to lose her resolve and began to wonder if it was the right moment to break the news. This doubt only lasted a moment and was soon erased, when she saw her opening she took the offensive.

"You better be careful, Aunt Em, you don't want John to get the wrong idea about English hospitality. With all these questions, he might begin to think he is being cross-examined and you are the judge."

"Sorry, Abby," her aunt replied. "I didn't think I was asking anything out of the ordinary."

"I don't mind," John said. "I understand that I am a bit of a curiosity."

"Well, anyway, you'll have plenty of time to get to know him. It's not as if you have to ask him everything in one sitting."

"What do mean?" her aunt asked.

"Yeah, what do you mean?" her mother chimed in.

"Well, now is as good a time as any," she looked over at John for support. "John has asked me to marry him and I have accepted," as she said it she held up her left hand showing the engagement ring sparkling on her finger.

Mrs. Featherstone and Mrs. Miller looked at each other a bit perplexed, but it was Mr. Brown who was the first to respond. "Congratulations, you two, that is wonderful news," he said before the other two even had a chance to react. "I'm very happy for both of you."

"Well, of course we're happy for you," Abby's mother stood up from her chair and stepped to her daughter's chair and leaned down to give her a kiss on the forehead.

"Let me get this right, you two are engaged, after only knowing each other for three weeks?" Abby's aunt asked. "Don't you think that is rushing it a bit? I mean, Abby, have you lost your mind?"

"Now, Em," Mrs. Featherstone cautioned. "Abby's a sensible girl, she must know what she is doing."

"Its okay, Mrs. Featherstone," John took the lead. "We totally understand you're questioning it. The reality is it does seem a little crazy. We don't totally understand it ourselves, how two people who have known each other for so short a time could fall so deeply in love, to know without any uncertainty, that we want to spend the rest of our lives together. I love Abby, and I can't imagine my life without her."

"And I love John," Abby added. "It's not as if either of us anticipated this happening. The truth of the matter is, until recently, I didn't think that I could ever love again. I never thought I would get over losing Mark. I was living each day, one at a time, not believing the future held much of anything for me. John changed all of that, not just for me, but for Maggie as well." Abby reached out and squeezed John's hand.

"But you're an American," Abby's aunt was not about to give in so easily. "You can't just come into town and sweep this girl off her feet, and then take her and our beautiful Maggie back to wherever it is you came from." This comment caused some concern to grow across Mrs. Featherstone's face, as well.

"No, you're absolutely right. I have thought about that as well. Northumberland is all that Abby has ever known. I knew that this meant I might have to consider living here. The last thing I wanted to do was disrupt all your lives, and as you put it, take Abby away from here. As chance would have it, I have been offered a fellowship at Edinburgh University. My advisor from back home arranged for it, and it will allow for me to complete my studies here."

"And what about after that?" Aunt Emily asked.

"After that, we will go wherever God wants us to go," Abby said. "No one ever knows what the future holds, but whatever it has for us, it will be something we will face together."

"We don't have all the details worked out," John continued. "There is a lot we still have to discuss. We haven't set a date yet, and we want you all to be a part of our future plans, but for now, we would very much like for you to give us your blessing," as he said it, he looked directly at Abby's mom.

"Em, they're absolutely right," Abby's mother intervened. "Abby can't be planning her life by what we think or want. She must live her own life." She patted John on the shoulder and place her other hand on Abby's. "I would be proud and honored to have you as my son-in-law."

"Thanks, Mum," Abby said, reaching out and patting her mother's hand as it rested on her shoulder.

"Now that's settled, who's going to help me wash the dishes?" Mr. Brown asked.

"I'll be glad to help," John volunteered, as he tried to get up.

"You stay right where you are young man, Emily and I can take care of it," Mrs. Featherstone insisted.

"That would be for the best, John. We actually need to be getting along. Mum, I hope you don't mind if we leave Maggie with you and Auntie Em, while John and I go riding. We have a little errand to take care of."

Aunt Emily picked up Maggie from her chair. "You go right ahead Abby. I have been looking forward to spending the morning with my favorite great niece."

*****

It didn't take long for John to adjust to being in the saddle again. Horseback riding was not one of his favorite activities, but he had done it enough to feel right at home. Abby took the lead, and he was not about to let her show him up, so he did the best he could to keep up. His mount seemed to be pretty well mannered, and John had little difficulty managing him.

They took a fairly direct line toward Rowfoot. It was pretty clear that Abby had made this journey on horseback many times before. They had been riding for just about an hour when they arrived in Rowfoot and John was beginning to feel the affects of sitting on a horse for longer than he was accustomed to. At Rowfoot, they took Hallbank Road toward Featherstone. As they came to the peak of the rise overlooking the castle and the river beyond, Abby signaled to stop. There was a nice shady spot beneath a large elm tree, so she dismounted and tied her horse to a small bush. John did the same.

"Why are we stopping here?" he asked.

"I just thought it would be a nice place to rest a bit. We don't have much further, but this is such a beautiful spot, a beautiful view." She sat down in the grass, facing the castle below.

"You said last night that there was something you wanted to show me," John said, with a slight questioning tone.

"Yeah, down at the castle. There was something about the poem we read in the letter by Scott that kept playing over and over in my mind. *Follow the ravens from the gate.* The only gate it could have meant is the front gate of the castle. But what did it mean, follow the ravens. At first, I thought it meant actual ravens, as in the story about Abigail. But then it occurred to me, it might be something else. That's when I went to the gate and began looking around. At the base of the gate I found what looked like some sort of engraving. It was in the form of bird, a raven, very old and barely discernable. That's when I thought it might be some sort of marker."

"You might be right, it could be some sort of marker, but what does it mean, to follow it? Where is it leading, or where is it pointing to?"

"I don't know, I thought maybe together we could figure it out. That is, if we should."

"What do you mean, if we should?" he asked.

"John, you and I both know that we are thinking the same thing, that somehow this mystery concerning the death of Abigail Featherstone and John Ridley may have something to do with the Blenkinsopp gold. You know it and I know it. But the question is, whether we should be looking for it at all. Wherever we've looked, it seems that tragedy has followed this treasure. Perhaps it's cursed, I don't know, but maybe it would be better to leave it alone."

"You might be right. I have thought the same thing, but, in the end, I keep coming back to the possibility, that maybe we were supposed to find it, if it exists at all. I think it is more than the gold itself, I think there is something more. It's about finding out what really happened, about finding out the truth."

"Maybe you're right. But you have to promise me one thing. Whatever happens, whatever we find, we don't let it change us as it has so many before. You know, we don't want to let it be the thing that controls us; the thing that directs our course."

"I understand. You're right, of course. I promise."

They sat and looked out over Featherstonhaugh for several more minutes. It was a moment to reflect, to gather their thoughts before going forward. They could not have known that it was the same place that John Ridley and Abigail Featherstone had met, three hundred years earier.

John finally broke the silence. "Come on Abby, let's go solve this mystery, once and for all."

When they arrived at the castle they circled around to the side facing the river and dismounted at the gate. After tying up the horses, Abby lead John to the place where she had seen the picture of the raven. John rubbed his hand over it. It was almost worn away, but it was clearly the picture of a bird. Then Abby took him to the other side of the gate and showed him a similar

368

picture at the base of the wall. There were two ravens, one on either side of the gate.

"Follow the ravens from the gate," John repeated. He thought for a moment and then looked at each one of them again. A smile crossed his face. "Look, Abby, notice how the beaks of both ravens are pointing in the same direction. If they were merely decorative, you would have thought that they would have been facing each other, you know, more symmetrical."

"You're right, I hadn't thought of that. If that's the case, maybe they are pointing toward something."

They started walking along the castle wall, to the north, in the direction that the ravens seemed to be pointing. John began pulling back some of the grass along the base of the wall. "Look here, there's another one." Sure enough, there was another raven, a perfect copy of the others, also pointing north.

They kept going. About every twenty feet or so they discovered another, and then another, until they rounded the wall and started going along the northern wall to the east. Here the wall ran parallel to the road and there was a significant amount of brush that had grown up against the wall, so the going was slower. Eventually they came to a place where the wall was entirely covered by brush, such that no part of the wall could be seen from the road. John pressed himself against the wall trying to slide between the foliage and the wall. It was difficult going, but just a few feet in, there was enough of a gap between the growth and the wall that he could move freely. He looked into the shadows at the base of the wall hoping to find another symbol. As he knelt down to feel along the wall, he could sense Abby looking over his shoulder. His eyes began to adjust to the shadows and he noticed that the base of the wall had a slight arch, suggesting a hole beneath the wall. He bent down and felt along the ground. To his surprise, he discovered that there was a sort of iron grate on the ground extending out from the wall. It had been completely overgrown by some ivy and was completely invisible. He started pulling the ivy back.

"What is that?" Abby asked.

"It seems to be some sort of grating, a drain perhaps."

Once he had removed as much of the vine as he thought necessary, he grabbed the grill and tried pulling upward. It moved slightly, but didn't give entirely. He looked around the edges, and then felt with his hands until he was able to discern some hinges on one side. He inspected the opposite side only to find a single bar latch. He turned the bar and then slid it away from its clasp. He then tried lifting the grating, this time with a little help from Abby. It gave way with a loud screech, evidence of years of rust and decay.

Beneath the grating was a large hole descending down into the ground. It appeared as if it was some sort of drain. John could hear the trickle of water on the rocks in the depths. He took off his back pack and pulled out a flashlight. The beam of light was enough to reveal the details of the hole, including a stone stair case leading down into the depths. There was just enough light to be able to discern the bottom which appeared to be at a depth of about ten feet.

"Shall we," John said stepping down onto the first stair.

Abby placed her hand on John's shoulder. "Are you sure, do you think we should? You never know what might be down there."

"We've come this far, it wouldn't make sense to stop now," John said. "Come on, where is your sense of adventure."

Abby smiled. "Okay, lead the way. But if we come upon any rats, I'm leaving."

John had already started down the stairs. When he arrived at the bottom, he stopped a moment to make sure Abby descended safely. Once they were both standing on solid ground, he scanned the passage with the flashlight in all directions. It appeared they were in some sort of tunnel. John was struck with a sense of déjà vu, but he brushed it aside. In one direction the tunnel seemed to lead underneath the road to the north. There was a small trickle of water flowing in a narrow ditch on one side. It was likely a drain leading to the river. In the other direction, the tunnel seemed to go directly toward the castle. He shined the flashlight down the passage, but it turned slightly just ten yards forward, not allowing them to see into its depths.

John took Abby by the hand, "I think we should go this way," he said pointing his lantern toward the bend.

"I think you're right," she said pointing to the base of the illuminated wall. There clearly etched in the base of the wall was another symbol of the raven, its beak pointing toward the darkened depths of the passage.

John started down the tunnel with Abby close behind. As they rounded the bend they could see that the tunnel continued for some distance. Slowly, they proceeded, pausing every few steps, as John panned the light up and down the walls on either side. They must have gone nearly sixty yards when the passage came to an abrupt end. There was a staircase hewn out of the rock wall that ascended to nowhere. John directed the light up the staircase to the ceiling. There appeared to be heavy wooden beams blocking what once was the opening to the world above.

"Where do you think that goes?" John said, barely loud enough for Abby to hear.

"It seems we are directly beneath the castle, perhaps the chapel end," she replied. "I think this may have been used as some sort of secret passage. These old castles often had tunnels that were used as escape routes in the event that the castle was under siege and in danger of falling."

"I think you're right," John agreed. "I found something similar to this at Willimoteswick. This one seems to go all the way beyond the exterior wall, but look at this over here." He pointed his lamp at the wall fifteen feet back down the tunnel. "Notice that the natural rock wall ends and there is a stone and mortar wall. It seems a little out of place. Why would there be a stone wall down here? It can't be for support."

"What's that there?" Abby said pointing to the top of the wall. They both stepped closer and John pointed the light directly where Abby had been pointing. Abby answered her own question, "it's a family crest, the Featherstone crest."

John kept the light on it for a moment, but then began scanning the remainder of the brick wall, pausing on each stone for just a moment, looking at every detail. "Look at this," he held his light on a rectangular stone, about shoulder height, on the far right edge of the wall. It had an iron ring hanging from a metal plate attached to the stone. He reached out and lifted the ring. It creaked as he lifted up. "Here hold this," he handed the flashlight to Abby. He then began rubbing the dust off the metal plate. As he cleaned it off, he could clearly discern an engraved image.

"What is that?" Abby asked.

"It's a raven," he answered. "Here, keep the light on it." He took hold of the ring and began to tug on it. He could feel the stone give just slightly. He tried again, it moved just a little more. He pulled again, a little harder and the stone began to give, sliding out from the wall entirely, leaving a whole about six inches square in the wall.

John took the flashlight from Abby and directed the light into the void created by the absent stone. The hole was less than a foot deep. At the back of it there was a large vertical iron bar. He took hold of it with his free hand. "Step back a little Abby. If this is what I think it is, you may not want to be to close to the wall." He gave the bar a quick jerk. It gave way without resistance, and suddenly they could hear something in the wall, something mechanical, iron grating against stone. Then, almost as if by magic, a three foot wide section of the wall began to move forward toward them. The two of them stood back in amazement. The stone wall kept moving outward until it extended out into the passage two to three feet. There was just enough space for a person to slide behind the wall. John started to step through the narrow passage.

"Where are you going?" Abby asked a bit nervously.

"Here, give me the light. Wait here just a minute. I'm not going very far, I just want to check it out."

Abby handed John the light and then stood still in the darkness as he disappeared behind the wall. A moment later he returned. "Here take my hand. Be careful, it is rather narrow in there. And whatever you do, don't touch anything. We don't want this thing closing up while were inside."

Although growing more and more apprehensive, Abby took John's hand and followed him through the opening in the wall. After just a few feet, they entered into what seemed to be a fairly large room. John's flashlight cast light throughout the room revealing its contents.

Abby and John stood motionless, silent, not believing what their eyes beheld. In the middle of the room there was what appeared to be a coffin. Just in front of it, on the ground, a small wooden chest. On one wall, was a pair of crossed swords in scabbards, beneath a large shield, emblazoned with the Featherstone coat of arm, still visible beneath the dust. Strewn throughout the room were other various items, all covered in centuries worth of dust.

"I can't believe what I am looking at," Abby finally spoke. "Is that a coffin? Is this some sort of a crypt?"

"It is a coffin, but not just any coffin," John said.

"What do you mean?"

"It is kind of small. I don't think it was meant for a man." John said as he stepped toward it. He used his hand to brush away the years of dust that had gathered on its surface. The top was decorated with a painting of a woman, lying face up, arms folded across her chest, eyes closed. She was wearing all white. Written across the top, just above the woman's head, were the words, *'Here lies our beloved Abigail.'*

Abby leaned over and read the words. "I don't believe it. This is Abigail Featherstone, *the* Abigail Featherstone."

"So it seems. Here, hold the flashlight for me," John handed the light to Abby.

"Why, what are you going to do?"

"Take a look inside," he answered, as he looked for a place to grip the lid.

"Do you think you should?"

"Why not? I don't think she'll mind, whoever she is." John then lifted hard on the lid. Surprisingly, it gave way fairly easily. They paused a moment, both in surprise, before speaking. Beneath the lid of the coffin lay the mummified remains of a woman. There were still the remnants of what could certainly have been a wedding dress. Near the breast it looked as if it had been stained with something. The arms of the corpse were folded across a small wooden shield. John gently removed it from the skeletal arms and brushed the dust from its surface.

The shield had three birds illustrated, separated by a single chevron.

"Are those ravens?" Abby asked.

"No, I don't think so," John was smiling, but it went unnoticed in the dark. "I think they are falcons, or hawks."

"What do you think it means?"

"I'm not sure, it looks like some sort of family crest, but I have never seen it before, have you?"

Abby thought for a moment, "You know, now that I think about it, it does look familiar, but I am not sure why. I think I have seen this before, but I don't know where…I think maybe you should put it back. It makes me feel a little weird, disturbing the dead, and all. Maybe you should close it up again."

"Okay, you're probably right," John admitted. "Perhaps we should leave her in peace." He replaced the wooden shield and then carefully slid the coffin's lid back into place.

"I imagine this is what we have come for," John said as he pointed the light down onto the chest on the floor. He bent down and placed his hand on the latch.

"Wait," Abby said as she knelt beside him, placing her hand on his shoulder. "Are you sure you're ready to see what's inside. Beneath that lid might be something wonderful, but if it is what we think it is, it could also be the source of evil and pain. Are you sure we can resist the temptation that comes with possessing anymore than those who have tried in the past. Are you sure you want to open it?"

John removed his hand and drew back slightly. "I know what you're saying, but I think we must find out what is inside. I am not sure how we got here, but I feel deep inside that what we are doing is right. I don't understand it, and I can't give any sound reason for it, I just know it somehow. We came here to find answers, and unless we take this last step, we will always be left wondering. I didn't begin this journey looking to fall in love, and yet it happened, and I know it is good and right. At the same time, I never once imagined being here, in this moment, possibly discovering something that has been lost for centuries. I have never really had any aspiration for riches. In my heart I know the danger that comes when placing our love in material things. It's not as if money doesn't hold any allure for me, and I'm not so naïve to think that I can't be held captive by it. But a man is never truly disciplined until he is in a circumstance in which his virtue is challenged. Perhaps this is such a moment."

"I trust you," Abby affirmed. "Just promise me, that whatever happens, we will not allow this moment to change who we are, to change what we believe, to change what is important."

"Don't worry, Abby, I know what is important. God, you and Maggie and then everything else, that will not change, I promise."

John turned and undid the latch on the chest. He then lifted the lid. When the light hit the contents, they were a bit taken back. Immediately on top was a large leather bound book. It was held together with straps that were tied on one side. John reached down and carefully lifted the book out of the chest. It was lying on a wood slat, an inner tray. He felt around the edges, getting his fingers between the slat and the edge of the chest. He slowly lifted it out. Abby directed the light on what was below. There was an immediate glare of yellow that emanated from the chest. Beneath the wooden slat were hundreds of gold coins, each a little larger than a nickel. John could not believe his own eyes; it was all a little surreal. He took one in his hand and held it to the light. It was stamped with the image of two individuals, one kneeling in front of what appeared to be a saint. The writing stamped on the coined looked like it might be Latin.

"Have you ever seen coins like these before?" Abby asked.

"No, too old," he replied. "There must be several thousand."

"What do you think they're worth?"

"I'm not sure." He tried lifting the chest, being able to raise it slightly from the ground for just a moment. "I don't think it is quite as much as described in the legend of the White Lady. It certainly would not have taken half a dozen men to carry this, but then again most legends have a little embellishment. I would guess that it must weigh at least 150 to 200 pounds." He thought to himself for a moment. "Just a rough guess, but by today's standard it has to be worth well over a million dollars."

"And it has just been sitting here all this time." Abby said in bewilderment. "Why hasn't anybody ever found it before?"

"I don't know, but my guess is that the Baron closed up the passage from above, after he placed his daughter here. Clearly, he didn't want it to be discovered. I suppose, the real mystery is how did Beardie Grey know about it? Certainly, without her poem, we would never have found it. In fact, I have a suspicion that she is responsible for the poem on the Raven Stone, as well. Maybe we can find some answers here," he said, holding up the book.

Gingerly, John lifted the book and undid the leather straps that bound the protective cover. Very gently, he opened the cover and turned the first page. Despite being obviously very old, it was in surprisingly good condition; no doubt the result of the cool dry air of the crypt. He browsed over the first couple of pages. "This seems to be some sort of history, a family history of the Featherstones."

"Incredible," Abby said. "Let me see." She leaned closer, holding the light directly over the pages, while John held up the book so she could look at it. Although written in an old hand script, she could make out the words '*A History of the Ancient Family of Castle Featherstonhaugh.*'

"We don't really have time to read the entire thing." John turned the book over and opened it from the back cover. The last entry was dated 18th of July, 1659. John started to read the entry aloud...

> *It is cold and dark and I am not much long for this world. I do not fear death's approach at my doorstep, I hold nothing dear that I might lose, and there is no one left to mourn my passing. I am the last of the heirs of Featherstonhaugh, and the only heiress has preceded me in leaving the earth. I have tried to remain diligent in adding to this chronicle of a family which has proudly and*

honorably protected these lands from the invading bandits from the north.

What shall become of Castle Featherstonhaugh? I do not know. Truth be known, I no longer have regard. It is a trivial thing, nothing more than stone and mortar and just as our beloved Lord taught, it is the fool who puts his trust in things which do not last.

Hear the wisdom of an old and dying man. Pride goes before the fall, and thus is a deadly vice. However, greed is a greater evil still. The first is a self love and remedied by simple humility, the second is the love of things, which is madness. Both shall lead to destruction, but it is difficult to know which one is the greater evil. I have known both, and as a result the end of my years has been painful and tragic. May God forgive me my sins and redeem my sickened soul. In Him, and only in Him, I find my hope.

Beware the treasure that is found here; its allure is addictive, and tenacious. At first glimpse, it secretly whispers to the heart, words of pleasure and happiness. However, it is cursed and will bring ruin to all those who seek to love it, rather than hate it; who will become the possessed, rather than the possessor. I have known it to twice bring ruin to those who tried to hold it. First, when the love of the White Lady was ignored, neglected, by one who was blinded by the brilliance of its glare; the second, when a young girl was lost and abandoned to an unjust fate, because of a father's foolish imprudence, having succumbed to the vanity of wealth and riches.

Beware its enchantment; do not keep it for thyself. Give it away, or put it to work to do what is charitable; and by these actions the White Lady and Beloved Girl might finally know peace. If only I possessed the courage to have done such, but even now at the twilight of life, I fear that I cannot let it go. Not that I possess it, but it possesses me. Only death can bring me freedom from its enslavement.

Search thy own soul. If thou findest not the strength to accomplish these things, then bury it once more in the depths of the earth. Remember this condemnation, that hast been known since ancient times; the worst crime against mankind was committed by him who was the first to put a gold ring upon his finger.

John paused for a moment, looking at Abby, and then down at the gold. He could see in her eyes that she was thinking the same thing he was. He looked back at the book, "perhaps it would be fitting for you to read this next part." He handed her the book and then took the flashlight from her hand and held it above the book.

The last entry was a letter addressed to Abigail Featherstone.

Dearest Abby,

Only by a miracle of our Lord's infinite mercy could this correspondence reach beyond the grave to thy waiting eyes and thereby grant this foolish old man one last opportunity to make amends for so grievous a transgression. How do I begin to convey my anguish, my despair of knowing it was I who put thee in harms way, who led thee to death's door, because of my prideful and stubborn heart. My eyes were blinded by the material and temporal vanity of opulence. What can drive a father to ignore his daughter's pleas for benevolence? Thou have always been a daughter of light, devout, loving and honorable in all things. Thou were, in life, the apple of thy father's eyes, the greatest gem amongst all he treasured, and yet, he turned his back on thy appeals for sympathy and understanding.

Allow this humble spirit to offer one last effort at recompense for so horrible a circumstance that lead to thy untimely demise. I do not ask for forgiveness, for I dare not imagine such a prospect, even though thy heart has always been one of grace and charity. I only can offer this, a promise that I have never or will never profit in any way from the ransom paid for thy marriage contract. And may I also give, although delinquent it may be, a father's blessing on thy love for John Ridley, of whom I now consider a lost son. I now know that I should have trusted thy heart, for it has always been true and noble. I was wrong to act with prejudice and malice toward a young man who obviously held thee in such high esteem, resulting in his own death, whence he could no longer go on with life, once he realized thy destruction.

My loving daughter, may thee find peace and rest, and may our Father in heaven grant thee and thy love, grace and eternal joy.

Thy Loving Father

Abby looked up from the letter with tears welling at the edge of her eyes, however, the darkness of their surroundings concealed her emotion. She felt strange reading such a letter. She could not help empathize with the intended recipient, not only because they shared the same name, but also because she was separated from her father by death, and as a result, he would never be able to share in the joy of her new found love. It was as if the letter had been addressed to her personally. She sensed the emotion of a father attempting to reach beyond the grave, and it left her wanting. She closed the book and held it to her chest. She felt connected to it, somewhere in the depths of it pages was her story, as well.

"So, it is true," John began, "the Baron of Featherstonhaugh had accepted this gold as a part of a marriage contract with the Blenkinsopps, only to see it end in tragedy. And this is the same gold or perhaps a part of the gold that was paid as the dowry for the White Lady of Blenkinsopp Castle. But the real treasure is not the gold. The real treasure is there," pointing to the book. "It is what I came here to find. In these pages we find the truth. This is a first person account, a primary source for events that took place more than three hundred years ago. Do you know how rare that is? It may be worth more than the gold, at least, it is to me."

"And to me as well," Abby said.

Epilogue

It is written in the good book that the sins of the fathers shall fall upon their children to the third and fourth generation.

John was sitting in the garden of Unthank, enjoying the shade of a large oak tree. There was a bird singing a morning melody, somewhere in the field beyond. In his lap lay the Featherstone histories. He had risen early this morning, found this quiet place, where he hoped to proceed undisturbed, and began reading from the beginning. The early part of the history gave a rather sketchy description of the Saxon origins of the family who had first settled at Featherstonhaugh. Featherstonhaugh means 'valley of the feather stones'. It was unclear as to what the feather stones actually meant, but it was described that the family had first constructed a castle on top of the rise, and it was later moved to its present location in the valley between the rise and the river. In the eleventh century, when William the Conqueror insisted on families employing the use of surnames, the residents of the castle chose the name de Featherstonhaugh. There were a couple of pages showing the family pedigree with the names of each generation of heirs for the first 200 years.

As John continued to read on, he came across a passage that was particularly intriguing. Just as he was about to read it a second time, Abby appeared.

"You're up early this morning," She said, as she sat down next to him.

"I woke up early, and I couldn't go back to sleep. I kept thinking about this book. It was no use avoiding it. I just had to dive into it. I kept wondering what else was contained within the pages."

"Did you find anything of interest?" she asked.

"Yeah, let me read it to you," he said.

> *In the thirtieth year of Henry II, a new family of Norman heritage took residence in the Tyne valley near Bardon Mill. They were an ancient family who had been rumored to be allied with William during the Norman invasion. A father and son gained rights to the Estate de Ridley, now Ridley Hall, as a result of the marriage of the son, by name John, to the daughter of Julian Burdett. Burdett was a Saxon of ill-repute who sought to protect his own interests by catering to the whims of the brutish Normans.*
>
> *The Ridleys were a proud and arrogant lot, quick to make enemies, and unhesitant to spill blood, when put to the test. In battle, they were fierce, making them a welcomed ally when defending the Tynedale from the marauding rogues from the north. However, they were quick to take advantage of this reputation and made use of it in intimidating their Saxon neighbors. Realizing this confidence, they sought to expand their already extensive territory. What they were unable to obtain by honest means, they did so by intrigue and deception.*
>
> *When Anthony Ridley, son of John, was of age, he sought the hand of what was believed to be the most beautiful maiden in all of Tynedale, the fair Alice, daughter of Odard de Willimoteswick, the greatest of the ancient Saxon estates of Tynedale. However, Alice, from an early age, had*

*been pledged to Alexander de Featherstonhaugh,
in order that these two great Saxon families would
be joined and Willimoteswick would come under
the arms of Featherstonhaugh.*

*Anthony de Ridley did not recognize this
contract, but instead chose to settle the dispute by
making a challenge of Alexander to mortal
combat. Ridley was of great stature and reputed to
be an impressive warrior. However, Alexander
could not refuse this open challenge for fear of
losing face. As a result, the two met on the field of
battle at Greenscheles Cleugh.*

*To his credit, Alexander fought hard and long
to defend his honor and the hand of his intended.
However, Ridley was much too strong and skilled
in all forms of weaponry. After a lengthy and
valiant struggle, the young Alexander succumbed
and was struck down by a mortal blow of the
broad sword.*

*As Anthony Ridley stood over the dead body,
possibly pausing due to the strain of battle, but
appearing to take pleasure in his conquest, the
kinsman of Featherstonhaugh maintained great
restraint, despite their desire to avenge their fallen
brother. Although remaining arrested, to a man,
they vowed to make revenge and to never again be
at peace until the Tynedale was rid of the entire
Ridley clan.*

*It was from this moment that the Ridleys
gained control of Willimoteswick Castle and that a
bloody feud began between the Featherstones and
the Ridleys.*

"And thus began 500 years of feuding and bloodshed,"
Abby said, shaking her head in dismay, "so much hatred."

"And so little reason," John affirmed. "It is
incomprehensible. I mean, it is not difficult to imagine the

384

feelings of revenge within a generation, but how did it continue across generations, and across centuries."

"That is the nature of revenge. One act of revenge prompts another, which prompts another. Before long, no one really remembers what started it all. They only remember the most recent event. Nothing else really matters. This is why we are told to love our enemies. It's not easy to love our enemies, but if we are unable to achieve this type of love, we are never able to fully understand forgiveness. It begins by letting go of the pain of the wrong. Carrying the pain, dwelling on it, so that it works through the heart, leads one to act with evil."

There was silence as both of them reflected. Then John spoke, "I once read somewhere, that if you act with forgiveness and grace toward someone, you will eventually grow to love them. But if you act with volition toward even your closest friend, you will eventually grow to hate them."

"Clearly, the Ridleys and Featherstones of the past never understood this," Abby said, "but tragedy, the kind of tragedy of a father losing his daughter, is sometimes enough to turn the tide. Come with me, I want to show you something."

John placed the book under one arm and then took Abby by the hand. She led him through the garden, to the front gate that faced the Tyne River. As they passed through the gate, Abby turned and pointed to the right side of the gate. There, right in plain sight was a family crest. The shield of the crest contained three falcons, separated by a single chevron.

"Do you recognize this?" Abby asked.

"Yes," John answered. "It's the same as the shield we found held in the arms of Abigail's corpse.

"I thought I remembered it from somewhere. Last night I asked Grandfather if he knew what it was from. He said that it was the original coat of arms of the Ridley family. It was placed on the gate when Unthank Hall was their residence."

"So, it was a symbol, a message, that in the end, the Baron of Featherstonhaugh was able to put an end to the cycle of revenge, to finally begin a new path toward forgiveness."

"Yes, I think that is what happened. Sadly, his change of heart only came after the death of Abigail and her lover, John

Ridley. In the end, their deaths became the ultimate sacrifice that finally put to end the years of evil and hatred."

"How ironic," John began, "that the feud began, not because of lost love, but over the possession of land. In the end the Featherstonhaugh was lost because there was no male heir, and just a few years later the Ridleys lost possession of all they owned because of their support of Charles II."

"The love of the material is always a foolish pursuit, it can never last. But when possessions are lost, love still remains, and through love, hope, healing and forgiveness can last forever."

The End

Unthank Hall, Northumberland, England

About the Author

Michael Rea was born in Eugene, Oregon and spent his entire youth living in the Pacific Northwest, where he enjoyed many moments camping, hiking and fishing in the Cascade Mountains of Washington and Oregon. He attended Westmont College in Santa Barbara, CA where he earned a B.A. in Chemistry and upon graduation, enrolled in a graduate program in Chemistry at the University of Illinois. Although expecting to complete his Ph.D. and begin a career as a research scientist, he unexpectedly fell in love with teaching, completed a M.S. in Teaching Chemistry and embarked on a career in secondary education.

Aside from his love for science, and his newly discovered passion for writing, Michael is also an artist, specializing in landscape and wildlife paintings in oil. He and his wife, Janet, love to travel and they make an effort to visit at least one national park every summer. These trips have greatly contributed many of the subjects for his paintings, while at the same time providing him with a time to get away to write. Together, he and his wife share a love for literature. A list of his favorite authors suggests a diverse influence on his writing: Isaac Asimov, C.S. Lewis, J.R.R Tolkein, Sir Walter Scott, Alexandre Dumas and Charles Dickens.

With over thirty years of experience in education, he has taught courses in all levels of mathematics and science, art, philosophy and religious studies. Science and the arts don't always mix well, but Michael's proficiency in both makes for an interesting combination, as does his eclectic background in coaching, teaching, and high school administration. He currently divides his time between his love of teaching chemistry and physics to his students and his love of oil painting and writing.

Today, Michael and his wife live in Temecula, CA. They have three children and three grandchildren.

www.ingramcontent.com/pod-product-compliance
Lightning Source LLC
Chambersburg PA
CBHW070753280626
47162CB00016B/216